ROMANTIC TIMES RAVES ABOUT *NEW YORK TIMES* BESTSELLING AUTHOR CONNIE MASON!

PIRATE

"Ms. Mason has written interesting characters into a twisting plot filled with humor and pathos."

THE LAST ROGUE

"A delight.... This is a must read for Mason fans."

SEDUCED BY A ROGUE

"Another wonderful story filled with adventure, witty repartee and hot sex."

THE ROGUE AND THE HELLION

"Ms. Mason has written another winner to delight her fans who want sexual tension that leads to hot explosion, memorable characters and a fast-paced story."

THE LAIRD OF STONEHAVEN

"[Ms. Mason] crafts with excellence and creativity...[and] the added attraction of mystery and magic. [The reader will] enjoy the facets of the supernatural that permeate this wonderful love story."

LIONHEART

"...upholds the author's reputation for creating memorable stories and remarkable characters."

THE DRAGON LORD

"This is a real keeper, filled with historical fact, sizzling love scenes and wonderful characters."

THE BLACK KNIGHT

"Ms. Mason has written a rich medieval romance filled with tournaments, chivalry, lust and love."

MORE *ROMANTIC TIMES* PRAISE FOR CONNIE MASON!

THE OUTLAWS: JESS

"Jess is filled with adventure and passion. Ms. Mason delivers."

THE OUTLAWS: RAFE

"Ms. Mason begins this new trilogy with wonderful characters...steamy romance...excellent dialogue...[and an] exciting plot!"

GUNSLINGER

"Ms. Mason has created memorable characters and a plot that made this reader rush to turn the pages.... Gunslinger is an enduring story."

BEYOND THE HORIZON

"Connie Mason at her best! She draws readers into this fast-paced, tender and emotional historical romance that proves love really does conquer all!"

BRAVE LAND, BRAVE LOVE

"An utter delight from first page to last—funny, tender, adventurous, and highly romantic!"

WILD LAND, WILD LOVE

"Connie Mason has done it again!"

BOLD LAND, BOLD LOVE

"A lovely romance and a fine historical!"

VIKING!

"This captive/captor romance proves a delicious read."

TEMPT THE DEVIL

"A grand and glorious adventure-romp! Ms. Mason tempts the readers with...thrilling action and sizzling sensuality!"

BURIED TREASURE

Still holding her wrists in one hand, he caressed her face with the other. His fingers grazed her cheek, her chin, his thumb rubbing her lower lip in a back-and-forth motion.

She was aware of his hard, masculine fingers, warm and firm against her mouth. He was so close she could smell the salt spray and sunshine on his clothing, feel the heat emanating from his body, almost taste his sexuality.

His words jolted her. "I want you, Bliss Grenville. I want your body. I want your soul. I want your heart."

Bliss nearly gagged on her panic. What did he mean? "No! Please let go of me. You're supposed to return me to my fiancé unharmed, remember?"

Hunter's face was as hard and cold as his voice. "Oh, you'll see Faulk again, but not until I decide it's time."

Hunter felt Bliss's soft body stiffen against his and smiled inwardly. She was frightened, but fear was good. Fear was a start. He couldn't wait to turn her fear into desire. The same desire she'd once felt for Guy DeYoung.

Other *Leisure* and *Love Spell* books by Connie Mason:

THE PIRATE PRINCE
THE LAST ROGUE
THE LAIRD OF STONEHAVEN
TO LOVE A STRANGER
SEDUCED BY A ROGUE
TO TAME A RENEGADE
LIONHEART
A LOVE TO CHERISH
THE ROGUE AND THE HELLION
THE DRAGON LORD
THE OUTLAWS: SAM
THE OUTLAWS: JESS
THE OUTLAWS: RAFE
THE BLACK KNIGHT
GUNSLINGER
BEYOND THE HORIZON
PIRATE
BRAVE LAND, BRAVE LOVE
WILD LAND, WILD LOVE
BOLD LAND, BOLD LOVE
VIKING!
SURRENDER TO THE FURY
FOR HONOR'S SAKE
LORD OF THE NIGHT
TEMPT THE DEVIL
PROMISE ME FOREVER
SHEIK
ICE & RAPTURE
LOVE ME WITH FURY
SHADOW WALKER
FLAME
TENDER FURY
DESERT ECSTASY
A PROMISE OF THUNDER
PURE TEMPTATION
WIND RIDER
TEARS LIKE RAIN
THE LION'S BRIDE
SIERRA
TREASURES OF THE HEART

LEISURE BOOKS NEW YORK CITY

A LEISURE BOOK®

February 2005

Published by

Dorchester Publishing Co., Inc.
200 Madison Avenue
New York, NY 10016

ISBN 0-8439-4456-0

Printed in the United States of America.

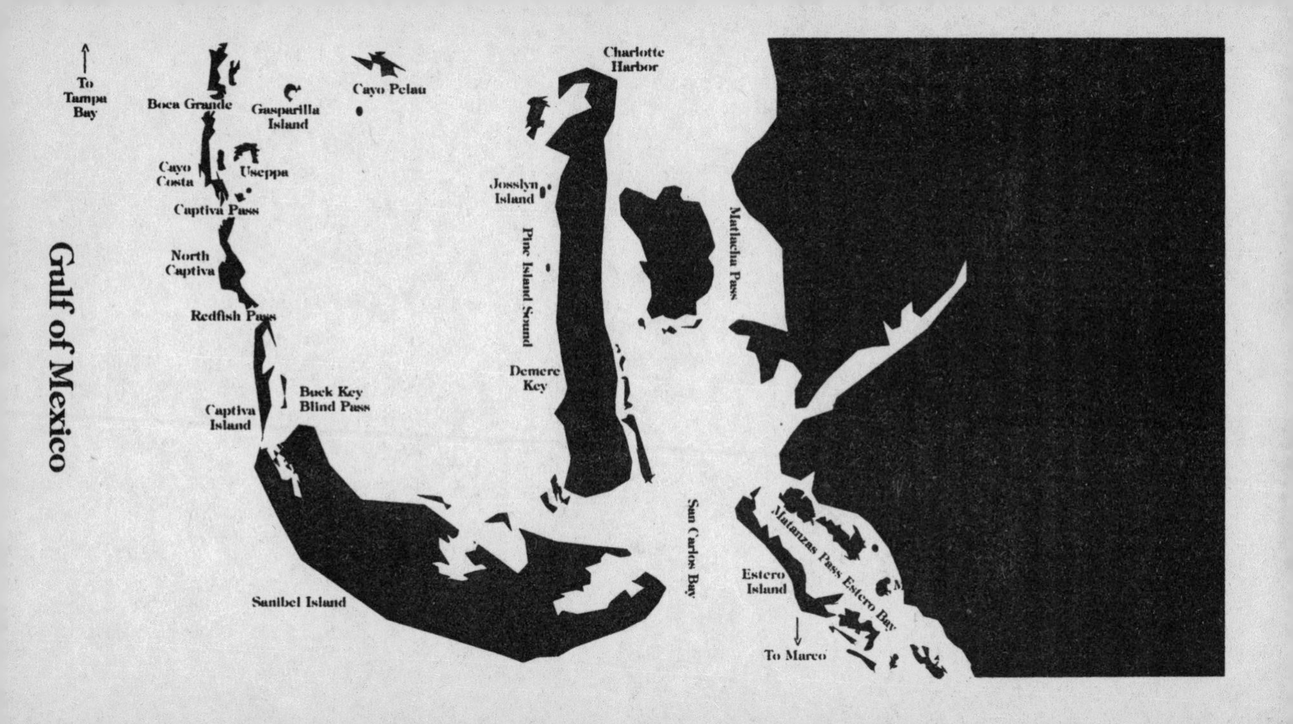
To Tampa Bay
Boca Grande
Gasparilla Island
Cayo Pelau
Charlotte Harbor
Cayo Costa
Useppa
Josslyn Island
Captiva Pass
Pine Island Sound
Matlacha Pass
North Captiva
Redfish Pass
Demere Key
Buck Key
Blind Pass
Captiva Island
San Carlos Bay
Matanzas Pass
Estero Bay
Estero Island
Sanibel Island
To Marco
Gulf of Mexico

Pirate

Prologue

New Orleans, 1804

Guy DeYoung didn't fear death. It was the thought of leaving Bliss to a man like Gerald Faulk that sent terror though his heart.

Clouds of thick, swirling mist nearly obscured the handful of men standing beneath the canopy of live oak trees known as Dueling Oaks. Eerie, gray tendrils of Spanish moss streamed downward in the damp, predawn morning, obscuring the view of the two opponents facing one another.

Guy DeYoung selected a pistol from the polished case held by his second, aware that his opponent intended to kill him. This was Guy's first duel; an *affaire de coeur*. He had unwisely fallen in love with Bliss Grenville the daughter of the man who had hired him as stable master. He'd been jubilant when he learned his affections were returned in full, and he and Bliss had secretly married without her father's approval and her former fiance's knowledge.

When Guy had informed Claude Grenville that he and Bliss were married and had consummated their vows, Grenville had been livid. Bliss's father had called Guy a penniless Cajun upstart with no future. Grenville had great expectations of the marriage he had arranged between seventeen-year-old Bliss and Gerald Faulk, a wealthy shipowner and exporter. Grenville was a prominent investor in Faulk's business and had counted on a long and prosperous association with his prospective son-in-law. When Faulk learned that his fiancee had married another man, he considered himself the injured party and challenged Guy to a duel.

They stood now beneath the Dueling Oaks, enclosed in a tent of green leaves dripping with morning dew.

Gerald Faulk sneered at Guy as he balanced his pistol in the palm of his hand. "You're a fool, DeYoung. You should have known better than to reach above yourself. No one will mourn your passing."

"Bliss loves me," Guy taunted. "That's more than you can say."

Faulk, a handsome, dapper man with light hair and a pencil-thin mustache, had the audacity to laugh at his tall, handsome opponent. "You poor, deluded fool. Bliss was but toying with you. What she perceived as love was simple infatuation. She's already begged my forgiveness for her rash act, and I magnanimously granted it." His words were lightly uttered but the look in his eyes bespoke his rage. "Bliss already regrets marrying you against her father's wishes. You're scum, DeYoung. Poor as dirt! Claude Grenville has already applied for an annulment."

"You're a liar, Faulk!" Guy spat. "Bliss loves me. She'd never play me false. Money means nothing to her."

"The outcome of this duel will decide Bliss's future," Faulk declared. "We both know it's her money you want. Are you aware that she doesn't come into her inheritance until she reaches twenty-five?"

"I don't want her money," Guy said, insulted. "I will make my own fortune."

"Make your own fortune? Ha! Doing what? Sweeping up horse dung? I hope you enjoyed Bliss, for you'll not get another chance at her," Faulk spat.

Suddenly a woman came riding out of the mist toward them, a cloud of russet hair flying behind her as she reined her mount to a skidding halt. "Wait!" she cried as she slid from the saddle and raced toward the duelists.

"Bliss! My God, what are you doing here?" Guy cried, catching the young woman in his arms and swinging her out of harm's way. "Nothing can be gained by your presence. Go home, sweetheart. Please."

"You don't understand," Bliss panted as she glanced fearfully over her shoulder. "Father . . . He said you . . . The police . . . I know you didn't do it."

"Dueling is frowned upon, but not illegal," Guy declared, unable to make sense of her words. "I might have to go away for a while but you'll come with me."

"Step away, Bliss," Faulk ordered brusquely. "Your young lover and I have unfinished business to settle. If you hadn't acted like a spoiled child, this wouldn't be necessary."

Bliss turned the full potency of her turquoise eyes on Faulk. "Don't do this, Gerald. I beg you. What if you're killed? Or maimed? What will happen to—"

"I will win," Faulk said with confidence.

Guy regarded Bliss with dismay. All her concern seemed to be directed at Faulk. Bliss was acting as if Faulk were the man she cared about. Had Faulk been right about Bliss all along? No, he couldn't . . . wouldn't think that way. Bliss loved him. She'd never play him false.

"Move away, love," Guy said.

"But Father—"

Guy didn't have time now to hear what Bliss was trying to say. She could tell him later, after he had dispatched Faulk. He motioned to his second, who strode briskly forward to remove Bliss from the dueling arena. Then Faulk's second read the rules while the opponents aligned themselves back to back, barely touching. Upon command, they marked off the required ten paces and stopped.

As the count ended, a second intoned, "Turn and fire at will." Both men turned, raised their pistols, and took aim.

Faulk's shot whizzed past Guy, nicking his ear. Guy's shot, intended for Faulk's shoulder, lodged in his chest when Faulk lurched to the right in a futile effort to escape Guy's bullet.

Bliss screamed as Faulk clutched his chest and fell to the ground. Lifting her skirts, she rushed forward, dropping to her knees beside him. Her frantic words to her former fiance would remain etched upon Guy's brain to the end of his days.

"Don't die, Gerald! Please don't die!" She tilted her tear-stained face upward, her terror palpable. Her lips had become bloodless in a face leached of all color. "Look what you've done!" she screamed at Guy. "Oh God, why did you do it?"

Guy felt as if he'd been ripped apart. He didn't want to believe it, but he realized now that Faulk had been right when he'd said Bliss had been toying with him. Their marriage meant nothing to her. His expression hardened and his heart turned to stone. Even though Guy had won the duel, he felt as if he had lost the battle.

Through a haze of seething rage, Guy became aware suddenly of a disturbance, a racket raised by shouting voices and pounding hooves. He tensed, his nerve endings screaming danger.

"There he is! Seize him! The bounder sold

two of my most valuable horses and pocketed the money. Now he's killed a prominent citizen of New Orleans."

The heavy mist was drifting away now, chased by the morning sun. Through the thinning vapor Guy saw Claude Grenville riding toward him with a dozen City Guards hard on his heels. There was but one thought in Guy's mind. Flee! He knew nothing about stolen horses, but was astute enough to realize that Bliss's father had concocted false charges in order to keep him away from Bliss. Guy sent a bewildered, hate-filled glance toward Bliss, convinced that she had known of her father's scheme all along. Then he spun on his heel and fled.

He sprinted across slick, wet grass, away from the magnificent oaks, unaware of the blood flowing down his neck from his nicked ear. His one chance of escape lay in the acres of swamps and bayous south of the city, where a man could lose himself forever. But it was not to be. He was but one man against many. He was soon run down, beaten, and dragged off to the Calaboso, that dark, damp prison where many a man before him had met his end.

Chapter One

New Orleans, 1805

"You can't go on like this, Bliss," Claude Grenville chided his daughter. "Your child is dead and buried and your lover is unlikely to leave the Calaboso any time soon. There is nothing to stop us now from obtaining an annulment of that disastrous marriage you made. You were underage and obviously coerced into running off with that young fortune hunter."

"I don't want an annulment, Father," Bliss said as she moved listlessly to the window to contemplate the sun-drenched gardens.

"We've gone over this time and again, Bliss," Claude Grenville said with an apparent lack of patience. "Gerald has fully recovered from his wound and is still willing to marry you, despite your reckless alliance with Guy DeYoung. I waited until after the birth of the child to start annulment proceedings, because I didn't want bastardy attached to our good name. Now that the impediment of an unwanted child no longer exists, I can petition for an annulment and you can plan a fall wedding."

Bliss raised her fan and waved it before her pale face in a desultory manner. Very little interested her anymore. Her attempts to visit Guy in the Calaboso had failed, foiled, she supposed, by either her father or Gerald Faulk. She knew they had used their considerable influence and high-placed friends to keep Guy from being brought to trial, and it only made her more determined than ever to resist her father's efforts to make her marry Gerald. She would never marry while Guy was still alive and languishing somewhere within the dank stone walls of the Calaboso. She knew exactly who was responsible for the injustice against Guy and she hated them for it.

After the stillborn birth of her child, Bliss had nearly lost the will to live. But her strong survival instincts and the belief that Guy would one day be released from prison sustained her, instilling in her the spirit to go on. Being reunited with the man she loved became the driving force within her.

"You can petition for an annulment if you want, Father, but you can't force me to marry Gerald Faulk," Bliss maintained. "They can't keep Guy in prison forever. When he's released, we will be together again."

Claude stared into his daughter's belligerent turquoise eyes and recognized defeat. He'd just been informed that the newly appointed magistrate had reviewed Guy's records and ruled that he had been imprisoned long enough, since a crime had never been proven. They were planning to release him very soon. Claude had sent an urgent message to Gerald Faulk and expected him momentarily.

"Even if DeYoung is released from prison, there is no way he can make a living," Claude argued. "He's a nobody. A hotheaded Cajun with a criminal record. He served as my stable master, for heaven's sake. Is that the kind of man you want for a husband?"

"I love him," Bliss said, raising her pointed little chin to a defiant angle. "We'll go away together, where no one knows him."

"Gerald Faulk can give you a good life," Claude persisted. "He's prosperous and respected in the city, despite being an American. Unlike some New Orleans natives, I have learned to live with the Americans who flooded the territory after it was sold to the United States. I've invested heavily in Faulk's shipping ventures and hope to make a fortune from my investment. He has loaned me funds to satisfy my debtors. When he asked for your hand, I saw no reason to deny him. Everything would have worked out if you hadn't fancied yourself in love with my stable master and run off with him."

"Guy intends to enroll at the university and become a lawyer," Bliss claimed.

"He's a fortune hunter after your inheritance," Claude contended. "Fortunately, you can't touch the bulk of your funds until your twenty-fifth birthday."

"I refuse to listen to your insults, Father," Bliss said, facing him squarely. "I'll never love another man. I'm prepared to wait for Guy forever."

"Am I intruding?" Gerald Faulk asked as he strode into the drawing room. "The butler let me in."

"Come in, come in," Claude invited as he held his hand out to Faulk. "I've been waiting for you."

"Excuse me," Bliss said, spinning on her heel. "I need to confer with the cook about tonight's dinner."

Gerald Faulk watched Bliss walk across the room and felt a tightening in his groin. He'd wanted her since he'd first laid eyes on her, and he would have had her if that damned DeYoung hadn't stolen her away from him. He'd even loaned her spendthrift father money in order to have her. He wanted Bliss for many reasons. He wanted her in his bed, he wanted her inheritance, and he wanted her because she would ease his entry into French New Orleans society. These Frenchmen were a clannish bunch who were leary of his American heritage. Once he married into the Grenville family, Faulk was confident his shipping business would flourish.

"Did you speak with Bliss about our marriage?" Faulk asked once Bliss had left the room.

"Of course I did," Claude said, gesturing impatiently. "But the outcome is the same as it has been since DeYoung came into her life. Annulment or no, she refuses to marry you."

"You don't need her approval to obtain an annulment," Faulk reminded him. "You're her father. You can force her to accept the marriage. I almost died because of her. You both owe me for that. You're my business partner. I've loaned you money when you needed it. I want Bliss and I aim to have her one way or another."

Claude heaved a pained sigh. "I don't have the heart to force her after . . . after what I've done to her. That's why I haven't pushed for the annulment. Bliss won't hear of it. Even if I did apply for an annulment, Bliss wouldn't marry you."

"You're too lenient with the girl," Faulk said with a snort of disgust. "You did what had to be done. We both agreed to it."

"I know," Claude said distractedly. "Don't worry. That part of our bargain still holds. A child sired by a man who is not her social equal would have ruined Bliss's life. I did what I thought best. But what's to be done now? DeYoung is likely to be released soon, and Bliss still fancies herself in love with him."

Faulk's attention sharpened. "Are you sure DeYoung is to be released soon?"

"I received word just yesterday from a source

I pay to keep me informed. One of DeYoung's numerous petitions for release must have reached the courts. I don't know why our influential friends failed to block it as they did the others, but it fell into the newly appointed magistrate's hands. He looked into the charges, learned that DeYoung had never been brought to trial, and ruled for his release. Apparently the magistrate decided DeYoung had been incarcerated long enough."

"Damnation! Something must be done, and quickly. Obtaining an annulment now isn't enough if Bliss remains opposed to our marriage."

Claude sent Faulk a dubious look. "What do you propose?"

Faulk's light eyes gleamed with sly determination as he stroked his mustache with a long finger. "Leave the particulars to me. You don't want DeYoung to have your daughter, do you?"

Indignant, Claude stiffened. "Absolutely not! Her mother, God rest her soul, would turn in her grave if she knew her daughter's inheritance would go to a penniless stable hand. Marie's ancestors were French aristocrats. You aren't the aristocrat Marie would have wanted for her daughter, but there are few of those left these days. At least you have the means to give Bliss a good life."

"It's settled, then," Faulk said. "I'll take care of DeYoung. With DeYoung out of the picture, Bliss will have no reason to wait for him. The only way DeYoung will leave the Calaboso is in a wooden box."

Claude blanched. "Wooden box! I don't want to know the details, Gerald. Do what you have to do, but don't expect me to help."

Above stairs in her room, Bliss paced nervously until she heard the crunch of Faulk's carriage wheels on the coquina driveway. She waited until the equipage disappeared through the plantation gates before rushing downstairs to confront her father. She found him gazing up at her mother's portrait, hands behind his back, a pensive expression on his face.

"Did you tell him I wouldn't marry him?" Bliss blurted out as he turned to face her. "You can get the annulment, but I won't marry Gerald as long as Guy lives."

"I told him," Claude said in a flat voice that sent chills racing down Bliss's elegant back. She'd never seen her father so distracted. What had transpired between him and Gerald?

"I don't suppose there is anything I can say to convince you to expedite Guy's release from prison, or to let me visit him. He doesn't even know about the child."

God willing, he never will, Claude thought. "I don't wish to discuss this with you now," he said. "I have other things on my mind. You're only eighteen, Bliss, and a great beauty. Why do you persist in throwing your young life away on a man who is a known thief?"

"Guy is no thief! You and Gerald trumped up

that charge. Don't you think I know you've kept Guy in prison through political machinations? I may be only eighteen, but I'm old enough to recognize manipulation when I see it. I'll never forgive you for what you've done to Guy and me, Father."

Whirling on her heel, she left the room with all the dignity she could muster. Claude watched her leave, his expression a mixture of determination and sadness. He loved his daughter and didn't want her to throw her life away on a man far beneath her in social rank. Guy DeYoung's parents had been impoverished sharecroppers and the son was no better. Furthermore, Claude's alliance with Gerald Faulk had to succeed, for he was on the brink of financial ruin. Crops had failed three years in a row, his mistress was demanding more than he could afford, and he'd borrowed from the bank in order to invest in Faulk's business venture. Bliss wouldn't receive her inheritance until she was twenty-five and Claude was damned if he'd let Guy DeYoung have it. Claude had already made a deal with Faulk to share Bliss's inheritance, and he wasn't about to give it up.

The Calaboso

Guy DeYoung turned painfully on his left side, careful not to aggravate the broken rib he'd suffered during his latest beating. Despondent, he gnawed on a hunk of bread and stared into the darkness. During the year he'd spent incarcerated in the Calaboso he'd received beatings regularly, each one administered with the compliments of the Grenvilles and Gerald Faulk, or so he'd been told by the sadistic guard who had wielded the club.

Each plea for an interview with the magistrate had been met with yet another beating. Guy had no idea whether any of his numerous petitions had ever reached the magistrate and he had almost given up hope. Thin to the point of gauntness, Guy barely existed in the dark, dank cell. He was a mere shell of the man he'd once been. His pale face sported a beard as thick and black as his long, matted hair. His silver eyes, once alive with the joy of living, now seethed with hatred and dreams of revenge.

His clothing hung on his sparse frame in tatters and his leather boots had long since rotted away. Despite privation, beatings, near starvation, and harsh treatment by sadistic guards, he had survived, kept from complete madness by dreams of revenge. What hurt most was the isolation, the feeling of being cut off from the outside world. Guy knew he had Grenville and Faulk to thank for that. Their powerful friends had seen to it that his petitions for a trial never reached the courts. How he wished he had killed Gerald Faulk when he'd had the chance.

Guy knew for certain that no evidence existed to substantiate the false charges of thievery against him. And he'd learned from a friendly guard that Gerald Faulk still lived, so no charge of murder hung over his head. Yet his hopes for a quick acquittal had dwindled with each passing day, until he despaired of ever being free again.

Guy would have remained completely ignorant of outside events if not for Andre Cardette, a childhood friend who was now a guard at the prison. Andre wasn't like the other guards. He never participated in the beatings. He provided Guy with what small comforts he could without sacrificing his job, which he needed to support his large family. During many of the beatings, Andre had prevented overzealous guards from turning a beating into a death. If Andre could have done more for him, Guy knew he would have.

Guy groaned and changed positions again, unable to find comfort in the pile of moldy straw that served as his bed. He no longer noticed the offensive odor emanating from both his bed and his body, but he knew others would find his stench intolerable. Between beatings he tried to maintain a program of exercise, fearing his limbs would wither from lack of movement if he didn't make the effort. His strength was nothing like it used to be, but thanks to his strict adherence to regimen, he was stronger than he looked. But last night's beating had been particularly brutal. Unfortunately, Andre hadn't been there to temper the viciousness. Guy didn't know how much longer he'd be able to survive in this hellhole.

Suddenly Guy heard a key scrape in the lock and he turned his head toward the heavy oak door. The door opened and he blinked at the sudden flare of light.

"Guy. Are you all right?"

Andre. Guy allowed himself to breathe again. He didn't think he could survive another beating. "Your friends nearly did me in last night. Have you come to gloat?" Andre didn't deserve that from him, but he couldn't help the jibe. He hurt so damn much that only his raging anger kept him sane.

"I'm sorry, Guy, there was nothing I could do." He walked into the cell and closed the door. Guy flinched away from the light. "How badly are you hurt?" Andre asked.

"I'll live," Guy grunted. "This time it was only a cracked rib." He shrugged, then winced and clutched his middle. "Who knows what the next beating will bring? Do you bring news?"

Andre moved closer and squatted down beside Guy. "Listen carefully, *mon ami*," he whispered. "The guards on duty tonight have been paid by your enemies to leave the key in the lock. You must prepare yourself for an unwanted visitor. An assassin will enter your cell tonight to kill you. Your death certificate will state that you died of jail fever, and you'll be buried with uncommon haste in pauper's field."

Guy spit out an oath. "How did you learn of this?"

"I know because I was assigned to discover your body in the morning. People with money can do as they please, even take a man's life, while the poor must suffer. I have done what I could for you, Guy, because of our childhood friendship. I wish it could have been more, but I have my family to think about. They need what little my job provides. The best I can do is warn you and give you this."

He pulled a wicked-looking blade from beneath his uniform jacket and handed it to Guy. "Take it and use it wisely. I'm going off duty now. I've orders to return at dawn with a pine box. It will be my sad duty to report your death. If you're still alive, perhaps we can figure out something."

"Andre." The guard was halfway to the door before he turned. "Thank you. If there is a God, he'll surely bless you for this. Unfortunately, I've lost all faith in Him."

Andre nodded, started to say something, thought better of it, then quietly let himself out of the cell, locking the door behind him.

Guy's fingers curled around the handle of the knife. It felt good in his hand. Solid and deadly. He flexed the muscles of his arm, testing his strength. It was definitely not what it use to be, but it was sufficient. Then he lay down on the straw and waited.

Hours later he heard shuffling outside his door. The metallic click of the key turning in the lock. A muted squeak as the door opened. Hushed footsteps as a shrouded figure stepped through the narrow opening.

After long months of living in the cavelike environment of black and gray, Guy was accustomed to the darkness. He tensed and mentally prepared himself as the assassin crept noiselessly toward him. Guy willed himself to rise above the pain of his aching ribs as he gauged the assassin's approach.

Guy tensed as the assassin crept closer. He held his breath when he sensed the man's presence looming over him. Guy knew the exact moment the assassin raised his arm; swiftly, he rolled away, leaping to his feet to face his enemy. The man appeared surprised, which was exactly what Guy had counted on. Guy used his momentary advantage to launch an attack of his own. The man seemed to recover himself as he fended off Guy's blow, driving Guy back by slashing his knife in a wide arc.

They circled one another in silent combat, feinting and retreating, each swipe of their blades drawing blood. Guy was panting, nearly at the end of his endurance, when suddenly he saw an opening. He feinted to the right. When the assassin parried, Guy buried his knife deep in the other man's chest. The assassin's blade, already in motion when Guy had struck, continued its deadly path, slashing downward across Guy's right eye.

Pain. Excruciating. Debilitating. Seething over him and through him. He fell to his knees, clasping his hand over his eye to stanch the blood. His breath came in short, uneven bursts as he bit his lip clear through to keep from screaming. With his good eye he saw the assassin lying motionless, blood streaming from his chest. He forced himself to place an ear to the man's breast. The assassin's lungs were still, his heart silent. He was dead.

Guy dropped to the foul straw, too spent to feel, too bitter to think past the loss of his eye. Another travesty to lay at the door of Gerald Faulk and the Grenvilles. Some way, somehow, he vowed to make them pay for the pain and suffering they had cost him. The love he'd once felt for Bliss no longer existed. It had hardened into a knot of intense loathing. The sight of her wailing over Faulk's body after the duel had been indelibly engraved upon his mind.

Guy didn't know how long he lay in the filthy straw holding his injured eye. Pain made the time seem endless. He barely roused himself when the cell door opened and Andre entered.

He sensed rather than saw Andre kneel beside him. "*Sacre bleu!* Are you dead, then? Have you killed one another?"

Guy raised his head with great effort. "I am alive, but perhaps not for long. The assassin is dead."

Andre gave an audible gasp when he saw blood streaming through Guy's fingers. "How badly are you hurt?"

"It doesn't matter. Have you brought the pine box?"

"It's sitting just outside the door. The men who delivered it are waiting in the guard room to carry it away. What do you propose?"

"Help me to exchange my clothing for the assassin's. You said the guards on duty have been paid to look the other way while the assassin slips in and out of the Calaboso. I'm going to take the assassin's place. I'll need you to stuff the assassin's body in the box, close the lid, and summon the men back to carry it away for a swift burial."

"I will do it, *mon ami*. Are you able to manage on your own? What has he done to you?"

"I will manage," Guy said grimly. "I think I have lost an eye, but I'll survive. My thirst for revenge will keep me alive."

Andre swiftly removed the assassin's clothing while Guy cast off his own tattered rags. After the clothing had been exchanged, Andre dragged the coffin into the cell and dumped the stiffening body into it. Then he hammered down the lid with the hilt of his sword.

"I owe you my life, Andre, but I would ask one more thing of you," Guy said as he prepared to leave.

"What would you have me do?"

"Breathe not a word of this to anyone. Everyone must believe that Guy DeYoung died an ignoble death in the Calaboso."

Andre nodded. "For my own sake as well as yours, I will say nothing. Where will you go? What will you do?"

"There is only one place I can go. The Lafitte brothers are known to help fugitives from the law. I will ask them to take me to their stronghold on Barataria. No one will look for me there while I recover and regain my strength."

"You would become a pirate? 'Tis a well-known fact that the Lafitte brothers, if not actual pirates themselves, broker goods in New Orleans provided by Caribbean pirates, and that Grande Terre is a pirate's haven. Rumor has it the brothers have grown fabulously rich off stolen merchandise."

Guy's ruined face hardened. "I will do whatever is necessary to survive. Farewell, Andre."

The Grenville Plantation

Bliss stared at her father in abject horror. "No! I refuse to believe it!" Her lips trembled, her face was white as a sheet. "Guy can't be dead. I would know in my heart if he no longer existed. You lie!"

"I will show you the place where he is buried," Claude Grenville said, "and take you to the Calaboso myself so you may interview the guard who found his body. Accept it, Bliss. Guy DeYoung succumbed to a debilitating illness while in prison."

None of the tragedies in Bliss's young life had been as soul-destroying as this. Guy's death forever doomed her dreams of a future with the man she loved. While he lived, hope existed. Each night she knelt in prayer, beseeching God to bring about his release from prison. Not once did she give up hope, or doubt that God would answer her prayer. But Guy's death ended life as she knew it. How could she go on?

"You no longer have a reason to deny Gerald Faulk," Claude observed. "Guy DeYoung will never return."

His insensitive words provided Bliss with the spirit to resist her father's plan for her future. She glared at him, her turquoise eyes narrowed with stubborn determination. "The only man I'll ever love has just died. I hold you and Gerald responsible for his death, no matter how he died. How can you even suggest that I marry another man? Nothing you can say will persuade me to marry Gerald."

"Whatever did I do to deserve such an ungrateful daughter?" Claude shouted. "Faulk's generous loans have paid for your gowns and the food you eat."

"Don't forget your mistress, Father," Bliss returned sarcastically. "That house you bought Yvette on the ramparts must have cost a small fortune."

Claude, still handsome and vigorous at forty-five, harrumphed at Bliss's bald accusation. "A man my age must have his pleasures, Bliss. It isn't as if I'm betraying your mother. She died long ago. I depend upon Faulk's business for my livelihood. The least you could do is please me by marrying him. It is what Faulk wants, and I wish to maintain a good relationship with him for obvious reasons."

"Gerald covets my inheritance. I wish my grandparents had never left me wealthy."

"I won't lie to you. Your inheritance is important to both Faulk and myself, but it won't be yours to claim for a long time. Meanwhile, Faulk will take care of you in the manner to which you're accustomed."

"And my inheritance will be his when . . . if I marry him."

Claude harrumphed again. "That's the usual way it works. Women aren't capable of handling large sums of money. That's why the law provides for husbands to manage their wives' affairs. DeYoung would have squandered your inheritance."

Bliss closed her eyes against hot tears as the shock of Guy's death suddenly hit her. She would never see him again. Never taste his kisses. Never feel his hands gliding over her body, loving her with his unique brand of passion. Never hear him whispering sweet words of love.

Guy was a man like no other, strong and powerfully built, despite his youth. He was a sensitive lover who always placed her pleasure above his own. He'd been barely twenty-one when they had met and fallen in love, but she'd known immediately that he was an exceptional man: kind, compassionate, unfailingly gentle; she'd never forget him. Their times together had been achingly brief, albeit sufficient to make a child. Now Guy would never know they'd had a child together and lost him at birth.

"Did you hear me, Bliss? Shall I tell Faulk you'll marry him?"

"No, Father. I'll never remarry." She meant it. Marrying another man would sully her memory of Guy. "Tell Gerald he'll never have my inheritance."

Chapter Two

New Orleans, 1811

"You must do this for my sake, Bliss," Claude Grenville said as he paced a well-worn path across the carpet. "I'm begging you to reconsider. It's no longer a simple matter. I'm ruined, ruined. And so is Gerald Faulk if you don't marry him and let him use your inheritance to recoup his losses. I haven't pressed you before, because you were still too young to collect your inheritance. You know the terms as well as I. You have to be married in order to receive the bulk of your fortune. If you are still single when you reach twenty-five, you are only entitled to a monthly allowance."

Bliss sighed wearily. "We've gone over this before, Father, and my answer is still the same."

"Our home is at stake, daughter. The bank will own it if I can't meet the mortgage payment. Neither Faulk nor myself anticipated the incredible losses his business has suffered of late. Every one of his ships has been attacked by pirates. By one pirate in particular, I might add. It's as if that damned thief has singled him out for attack. Months later his stolen goods turn up in the city, offered to buyers by those incorrigible Lafitte brothers at outrageous prices."

"Where is the American Navy? Why do they allow these atrocities to continue?" Bliss wondered.

"The few ships the Navy owns are engaged in keeping the British from our shores. The Navy has neither the money nor the time to chase pirates from our waters. Gasparilla is the worst of the lot. He's formed a Brotherhood of pirates to sail under him. Their attacks upon our ships are intolerable. A pirate known as Hunter seems bent upon destroying Faulk Shipping."

Bliss shivered, recalling the latest gossip she'd heard in town concerning Gasparilla and the Brotherhood. "I've heard that Gasparilla keeps women hostages on a separate island. The women on Captiva Island are lucky in one respect, for they usually are ransomed and sent back to their families."

"Only God knows what happens to those poor wretches while awaiting ransom," Claude contended. "But I digress. What's important here is the fact that in six months you will come into your inheritance. If you're still unwed, all you'll receive is a monthly allowance, so you need to marry. Faulk is desperate for funds to place additional cannon on his remaining ships. The bank refused his request for a loan and he has nowhere else to turn."

"There are other heiresses in town, Father."

"You're the one Faulk wants. It's always been you. It's time you married, Bliss. Who will take care of you after I'm gone? You're going to be twenty-five soon. Men want wives young enough to bear them several children. Consider this. Unless you marry, you will never know the joys of motherhood."

Bliss winced. Claude had hit a sore spot. Nearly seven years had passed since she'd lost her child, and six years since Guy's death. She'd never forgotten either. Her life was a progression of empty days, filled with dreams of the man she had loved more than her own life, and of the child they had made together. Did she want another child? The answer was a resounding yes. Unfortunately, the only way to have that desperately wanted child was to marry.

"I do want children," Bliss admitted with a wistful sigh. "If my son had lived—"

"But he didn't," Claude cut in harshly. "You've mourned long enough. Agree to marry Gerald Faulk and you could be holding a child in your arms by this time next year. You're nearly twenty-five, long past the time most girls marry. I'm desperate and so is Faulk. He needs your inheritance to keep his shipping business afloat. If he goes under, so do I.

"I've asked very little of you, Bliss. The least you could do is comply with my wishes. I assured Faulk that you would accept his proposal this time. I won't let you make a liar out of me."

Bliss's gaze turned inward as she pictured the face of the man she had loved and married long ago. Seven years was a long time and Guy's beloved features had dimmed over the years, but she'd never forget the brief but passionate love they had shared. She had admired and loved everything about him, the softness of his dark, shiny hair, the luminous sheen of his silver-gray eyes, and the solid strength of his muscular build.

Guy DeYoung was dead.

Her child was dead.

There would never be another Guy, but she could have another child.

"You will obey me in this, daughter," Claude repeated. "Gerald has applied for a license and the banns are to be read in St. Louis Cathedral this Sunday. The wedding will take place in three weeks."

"I can help pay your debts with my monthly allowance, Father," Bliss offered. "I understand it's a generous stipend."

"It's not enough for our purposes. Faulk has waited a long time for you and he's running out of patience. He loaned me money when I needed it. I must honor that debt. He needs substantial funds to keep his business afloat. He must arm his ships."

"With my money," Bliss said bitterly.

"There is no other way," Claude said, shrugging. "Since you have no husband, you are ineligible to receive the bulk of your inheritance upon coming of age."

"How can I marry Gerald when I don't even like him?" Bliss complained bitterly. "Guy would still be alive if Gerald hadn't challenged him and you hadn't used your influence to keep him in jail until he sickened and died of fever."

"That's water under the bridge. The wedding will take place in three weeks and that's final."

"I'll agree but I don't have to like it," Bliss said with ill-grace. "If marrying Gerald is the only way to save my home, then so be it. Having a child will make my sacrifice worthwhile. Just make sure Gerald knows I can never love him. I'm sure he won't mind since it's my money he really wants."

Claude heaved a sigh of relief. His greatest fear had been that his daughter would refuse to marry Faulk. It seemed incredible that Bliss would mourn Guy DeYoung six years after his death, and still pine for the son she had borne him. She'd been so young at the time, and he'd felt certain she would forget the past and accept Faulk's proposal before she turned twenty-five. He'd had no idea his daughter would prove so stubborn. Thank God he had finally worn her down.

* * *

Bliss posed before the mirror in her wedding dress, gazing at the image she would present to all their friends in less than two days. She had gained a certain maturity since her marriage to Guy seven years before. Her burnished hair still retained its sheen and her eyes were the same bright turquoise they had always been, but her figure had ripened to lush maturity over the years.

"You'll make a dazzling bride, Bliss," the dressmaker sighed as she placed the last pin in the hem. "The color suits you. I'm glad you decided on blue instead of white."

"It's a lovely dress, Claire," Bliss said, recalling the day she had run off with Guy. She'd worn a frilly white organdy dress. It was a child's dress, she realized now, but Guy had loved it.

"Take it off and I'll do the hem in the shop and have it back in plenty of time for the wedding."

Bliss could find little joy in either her wedding or the dress she was to wear. After the dressmaker left, she sat listlessly on the bed and stared at the ceiling, her thoughts anything but placid. How could she allow Gerald to touch her in the same way Guy had? After their wedding Gerald could do anything he wanted to her and she'd have to submit. A shudder of revulsion rolled down her spine.

She recalled how eager she'd been to consummate her marriage to Guy. How his tender words and gentleness had erased her fears and eased her embarrassment. There had been pain, but Guy had made it so beautiful she'd hardly noticed. A sob worked its way into her throat and lodged there. Her eyes grew misty with tears as her thoughts turned to Guy. After all these years, she still couldn't accept Guy's death. Had she seen his body, she might have been more accepting, but all she'd seen was a gravesite.

The clock on her dresser chimed the hour and Bliss forced herself to dress and descend the staircase. She intended to take the carriage to town to purchase gloves and slippers to match her dress. In the hallway, she met Mandy, the slave who had been like a mother to her after her own had died.

"Where you going, honey?"

"To town, Mandy."

"Not alone, you ain't. Wait here while I get my shawl."

"I'm not a child, Mandy, I don't need a chaperone," Bliss said.

Mandy looked unconvinced. "If you say so, honey. Have Henry drive the carriage. He'll see that you come to no harm."

"If you insist. Have you seen my father?"

Mandy rolled her eyes. "He's in the study with Mr. Gerald. Are you sure yore ready to marry that man? I know you well enough to tell you ain't happy," Mandy confided.

"I haven't been happy for a long time," Bliss admitted with a sigh. "This marriage is necessary or I wouldn't have consented. I'll tell father

I'm leaving," she said as she headed for the study.

The study door was ajar and Bliss started to push it open when she heard her name mentioned. She went still, her hand poised on the doorknob. She knew eavesdropping was unethical, but she quickly discarded the thought as she flattened herself against the door to listen.

"The greedy fool is demanding more money," Claude said, slamming his hand down on his desk to emphasize his words. "I received the letter just today. Will he never be satisfied? If the boy wasn't my grandson, I'd tell him to go ahead and abandon the brat as he threatened."

"How much does he want this time?" Faulk asked, apparently aware of what Claude was talking about.

"Twice the yearly stipend. He said the boy is getting older now and eating more."

"Tell Holmes to make do, that you'll send him no more money," Faulk advised. "Mobile is a long way off, chances are you'll never encounter either him or the boy."

A tingling sensation crept down Bliss's spine. Boy? What boy? Why was her father paying someone to care for a child? The answer was too painful to contemplate. It couldn't be. Her father could never be so cruel, so heartless, could he? Claude's next words sent her world crashing down around her.

"The boy is Bliss's son. I can't just ignore him, or see him mistreated."

"I don't have money to give you, Claude,"

Faulk said with finality. "Even if I did, I wouldn't waste it on DeYoung's bastard."

"I suppose you're right," Claude said uncertainly.

Bliss's head began to spin and she had to hold onto the wall to keep herself from fainting. *Her child wasn't dead!* Her father had lied to her. He'd taken her baby from her when she'd been too ill to ask questions about his death. Then her father had sent her son away to be raised by strangers. She recalled now that Mandy had been away at the time of the birth, and the colored midwife who had delivered her baby had been sold shortly thereafter. She wanted to scream. To rage at the unfairness of life.

She wanted her son. Guy's son. The child she had mourned all these years. Gerald and her father had perpetrated a grievous sin against her. She would never forgive them.

"Put that letter away and forget you ever received it," Faulk advised. "Come to the office with me. I'll bring you home this evening when I return to take dinner with you and Bliss. We need to discuss the new ship I've ordered. I promised the shipbuilder full payment after Bliss receives her inheritance."

Claude mumbled something Bliss didn't hear. Then she heard a drawer slam, followed by the sound of footsteps approaching the door. Gathering her wits, she scooted out of sight around the corner and waited for them to leave. The front door slammed, galvanizing her into action. No one was in sight as she slipped into the study and started opening drawers until she found the letter. Snatching it up, she memorized the name and address, then carefully replaced it where she'd found it.

Without considering the right or wrong of her act, Bliss went unerringly to her father's cash box and emptied it of all its cash. It wasn't a great deal, but it was sufficient to buy passage to Mobile. Rushing upstairs, she packed a small valise and quietly left the house without being seen.

Faulk's carriage was just clearing the front gate as Bliss made her way to the stables. The stableboy was occupied elsewhere, so she saddled her own horse rather than alert anyone to her plans. After tying her valise to the saddle, she mounted and took off down the road.

After spending two days in a run-down boardinghouse close to the levee, waiting for her ship to sail, Bliss boarded the *Sally Butler*, a freighter carrying slaves to Mobile, Alabama. She'd felt no remorse at selling her horse to the hostler and keeping the money. Her father owed her that much and more. As for her inheritance, it did her soul good to think that Gerald Faulk would never get his hands on it. She and her son could live comfortably on her monthly allowance.

But disaster struck on her second day out of New Orleans. A pirate ship appeared suddenly from behind a small island and gave chase. When they were within range, the pirates fired a shot across the *Sally Butler*'s bow. The ship was unarmed and gave up without a fight.

Bliss felt blood rush to her head as pirates swarmed over the ship. Her knees began to buckle when a fierce buccaneer grasped her about the waist and dragged her to the railing.

"This one belongs to me!" the pirate bellowed as he tried to kiss her.

Suddenly she was torn from his grasp, only to find herself in another pirate's arms.

"No one takes her until I, Gasparilla, decide if she's worth ransoming."

Bliss recognized the name and felt herself spinning away into suffocating blackness.

Chapter Three

The Barrier Islands off the Coast of Florida, 1811
Gasparilla Island

The pirate called Hunter sprawled in a wicker chair, waiting for Gasparilla to appear from his bedroom where he dallied with one of his women. Hunter's one-eyed gaze took in every aspect of the opulent mansion Gasparilla had built, mentally comparing it with his own home on Pine Island. Gasparilla possessed every luxury known to mankind within the sprawling house. Almost everything Gasparilla owned had been taken as plunder from rich Spanish galleons and other ships unlucky enough to cross his path.

Over the years Gasparilla had set up his elaborate complex on several islands in Charlotte

Harbor, keeping and naming the largest for himself. Because of his regal way of life, fashionable clothes, and elegant manners, he was referred to by the Brotherhood as King of the Pirates. He was fearless in battle, ruthless and cruel. A fickle lover, he kept a harem of the most beautiful women captives, using and replacing them when they fell out of favor. Only those women wealthy and important enough to bring ransom were left untouched.

Hunter's single eye gleamed like pure silver as his mind skipped back over the past six years. He counted his life from the day he had encountered Gasparilla on Barataria. The meeting had proven fortunate as well as profitable. Wounded and near death, Hunter had reached the Lafitte brothers and they had taken him to Grande Terre to recover his health after his almost miraculous escape from prison. His right eye had been totally destroyed, and the eyepatch he wore now covered the scars. Since real names were rarely used among pirates, he'd called himself Hunter because of his determination to hunt down and destroy every ship belonging to the Faulk line. As names went, it wasn't a bad one. Since the supposed death of Guy DeYoung, Hunter had no desire ever to use that name again.

Hunter's thoughts scattered as Gasparilla strutted out of the bedroom. Swarthy and small of stature, Gasparilla was of Spanish heritage. It was rumored that his name was really Jose Gaspar, and that he had once been an admiral in the Spanish Navy and had fled his country after being accused of stealing the queen's jewels. Gasparilla was not unhandsome, and he definitely had a way with women, but he was greatly feared for his cruel nature.

"Sorry to keep you waiting, Hunter," Gasparilla said as he pulled a dainty lace handkerchief from his sleeve and touched it to his forehead. "A woman I took from a ship several days ago caught my fancy and this is the first opportunity I've had to try her out."

Seven years ago Guy DeYoung would have felt sympathy for the woman, but Hunter had no conscience, felt no compassion, no charity for anyone weaker than himself.

"Did she please you?" Hunter asked conversationally.

Gasparilla sighed. "I think I am in love. But she spurns me. I've given her precious gems, cloth of gold and silver, and baubles that most women would envy. I do not understand women, my friend."

"You aren't the only one," Hunter said grimly. "Women can be treacherous. But that was in another life, another time. I was reborn six years ago and nothing remains of my former self."

"A wise decision," Gasparilla agreed.

"I have something for you from our agent in Havana. I carried it up from my ship," Hunter said, gesturing toward the small chest sitting on an ornately carved table.

Gasparilla strode to the chest and flipped

open the lid. The sparkle of gold was unmistakable. "Ah, ransom. Which one of my women captives has been liberated by her family?"

Hunter removed a thick missive from inside his black silk shirt and handed it to Gasparilla. "This should tell you."

Gasparilla scanned the letter. "Ah, the copper-haired wench from New Orleans. Her fiance has finally come through with the ransom and delivered it in person to my agent. He is awaiting her in Havana. I was hoping he wouldn't be able to raise it so I could sample that tempting morsel myself. But you know my policy. No woman awaiting ransom is to be harmed in any way. 'Tis a promise I made and one I've always kept."

Hunter laughed. "A pity the Brotherhood doesn't share your views. Before you moved the women captives to a guarded stockade on Captiva Island, they were at the mercy of your men, who thought nothing of kidnapping and using them for their own pleasure."

"Aye, 'twas a good move. But back to the Grenville woman. I can't spare the time to take her to Havana myself. Unfortunately, most of my captains are either unavailable or untrustworthy. I wouldn't want it said that Gasparilla reneges on his promises. Can I rely on you to deliver her to her fiance in good condition?"

Hunter had stopped listening when he heard the woman's name. *Grenville.* Surely it was a common enough name. It couldn't be Bliss Grenville, the woman whose name he hadn't spoken in seven years. Bliss Grenville would have no reason to be traveling alone on a ship. And her name would no longer be Grenville. She would have married Faulk long ago.

"Will you do this for me, Hunter?" Gasparilla inquired.

Hunter mentally shook himself, realizing that Gasparilla was speaking to him. For a moment long repressed feelings had inundated him with forgotten memories. "What is it you want me to do?"

"Haven't you heard a word I've said? Take the Grenville wench to Havana for me and I'll share the ransom with you. You'll find her in the stockade on Captiva Island. The guard can point her out to you."

Hunter shrugged. "I have nothing better to do right now."

"I do. I'm to meet with Jean Lafitte on Sanibel Island to transfer slaves taken from a galleon into his keeping. He has buyers in New Orleans clamoring for slaves, and I stand to gain a small fortune from their sale."

"I'll spend the night aboard my ship and sail to Captiva tomorrow," Hunter said, ignoring the warning bells ringing inside his head. Something he couldn't explain told him that his life was about to change.

The next day Hunter rowed ashore in his skiff and beached it upon the white sand of Captiva Island. Shells crunched beneath his boots as he followed the well-worn path through a mangrove forest to the stockade where the women captives lived in closely guarded thatched houses built of rough palmetto logs.

Two elderly pirates snapped to attention when they heard Hunter approaching. When they saw it was Hunter, not Gasparilla, they relaxed and greeted him jovially.

"What brings you to Captiva, Hunter?" one of the old pirates asked.

"Orders from Gasparilla," Hunter answered. "The ransom arrived for the Grenville woman. I'm here to take her to Havana. Can you point her out to me?"

One grizzled pirate flung open the gate and cast about for the woman in question. Hunter followed his gaze, skipping over a dozen or more women engaged in various mundane chores. Some were bent over cook fires preparing food while others were washing clothes in large wooden vats. A few were engaged in ordinary housekeeping chores. Most of the women wore tattered remnants of past finery that exposed large portions of pale skin. All were covered with angry red mosquito bites.

"There she be," the old pirate said, pointing to a woman bending over a tub.

Hunter spared a moment to admire her backside before recalling his mission and striding toward the woman. The buzz of conversation came to an abrupt halt as the women captives followed his progress across the compound.

He was dressed all in black, from his blousy silk shirt open at the neck to his tight black trousers and thigh-high boots. The single splash of color in his somber outfit consisted of a bright red neckerchief tied about his throat. His hair was long, straight, and black as sin. It covered both his ears, then was swept back and tied with a cord at his nape. His tall, muscular body moved with graceful precision, a visual feast for the women captives of Captiva. The bold slash of his eyebrows, strong features, and handsome face were enhanced instead of diminished by the eyepatch he wore, which intensified his mystique and charisma.

The bolder women preened for his benefit, while the shy ones looked at him from beneath lowered lids and smiled timidly. Hunter looked neither right nor left, his silver-gray eye focused on the woman bent over the washtub.

Bliss became aware of the unusual silence among her fellow captives but paid it little heed. Her mind was on more important matters. Such as why Fate kept dealing her one terrible blow after another. First she'd lost the man she loved. Then her child, or so she'd been led to believe. When she'd learned that her child wasn't dead after all and had run off to rescue him, her ship had been attacked by pirates and she'd been taken captive. She'd been held prisoner on the isle of captive women, where she'd had countless hours to worry about her son. It hurt to think she didn't even know his name.

The heat, the mosquitoes, the lack of wholesome food, the storms, all had combined to make life unbearable. She'd been told she was being held for ransom, but she seriously doubted that either her father or Gerald Faulk could raise funds to ransom her. Her birthday had come and gone, forgotten in the midst of all her troubles. She had turned twenty-five and was now eligible to collect her monthly stipend. Were she married, she'd have full control of her inheritance, but marriage was out of the question. She'd never marry Gerald Faulk after what he'd done to her.

Hunter halted a few steps behind Bliss, shocked at the way his heart was jumping in his chest. Sweat popped out on his forehead as he stared at the woman's back. Her dress was in tatters, baring one delicate shoulder and her shapely legs to her knees. A prickling sensation began at his lower spine and continued upward. He couldn't ever recall feeling like this before. As if Fate had brought him to this moment in time.

Bliss spun around, suddenly aware of a presence behind her. The pirate was dressed all in black, his tall, imposing form striking fear in her heart as he stared at her with one brilliant silver eye. His right eye was covered with a black patch; Bliss could see the faded white line of a scar both above and below the patch. She shuddered. The injury must have been horribly painful, and briefly she wondered if he had sustained the injury while engaging in battle with his hapless victims.

All sorts of gruesome atrocities came to mind

as she eyed the sword at his side and the brace of pistols protruding from his belt and the wicked-looking knife stuck in his boot. He looked hard and brutal, and she took an involuntary step backward.

Hunter stared at the woman he'd vowed to forget and felt the years slide away. He recalled the taste and scent of her, her innocent passion, the softness of her skin, the incredible heat and tightness of her as he brought her to climax. Damnation! He'd thought he had cast her from his heart and mind. Put her behind him the day he was reborn as Hunter. But seeing her again brought all those forbidden memories back in a rush of violent recollection. Once he had loved her fiercely, with every fiber of his body and soul. That love had shriveled and died when he'd seen her crying over Faulk and begging him not to die.

He wasn't surprised that Bliss didn't recognize him. He had changed over the years and so had she, albeit much less than he. The color of her hair was darker than he recalled, but no less vibrant. Her figure had ripened with age, he noted. She was far more alluring now than she had been at seventeen. On the other hand, her turquoise eyes had changed little. They were still as captivating as they had been seven years ago.

"What do you want?"

Her voice startled him. It was slightly throaty, with a huskiness to it that made him think of sultry nights and sex. And it was as deceptive as the name he now bore, he thought. He wasn't the gullible fool he'd once been. He'd lost whatever goodness he'd possessed. He'd committed heinous acts that any man with a heart and soul would deplore. But he had neither heart nor soul. Compassion and sentiment didn't belong in the world in which he now lived. His sole purpose in life was revenge.

Hunter had already had a good dose of vengeance. Gerald Faulk and Claude Grenville had cost him his eye. An eye for an eye was the code he now lived by. He'd made Faulk's ships his particular prey. Few of them got by him intact. The Lafitte brothers had told him that Faulk and Grenville were tottering on the brink of total ruin. The news was sweet indeed.

"Your family has sent the ransom," he said in answer to Bliss's question. "Your fiance is waiting for you in Havana."

Bliss started violently. That voice! Where had she heard it before? The deep, almost sensual quality flowed over her like fine wine. She shivered and backed away. It was eerie, as if someone had walked over her grave. No! More as if she had just walked over someone else's grave.

"I don't want to go to Havana," Bliss said, unable to turn her gaze away from that fascinating silver eye.

Hunter's dark brow lifted. "What have we here, a reluctant bride?" He looked her up and down. "At your age one would think you'd be eager to marry." He made the words sound like an insult.

Bliss's gaze slid away from his face. "You don't understand. I can't marry Gerald Faulk. There is something I have to do first. I can't go to Havana. Gasparilla has my ransom; why can't I be taken where I wish to go?"

Hunter's face hardened into uncompromising lines. "Gasparilla prides himself on keeping his word to the families of his captives. He promised your family you'd be taken to Cuba and released unharmed."

"Who are you?" Bliss asked. She had the distinct feeling that she'd met this man before. How could it be? Surely she'd remember someone as imposing and . . . yes, as handsome as this fierce pirate.

"Call me Hunter."

"Mr. Hunter, I—"

"Just Hunter."

"You seem more . . . refined than the usual lot of cutthroats I've encountered around here. Can't you find it in your heart to take me to . . . say, Mobile, instead of Havana? I have a small allowance I can draw upon. I can make it worth your while."

Hunter sent her an amused look. "Don't mistake me for a gentleman. I'm the same as any other member of the Brotherhood. I have no heart, and it will do you little good to appeal to my conscience, for I have none. If it's compassion you're seeking, forget it. I lost it long ago."

"I thought . . ." She shook her head and looked away.

"What is so important in Mobile?" Hunter inquired. "Is one of your lovers waiting for you there? Are you running away from your betrothed? Is that why you were on a ship without a chaperone?"

"I owe you no explanation," Bliss said on a rising note of panic. She couldn't return to Gerald! Not now, not after he'd shown her what a true bastard he was.

"Gather your belongings, we've tarried long enough."

"Please," Bliss said. "If you won't take me to Mobile, then release me in New Orleans."

"You're appealing to the wrong person, Bliss. I'm merely doing Gasparilla a favor by taking you to Havana."

Bliss went still. "How do you know my name?" The same eerie, haunted feeling she'd experienced upon meeting the one-eyed pirate sent a shudder down her spine.

Thinking fast, Hunter said, "Gasparilla's agent in Havana provided your full name and it was relayed to me. I suppose the agent learned it from your betrothed."

Bliss hesitated but a moment. Leaving this stockade of captive women wasn't the worst thing that could happen to her. Even if she was returned to Gerald, she could always skip out again, just as she'd done before. This time she'd do things differently. She'd confront Gerald and her father with what she knew about her son and make them get her child for her. Had she thought it out more thoroughly, instead of running off to Mobile herself, that's what she would have done.

"I'm ready," Bliss said, raising her chin. "There is nothing I want to take with me." She glanced down at her tattered dress and frowned. "Will I be given something decent to wear when I'm set ashore?" She touched her tangled mass of burnished curls. "I'll also need a comb and brush."

Hunter thought she'd never looked lovelier, but stifled the urge to say it. "There is an assortment of clothing and grooming supplies for you aboard the *Predator*. You'll have plenty of time before we reach Cuba to primp. Come along now, my skiff is beached nearby."

Bliss had a hard time keeping up with Hunter's long-legged stride. He reminded her of another man whose long legs and lithe body had never reached its full potential. A man she'd loved more than herself. But Guy hadn't been as brawny as Hunter. If there was one similarity between her dead husband and the infamous buccaneer, Bliss decided it was their silver eyes. But the resemblance stopped there. Whereas Guy's eyes had been windows into his compassionate and loving soul, Hunter's visible eye gave eloquent witness of brutality, bitterness, dissipation, and things she couldn't even guess at.

The sun beat fiercely down on Bliss's bare head; her face was shiny with perspiration as it ran down her neck and puddled between her breasts. She tried to concentrate on anything but the fierce pirate walking in front of her and was vastly relieved when they finally arrived at the place where his boat was beached.

Hunter pulled the skiff out into the surf, scrambled aboard, and held it in place with an oar while Bliss climbed inside. Once she was settled, he began to row. Hunter's ship rode at anchor just beyond the breakers, and Bliss admired it from afar. It was a brigantine, two-masted and square-rigged. Hunter had named it *Predator*, and Bliss thought the ship looked as strong, dangerous, and deadly as its captain.

"You'll have to climb the rope ladder," Hunter said as the skiff bumped against the *Predator*. "I'll be right behind you, so don't worry about falling." He tied the skiff to the ship, then grasped her around the waist and lifted her up to the rope ladder.

It seemed like a long way up and Bliss didn't look down as she began the perilous climb. Hunter was behind her; she could feel the heat of him against her legs. She had almost gained the top when hands reached down to haul her onto the deck. Hunter leaped up behind her, landing agilely on his feet.

Bliss eyed the crew of fierce pirates and shrank back against Hunter. They were the scurviest lot Bliss had ever laid eyes upon. Dressed in an odd assortment of finery and rags, they leered at her as if she were a tasty morsel to be devoured.

"Heave to, mates," Hunter said, placing himself between Bliss and his men. "We've a job to do for Gasparilla. Helmsman, set a course for Cuba."

Bliss breathed a sigh of relief as the crewmen scrambled to obey Hunter's orders. She heard the anchor chain creak in protest as it slowly rose from the water. Moments later, wind caught the billowing sails and the ship moved forward. They were under way.

"Come along," Hunter said gruffly. "My crew are damned good at what they do, but they are all unprincipled men. 'Tis best you remain in my quarters while you're aboard."

"Your quarters?" Bliss repeated, eyeing him warily.

"The captain's cabin is the only private quarters on the *Predator*. You'll find the arrangement comfortable."

"Where will you sleep?"

He gave her an enigmatic smile. "In my bed, of course. I said there is but one cabin aboard the *Predator*. The crewmen sleep on deck when the weather is good or down below when it's not. Any other questions?"

"Just a request."

"You are in no position to request anything. But go ahead, I have a feeling I'll find it amusing."

Color flooded Bliss's face. Only a man without a heart would find amusement in her predicament. "Don't take me to Cuba," she pleaded. "If you can't set me free in Mobile, then New Orleans will do. Anyplace but Cuba."

Hunter regarded her curiously as he opened

the door to his cabin and ushered her inside. He shut the door firmly behind him, his gaze roaming freely over her ill-clad form as he suddenly saw her through the eyes of his crewmen. One golden shoulder was completely bare, and the tattered material of her bodice provided a tantalizing glimpse of a white breast. Her skirt had been shorn at the knees and her bare calves were the same smooth tan color as her one bare shoulder. Her disheveled beauty was riveting.

Just as riveting as he remembered from long ago.

She must have been aware of her disheveled appearance, for she tried to cover the gaps in her clothing with her hands. Hunter smiled at her futile efforts and asked, "Why are you running away from your betrothed? What's so important in Mobile?"

"It's a long story, I'm sure you wouldn't be interested. I've been a captive for several weeks. Time may be running out. It's imperative that I reach Mobile as soon as possible."

Hunter stared at her askance. Who was waiting for her in Mobile? he wondered. A lover? Bile rose up in his throat at the thought of other men touching her. Seven years was a long time. He knew Faulk must have had her, as well as others, and intense rage blotted out all reason. Faulk and Grenville were the cause of all his suffering. He'd have two good eyes if not for the assassin they'd sent to kill him. Bliss must have known about it, condoned it even. He'd thought that attacking Faulk's ships and ruining him financially would satisfy his thirst for revenge, but he'd been wrong.

The passing years had done nothing to ease his bitterness or erase his hatred. In truth, they had increased a thousandfold, making him more determined than ever to find other ways to punish Faulk and the Grenvilles. It suddenly occurred to him that he had in his hands the ultimate instrument of revenge. Bliss Grenville. With little effort he could use her to humiliate his enemies. Suddenly life was good.

"You're not exactly a young woman," Hunter said, curling his lip in derision. "Why haven't you married before now?"

Bliss's chin shot upward. "I wasn't ready," she said, refusing to divulge her innermost secrets to a heartless pirate who wanted answers to questions he had no business asking.

"I'm surprised your fiance was willing to wait for you. Most men wouldn't be so patient."

"Gerald Faulk is not like most men," Bliss said dryly. Hunter frowned, mistaking her words for praise. "Why should it matter to you? I made a simple request. What is your answer?"

"I'll think about it," Hunter said as he let himself out the door. "Meanwhile, I'll see that you have something decent to wear when you're set ashore. We wouldn't want your family to think you've been mistreated. Gasparilla is very meticulous about following the ransom terms. He becomes enraged when they are breached."

Hunter closed the door behind him and climbed the half dozen steps to the deck. He breathed deeply of the tangy salt air, clearing his nostrils of the scent of woman. The scent of Bliss . . . his wife. Was she still his wife? he wondered. Or had she obtained an annulment after he'd been thrown in jail? Most likely her father had been relentless in dissolving the short-lived marriage between Guy DeYoung and his daughter. Hunter had discovered that Gerald Faulk hadn't died of his wounds, but he'd learned little else during the year he'd been shut away from the outside world.

He'd briefly considered returning to New Orleans before he'd joined the Brotherhood, but he'd known nothing good would come of it. As a result he had severed all ties with anyone who had once known the man named Guy DeYoung. The only thing left to connect him to that man was his hunger for vengeance.

Ah, revenge, how sweet it tasted.

Hunter smiled as he contemplated the ramifications of his plan. Once he was considered a charming fellow. It would be a simple matter to use that charm on Bliss, to make her fall in love with him. She'd loved him as Guy DeYoung, why not as Hunter? He would seduce her, bed her, oh yes, he looked forward to that with relish, then return her to her fiance and father with a pirate's get in her belly.

Hunter laughed aloud, pleased with his plan. The only thing that could go wrong was having Gasparilla learn that Bliss hadn't been returned to her family as he had instructed. But Hunter would cross that bridge when he came to it. More than likely Gasparilla would never know.

"Change the course for Pine Island, Greene," Hunter told his helmsman.

Greene gave him a gap-toothed look of surprise. "Pine Island, Hunter? Are ye certain sure? Gasparilla ain't gonna like it."

"The men have earned time on shore with their women and children, and the *Predator*'s hull needs scraping."

"But the captive—"

"She's mine right now. She'll be delivered to her family when I'm good and ready to give her up."

Greene sent him a knowing grin. "Like that, huh? She's a comely wench, all right. I envy you, Cap'n."

Bliss dashed wayward tears from her eyes as she fought the urge to cry. It seemed there was no way to avoid being taken to Cuba. Dear God! It was too far away from her son.

Bliss walked to the back of the cabin and stepped through double doors onto the tiny balcony. The day was fine and sunny; a brisk breeze propelled the ship. She stared at the rippling waves and wondered what would happen if she jumped overboard and swam to the nearest island. There were so many islands and cays off Florida's west coast, she doubted she'd have trouble reaching one. But then what? Would she trade one pirate's lair for another?

She sighed deeply, her thoughts turning to

the man called Hunter. Who was he really? she wondered. Swathed in unrelieved black and wearing an eyepatch, he could be the Devil himself. When she looked into his silver eye she had the strangest feeling of déjà vu. His scent, and the way he carried himself, were hauntingly familiar. Yet, had she met Hunter before, she knew she would never have forgotten him.

"Not thinking of jumping overboard, are you?"

Bliss started violently. Hunter had come up behind her while she'd been lost in thought.

"It's something to consider," she replied.

"It wouldn't work. I'm an excellent swimmer; you'd not get far."

"Have you decided to honor my request?"

"Aye."

Bliss didn't like the glint in his eye, but she was so elated she chose to ignore it. "You're going to take me to Mobile?"

"I didn't say that."

Bliss's spirits plummeted. What kind of game was he playing? Did baiting her amuse him? "New Orleans will do if you can't see your way to taking me to Mobile."

"I have no intention of taking you to New Orleans."

Fueled by anger, driven to the limits of her patience, Bliss gave a cry of outrage and pounded her fists against Hunter's chest. "What kind of man are you? Have you no compassion, no heart? Does my predicament amuse you?"

Apparently taken by surprise, Hunter suffered her pounding for several moments before capturing both her wrists in one of his powerful fists and jerking her against him. For a moment he seemed to savor her softness, then he gave her a rough shake.

"Never mistake me for anything other than what you see before you. My heart was ripped from my body just as my eye was destroyed long ago. I have no conscience, no soul, feel no remorse. I've done things, seen things that would make you cringe. Sometimes they even make *me* cringe. When I see something I want, I take it."

Still holding her wrists in one hand, he caressed her face with the other. His fingers grazed her cheek, her chin, his thumb rubbing her lower lip in a back-and-forth motion.

She was aware of his hard, masculine fingers, warm and firm against her mouth. He was so close she could smell the salt spray and sunshine on his clothing, feel the heat emanating from his body, almost taste his sexuality.

His words jolted her. "I want you, Bliss Grenville. I want your body. I want your soul. I want your heart."

Bliss nearly gagged on her panic. What did he mean? "N . . . no! Please, let go of me. You're supposed to return me to my fiance unharmed, remember?"

Hunter's face was as hard and cold as his voice. "Oh, you'll see Faulk again, but not until I decide it's time."

Hunter felt Bliss's soft body stiffen against his

and smiled inwardly. She was frightened, but fear was good. Fear was a start. He couldn't wait to turn her fear into desire. The same desire she'd once felt for Guy DeYoung. Hunter stared into Bliss's beautiful face and made a silent vow never to fall into the same velvet trap that had destroyed Guy DeYoung. This captivating woman in his arms was a means to an end, nothing more.

Roughly he pushed her away from him. "I'm taking you to my private island."

Bliss stared at him. "Why?"

His silver eye gleamed. "I have my reasons."

Whatever his reasons, Bliss knew she wasn't going to like them.

Chapter Four

The *Predator* sailed though Pine Island Sound into a lagoon enclosed by a natural seawall consisting of layers of oyster-shell deposits. Bliss stood on the ship's small balcony, watching porpoises and sharks chase fish into the shoals, where hundreds of pelicans, cormorants, and gulls waited to engage in a feeding frenzy. The poor fish hadn't a chance, attacked from both the air and the sea. On shore, a regal heron lifted its huge wings to join the melee.

From her vantage point on the ship, all Bliss could see of the large island were mangrove thickets and pine trees. She watched in dismay as the ship sailed toward the shore, as if it meant to beach itself. Just when it appeared the ship would crash into the mangrove swamp, a river passage opened up, cutting a swath through the swamp large enough to allow a ship to enter. She held her breath as the ship glided effortlessly into the river, scraping trees on either side as it sailed into the dense interior of the island. A short time later the river opened into a large lake and the helmsman skillfully maneuvered the ship toward a stone jetty.

Bliss made her way on deck during the docking process. Hunter was waiting for her.

"Welcome to my home," Hunter said. "I'll escort you ashore."

As he ushered her down the gangplank and onto the stone jetty, Bliss was surprised to see a village nestled along the shore of the lake. Small cottages constructed of latticed pine saplings chinked with clay plaster and thatched with marsh grass were clustered together in disorderly rows. Fishing skiffs lined the shore and racks of drying fish baked in the afternoon sun. The heat was oppressive and the stench of fish offensive to her nose. Bliss followed Hunter down a shell-lined street.

"Which house is yours?" Bliss asked, eyeing the huts with misgiving.

They walked through groups of excited women hurrying to the jetty to greet their men. They were a rough-looking lot, Bliss thought, as crude in speech and unkempt as their men. Their finery had probably been taken from plundered ships, but the once-rich silks and satins were ripped beyond repair and worn upon dirty bodies.

"I built my house farther inland, away from

the carousing that usually goes on in the village."

"And you don't carouse?" Bliss taunted.

"At times. But there are times I prefer privacy and quiet. Come along," he said, taking her elbow. " 'Tis but a short walk."

They pushed their way through a milling crowd of men and women shouting out greetings to Hunter. Bliss shrank away from groping hands as vulgar suggestions about what Hunter should do with her were freely offered. She was vastly relieved when they took a path through the forest, leaving the village behind.

The path cut a swath through thick underbrush and skirted numerous shallow basins lined with crushed shells. Bliss was curious about their function and asked Hunter about them.

"They're used to collect rain water," he explained. "Compliments of the Calusa Indians who once inhabited these islands before their Spanish masters killed most of them. Only a few are left now. The island is dotted with Indian burial mounds and remains of temples, dwellings, and storage buildings of tribes now extinct. I've seen remnants of Indian settlements stretching more than three-quarters of a mile along the north shore of the island and one-quarter of a mile wide."

Bliss was intrigued. "Burial mounds? Have you dug into any of them?"

"No, and I don't intend to. I have no desire to disturb the dead. Let some future generation discover their secrets. As for myself, I'm content to live in peace among the living."

Bliss's skin was slick with perspiration by the time they reached Hunter's house. But as she stared at Hunter's home she decided it was well worth the walk. It was a palace compared to the small huts on the beach. The dwelling was built on a grand scale, constructed of sawed boards instead of rough pine saplings. It sat on a slight rise beneath an umbrella of palm trees that provided abundant shade. A wrap-around porch allowed the breeze to waft through the open windows. Another building, probably a kitchen, was connected to the house by a covered dog run.

Hunter held the door open and she stepped inside. She came to an abrupt halt as her startled gaze encountered a room as luxuriously furnished as some of the grandest homes in New Orleans. Works of art hung on the plastered walls above richly polished furniture and thick, woven carpets. Dainty curtains billowed gently in the tropical breeze, and delicious cooking smells drifted to her on the humid air.

"Do you like it?" Hunter asked. Somehow it mattered that Bliss should like his home.

"It's . . . I can't believe such a home exists on this remote island inhabited by pirates and cutthroats."

"I like to be comfortable," Hunter said as he watched Bliss pick up a gold-encrusted vase and examine it.

"At the expense of other people?" Bliss challenged as she set the vase down. "How many ships did you plunder to furnish your house? How many lives were lost?"

Hunter looked away, ignoring her probing questions. Her words unsettled him more than he cared to admit. There had been too many ships. Too many lives lost to count. He'd be a liar if he said they hadn't mattered at first. But after so many ships and so many lives, one tended to forget the numbers. Though he usually tried not to take innocent lives himself, he'd done nothing to stop Gasparilla and others like him from committing cold-blooded murder.

Crews taken from the ships he'd personally attacked had been set adrift in boats, not simply slain for the joy of killing. He liked to think that small kindness set him apart from men like Gasparilla, but he knew he was fooling no one but himself. He was no better than his fellow pirates. In some ways he considered himself worse, for he'd once had a conscience. He knew right from wrong and had learned to ignore his conscience.

"Don't judge me, Bliss," he said harshly. "Were you to look deep into your heart, I'm sure you'd find something to regret, too."

Bliss flinched beneath his scrutiny. She had the uncanny feeling that Hunter could see into her soul, read her mind. It was as if he knew things about her that not even those close to her knew. *Who was this man?*

"No one is perfect," she allowed.

"What do you regret, Bliss?"

Bliss opened her mouth, then clamped it tightly shut. The urge to unburden herself to this man was so compelling, she'd been ready to tell him about the child she'd never even held in her arms.

He gave her an enigmatic smile. "Keep your secrets. Come along, I'll show you to your room."

They had just started down a long hallway when they were met by a handsome black woman. She was tall and slender, with expressive brown eyes and a generous mouth. She grinned from ear to ear when she saw Hunter.

"We weren't expecting you, Cap'n. How long will you stay this time?" Her dark-eyed gaze, bright with curiosity, settled on Bliss.

"I'm long overdue for a rest, Cleo," Hunter said, placing a proprietary arm around Bliss's waist. "My ship's hull is in need of careening and my men need time with their women and children." His gaze fell on Bliss. "The length of my stay depends on Bliss."

"On me! You can leave tomorrow for all I care."

"Too soon, Bliss. Far too soon for my purposes." He turned to Cleo, saying, "Find Caesar and Tamrah. I wish to introduce all three of you to your new mistress."

Bliss started violently. Mistress? What kind of game was Hunter playing? He'd made no move thus far to hurt her, but she was astute enough to realize he wanted something from her.

I want your body. I want your soul. I want your heart.

His words hung between them like a curtain of choking smoke, stealing her breath. His sexual innuendos were too blatant to be misconstrued. He'd brought her to his island to make her his mistress. Nothing else made sense.

Cleo left them. Hunter opened a door and ushered her inside a sunny room whose two large windows overlooked a vegetable garden. Beyond the lush garden Bliss could see the glimmer of sparkling water. Hunter watched her closely as she gazed about the cheery room. He followed her when she walked to the window and gazed longingly toward the sea.

"There are panthers on the island. You wouldn't get far." He was so close she could feel his warm breath upon her neck.

Could he read her mind? She had indeed been thinking about escape.

"Bliss, turn around and look at me."

She turned slowly.

"Do you know why I brought you here?"

"I'm not stupid. I know exactly what you want."

"I'll bet you do," he mocked.

"I won't do it!" Her chin rose belligerently.

He moved closer. She stepped backward but there was nowhere to go. She was hemmed in by the window behind her and Hunter in front of her. The heat from his body scorched her; she felt the appalling urge to melt against him, to give herself up to him in total surrender. His face was so close she could see tiny squint lines fanning out from the corner of his good eye. Her gaze fell to his lips. They were slightly parted, full and moist. Her mouth went dry and she licked moisture onto her lips with the tip of her tongue.

"Yes, you will," he breathed against her mouth. "You'll beg me for it."

Before she could form a cutting reply, his mouth closed over hers. His kiss was demanding, yet oddly tender. It was exquisitely, unbearably intense. He ended it before she was ready. She could have almost imagined it, if not for the way her lips tingled and burned.

Her fingers flew to her mouth. She had the strangest feeling that she had kissed him before, which was utterly ridiculous. Then she became aware of a different heat and pressure. With a sudden intake of breath she realized that Hunter's hands were on her breasts. He was caressing them, stroking her nipples, his silver gaze intent upon her, gauging her reaction.

"Don't do that!"

"Don't you like it?"

"No!"

"Perhaps you prefer Gerald Faulk's caresses."

The thought of Gerald's hands upon her like this made her shiver in revulsion. "Perhaps," she hedged.

"Liar! I believe you prefer me and the way I make you feel," Hunter said with a hint of arrogance.

"No! That's not what I mean at all. You're confusing me."

It was true. Bliss could barely think, let alone speak. The sensations Hunter evoked in her were becoming unbearable. Only one man had ever made her burn like this, and that man was dead. Allowing this vile pirate intimate liberty with her body was a defilement of her one true love's memory. Ignoring her dangerous position, she slapped his hands away and retreated into the farthest corner of the room.

Hunter knew he was deliberately provoking Bliss, but couldn't seem to stop himself. The moment he'd touched her, long forgotten memories assailed him. Seven years ago he'd unleashed her sexuality. Now he intended to devote countless hours to exploring it, tasting it, savoring it. He had seven years to make up for.

He remembered every fascinating detail of her body. That intriguing little mole beneath her left breast that he'd loved to kiss and caress with his tongue. Her tiny waist. Her long, supple legs. The abundance of copper hair shielding the succulent pink flesh of her most secret place. Her tiny gasping moans when he suckled her nipples. He groaned. He'd grown hard as stone. If he didn't stop fantasizing, he'd end up tupping her on the bed with her skirts thrown over her head. And that wasn't the way he'd planned it.

After he returned her to Faulk and her father, he wanted her to remember that she had wanted it, begged for it, burned for it. When he finally revealed himself to her, he wanted her to feel the same kind of pain he'd suffered the day of the duel when she'd chosen Faulk over him.

Quelling his sexual urges, Hunter gave Bliss a mocking salute. "As you wish, Bliss. For now," he added cryptically.

The tension between them was so thick, Bliss nearly choked on it. She couldn't imagine what had come over her. Or why this pirate aroused feelings in her she'd thought impossible with any man but Guy DeYoung.

A discreet knock on the door diffused the tense atmosphere. Bliss nearly collapsed with relief when Hunter turned away from her to answer the door.

"Come in," he invited, holding the door wide. "I've summoned you here to introduce all of you to your new mistress."

Cleo entered the room, followed by a gigantic man whose skin was the same shiny black as Cleo's. The last to enter was a young woman barely out of girlhood. Her flawless coffee-and-cream skin and long black hair were a perfect foil for her expressive, almond-shaped eyes. She wore a sarong-like garment that left little of her voluptuous figure to the imagination.

"You've already met Cleo," Hunter said. "The big fellow behind her is Caesar, her husband. I married them myself."

"Are they slaves?" Bliss asked.

"I found them aboard a Spanish slaver and brought them here. They are free, but choose to remain on Pine Island and serve me for wages. Cleo is my housekeeper and cook and Caesar is caretaker. I couldn't do without either of them."

Bliss turned her turquoise gaze on the young woman, who was staring at Hunter as if she wanted to devour him. Bliss thought she already knew what the woman was to Hunter and wondered how he would explain the dusky beauty's presence in his home.

"This is Tamrah," Hunter explained. "She's one of the few Calusa Indians remaining on the island. She helps Cleo with the chores," he said, offering no other explanation.

Bliss wasn't stupid; she knew exactly where Tamrah fit into the household.

"Bliss is your new mistress," Hunter told the servants. "Obey her wishes as you would mine. Are there any questions?"

"No, Cap'n," Caesar said, answering for both himself and his wife. He aimed a wide grin at Bliss, revealing straight white teeth. "Don't worry, me and Cleo will take good care of the little missy. Is she your wife?"

Though Hunter seemed to hesitate over the question, Bliss had no difficulty answering. "No, of course I'm not his wife. I'm his captive. I'm not here by choice."

Both Cleo and Caesar pretended they hadn't heard Bliss's outburst. "Is that all, Cap'n?" Cleo asked.

"Aye, you can go now. I just wanted to make you aware that Bliss is my guest and should be treated respectfully."

Cleo and Caesar padded from the room on bare feet. Tamrah remained, her eyes dark with malice as they settled on Bliss.

"You can help, too, Tamrah," Hunter continued blithely. "Bliss needs a personal maid. I know you haven't been trained for the job, but I'm sure Bliss can teach you whatever you need to know."

"Personal maid?" Tamrah repeated in broken English. "I am a Calusa princess. I wait on no one." Indignant, she turned and swept regally from the room.

"Tamrah tends to be a little haughty," Hunter said, chuckling.

"I don't need a maid," Bliss returned shortly. "I can manage on my own just fine, thank you."

"If you need help, open the connecting door over there. I'll be happy to oblige."

"Connecting door?" Bliss turned her head, noting for the first time the door at the opposite end of the room.

"My room lies just beyond that thin panel," Hunter said smugly. "I find the arrangement convenient at times."

Bliss remembered the way her breasts had tingled and burned when he'd touched them and she suppressed a shudder. "Convenient for what?"

Hunter gave her a smile lavish with innuendo. "Figure it out." Then he strode through the door, closing it quietly behind him.

Bliss was still staring at the door long after

he'd left. She didn't move until Cleo rapped and stuck her head inside.

"It's Cleo, missy. Caesar is here with the tub for your bath."

"Bath? Oh, do bring it in," Bliss called, eager to soak in a real tub after being denied that luxury for so long.

Soon the tub was set up and filled with tepid water. A bar of jasmine-scented soap and a thick drying cloth had been placed on a bench beside it. Cleo lingered behind. "Is there anything else you wish, missy?"

"No, thank you, unless you can find me something decent to wear."

"The master has already instructed me to find clothing for you. While you're soaking, I'll sort through the trunks in the storeroom. Enjoy your bath, missy."

Bliss quickly stripped and stepped into the tub, sighing contentedly as she lowered herself into the water. The tepid water felt wonderful on her overheated skin,.as she soaped her hair and scrubbed vigorously. After washing and rinsing her hair twice, she lathered and rinsed her body, beginning with her face and continuing down to her toes. Then she lay back, closed her eyes, and let the water soothe and relax her.

A jarring voice intruded upon her thoughts. "Why are you here?"

Bliss hadn't heard the door open but she recognized the voice. Her eyes flew open. Tamrah. Bliss turned her head toward the door and saw the exotic beauty standing just a few feet away.

"Why don't you ask Hunter that question? This isn't where I want to be. I had no choice in the matter."

"Hunter has never brought a woman here before."

The question that burned on the tip of her tongue had to be asked. "What are you to Hunter?"

"I belong to Hunter," Tamrah declared smugly. "Father gave me to him. Father was the last great Calusa chief left on the island. Nearly all our people, except for those living in a small village at the north end of the island, were annihilated by the Spanish who came to our island many years ago. Father trusted Hunter. Before Father died he asked Hunter to find me a suitable husband from among our people when the time came. I want no one but Hunter," she said fiercely.

Bliss didn't ask, but it was obvious to her that Tamrah and Hunter had become lovers.

"Hunter will kill you when he tires of you," Tamrah said with grim satisfaction. "He has taken women before, but they quickly bore him and then he returns to me."

Bliss heard a noise at the connecting door and swung her gaze in that direction. Was she to be allowed no privacy? she wondered as Hunter entered the room. She scooted as far down into the water as she dared without drowning.

"Have you changed your mind about serving as Bliss's maid, Tamrah?" Hunter asked. "If not, you may leave now. I'll see to Bliss myself. And close the door behind you."

"I have not changed my mind," Tamrah threw over her shoulder as she flounced out of the room, slamming the door behind her.

"Your mistress was just regaling me with stories of your exploits," Bliss said sarcastically.

Hunter gave her a lopsided grin. "Your jealousy is charming. Tamrah fancies herself in love with me, but she is not now nor has she ever been my mistress. She's more like a sister to me."

"Some sister," Bliss muttered beneath her breath. She was more inclined to believe Tamrah than she was Hunter. Not that it mattered. She wanted nothing to do with the heartless pirate, who had not denied committing vile crimes upon the high seas.

"What are you doing here? Am I to be allowed no privacy?"

"This is my home, I go where I please. I returned to tell you that I won't be able to dine with you tonight. My men have invited me to a celebration down in the village and I don't think you'd care to attend. Their revelries tend to get pretty rowdy."

"Go where you please"—Bliss shrugged—" 'tis no concern of mine. Are you taking Tamrah?" Hunter's smug smile made her want to bite her tongue.

"No, Tamrah never attends events in the village. She is too good to be wasted on undisciplined pirates who despoil everything good and pure."

"Are you not a despoiler yourself?" Bliss taunted against her better judgment.

Hunter gave her an enigmatic look. "I suppose you might say that." He reached for the drying cloth and held it out. "Step out of the tub. As long as I'm here, I'll provide maid service."

"No, thank you."

After what seemed like an eternity to Bliss, he dropped the cloth. "Have it your way . . . for now. But don't expect it to last." Then he turned on his heel and strode away.

Bliss dined alone in her room. The worst of the heat had dissipated with the setting sun, leaving behind a soft, starlit evening stirred by sea-scented breezes. Night sounds wafted through the balmy air; concertina music and loud voices raised in lusty celebration floated to her on the breeze.

Bliss had no idea what was taking place down on the beach and didn't want to know. Nevertheless, she moved to the window, enchanted by the almost magical display of dancing shadows and dappled moonlight. Bursts of laughter and noises made by couples engaging in sexual activity in the underbrush close to the house drifted through her window. Was one of those grunting men Hunter? she wondered distractedly.

The night sky was brilliant with sparkling stars when Bliss finally changed into one of the nightgowns Cleo had brought her, climbed into bed and pulled the mosquito netting around her. The bed proved to be as comfortable as it looked and she fell instantly asleep.

Bliss was sleeping deeply when Hunter returned home. He'd drunk too much rum and his head spun dizzily. He found his room with some difficulty and stripped off his clothing. He struggled with the mosquito netting, then fell onto the mattress. It wasn't until he happened to glance at the connecting door that he recalled the woman sleeping on the other side of that door.

His wife.

He groaned, turned over on his stomach and tried to ignore the erection that had plagued him from the moment Bliss had claimed his thoughts. To his dismay, sleep eluded him. His nights were sleepless more often than not, his dreams fraught with terrifying memories of prison cells and assassins. Over the years he'd learned to live without sleep. It was simpler than reliving the same nightmare night after night. And the cause of those nightmares lay just beyond the connecting door.

Hunter rose slowly so as not to jar his aching head, fought the mosquito netting, found the opening, and struggled to his feet. He walked unsteadily to the connecting door and turned the knob. The panel swung open on noiseless hinges and he stepped inside. The bed was bathed in moonlight. Behind the thin veil of mosquito netting lay the woman whose body he had once known as intimately as his own. The woman he had married in good faith, the one who had sworn undying love, then shattered his life by abandoning him for another.

The outline of her slight body within the bed drew him like a moth to flame. He padded across the floor and shoved aside the netting. She was lying on her back, one arm curved upward over her burnished head like an innocent child. He stared at the steady rise and fall of her breasts, and at the lush outline of her pink nipples pushing against the thin material of her nightgown. The buzzing in his head increased. He had to forcibly restrain himself from reaching out to touch her. Soon, he thought with grim determination, soon he'd have her in his bed.

Bliss had no idea what had awakened her, but abruptly she knew she wasn't alone. Her eyes opened slowly and she started violently when she saw Hunter bending over her. He was as naked as the day he was born. She was too stunned to speak coherently. Her throat worked convulsively as she tried without success to swallow the lump in her throat.

He was bathed in moonlight and shadows, his powerful body a perfect blend of muscles and taut flesh. She smiled groggily as time sped backward. She imagined herself with the man she loved more than her own life. She whispered his name, vaguely aware of her mistake.

"Guy . . . Oh, Guy . . ."

Hunter went still. "What did you say?"

Bliss's eyes widened and she shook her head, her wits returning as she rose up on her elbows and glared at him. She was fully awake now and clearly aware of what and who he was.

"What are you doing here?"

"I came to bid you good night." The words twisted about his tongue and came out somewhat slurred.

"You're drunk! What do you want?"

"You." The bedsprings groaned as he lowered himself to the mattress.

She shoved him away but he wouldn't budge. "Go away."

No answer.

"I'm not going to make this easy for you."

Still no answer.

"Damn you! Go find Tamrah if you want someone in your bed."

This time Hunter made a snorting sound and Bliss realized he'd fallen asleep. She tried to roll away from him, but her nightgown was stuck beneath him. When she attempted to pull it out, he turned abruptly and threw one leg and an arm over her, making escape all but impossible. Bliss had no recourse but to remain pinned beneath him until morning and pray that he wouldn't awaken. She waited until she was certain he was sleeping soundly before drifting off to sleep herself.

Hunter groaned and tried to open his gritty eye. His mouth tasted like yesterday's fish and his head felt as if it were being pounded by a hundred hammers. And he was hot. Rivers of sweat gathered in places where something soft and warm was pressed against him. He was also, he quickly discovered, painfully aroused. Something beneath his right hand moved and he squeezed reflexively. A soft feminine sigh brought him abruptly awake. Whose bed was he in? he wondered groggily. What woman had favored him with her body last night? The voluptuous redhead who was newly arrived on the island? The sightly aging but sexy-as-hell brunette who often came to him when he needed a woman? The little blonde with big, pillowy breasts? Aye, the blonde, he decided as he gave the soft mound another squeeze.

Hunter finally managed to open his undamaged eye. Bright sunlight flooded the room and he closed it again. When he found the courage to face the day, he was stunned to see Bliss lying beside him. She was still sleeping soundly, and he wondered why he couldn't recall what had happened the night before. He didn't even remember how he'd ended up in her bed. Had he taken her? He hoped not. It wasn't the way he'd planned it. He wanted them both awake and aware of every nuance of his lovemaking. Then he saw his eyepatch resting on his pillow where it had fallen, and he groaned with dismay. Had Bliss awakened and seen him without it, she might have recognized him.

He rose slowly so as not to disturb her sleep, retrieved his eyepatch, and tiptoed from the room. Then he donned his breeches and boots and walked the short distance to the beach for his morning swim. But no matter how deep he dove into the pounding surf, he couldn't forget how good Bliss's breast had felt in his hand. Or how sweetly she had sighed when he'd tested its weight and shape within his palm.

Bliss awakened shortly after Hunter's departure, surprised that she hadn't wakened when he'd left the bed. She rose and washed herself from head to toe, cleaned her teeth with a cloth, and donned a simple dress of yellow sprigged dimity that Cleo had left for her draped over a chair. Then she left the room to explore the house and grounds. She wanted to learn the lay of the land in order to prepare herself for any eventuality. Each day spent as Hunter's captive meant one day longer away from her son.

"Can I help you, missy?" Cleo asked when she saw Bliss walk out onto the porch. "Cap'n says you should wait for him. He wants to take breakfast with you. I'm setting a table on the porch. The mornings here are cool and pleasant compared to the afternoon heat."

"I'll just have a look around while I'm waiting, Cleo," Bliss said, stepping down from the porch.

"Don't go far. It's easy to get lost in the jungle."

Bliss limited her morning exploration to the grounds surrounding the house. She found animal sheds holding pigs and chickens, the garden she'd seen from her window, several storage sheds, a tool shed, and a small cottage built in a clearing not far from the main house. She assumed it was where Cleo and Caesar lived. She was just rounding the corner of the house when she met Hunter coming from the beach.

"Did you sleep well?" he asked with surprising good humor considering his drunken state the night before.

Bliss eyed him narrowly. "As well as could be expected under the circumstances."

He gave her a cocky grin but said nothing about sleeping in her bed. "Are you ready for breakfast? I'm starved. I'm glad you waited." He took her arm and guided her up the stairs onto the porch. He held the chair for her as she seated herself at the table.

Bliss wondered why he was being so agreeable. Was he having second thoughts about keeping her captive? Perhaps this was a good time to revisit the subject of her release. She waited until Cleo placed a platter of fresh fruit on the table and left before taking a deep breath and saying, "Are we leaving today? Have you decided to set me free? I'd prefer to be released in Mobile, if it isn't too much trouble."

Hunter's fork paused in midair. "What makes you think I'm taking you anywhere? We just got here."

"You were being so nice, I thought you'd had a change of heart."

He gave her a look that sent shivers clear down to her toes. "I'm only nice when it suits my purposes. I find lovemaking far more pleasurable when there is no animosity between bed partners. I intend to be nice to you, Bliss. *Very* nice," he emphasized. "And there *will* be pleasure. More pleasure than you've known with any other man."

What he didn't say was that he fully expected his lovemaking to result in pregnancy. He intended to return her to Faulk and her father, all right, but not until she quickened with his child.

A niggling little voice in his head whispered that he hoped she wouldn't become pregnant too soon. He was going to enjoy having her in his bed.

Chapter Five

Under any other circumstances Bliss would have loved the island. The afternoon heat was tempered by ocean breezes and the nights were soft and sultry. Mornings were pure pleasure and she tended to rise early simply to enjoy the pine-scented coolness that preceded the stifling afternoon heat.

Since her arrival on Pine Island three days before, Bliss had been on edge, wondering about Hunter's plans for her. He seemed to enjoy keeping her in suspense. Each night she listened for his footsteps in the hall and ended up falling asleep before he returned to his room. She'd even begun to look forward to the times she would see him again. He normally spent long hours on the beach with his crew, overseeing the careening of his ship; then he would join her for dinner and afterward accompany her for a walk on the beach, until the mosquitoes drove them inside.

Bliss stood before her mirror, giving her hair a final pat before meeting Hunter for lunch. Her mind skipped along a path that eventually led to thoughts of her son. Her eyes grew misty as a mental image of him formed in her mind. She pictured a miniature Guy and smiled dreamily.

"I trust that smile is for me."

Bliss's eyes widened in her surprise to see Hunter's reflection join hers in the mirror. His face was striking despite, or perhaps because of, the eyepatch he wore. His well-honed features were framed by inky dark hair clubbed at the nape with a leather thong. She started to whirl around to face him, but he grasped her shoulders and held her in place, forcing her to view the two of them in the mirror.

"Tell me what you were thinking." His voice was a husky purr that sent chills down her spine. "Were you pining for your betrothed?"

Bliss gazed at his reflection, puzzled by his sudden tenseness. Since there was no answer she was comfortable sharing, she gave him none.

His hands tightened on her shoulders. "Answer me, Bliss. Were you dreaming of Gerald Faulk? Was your smile for him?"

"You're hurting me! I was merely smiling at my own image; does that satisfy you?"

His grip eased, but he didn't let go. She could

feel his hard body pressed against her, his breath hot upon her neck.

"For the time being."

His callused palms slid down her arms. She held her breath as they skimmed her waist, lingered, then moved inexorably upward to caress the sides of her breasts. She shivered and closed her eyes. She opened them abruptly when she felt his hands cupping the full mounds. The crests immediately tautened in automatic response.

"Don't."

His thumbs rubbed over her nipples through the material of her dress, causing a wildly erotic friction that made Bliss want to melt against him. She offered half-hearted resistance.

"I know you like this, Bliss. Your breasts have always been sensitive."

It took Bliss a moment to realize what he'd said. How could he possibly know that? Only one man had ever touched her breasts in such an intimate manner. Oh, God, she was going mad. Hunter was nothing like her beloved Guy.

"Look in the mirror, Bliss. Watch me love you."

Bliss shook her head, but nevertheless her gaze was drawn to their reflection in the mirror. She saw a woman whose eyes were glazed, her mouth slightly open. She had the look of a wanton. She couldn't look away.

She felt his fingers on the back of her gown. Moments later her bodice fell away, revealing the peaked crests of her breasts beneath her sheer shift. He caressed them through the flimsy cloth, and her gaze fused to that place where his large hands fondled her. She hated herself for wanting him to tear away the thin material and touch her bare flesh.

She felt his lips on her neck, and a small, sobbing moan escaped her throat. She closed her eyes again, and when she opened them she saw that he had unfastened her shift, pushed the edges aside and bared her breasts. The contrast between his dark, tanned hands and her white flesh was startling. Erotic. Arousing. Her head fell back against his shoulder; she was lost in that timeless place where sensual pleasure ruled.

She gave a gurgling cry of protest when Hunter's hands left her breasts so he could work her gown down her hips. The cry died in her throat when she felt his hands on her thinly clad body again, one of them traveling downward to press intimately between her legs. The sensation was more arousing than anything she could imagine. When he began to massage gently, she couldn't stop herself from grinding her buttocks against his loins. It had been so long since she'd experienced genuine arousal that her body acted independently of her mind.

Hunter returned the courtesy by bracing his legs and thrusting forward, giving her the full benefit of his erection. Bliss knew she was courting trouble by responding so blatantly, but she had neither the will nor the inclination to free herself from his seductive power. And it *was* seduction. He'd already announced his intention to seduce her.

God help her, for it was working.

"It's time," Hunter whispered as he kissed and nibbled her ear. "Do you want me, Bliss?"

"I . . ." If she said yes she feared she would lose that part of herself she'd held in reserve for her dead husband's memory.

"Tell me, Bliss."

She felt him grasp the skirt of her shift and raise it. Without volition her gaze returned to the mirror. She saw long pale legs, dimpled knees, and white thighs against a backdrop provided by Hunter's black-clad body. An inch higher and the copper curls concealing her womanhood would be fully exposed. She prepared herself for Hunter's reaction to all her secrets revealed in the mirror.

That moment never arrived. Abruptly Hunter released his hold on her shift and turned her to face him. He wedged his powerful thigh between her own and lowered his head to her breasts. The tips of his fingers stroked her back and buttocks as he pressed the hard length of his erection into the cradle of her thighs and lowered his head to suckle one of her pink nipples.

How much could she take before she surrendered to the sensual web he was weaving around her? Bliss wondered distractedly as he continued to draw on her, tugging on the sweet tip with his white teeth.

Hunter's control was quickly eroding. He

knew from experience that Bliss was a passionate woman, and her response was everything he remembered. He had to keep a tight rein upon his emotions, he told himself. Losing control now would cost him everything he'd gained in the last seven years. Fortunately, he wasn't worried about engaging his heart, for nothing but a hole existed where it had been ripped from his body.

Hunter had to keep reminding himself, however, that his prime objective was to seduce Bliss, make her pregnant, and return her to her fiance. In order to accomplish that he had but to keep a cool head, have sex with Bliss as often as possible, and remain far removed from every emotion. He was determined not to think of what he and Bliss were about to do as making love. Calling it lovemaking would be a mockery and a blatant contradiction of his purpose.

Hunter backed Bliss against the wall, intending to take her standing up. When she made little mewling sounds of protest, he kissed her sweet lips until she became quiescent in his arms. Unwittingly, the unique taste of her jogged his memory, bringing to mind those nights of passion they had shared in another life, another time, and suddenly he was unable to get enough of her.

Hunter wasn't the only one plagued by intensely profound recollections. Hunter's kisses sent Bliss spinning back to the past. To the man who had taught her passion. Hunter's kisses, his scent, his adeptness, were so reminiscent of

Guy's that for a moment she forgot she was kissing an uncivilized pirate. She imagined she was in Guy's arms; it was Guy's lips making her dizzy, Guy exploring her mouth with hot, thrusting strokes of his tongue. He even tasted like Guy.

But he wasn't Guy. Guy was dead. This man was her captor, her seducer. He intended to use her body for his own pleasure, then kill her when he tired of her. She'd heard too many stories about Gasparilla and the Brotherhood to believe otherwise.

Bliss fought for control of her senses. When she felt the wall pressing against her back, she found the strength to launch a vigorous protest.

"No! I don't want this."

Apparently Hunter was too far steeped in lust to stop as he fumbled with the fastenings on his breeches. "I want you, Bliss, and I always get what I want." He groaned in obvious frustration when the strings on the placket of his breeches knotted. He spit out an oath and reached for his knife.

Neither occupant of the room heard the door open, or saw the uninvited guest step inside. Suddenly a squeal of outrage rent the air, destroying the moment. His face white with rage, Hunter whirled to face the intruder.

"Don't you ever knock, Tamrah?" he snarled. "Get out. Can't you see I'm busy?"

"I can see very well what you're doing," Tamrah spat, sending Bliss a venomous look. "Cleo sent me to fetch Bliss for lunch. You must not have heard me knock. Why did you bring her here, Hunter? I could be all the woman you want if you'd let me."

"You're still a child, Tamrah. How old are you? Fourteen? Fifteen? I'm a grown man. I have done many despicable things in my life, but I'm not a despoiler of children. When it's time I will find you a husband from among your own kind."

"I'm no child. I'm sixteen," Tamrah informed him haughtily. "I can wait until you tire of Bliss." Her dark eyes gleamed with malice. "Will you kill her when you finish with her?"

Bliss blanched.

"Nay. In due time Bliss will be returned to her fiance. After—"

"After what?" Bliss blurted out. "What do you want from me?"

Tamrah gave a snort of disgust. "Even I know what he wants from you. What I don't understand is why. Hunter has had women more beautiful than you. You are not even young."

"Enough!" Hunter roared. "Don't try my patience, Tamrah. Go help Cleo in the kitchen. I'm sure she can find something for you to do."

Tamrah left in a huff. Hunter turned back to Bliss, but the moment had been lost. She was staring at him warily. The passion he'd aroused in her was now replaced by fear.

"You lied to Tamrah," she accused. "You're going to kill me after you . . . after you get what you want."

"My plans for you don't include your death,"

Hunter assured her. "You'll be returned to your fiance when I'm good and ready to let you go."

"Why don't you return me now? What possible reason could you have for keeping me here?" She squared her shoulders and regarded him solemnly. "Bed me, if that is your intention. I'll not fight you if you promise to take me to Mobile afterward. The sooner you have what you want from me, the sooner I can leave here."

"You remind me of a martyr about to face the lions," Hunter said. "That's not the way I want you. I want you hot and willing. Soft and giving. The way you were with . . . Gerald Faulk." He almost said Guy DeYoung but caught himself in time.

"I fully intend to bed you, Bliss, in my own good time. If you think you can get away with lying beneath me like a board, forget it. I'll have your passion and everything else you're capable of giving."

"I'm capable of giving nothing to you," Bliss retorted. She stared into space, her turquoise eyes misty with unshed tears. "There was a man once—" Her voice broke on a sob and she turned away. A moment later she regained her composure and said, "Didn't Tamrah say lunch was ready? We shouldn't keep Cleo waiting."

Hunter helped her to dress. She thought his fingers remarkably nimble and decided it was because he had intimate knowledge of women's bodies. When she was decently clothed, he offered his arm and escorted her to the sunny porch, where Cleo had set out food for their lunch.

Bliss ate heartily of fresh fruit, boiled shrimp, crab, and spicy gumbo. The meal ended with a dessert made from plantains. When Cleo returned to clear away the plates, a worried frown marred her brow.

"Is something wrong, Cleo?" Hunter asked. "You look perturbed."

"I can't find Tamrah," Cleo said. "I sent Caesar to look for her." She shook her head. "Silly girl, I don't know where she gets her ideas. She is just turned sixteen and has decided she is old enough to become your woman. But I've told her she is still too young for you."

"I told her the same thing. Where do you think she went? It's a large island."

Cleo didn't appear overly concerned. "Caesar will find her. Perhaps she went to visit her people at the north end of the island. Good riddance, I say; it's where she belongs."

Hunter had intended to find Tamrah a mate from among the Calusa when she was old enough. Now it seemed as if she'd taken the matter into her own hands. Nevertheless, after lunch he went in search of the headstrong girl.

Tamrah was not in the Calusa village. Hunter spent an hour or so in private conversation with a young warrior who had expressed a desire to speak to him. Afterward he spent the remainder of the day and far into the night searching the pine forests for her. When he failed to find her, he feared that she'd either gotten lost in the mangrove thickets or stumbled into quicksand. Poisonous snakes, panthers, and wild pigs inhabited the forest. Any number of things could have happened to the girl.

Even Bliss was worried about Tamrah, though the girl hadn't been the least bit friendly to her. Cleo had already retired to the cottage she shared with Caesar, leaving Bliss alone in the house. Far into the night. Bliss waited in the parlor for Hunter to return with news of Tamrah. Finally she heard a footfall upon the wooden porch and looked expectantly toward the door, expecting to see Hunter. Instead, three pirates she recognized from the ship burst into the room. Tamrah was with them.

"There she is," Tamrah said, pointing to Bliss. "She's yours. Hunter is bored with her and has given permission for other members of the Brotherhood to enjoy her."

One of the pirates leered at Bliss, unable to believe his good fortune. "Are ye sure?" he asked Tamrah. "Where is Hunter?"

"He left so he wouldn't have to deal with her when you took her away."

Stunned, Bliss finally found her voice. "You lie! Hunter is out looking for *you*. Why did you run away?"

Tamrah gave her an innocent smile. "I don't know what you're talking about." She turned to the pirates, who were staring at Bliss with greedy anticipation. "Do you want her or not?

Better take her now, before the others get wind of Hunter's generosity and demand that you share her. Take her into the forest where her cries can't be heard."

"I get her first," an ugly pirate with spiky red hair said.

"Aw, Red, ye always go first. Ain't much left after you get through."

"It's my turn to be first, Salty," the third pirate argued.

"Who says, Butch?" Salty challenged, scowling.

Red drew his knife. "This says I'm first."

"Are you all mad?" Bliss cried. She felt as if she were living a nightmare. "Get out of here! If Hunter learns of this, he'll kill you." She started to back away.

All three pirates returned their attention to Bliss. Then as if on signal they lunged at her. Bliss turned to flee, but was brought up short. They grabbed her and passed her from man to man, pawing her with their filthy hands.

"Tamrah! Make them stop. You can't do this."

"I'm only saving Hunter the trouble of doing it himself," she said smugly. "Hunter tires of women quickly. He likes variety. Just because he brought you to the island doesn't mean he intends to keep you."

Bliss resisted violently as Red began to drag her toward the door. Salty and Butch added their strength, and between the three of them they hauled Bliss unceremoniously through the front door and down the steps. Following Tamrah's advice, they plunged into the dark forest.

Bliss decided it was a good time to scream. If she was lucky, Caesar would hear her and come to her aid. Red must have read her mind, for he placed a grubby hand over her mouth. The darkness was oppressive, but they seemed to know precisely where they were going. When they came to a small clearing, they tossed Bliss down upon the marsh grass and began to argue over who would have her first.

Taking full advantage of the distraction, Bliss gathered her wits and leapt to her feet. She ran blindly through the thick underbrush, tripping over roots and dodging trees whose limbs pulled at her hair and left scratches on her tender skin. Behind her she heard a roar of rage, the harsh rasping of breath, and knew they were almost upon her. Panic-stricken, she glanced over her shoulder to confirm her worst fears and ran headlong into an unmovable object. It was too soft to be a tree and too solid to be a bush. It was . . .

Hunter.

She collapsed against him, sobbing into his chest as his arms surrounded her. She had no idea if she was racing from the fire into the frying pan, but she preferred the devil she knew to those she didn't know.

Hunter focused his good eye on the three pirates, who had stopped dead in their tracks when they saw him.

"What's going on?" Hunter asked, pinning the

pirates with the intensity of his gaze. "Who gave you the right to take my woman?"

"We was just following yer orders, Cap'n," Red said, glancing nervously from Hunter to Bliss.

"What orders?" he asked tightly.

"Ye gave the woman to us, but she didn't take kindly to it."

Hunter went still. He lifted Bliss's chin and stared into her frightened eyes. "Did they hurt you?"

She shook her head, unable to speak past the lump in her throat. Hunter regarded her solemnly, then nodded, apparently accepting her answer. It was the pirates on whom he vented his rage.

"Who told you I no longer wanted this woman?" he roared. "I should kill you for touching my property."

Carefully he set Bliss aside and drew his sword. "Who's first?"

The pirates eyed him warily, aware that Hunter could send them all to hell and back without working up a sweat.

"Aw, Cap'n, 'twere a mistake. That little Injun wench came to the village and said you were tired of the woman. She told us to come and get her."

"Tamrah said that?"

"Aye, Tamrah, that's her name. We wouldn't have taken yer woman if we thought ye still wanted her."

Hunter's hand tightened around the hilt of his

sword. The thought of what these brutal savages had meant to do to Bliss made his blood run cold. Yet the situation was not much different from what he'd seen and experienced on countless other occasions, so why should he act outraged now? he wondered. He'd seen so many women ravaged that he'd learned not to cringe anymore, to accept it, even though he took no part in those barbarous orgies. But this was different. This time Bliss was the woman the men were manhandling.

"Bliss, is Red telling the truth?" Hunter asked. "Did Tamrah tell them I was tired of you and wanted to be rid of you?"

"I . . . yes. She brought them to the house and told them to take me away, that you were bored with me."

"I never thought to look for Tamrah down in the village," he muttered. He returned his attention to the pirates. "Get the hell out of here. Pass the word around. If I see any of you or your mates sniffing around my woman again, I won't be as lenient the next time."

Red belligerently stood his ground, glaring at Hunter as if he meant to challenge Hunter's authority. But he must have realized he was no match for Hunter's superior skill, for he turned abruptly and followed his mates back the way they had come.

Hunter sheathed his sword and drew Bliss back into his arms. "Are you all right?"

"I'm fine."

"You don't look fine."

"If you hadn't arrived when you did . . ." A tremor passed through her body.

"Let's get back to the house. I have business to conduct with Tamrah."

"What are you going to do? She's young. She didn't know what she was doing."

"She knew exactly what she was doing." His voice was hard, implacable.

"You're not going to hurt her, are you?"

He supposed he deserved that. "No. Her father would haunt me if I harmed her. I had planned to find her a mate, but not until she was older. Now I think it best to do so immediately. She already has a suitor. A young Calusa warrior has asked for her, and I'm of a mind to send her to him." He searched her face. "Can you walk?"

"Of course." She took a step forward and tottered. Her wobbly knees belied her words, and Hunter swept her up into his arms and strode through the forest, relying on the stars and moon to guide his steps.

"I can walk."

He ignored her.

"Hunter, may I ask you a question?"

"If you must."

"How many women have you given to your men after you tired of them?"

The play of shadows and light upon his face all but concealed his expression. Bliss thought she saw him grimace, imagined a shadow pass over his good eye, but couldn't be sure. When he finally answered, his voice was flat and hard, devoid of all emotion.

"I've seen and done many things I'm not proud of. At first they bothered me, but after a time, what was left of my conscience ceased to exit. I can speak only for myself when I say I've never knowingly caused the death of a woman. Most of my female captives were ransomed to their families. Nevertheless, I'll probably burn in hell for having knowledge of the things that Gasparilla and members of the Brotherhood did to women."

Bliss mulled that over and decided to accept it as the truth. But that didn't make him any less a criminal. Hunter and his kind had made paupers of her father and others who tried to make an honest living from shipping. She knew she should fear him, but, incredibly, all she feared was the command he had over her senses. Before she could form another question they had reached the house. Hunter carried her through the dark, silent rooms, bypassing her bedroom as he took her to his.

His boots echoed hollowly on the wooden floor, solid and determined. Bliss knew what was going to happen, and a delicious shudder slid down her spine.

The flickering light from a single candle guided him to his bed. As he pulled aside the mosquito netting, a sweet voice said, "Hunter, you've come at last. Hurry, I've been waiting for you."

Hunter stopped dead in his tracks. He bit out

an oath when Tamrah rose up on her elbows and beckoned to him.

"What in bloody hell are you doing here?"

Tamrah saw Bliss in Hunter's arms and blanched. "What is *she* doing here?"

Hunter carefully set Bliss down on her feet, then reached inside the netting and pulled Tamrah out. She was naked, her satin skin shining like antique gold in the candlelight. "I ought to beat you for what you did to Bliss. You're no longer welcome in my home, Tamrah."

"You don't mean that. Where will I go?" Tamrah wailed.

"Where you belong. With your own people. I looked for you in the Calusa village today, thinking you might have sought your own kind. You remember Tomas, don't you? The young warrior expressed his desire to take you as his mate. I told him I'd think about it. Thanks to your machinations, I've reached a decision. I'm sending you to him tomorrow. It's either that or risk having you corrupted by one of the men from the village. I don't think you'd enjoy joining the prostitutes down there."

"I don't want Tomas," Tamrah said sulkily.

Bliss decided to add her opinion, whether or not it was appreciated.

"Perhaps you're being hasty, Hunter."

Hunter shot her a quelling look. "Keep out of this, Bliss. How can you defend her after what she did to you?"

"She's young. And she fancies herself in love with you."

"Tomas is a fine young warrior," Hunter claimed. "Better than she deserves. Tomorrow Caesar will take her to him."

Tamrah wasn't really all that disappointed. She knew Tomas and thought him handsome. Her punishment could have been far worse. Hunter could have beaten her to within an inch of her life had he wanted to. Young as she was, she now realized something about Hunter he did not even know about himself. His protectiveness and uncommon kindness toward his female captive were totally contradictory to his usual behavior. It spoke volumes about the man known for his unyielding nature and his lack of compassion. This woman was someone special to Hunter, Tamrah realized. He might not know it, but Tamrah did and finally accepted it as the Spirit God's will.

"Go to your room," Hunter ordered harshly.

Tamrah sent a sidelong glance at Bliss as she sidled past and marched in all her naked glory from the room. Hunter followed her to the door.

"Don't attempt to run away again, for there is no place you can go where I won't find you." So saying, he slammed the door behind her.

Bliss thought it a good time to return to her own room and started toward the connecting door.

"Where do you think you're going?"

"To my room."

"From now on, this is your room." He sent her a look so charged with sexual energy, Bliss felt overwhelmed by it.

"Hunter, I . . ."

She gazed into his eye. It was narrowed and hazy with passion. "Come here, Bliss."

His voice was a potent blend of erotic promise and sexual innuendo. Low and seductive and extremely provocative. And Bliss had the strangest feeling she had heard it before. Somewhere. Someplace. She racked her brain but memory failed her. His allure was so compelling that she couldn't think beyond this room, this man, and what he wanted of her. She approached him with slow, dragging steps.

"It's time, Bliss," he whispered when she was close enough to feel the scorching heat of his body. "I've waited patiently for this moment. You're not going to fight me, are you?"

Time hung suspended as Bliss considered his words. Fight him? She hadn't the strength to breathe, much less fight him. She watched in a daze as his weapons clattered to the floor. First his scabbard and sword, then his knife and pistols.

"I'm sorry for what happened tonight," he continued as he unbuttoned his silk shirt. "It was never my intention to give you to my men. I always meant to return you to your fiance once you quickened with my—" He stopped abruptly, as if he'd realized what he was going to say and decided against it. "After I'm ready to let you go," he quickly amended.

Bliss hadn't caught his slip. Both her gaze and her mind were focused on his bare chest. When he sat down on the bed to remove his boots, she swallowed convulsively, aware that in a few moments he'd be nude. The boots hit the floor and he stood, his hands on the waistband of his breeches. Her cheeks flamed and she looked away. Moments later she heard the rustle of cloth.

"Look at me, Bliss."

"No. I'm not ready for this." But she turned her head anyway.

He was magnificent. All taut skin and sleek muscles. Her gaze traveled down his body . . . and skidded to a halt when it reached his loins. He was fully aroused. His sex was thick and long, rising at full mast from black curls.

"I'll make you want me," he promised confidently. "Touch me, Bliss."

When she hesitated, he reached out and took her small hand, pulling it to the scalding heat of his loins and wrapping her fingers around him.

Bliss tried to withdraw her hand, but he wouldn't let her. Then she heard him gasp and looked up at him. His face was contorted and he appeared to be in pain.

"Did I hurt you?"

"Nay, I was beginning to enjoy it too much." He placed one knee on the mattress and sank down on it. "Now 'tis your turn."

Chapter Six

Bliss inhaled a tremulous wisp of air. Her chest was so tight she could barely breathe. Did she want this? Did she truly want this? Did she have any choice? Hunter was determined to have her, and there was little she could do to stop him. She tried to think of something to say that would delay the inevitable, but all she could think of was, "Take off your eyepatch."

He reached for her. "I don't want to frighten you."

"You won't frighten me."

His hands undid the top two buttons on the front of her gown. "Let me be the judge of that."

"I can't let you do this."

Two more buttons slipped from their openings. "You can't stop me."

"I . . . I've never been with a man before," she lied.

He freed the remaining buttons and chuckled, as if vastly entertained by her words. "You're twenty-five years old. Am I expected to believe you're still a virgin?"

"I—" Suddenly she realized what he'd said. "How do you know my age?"

He yanked her bodice down past her arms to her waist. "A lucky guess."

"Do you rape all your women captives?"

His hesitation cheered her; then he unlaced the ties holding her shift together and her hopes collapsed. "If I wanted to rape you," he said, "it would have happened long ago. This won't be rape, Bliss."

He pushed her skirts down past her hips and lifted her out of them. Then he knelt to remove her shoes and stockings. She wore only her knee-length shift now, and she feared she wouldn't have that for long.

"How long have you been a pirate?" she asked in an attempt to divert his attention elsewhere. It didn't work.

Still on his knees, he skimmed his hands upward beneath her shift, slowly raising the thin cloth to her slim waist. Suddenly he stood and yanked the shift over her head, baring her to the liquid heat of his gaze. With a swift intake of breath, she brought one hand across her breasts while the other moved down to shield her sex.

"It seems as if I've been a pirate forever." He

grasped her hands and pulled them down to her sides. "No, don't hide from me. Let me look at you. I want to see if you look the same as you did—"

"As I did when?" Bliss whispered, blushing furiously. No one but Guy had ever seen her nude. With him it had seemed natural and right, and she had enjoyed his honest appreciation of her youthful innocence.

"Yesterday, when Tamrah interrupted us," he hedged. He brought his hands to her breasts, caressing them.

Bliss flinched away from his touch. She felt the strangest longing every time he placed his hands on her and was both puzzled and worried about it. "Why are you looking at me like that? I'm sure you've seen hundreds of naked women before." She hoped that maintaining a false bravado would see her through this ordeal.

"At least hundreds," he concurred.

There was an edge to his voice she hadn't noticed before. She offered a silent prayer for courage, then said crisply, "Very well, let's get this over with. I've important matters to attend to and have already been kept away from them too long."

He gave her a look of astonishment. "This isn't going to be a quick coupling. When I make love . . . er . . . take your body," he amended, "I want your senses fully engaged. You will be aware of everything I do."

"Why? Why is it important that I respond?"

"I have my reasons." He gave her an amused smile. "It's not going to work."

"What isn't going to work?" *Could he read her mind*?

"I won't be diverted from my purpose. I'm determined to have you, Bliss."

Bliss thought his words confusing and somewhat threatening. "What *is* your purpose, Hunter?"

He stared at her, this woman he had once loved more than his own life. She had let him rot in prison, doing nothing when her fiance and father hired an assassin to kill him. The time had come to seek retribution for all the injustices done to him. Putting a pirate's babe in Bliss's belly would be a fitting punishment for the destruction of Guy DeYoung. Because of Bliss he had been turned into a man he neither recognized nor liked. Revenge would taste all the sweeter if he could make Bliss fall in love with him, he thought, imagining the pleasure her seduction would afford him.

"My purpose," he said with a careless shrug of his bare shoulder, "wouldn't interest you."

He traced a finger along her cheekbone in a tender caress, finding surprising enjoyment in the satin smoothness of her flesh. Tenderness was an emotion totally foreign to him, one he'd forsworn seven years ago, and it had no place in a relationship provoked by vengeance. His hand fell away from her face.

"Come," he said, urging her to the bed with a light touch upon her elbow.

* * *

Bliss felt helpless against the seduction he was weaving around her senses. Her mind wanted to reject him, but her body refused to obey. Something familiar and right stirred within her. Something long forgotten and utterly desirable. She made a moaning sound when Hunter lifted her into his strong arms and carried her to his bed. Still holding her against him, he followed her down upon the mattress.

Bliss's resistance splintered when Hunter's mouth brushed hers, sweetly tracing the lush contours with the tip of his tongue, then gliding along the moistened seam before he deepened the kiss. Strange memories added a unique flavor to his kisses, and a feeling of having been with Hunter before, perhaps in another life, added an element of rightness. Then her thoughts scattered as he plunged his tongue inside to ravish her. With a will of its own her mouth opened to him, wanting more of his drugging kisses.

His mouth was hot, hungry, his tongue thorough and wildly arousing. She mewled in protest as his mouth left hers, then purred when it moved down the slender column of her throat to kiss and nibble the pulsing vein at its base. Bliss's heart thumped a wild tattoo as his hands skimmed her flesh, leaving a trail of fire in their wake. She swallowed a moan, unwilling for Hunter to see how profoundly his touch was affecting her. But he would not allow her to pretend coldness as his tongue licked a scorching path to her breasts.

She felt the soft mounds swell beneath the wet heat of his mouth, felt her nipples harden into taut buds as he suckled and pulled upon them. Time and place faded as Bliss imagined herself in Guy DeYoung's arms, dreamed he was the man loving her instead of an uncivilized, one-eyed pirate. In her aroused mind Hunter became Guy, and it was Guy to whom she was eagerly responding.

Reckless, desperate, wild, she clung to him, seeking something she hadn't experienced in seven years with any man. Apparently Hunter knew exactly what she wanted, what she liked, as his hands played upon her flesh and sifted down through the burnished curls between her thighs. He found her slick cleft and stroked her with the rough pads of his fingers.

"Is this what you want?" he whispered against her breast.

She jerked violently upward into his cupped palm when he found the tiny button of her femininity with his thumb. "Oh, God! I can't . . . I don't . . ." Words stuck in her throat.

"You can," Hunter urged. "And you will."

Though dazed by passion, Bliss still had the presence of mind to wonder how he knew what she was capable of. With Guy she had given her all, holding back nothing. But this man wasn't Guy, would never be her beloved Guy. Oh God, she was dying!

"Let it come, Bliss," Hunter commanded. "Don't hold back."

He sensed her resistance and refused to allow it. His own heart was pumping so loudly he feared she would hear it and know how deeply he was affected by her response to him. He couldn't stop desire from carrying him away, unwelcome though it was. He feared that losing himself in sexual gratification would elevate the deed, making the sexual act more complex than a simple act of procreation, which was what he intended it to be. Neither making love to Bliss Grenville nor engaging his heart was his purpose. Oh, there would be pleasure, there always was, but he wouldn't allow it to become necessary to his well-being. He never wanted to be that vulnerable to a woman again.

Bliss's body thrummed with sensations long forgotten. Her breasts felt swollen, her nipples tender and distended. That sensitive place where Hunter's fingers stroked was slick with dewy moisture and throbbing. She felt tremors begin deep within her core and arched against him, making mewling sounds of desperate need. Her climax was sudden and explosive. Wave after wave of pure ecstasy kept her trembling with little aftershocks as he rose up above her and nudged her opening with the velvet tip of his staff.

Hunter pushed his hips forward and slid just past the entrance. She was so hot and tight he could barely contain his excitement; he took slow, deliberate breaths in order to slow the quick acceleration of his heartbeat. He pushed deeper, nearly overcome by pleasurable sensations he hadn't been prepared for. He shook his head to clear his mind, trying to remain focused on the act and not the woman. Disregarding the waves of pleasure coursing through him, he flexed his hips and thrust himself to the hilt.

He heard Bliss cry out as if in pain, and the sound rocked the foundations of his soul. He hadn't intended to be touched on an emotional level but he was, and he damned himself to hell for it. Then he became aware of something else. Something puzzling yet thrilling. Bliss was narrow and very tight. Almost virgin tight. Though he knew she was no maiden, her passage fit him so snugly, he would have sworn she'd not had a man since . . . Guy DeYoung.

Then the need to thrust, to push himself in and out, to create a friction that would ultimately lead to blinding pleasure, seized him and his thinking process gave over to instincts older than time. With a cry of surrender he began to thrust wildly, rotating his hips in a frenzy of motion that would bring him to his ultimate goal.

Bliss lifted her hips to meet his thrusts, learning his tempo and imitating it as she became hopelessly ensnared in the sensual web he had woven around her. She was lost in confusion and jolted by memories. Her eyes told her this wasn't her beloved Guy, but by some odd quirk she had discovered similarities between Guy and Hunter that captivated her senses. His breathing was harsh and grating, exploding like thunder against her neck, and without her knowledge her hands buried themselves in the silky softness of his hair.

She thought she heard him whisper her name, but the thundering of her heart was so loud she couldn't be sure. She *did* hear him when he said, "Put your legs around my waist."

She obeyed blindly and cried out when she felt him penetrating her more deeply. The delicious friction was almost more than she could bear. She felt her body start to disintegrate again and coherent thought fled.

"Come with me, Bliss," she heard him say scant seconds before she broke apart and scattered into a million pieces. Moments later, as if from a great distance, she heard Hunter shout, felt his body tense and release a stream of thick, hot liquid deep inside her.

Bliss stared at the beam of moonlight dancing upon the ceiling. The bitter taste of remorse was sharp upon her tongue. She had responded wantonly to Hunter and she felt as if she had betrayed Guy's treasured memory. She turned her head to look at Hunter. He lay on his back, one arm bent upward over his head. Moonlight cascaded over his shoulders and glinted through his dark hair. He looked peaceful, and younger than she had originally thought. But Bliss knew that a soul as black as Hunter's would never be at peace.

Her gaze was drawn to the smooth, curved arch of his brow, the elegant line of his nose, the proud tilt of his jaw. Dim images stirred her memory but were quickly lost. She sighed and turned away. She thought about returning to her own bed, but Hunter turned abruptly and brought her into the curve of his body.

"Stay," he whispered sleepily. "This is where you'll be sleeping from now on."

Bliss searched for a stinging retort, but the even cadence of his breathing told her he had fallen asleep. She sighed and closed her eyes, trying to make sense out of what had just happened between them. She knew *why* it had happened. Hunter's extraordinary power of seduction had woven a magic spell upon her senses. Somehow, someway, he had made her believe she was actually making love with her dead husband. That shocking ability made him more dangerous than anything she had ever faced before.

Sleep finally came, and with it vivid dreams. Bliss wasn't even aware she had cried out in her sleep until Hunter shook her awake.

"Wake up, Bliss, you're having a nightmare."

Two fat tears slipped from the corners of her eyes. "It wasn't a nightmare."

"Do you want to tell me about it?"

"No. Go back to sleep."

His warm hand caressed the curve of her hip and bottom, then slid between her legs. "I'm wide awake now and ready for you again." He turned her to face him, found her hand, and placed it on his erection.

She drew in a startled breath. He was smooth as velvet and hard as stone.

"Again?"

"And again and again. As long as it takes."

Bliss frowned. "As long as it takes for what?"

"For you to admit that you want me, that you love me between your legs," he hedged.

"That will never happen."

He thrust a finger inside her. "I think it will. And sooner than you think."

Bliss stifled a moan as his fingers worked industriously inside her. "Why do you even care? There are hundreds of women who would welcome your attentions. I don't understand this insatiable need of yours to have me in your bed."

His eye glinted in the moonlight, a flash of silver that sent shivers down her spine. "I promise you, Bliss Grenville, one day you will know everything there is to know about me."

Before she could question his baffling statement, he pulled her on top of him, spread her legs, and thrust upward. Neither uttered anything beyond unintelligible gasps and groans as passion spoke to them in words that needed no interpreting.

Hunter awoke to bright sunshine playing against his eyelid. He untangled himself from Bliss and sat at the edge of the bed, surprised that he had slept so late and so soundly. Too many uncomfortable nights in prison had made him a poor sleeper, but apparently Bliss had cured him in one night. He almost laughed aloud at that incongruous thought.

He straightened his eyepatch and turned to watch Bliss sleep. She slept deeply and innocently, her face smooth and guileless. He recalled their passion of the night before and smiled. He had enjoyed Bliss immensely, and he was astute enough to know she had enjoyed him. If there was a God of Vengeance, then his seed was already growing inside her. Nevertheless, he would bed her regularly, until she quickened with his child.

Without volition his mind traveled backward in time, recalling the pure, uncomplicated joy of their innocent young passion. Then it had been explosive and all-consuming. Now it was riveting. Suddenly he recalled how tight she felt, almost virginal, and he wondered about it. Surely she hadn't remained celibate for seven years, had she? He certainly hadn't.

Just thinking about their torrid coupling had made his loins swell and his head spin, but he knew he couldn't stay in bed with Bliss all day, no matter how much he wished it. Sighing ruefully, he pulled on his breeches and boots. It was time for his morning swim in the lagoon.

Bliss awoke long after Hunter had left. She stretched lazily, wincing when she felt an unaccustomed twinge between her thighs. Pain wasn't all she experienced. She suffered from guilt and remorse. During those passion-filled hours last night, she'd given her body freely to a conscienceless pirate, a man who intended to use her, discard her, and move on to another hapless female. How could she have been so gullible as to fall victim to his seduction?

A discreet knock on the door interrupted her glum thoughts. Cleo stuck her head inside and announced that Caesar was in the hall, waiting to bring in the tub for her bath. Bliss pulled the sheet to her neck and told them to enter. Then she recalled she was in Hunter's bed and wanted to sink into the woodwork. What must Cleo and Caesar think of her?

"You've slept away the morning, mistress," Cleo said, bustling into the room with a pot of chocolate and a tray of fresh fruit.

A streak of red crawled up Bliss's neck. Cleo seemed to expect no answer, so she gave none. Caesar entered behind Cleo, rolling in a large brass tub.

"I'll have this filled in no time, missy," Caesar said, giving her a cheeky grin.

"Have either of you seen Hunter?" Bliss asked. The moment she asked the question, she wanted to call it back. She didn't care where Hunter had gone.

"The cap'n went down to the lagoon to bathe," Caesar said. "By now he's probably giving his men a hand with the ship." His grin seemed to grow wider. "I can get him for you if you want him for something special."

"No!" She didn't want him at all. "I was just . . . curious."

Later, after the tub had been filled and the servants had gone about their chores, Bliss lay back in the water with her head resting on the rim of the tub and felt herself blushing again at Cleo's suggestion that she strip the bed of the soiled sheets before she left the room. The scent of sex must have been overwhelming indeed for Cleo to suggest changing the sheets when Bliss knew for a fact that Cleo had put fresh ones on yesterday.

Bliss washed quickly and stepped from the tub, wrapping the linen drying cloth about her as she searched for her discarded dress and shift. They were gone. Cleo must have carried them off with the soiled sheets, she decided as she entered her own room through the connecting door. She found Cleo inside, gathering up her belongings.

"What are you doing?" Bliss asked. Perhaps that one night was enough for Hunter and he was sending her home. She prayed it was so.

"Moving your things into the cap'n's room," Cleo said as she carried an armful of clothing toward the connecting door.

Bliss blanched. "Wait! I wish to remain in my own room."

"Cap'n's orders, mistress," Cleo said as she strode briskly into Hunter's room. Bliss followed.

"Wear this dress, mistress," Cleo said, holding up a lovely turquoise blue gown. "The color is perfect for you. I found it and several others that will suit you in the storeroom."

"What's going on?"

Bliss glanced up and saw Hunter leaning against the doorjamb, arms folded across his chest, legs crossed at the ankles.

"I want Cleo to take my things back into my room."

He shoved himself away from the door. "This is your room." He waved Cleo away and she made a discreet exit, closing the door quietly behind her. Once she was gone, Hunter grasped the linen drying cloth and whipped it away from her body.

Bliss gave a squawk of protest and tried to tug it from his hands. It wouldn't budge. "Why did you do that?" she demanded. "You had what you wanted from me, why can't you leave me alone now?"

Hunter's silver eye narrowed as he opened his fingers and let the linen cloth fall to the floor. "I have complete power over you. I intend to know your body as intimately as I know my own. I will bare it and take you whenever it pleases me to do so. And you'll know when I've become bored with you," he said in a husky voice tinged with passion. "I doubt it will be any time soon."

Bliss snatched the cloth from the floor and wrapped it around herself. "Cleo said I was to share this room with you."

"That's right. I gave those orders myself."

"I prefer to sleep in my own room," Bliss argued.

"And I prefer you in my bed."

She was a captive, Bliss thought with resentment. She could argue all day with Hunter and get nowhere. Nothing about his apparent fascination with her made sense. Not Hunter's strange obsession with bedding her, nor his desire to keep her with him. If she lived to be one hundred she'd never figure out how Hunter had wrung such a passionate response from her. She had thought no man would ever engage her emotions as her dead husband had.

Complicating Bliss's distress was concern for her son. She had no idea what was happening to her child while she was a captive on Hunter's island.

"This is your room from now on," Hunter said firmly. "Get dressed. I've some spare time today. Would you like to take a tour of this end of the island?"

"Oh, yes," Bliss said with alacrity. She wanted to learn anything that might help her to devise an escape plan.

Two hours later Bliss had lost all hope of escape. The island was a tropical jungle suited only for wild animals, insects, and pirates. The thick tangle of mangrove and pine forests was all but impenetrable. Hunter pointed out several deceptive-looking patches of quicksand on either side of the winding path they had been following. Yet despite her dour mood, she couldn't help admiring the natural beauty of the island.

Colorful tropical birds flitted in the trees

while eagles and ospreys soared high above them in a cloudless blue sky. The numerous Indian mounds were both mysterious and intriguing, topped with shells that had blackened with age. The beaches were pristine crescents of white sand, marred only by gulls, pelicans, and egrets searching for their dinner in the shallows.

Hunter led Bliss to the edge of the water on a deserted stretch of beach and pulled her down beside him on a small hillock of sand.

"What do you think of my island?" he asked conversationally.

"It's beautiful," she said wistfully, wishing she were here in any capacity but a pirate's captive. "Where is the Indian village?"

"At the north end of the island. We rarely disturb them. My men have learned to leave them alone. The Calusa are remnants of an ancient warlike tribe who allow us to share their island. The chief and I were on very friendly terms before he died. Younger warriors are in charge now, but they still honor their old chief's pact with me. I provide the tribe with much-needed supplies in exchange for the privilege of living here in peaceful coexistence. It works to everyone's advantage."

Abruptly Hunter rose and stripped off his silk shirt.

"What are you doing?" Bliss asked, staring at his rippling muscles and suddenly finding it difficult to breathe.

"Going for a swim. I'm hot and sweaty from

our walk. Once winter arrives we'll lose this stifling humidity," he said. "Winter is a pleasant time of year in the islands." He sat to pull off his boots. "Will you join me?"

"No, thank you," she said primly.

He pulled her to her feet and turned her around so he could reach the buttons on the back of her dress.

"Stop!"

"Why? I don't like to swim alone." He worked her dress down her arms and pushed it and her single petticoat over her hips to the ground. "You can keep on your shift if you're so concerned about modesty. You've nothing to worry about, though; we're quite secluded here."

Apparently Hunter didn't give a fig about his own modesty for he promptly shed his breeches and reached for her hand. She held back but a moment before placing her hand in his. He was right. Their walk had worked up an unladylike sweat and the water looked inviting. Together they raced into the surf, allowing the cooling waves to wash over them.

Bliss hoped he might take off his eyepatch, but he merely tugged it more snugly in place before ducking beneath the surface. He came up sputtering and pulled her with him into deeper water.

"Can you swim?" he asked.

"I swim very well," Bliss said proudly.

"See that rock just this side of the breakers? I'll race you there," Hunter challenged.

"Will you free me if I win?"

He stared at her, his silver eye narrowing. "Do you think you're good enough to outswim me?"

"I think so. I'm an excellent swimmer."

"Very well. But if I reach the rock first, I demand a forfeit." She cocked an eyebrow but said nothing, waiting. "If I win I intend to have my way with you on the beach."

She gave him a smug smile. "You won't win." Then she was off like a shot. Apparently her strong showing surprised him, for it took him several minutes to catch up with her. They swam apace for a time, and when Bliss pulled ahead, Hunter unleashed his reserved strength and easily outdistanced her. To Bliss's chagrin, he reached the rock first, treading water as he waited for her.

His unrestrained burst of laughter startled her. It was the first time she'd ever heard him laugh. A distant memory nudged her brain but quickly disintegrated when Hunter said, "It appears you won't be going anyplace anytime soon." He caught her against him. "Now it's time to pay the forfeit." Placing an arm around her waist, he towed her back to shore.

He stopped to catch his breath and to rest in the shallows, anchoring his feet in the sandy bottom and holding Bliss in place within the cradle of his legs. Water lapped around their waists as Hunter lowered his face and touched her wet mouth with his.

"You taste of salt," he whispered, licking her lips with a bold sweep of his tongue. "Open your mouth."

"No." Despite her refusal, her mouth opened beneath the hot demand of his probing tongue. His groan of pleasure was all but obscured by the cry of a soaring seagull as his tongue thoroughly explored the moist sweetness of her mouth.

The heat of his kiss warmed the water around her as Bliss surrendered to the torrid seduction of his hands and mouth. The kiss went on so long her legs buckled beneath her and she would have fallen if Hunter hadn't grasped her bottom in both hands and cradled her snugly between his strong thighs.

"Put your legs around my waist," he murmured against her mouth.

"You'll fall."

"I won't. Do it, Bliss, I want you . . . now."

"Do you always get what you want?"

"I do where you're concerned."

He raised her slightly and she wrapped her legs around him. Then he flexed his hips and slid smoothly inside her wet passage. She felt herself stretch and fill with him, the sensation so exquisite she could not prevent herself from crying out at the pure pleasure of it. His strength was incredible. She could feel the powerful muscles of his legs contract as he supported her weight and began the sliding in-and-out movement both their bodies craved.

Bliss couldn't hold back. Her body knew what it wanted and demanded no less than total satisfaction. She thrashed wildly against him, meeting his thrusts with savage enthusiasm and fierce abandon. Then she was there, breaking apart as brilliant lights exploded around her. Her climax was so violent she barely heard Hunter's shout of completion, or felt the hot splash of his seed inside her.

She was still lost in the throes of passion when Hunter carried her to the beach and laid her down in the shade of a swaying palm tree. She was just returning from the lofty place where Hunter had taken her when she heard him whisper, "This time I know it happened."

His startling words brought her drugged senses into focus. Her eyes shot open and she stared at him. "What are you talking about? What happened?"

Hunter went still. He hadn't realized he had spoken aloud. His mouth worked wordlessly. At length he said, "We could have just made a child."

All the color drained from Bliss's face. "A child? What a horrible thing to say! I'd rather bear Gerald Faulk ten children than bear you one. At least Gerald doesn't have a price on his head."

It was definitely the wrong thing to say.

Chapter Seven

Hunter leapt to his feet. The thought that Bliss would prefer to bear Faulk's children made him crazy. It would never happen if he had anything to say about it. If he had his way, Bliss would never see her betrothed again. She'd remain his captive, bear his children, and live here with him on his island.

Fortunately, his good sense returned and he realized how impractical that arrangement would be. Bliss was here for one purpose. Revenge. He would keep her until she quickened with his child, then return her to Faulk and Grenville. That was his plan and that was the way it had to be.

Deliberately he reined in his temper. It wouldn't do to let Bliss know how deeply her words had affected him. He was supposed to be stirring her passion, not her anger. He wanted her to fall in love with him. When he revealed his identity, he wanted her to feel the same kind of desperation he'd felt when she had abandoned him for Faulk.

"A child is the last thing I want from any woman," he lied coolly. He held his hand out to her. "Come. It's time we returned to the house."

"I'm glad we're in agreement," Bliss muttered, wondering what would happen to her if she actually did become pregnant. The thought occurred that she wouldn't have to worry about Gerald Faulk still wanting her should she conceive Hunter's child.

"Do you need help dressing?" Hunter asked.

"Just with the buttons."

They dressed quickly and started back to the house. The sun was high overhead and the heat stifling. Bliss was eager to relax on the wide porch with a cool drink and the ocean breezes fanning her heated flesh.

With the passing of the days Bliss came to the realization that she no longer feared Hunter. He had become as familiar to her as her dead husband had been. During her idle moments she found herself comparing the two men. Outwardly there were few similarities. But sometimes, in ways she couldn't explain, the resemblance was uncanny. The way Hunter cocked his head. The color of his eyes. The familiar ring of his laughter. No matter how long she pondered the puzzling parallels between the two men, no plausible explanation was forthcoming. Despite the knowledge that Hunter was a pirate with whom she had nothing in common, she began to look forward to the times they spent together.

Her growing fascination with the pirate did nothing to diminish her concern for her son. Her heart would never be healed until Guy's son was with his mother, where he belonged.

One night after making love, Hunter must have noticed her preoccupation, for he asked, "Is there something you wish to tell me?"

"No, why do you ask?"

"You seem pensive. Is something bothering you? You're not ill, are you?"

"I'm fine. It's just . . ."

"Just what?" Was she going to tell him she was pregnant? he wondered as he stroked her hair, savoring the feel of the silky strands slipping between his fingers.

Bliss stared at him, longing to confide in this pirate she knew intimately yet didn't actually know at all. She wondered if he might agree to help her if she explained her dilemma to him. At times he seemed quite taken with her, which puzzled her. She understood nothing about this strange relationship except that it would be very easy to care for Hunter. Especially when bizarre moments of recollection jogged her memory of another man, who somehow became Hunter in the confused chambers of her mind.

"Do you really want to know what's bothering

me?" Bliss asked, rousing herself from her introspection.

"I asked, didn't I?"

She searched his face. "Who are you, really? Have we ever met before? Sometimes you act as though you know me. I'm not stupid. I know you're keeping me here for a reason. I'm constantly plagued by questions whose answers defy logic."

"Is that all that's bothering you? One day I'll tell you everything you need to know," he said obliquely. His hands made a leisurely journey down her body, as familiar to him now as his own. "I can make you forget your problems," he whispered huskily.

She stiffened. "You seem to think sex is the answer to everything. Well, it isn't, not for me, anyway."

Hunter sighed and flipped over on his back, staring at the ceiling. "How can I help if you don't tell me what's wrong?"

"I can't stay here. I have to reach Mobile as soon as possible."

"I told you, you'll leave when I'm ready to release you and not before. What's so important in Mobile? Perhaps if I knew, I could help with your problem."

Plagued by indecision, Bliss contemplated her situation. She had no reason to trust this unscrupulous pirate. By all accounts he had murdered countless innocent men and women and broken every law known to mankind. Yet he had done nothing to hurt her except to hold her captive against her will. If she were truthful, she'd admit to being grateful to Hunter for proving she wasn't dead emotionally or physically. Since Guy's death she'd existed in an emotionless void, without love and affection. She didn't know whether to thank or curse him for teaching her how to feel again.

"Bliss, I've done many things I'm not proud of, but I truly do want to help you if there's a problem."

His sincerity surprised him. In the last seven years he'd found little to admire in himself, and his sudden desire to help Bliss returned a small piece of his soul he had thought irrevocably lost. He was aware that he was using Bliss as an instrument of his revenge, and that he was going to abandon her when she quickened with his child, but there existed a tiny part of him that remembered the powerful love they had once shared. If only she hadn't betrayed him. She had rushed to see to Faulk's injuries on the dueling field instead of exhibiting concern for her own husband.

The memory remained, though the physical pain had receded into a dull ache. What hurt the worst was Bliss's failure to visit him in prison. If there had been an explanation for her actions, she should have confided in him, but he'd heard nothing from her during the entire year of his imprisonment.

Had her father poisoned her against him? he wondered. Had she suddenly decided she loved Faulk and wanted to escape their marriage? She didn't seem overly anxious now to marry Gerald Faulk. If she loved Faulk, why hadn't she married him long ago? There were so many unanswered questions, he was as confused as Bliss appeared to be.

"You *can* help me," Bliss finally said, capturing Hunter's attention. "But I don't think you will."

"Try me."

"I don't know where to start."

"From the beginning."

"The beginning is painful. It began with my marriage seven years ago."

"You were married?" Hunter asked, feigning surprise.

"His name was Guy DeYoung. I loved him with my whole heart. He was everything to me. We ran off and married without my father's permission. I was seventeen. We were both so young."

"Why did your father refuse permission? Seventeen isn't too young to marry."

"It is when one's father is adamantly opposed to the match. Father had promised me to Gerald Faulk, his business partner. Guy was working in Father's stables at the time. He had no money or position in society. But that didn't bother me. We loved one another and wanted to be together."

Hunter stiffened with resentment. How dare she spout words she didn't mean! "What happened?" he asked through clenched teeth.

"There was a duel. Gerald challenged Guy

and was seriously wounded. Then Father arrived and accused Guy of stealing a valuable horse. Guy was taken to the Calaboso to await trial. He had seriously wounded a prominent citizen and, according to my father, had stolen a horse." She paused, the memory painfully vivid even after all these years. "Father and Gerald used their influence to delay Guy's trial indefinitely. I tried to see him countless times, but was turned away."

"Are you saying your husband is still in prison? Didn't your father have your marriage annulled? Why haven't you married Faulk before now? Seems unlikely that he would wait years for a woman." His voice was ripe with accusation, but in her despair, Bliss failed to notice.

"Guy died before he could be brought to trial. They told me he died from prison fever. Father wanted to have the marriage annulled immediately after the duel, but I discovered I was carrying Guy's child and the annulment was postponed."

Hunter started violently. "You have a child?" The words sounded as if they had been ripped from some private hell inside him.

"This part is going to be difficult to understand, so bear with me," Bliss said. "Since I was pregnant, an annulment was out of the question. The family honor, you know. Then Guy died in prison, ending the marriage legally, and it was no longer necessary to obtain an annulment."

"Where is your child now?" Hunter asked sharply. He had a child! He and Bliss had a child together. "Is it a boy or girl?"

"A boy," Bliss said. "A son I never knew was alive until just recently. Father told me he had died at birth, and I had no reason to doubt him. I was recovering from a difficult birth and very ill at the time. For years I mourned the child. But in truth my son had been given to distant relatives to raise. I had no inkling my son was alive until shortly before I took a ship for Mobile and was captured by Gasparilla.

"Father finally convinced me to marry Faulk shortly before my twenty-fifth birthday. I'm an heiress, you see, and due to inherit a fortune upon turning twenty-five. Gerald needed my inheritance to save his shipping business. Pirates had destroyed his ships and stolen his cargos. Father was his partner, so he was as desperate for my money as Gerald was. There was a catch, though. I could only collect a monthly allowance if I remained unmarried after I reached twenty-five. I needed to marry to gain access to the entire sum. I couldn't bear to see my father evicted from his home, so I agreed to marry Gerald for Father's sake."

"How did you learn about your child?" Hunter asked.

"I eavesdropped on a conversation between Father and Gerald. A letter from the man who is raising my son had arrived. They were discussing the contents. That was the first I knew that my child was alive. Later, I found and read the letter. That was when I learned that my child was being raised by a man named Enos Holmes. I memorized the address. He lives on Water Street in Mobile. His letter demanded additional money for my child's upkeep. If the funds failed to arrive, he was going to abandon my son. I was so desperate to rescue him, I wasn't thinking clearly. I stole money from Father's strongbox and booked passage on the first ship to Mobile. The ship was attacked by Gasparilla, and you know the rest."

Her narration was met with profound silence.

"Hunter? Did you hear nothing of what I said?"

"I heard," he said in a strangled voice. He had a son. A son! The word reverberated in his brain. A boy abandoned by his mother at birth and raised without love by uncaring strangers. Damnation! Very few things had touched him emotionally since his resurrection as Hunter, but Bliss's revelation affected him profoundly. And with good cause. His own flesh and blood could be out on the streets this very minute begging for food. He was so angry, he couldn't speak. Damn Bliss and damn her father!

"Will you take me to Mobile to find my son?"

"I . . . I need to think." His feet hit the floor. She heard him rummaging around for his breeches.

"Where are you going?"

"I'm going to take the skiff out for a while." He needed time away from Bliss. Time to think.

"You're leaving *now*? It's dark outside."

"It will be light soon. Don't worry if I don't return right away." The door slammed, leaving a bewildered Bliss staring after him.

Hunter pulled the skiff out into the water and grabbed the oars. The wind picked up a short time later and Hunter abandoned the oars and set the sail, heading west toward Sanibel Island with the wind at his back. He needed to visit the island anyway to check on the plunder he had left there under guard for the Lafitte brothers to pick up. All his business with the Lafittes was conducted on Sanibel. After the plunder was transferred aboard Lafitte's ship, it was taken to New Orleans to be offered at exorbitant prices to wealthy citizens. The arrangement had proven profitable for all concerned.

As the skiff skimmed across the water, Hunter's mind wandered back to all he had just learned from Bliss. He had a son and he still had a wife. Since Guy DeYoung was very much alive, he and Bliss were still legally married. Faulk couldn't have her, he thought fiercely. According to Bliss, Faulk wanted her for her money. Money was something Hunter had no need of. He had plenty of gold and specie buried in various sites around his island. He was an extremely wealthy man.

By the time the shores of Sanibel came into view, Hunter had reached a decision. He was going to take Bliss to Mobile to rescue their son. He had no idea what the future held for him and Bliss, or if there was a future, but he hoped he would have a clearer picture when his son was with his family again.

The sun was high in the sky when he beached the skiff and greeted the men he had left on Sanibel to guard his goods. He intended to head back to Pine Island after a short rest, but his plans were delayed when Jean Lafitte arrived to pick up the plunder and transport it to New Orleans. Though eager to be off, Hunter was obliged to remain an extra day, until all the goods had been transferred aboard Lafitte's ship and paid for in gold.

The evening after Hunter's departure, Bliss sat on the porch fanning herself. Cleo was busy in the kitchen and Caesar had gone to the village to help the crew float the newly careened *Predator* into the lake on the evening tide. Bliss was still puzzled and hurt over Hunter's abrupt departure. He had seemed stunned after she'd broken down and told him about her marriage and her missing son. And he had disappeared before telling her whether or not he'd take her to Mobile.

Hunter was a thoroughly confusing man, Bliss reflected. His reason for keeping her on his island was still a mystery, and that made her nervous. He hadn't hurt her or threatened her in any way. He made love to her as if he truly cared, but she was astute enough to know there was a purpose behind his seduction. For the life of her, she couldn't imagine what that purpose could be.

Even more puzzling was the haunting familiarity of Hunter's kisses. She no longer felt crushing guilt for wanting him. It was such a natural thing now that all she felt was the raw ache of needing him.

Bliss's mind wandered along a sensual path, unaware of the drama taking place on the beach below the village. It wasn't until Caesar burst through the mangrove trees that she became aware of trouble brewing on the island. She leapt to her feet, fear racing through her.

"Caesar! What is it? Has something happened to Hunter?"

"Gasparilla!" Caesar gasped, panting from his run through the forest. "He's on his way up here, missy. He's mad. Real mad at Hunter for bringing you to Pine Island instead of taking you to Cuba."

The words were no sooner spoken than Gasparilla and several of the more disreputable members of the Brotherhood strode up to the house.

"Where is Hunter?" Gasparilla barked.

For all his small stature, Gasparilla was an imposing man. Though he dressed like a dandy in red coat and silk shirt with lace cuffs, he was known to be ruthless and vengeful when crossed.

Bliss swallowed past the lump of fear lodged in her throat. "He's not here."

"So his men were telling me the truth," Gasparilla said with a disdainful sniff. He looked Bliss up and down and dismissed her with a wave of his hand. "I've seen women more beautiful than you; you must have *something* to commend you, else Hunter would not have compromised his loyalty to me. I would have trusted him with my life. What did you do to him, woman?" he roared. "He would not have betrayed me had you not enchanted him. You must have powerful magic between your thighs."

Bliss blanched, shocked by his crude words. "I did nothing."

"I am meticulous about keeping my word where my captives are concerned. I promised your betrothed you would be promptly returned upon receipt of your ransom. Hunter made a liar of me. I was livid when my agent informed me you had failed to arrive in Cuba. Your ransom was already in my hands. I had no recourse but to come here myself to find out why Hunter failed to take you to Cuba as he promised. When do you expect him to return?"

"I . . . I don't know," Bliss lied. "He didn't tell me."

Gasparilla scowled, his dark face growing even darker. "I can't wait. My honor is at stake. Others will be reluctant to send ransom the next time I demand it once word is spread that you weren't returned as I promised. Gather your belongings, I'll take you to Cuba aboard my own *Dona Rosalia*. I'll deal with Hunter when I return."

"No! I'd rather wait for Hunter."

Gasparilla grasped her wrist and yanked her off the porch. "Do as I say, wench! It makes no difference to me whether I take you to Cuba with or without your belongings."

"I will help you, mistress," Cleo offered from the doorway.

Gasparilla released Bliss's wrist and gave her a shove toward Cleo. "Hurry, wench. I don't want to lose the tide."

Brisk winds and fair weather brought the *Dona Rosalia* to Cuba five days later. Flying the Spanish flag, the ship entered Havana harbor beneath the threatening guns of El Moro Castle. Bliss's mood was as black as her thoughts as she watched the docking process.

The last person on earth she wanted to see was Gerald Faulk. She hated him. What he and her own father had done to her was despicable. They had taken her child from her and told her he had died. They had conspired together to keep Guy in prison until he was stricken with prison fever and died of his ailment. They had made a complete shambles of her life to satisfy their need of money. She silently vowed that neither Gerald nor her father would ever see a penny of her inheritance.

The gangplank was run out, and Bliss stiffened when Gasparilla came for her. "Where are you taking me?"

"I'm not taking you anywhere. I'm too well known and have attacked too many Spanish ships to show my face in Havana. One of my men will take you to my agent. Don Alizar will handle the reunion with your betrothed. I've sent a runner ahead so he'll know to expect you."

As she traversed the crowded streets of Havana, Bliss considered fleeing from her pirate escort, but soon discarded the idea. She had no money and no friends here to help her. She dreaded the reunion with Gerald, but at this point there was nothing she could do to prevent it. She would rather stay with Hunter than be reunited with Gerald and her father. The lengthy voyage from Pine Island to Cuba had given her many idle hours in which to think about Hunter and the curious connection that seemed to link her to the one-eyed pirate.

The bond was so strong that at times she felt as if she'd known him forever. No matter how hard she tried, she couldn't explain the affinity that existed between them. When he made love to her, the aching familiarity of his lovemaking brought tears to her eyes. And as much as he tried to deny it, she knew Hunter shared those feelings.

"Here we are, wench," said the rough pirate who had escorted her through the streets. "Felix Alizar's office is on the second floor. Open the door."

The door was set in a crumbling stucco building in a less than respectable neighborhood. Bliss pulled it open and saw a narrow dark stairway rising upward to the second floor.

"Go on," the pirate said, urging her up the

stairs and following close behind. "Alizar is expecting you."

Bliss hesitated on the upper landing and stared at the closed door. Her legs had turned to stone. If Gerald was behind that door, she feared she'd have a terrible time controlling her rage. The pirate opened the door and shoved Bliss inside. A small Spaniard sat behind a desk, perusing a sheaf of papers. He looked up, saw Bliss, and smiled.

"Ah, at last. *Gracias*, Ramon. Tell Gasparilla I expect word on Don Cobre's wife soon. When the ransom arrives, I'll send it by the usual route."

"*Sí*, Don Alizar, I will tell him. Gasparilla is anxious to take his leave before the authorities recognize the *Dona Rosalia*. We aren't exactly welcome in Spanish territory. Gasparilla sends his apologies to Gerald Faulk for the delay. It was not his doing." He placed the bundle of Bliss's clothing on the desk and took his leave.

Alone now with the agent, Bliss turned her attention to the man who had arranged for her ransom. He was short and thin, his thick black hair and mustache slicked down with pomade. His smile made her think of a weasel, and she shivered in revulsion.

"So you're the woman who drove Hunter to defy Gasparilla," he said, looking her over with a critical eye. "You're beautiful, but I don't know if *I* would have opposed Gasparilla to have you." He shrugged. "I do not envy Hunter. Gasparilla is not an easy man to placate. But you are here now and appear unharmed," he said cheerfully. "I took the liberty of notifying your betrothed; he should arrive shortly."

Bliss's reply was forestalled when the door opened and Gerald Faulk stepped inside. He gave Bliss a look of utter contempt, quickly replacing it with a false smile.

"Ah, my dear, I was crazy with worry for you. I've been waiting weeks for your arrival in Havana. I'm anxious to take you home so we can be wed. Why did you run away? If there was a problem, you should have sought my help."

As if sensing that his presence was not needed, Alizar rose abruptly. "I will leave you two alone. I'm sure you'd like to greet one another privately."

"Thank you for all you have done to reunite me with my fiancee, Don Alizar," Faulk said smoothly.

"It is nothing," Alizar said. Then he stepped out the door and closed it behind him.

Faulk turned back to Bliss, his light eyes narrowing on her with insulting intensity. "Well, you don't look any the worse for wear. Can I at least assume you're not with child?"

Bliss's chin rose slightly. "Assume what you like. It will be a cold day in hell before I marry you."

"Why did you run away?" Faulk asked with remarkable control.

Embers of resentment glowed brightly in Bliss's turquoise eyes. "You and Father took my child from me and gave him away!" She almost screamed the words at him. "He isn't dead. He's very much alive and living in Mobile. I will never forgive either of you for what you've done to me."

Faulk staggered backward beneath the blast of Bliss's enmity. He had had no idea Bliss knew about the boy, and it took a moment for him to recover from the shock. After a long pause his aplomb returned and he sought to placate Bliss.

"We did it for your own good," he said defensively. "You were too young to raise a child. He was placed in a foster home where he could be looked after properly. I knew we would marry one day and didn't want another man's child underfoot. We'll have our own children. You should be grateful to me for allowing you sufficient time to grieve and become accustomed to the loss. I haven't pressed you for marriage these past six years, have I?"

"You didn't press for marriage because I was still too young to collect my inheritance," Bliss charged.

"I've always wanted you, Bliss. Unfortunately, you wanted a man totally unsuitable. What happened was for the best. Your father is anxiously awaiting your return. We'll be married immediately upon reaching New Orleans. I have the license; all is in readiness."

"Over my dead body! I'll *never* marry you, Gerald."

"You don't mean that," Faulk cajoled. "You're tired. You've been under a great strain. These past weeks couldn't have been pleasant for you.

No one in New Orleans need ever know you were a pirate's captive. I'm taking you back to my ship, where you'll have time to rest and recover. I'm sure you'll come to your senses once you've thought this over."

"I've never lost my senses, only my blindfold. I see you clearly for what you are now. I never liked you, but now I hate you. You can take me back to New Orleans, but I won't stay there. As soon as I can, I'll book passage to Mobile."

"You're understandably upset, my dear. We'll talk further after you've eaten and rested. We're stuck here for at least another day. I've found a cargo of rum to fill my hold and it won't be loaded until tomorrow." He took her arm. "Come along. We can discuss our wedding plans later. Perhaps we can agree on something that will please you."

Bliss seriously doubted it, but she was too weary to belabor the point.

Pine Island

Anxiety pricked Hunter as Pine Island rose up before him. He aimed the skiff toward the shore below the village, maneuvered the breakers successfully, and beached the skiff on a stretch of pristine white sand. The moment he stepped ashore, he knew something was wrong. Nothing appeared disturbed, but the feeling persisted. Then he saw Caesar walking down the beach to meet him and his heartbeat accelerated.

"Is Bliss all right?" he asked as Caesar drew abreast of him. Damnation! If something had happened to Bliss, he'd never forgive himself. That thought gave him pause. When had Bliss come to mean so much to him?

"Gasparilla took her, Cap'n," Caesar said. "He found out she never reached Havana and came here to investigate. He sure was mad. I'm glad you weren't home when he arrived. Don't know what would have happened had he found you on the island. His men were armed to the teeth and itching for a fight. When he found you gone, he said he was gonna take the little missy to Havana, and then come back and take care of you for betraying his trust."

"When did all this happen?" Hunter asked. The thought of Bliss and Faulk together made him physically ill. She didn't belong to Faulk; she would always belong to Guy DeYoung.

"The *Dona Rosalia* sailed from our shores on yestereve's tide. You can catch them, Cap'n. I knew you'd want to go after them, so I ordered the crew to prepare the *Predator* for a voyage to Cuba. Provisions have already been carried aboard and stored in the hold."

Hunter gave him a grateful pat on the shoulder. "You're a good man, Caesar. You did exactly right. How soon will she be ready to sail?"

"She's ready now."

"Alert the crew. I'll get my weapons from the house and meet them on the beach."

Caesar gave him a white-toothed grin. "No need, Cap'n. Everything you need is already aboard. Me and Cleo seen to it. The tide's coming in. You'd best go now. Just bring the little missy back safe and sound."

Hunter hurried off. He intended to do whatever it took to find Bliss and his son.

Hunter reached Cuba scant hours behind Gasparilla. His heart sank when he noted that Gasparilla's ship was neither docked beside one of the stone piers nor anchored out in the harbor. Then he recognized a ship of the Faulk line moored at the far end of the quay and his mood lightened considerably. Chances were good that Bliss had been taken aboard the *Southern Star*. There was only one way to find out and he had to do it before the *Southern Star* left port.

Hunter waited for full darkness to arrive, then he ordered all lights doused and the *Predator* anchored just off shore behind the *Southern Star*. The night was so black the *Predator* appeared as a dark shadow against the inky sky. Dressed all in black, Hunter climbed down the ladder and slipped into the murky water.

Chapter Eight

Bliss sat in the tiny cabin aboard the *Southern Star,* listening to Gerald harangue her about their marriage. The cabin boy had just carried away the remnants of a late supper and Gerald showed no signs of leaving despite the lateness of the hour.

Bliss had refused food earlier and fallen asleep shortly after boarding. It was dark when she awoke. By then she was ravenous and had welcomed the tray of food Gerald had carried into her cabin. What she did object to was sharing her meal with a man she despised. And now, long after the meal had been consumed, Gerald remained to discuss their marriage despite Bliss's stoic refusal to wed him.

"I've come all this way to rescue you, my dear," Gerald said, pacing back and forth before her. "The least you can do is show your appreciation. It wasn't easy to come up with your ransom. I mortgaged my home to obtain the money. You owe me an enormous debt. I still want you, even though I'm fully aware that you were that pirate's doxy," he said brashly. "I'll never forgive your captor for taking what was rightfully mine. Did he rape you? Don Alizar told me the pirate took you from Gasparilla and kept you on his island."

A streak of red crept up Bliss's neck. It was true that Hunter had seduced her, but she hadn't been unwilling, though she'd never admit it to a villain like Gerald Faulk. "Believe what you want, you will anyway. I'll repay my debt from my monthly allowance," she promised. "It's late, Gerald, I suggest you leave. I have nothing more to say to you."

"Your monthly allowance, bah! At that rate it will take years to repay the money I borrowed. When we marry, your entire inheritance will compensate nicely for everything you have put me through. I'll even forgive your transgressions. Most men would hold your colorful past against you. Few men would be willing to wed a pirate's leavings. Accept it, Bliss. I'm your only hope for a normal marriage."

Dots of rage exploded behind Bliss's eyes. "How dare you speak to me like that! Nothing will convince me to marry you," she declared firmly. "You and Father deserve every adversity visited upon you. For six years you let me believe my son was dead. I'll never forgive either of you for depriving me of my precious baby."

"The child was Guy DeYoung's," Faulk said, as if that simple fact excused his despicable behavior.

"He's all I have left of Guy," Bliss maintained. "I'm going to find him, you know. You can't stop me."

Faulk stared at her thoughtfully. He knew from past experience how stubborn Bliss could be. If she said she wouldn't marry him, she meant it. His mind worked furiously. There had to be some way to change her mind. Suddenly he seized upon an idea, and after mulling it over, he knew exactly how to bring Bliss to heel.

"How badly do you want your son, my dear?" Faulk asked smoothly.

"He's the most important thing in my life right now." She realized she spoke the truth despite her powerful attachment to Hunter. Their relationship was all passion and no substance. One that had no place in the real world. Her feelings for Hunter were strong, but not as strong as the ties that bound her to her child.

"Then heed me well, Bliss," Faulk said, pausing before her and pulling her to her feet. "I will take you to Mobile to get your son in exchange for your promise to marry me upon our return to New Orleans."

"Why should I believe you?" Bliss asked warily. "You've lied to me before. Besides, the idea of marrying you appalls me."

"I'll not pressure you to marry me until I've

kept my bargain with you. That should prove I'm sincere."

"How am I to know you will never attempt to separate me from my son again?"

Lies leapt easily to Faulk's lips. "I wouldn't dream of doing such a thing."

"You would promise to treat him kindly?" Bliss said, unwilling to believe a man who had proven false in the past.

"I swear it," Faulk vowed, reaching for and finding the perfect blend of sincerity and contriteness. "I will do my utmost to reunite you with your son." And to separate you the moment you become my wife, he thought. No woman was going to tell him what to do. As soon as he had his hands on Bliss's inheritance, he would teach her to obey him.

Bliss searched his face, struggling with indecision. She did have one thing in her favor, however. She wouldn't have to marry Gerald if he didn't keep his word. And once her son was with her, she could do as she pleased, and marrying Faulk didn't please her. Somehow she'd find a way to fend him off until he became bored with waiting for her. But first they had to find her son.

"There will be no marriage until my son is returned to me," Bliss insisted.

"So I have said."

Faulk bowed his head in angry acquiescence. He needed the money; he had no choice. Once they were wed, he'd make her understand that she couldn't dictate to him. What Bliss Grenville needed was a proper beating, and he was just the man to do it. But first things first. Convincing her of his sincerity was his first priority.

"See how agreeable I am? We will set a course for Mobile as soon as the cargo is loaded tomorrow."

Satisfied, Bliss turned away, expecting him to leave. Remaining in the same room with Gerald made her physically ill.

Faulk wasn't so easily dismissed. His hands tightened on her shoulders and he pulled her against him, his eyes flaring with desire. "Not so fast, my dear. I've waited a long time for you. The least you can do is seal our bargain with a kiss."

Neither Bliss nor Faulk was aware of the dark-clad man who had scaled the ropes as they spoke and quietly climbed aboard the *Southern Star*. Nor did they know he had slipped past the night watch and was spying on them through the open porthole. He had arrived in time to hear Faulk say he wanted to seal their bargain with a kiss.

What kind of a bargain? Hunter wondered. He didn't have long to wonder. Faulk's next words sent hot rage seething through him.

"After we're married we'll be doing more than kissing. If the pirate taught you bed sport I'm not aware of, I want you to show me. First I'll take you to Mobile, then we'll be married."

Before Bliss could protest, Faulk wound his fingers through her long hair and pulled her face close to his. Then he kissed her, using his tongue to push past her teeth and into her mouth. Bliss made a gagging sound but couldn't escape the abomination of his kiss.

Hunter continued to watch the unfolding scene, driven nearly wild with jealousy. Until now he'd been ready to forgive Bliss anything. He'd planned to take her to Mobile to find their child. But this was too much. He couldn't find it in his heart to forgive her easy acquiescence to Faulk, and he despised her apparent willingness to allow Faulk to raise Guy's child. Once Bliss and Faulk were married, Faulk would become his son's legal guardian. No!

Hunter knew his ship was fast. Unburdened by cargo, it could outrun anything afloat. He would sail to Mobile himself and rescue his son before the *Southern Star* arrived. As for Bliss, she could spend the rest of her life with Faulk for all he cared. Or so he tried to tell himself.

God, it hurt. He had thought he'd lost the ability to care, but seeing Bliss in Faulk's arms proved he was still vulnerable, still capable of being hurt by this woman, and the realization angered him. Silently he vowed to purge himself of the tiny scrap of caring he'd discovered within himself.

Hunter returned his attention to the scene inside the cabin, saw the lovers break apart, and realized Faulk was preparing to take his leave. Hunter was more than a little surprised. He had thought Bliss would take Faulk to her bed, but apparently she was turning him away. His mouth curved upward in a grim parody of a smile as he backed into the shadows and waited for Faulk to clear the passageway. He allowed enough time for Faulk to reach his cabin before entering the passageway and making his way to Bliss's cabin. Then he opened the door and stepped inside.

She was standing before the porthole, staring out into the dark night. She must have sensed his presence, for she turned, searching the shadows for him. He heard her sudden intake of breath as he stepped into the halo of light provided by a hanging lantern.

"Hunter." His name trembled from her lips on a sigh.

"Aye. 'Tis me."

"How did you get here? You must leave before Gerald finds you."

He advanced slowly toward her, his upper lip curled into a mocking smile. "I have every intention of leaving. I was a fool to consider rescuing you when you don't need rescuing."

"Rescue me?"

Was he jesting? By rescuing her he meant he would take her straight back to his island, where they would continue on as they had been before she left. At least Gerald had promised to take her to Mobile to find her son. That was more than Hunter had done. When she'd told him about her son and asked for his help, he had reacted by running off.

"You're right. I don't need rescuing." God forgive her for lying. If not for her son, she would have been genuinely happy to go anywhere with

Hunter. Her life had been so very empty for so very long.

"I shouldn't have come." He turned to leave.

"Hunter! Wait."

He turned back to her, his face starkly outlined by flickering light and shadow. Only the flash of his silver eye gave any hint of his roiling emotions. "What is it?"

"I . . . Oh, God, I don't know. Just go."

Her unfeigned anguish touched a place inside him he didn't want to acknowledge. He moved toward her with weighted steps, his mind utterly rejecting what his body was demanding. He wanted her. He wanted his wife with every fiber of his being. He reached for her, bringing her hard against him. She raised her eyes to him. He searched her beautiful face, savoring those perfect features he had fallen in love with a lifetime ago. Her hands came up between them, pushing at first, then grasping the silk of his shirt to bring him closer. Hunter groaned in surrender and covered her mouth with his.

He felt her heart thundering in the same staccato beat as his own as he plundered her mouth with his tongue. He drank the throaty moans from her lips as he swept her up into his arms and carried her to the narrow bed, cursing his weakness for Bliss. He couldn't leave without tasting her sweet passion one last time. She was like an addiction. He knew she wasn't good for him, but the ecstasy he found within her arms was a powerful inducement.

Bliss felt herself being lowered onto the bed,

felt Hunter's hard body cover hers, and suddenly she wanted this as much as he did, despite the niggling voice warning her that she was unlikely to emerge from the encounter with her heart intact. Then a frightening thought occurred to her. If Hunter was caught with her, it could mean his death.

"Hunter, we can't. Go now, before you're caught."

"Tell me something first, Bliss. Are you carrying my child?"

Bliss gasped, shocked by his startling question. Why did he want to know? It *was* possible, though highly improbable. "I don't know."

"Too bad," he mumbled.

She was about to ask what he meant when she felt a cool dampness against her lower body and realized that Hunter had worked her skirts up to her waist. His clothing was still wet from his swim and she shivered. Then she felt the blunt tip of his sex prodding between her legs.

"I thought you were going to leave."

"Not yet. Not until I finish what I came to do. Open for me," he whispered, nudging her legs apart with his knee.

There was a harsh edge to his voice that she recognized as desperation, and when she looked up at him she was surprised to see that his face wore a haunted look that had little to do with pleasure. Then he thrust into her and her thoughts scattered.

Cradling her hips in his big hands, he adjusted her body to fit his and began to move inside her. "Take me deeper," he groaned against her lips.

She arched her back and felt him slide deeper, creating a clamoring inside her that accelerated with each swift, sure stroke. She could feel her body stretching taut as a bowstring as his sex reached deep inside her core, touching her soul. Higher and higher she climbed, until shards of brilliant lightning splintered through her, scorching her with dazzling sparks of pleasure.

Hunter blazed hotter with each thrust; the need to pour himself inside her was so intense he had to grit his teeth to keep from spilling his seed before Bliss attained her own pleasure. His mouth seized hers, his tongue delving and retreating, mimicking the thrusting of his sex. When the churning inside him grew unbearable, he brought his hand between them and found her most sensitive place.

Still maintaining the frantic tempo of his thrusting loins, he massaged the tiny nub, flinging Bliss to the sharp edge of climax. Then he pushed her over with a thrust so deep that the pleasure of it sent him tumbling after her as wave after wave of luminous ecstasy rushed through him.

He heard Bliss cry out, felt her tremble beneath him, and knew she had found her own pleasure. He remained embedded deeply within her until her contractions diminished and her legs released their hold on him. Then he rose from the bed and straightened his clothing. He couldn't resist turning back to look at Bliss one last time and immediately regretted it. She looked adorably wanton, lying there with her lips swollen from his kisses and her thighs wet and glistening with his seed. He turned away.

"I don't seem to have much control where you're concerned," he said harshly, "but you already know that."

"Where are you going now?"

"Back to doing what I do best." He gave her a mocking grin. "Are you sure you won't come with me? We can take up where we left off."

"I . . . No, I can't. Gerald has promised to take me to Mobile to find my son. I can't give him up. I've come too far."

"When you marry, Faulk will become your son's stepfather and guardian," Hunter said with a snarl.

"That's how it usually works," Bliss responded tartly.

But that's not how it's going to be, she thought to herself. She had no intention of marrying Gerald Faulk, not now, not ever.

"Heed me well," Hunter advised. "Make damn sure your husband is dead before you marry Faulk."

Bliss leapt from the bed, her face drained of all color. "What do you mean?"

"Figure it out for yourself."

He opened the door and peered into the passageway.

"You can't say something like that and just leave!" Bliss charged.

He gave her an oblique smile that stirred the depths of her memory and left her shaken.

The click of the latch galvanized her into action and she rushed to the door to stop him from leaving, but he was gone, disappearing as silently and mysteriously as he had come. His startling words hung in the air like a dark cloud. What did Hunter know about Guy that she did not?

Hunter left the ship as silently as he had arrived. He slipped into the water and swam back to the *Predator* without being detected.

He was determined to find his child before Bliss and Faulk reached Mobile. Until he'd seen Bliss and Faulk kissing, he'd intended to reveal his identity to Bliss, remove her from Faulk's ship, and sail with her to Mobile to rescue their son. He tried to tell himself that he had followed Bliss to Cuba for his son's sake, but he knew he was lying.

Don't lie to yourself, a little voice inside him whispered. You were willing to move heaven and hell to get Bliss back because she's your wife and you still want her. You seduced your own wife and treated her like your whore! You tried to make her pregnant as part of your revenge. How strange, Hunter thought as he climbed aboard the *Predator*, that he still had a small bit of conscience left. He would have to do something about it.

* * *

The *Predator*, newly named the *Boston Queen*, sailed into Mobile Bay a week later. She flew the American flag, one of many flags from various countries that Hunter kept on hand and used upon occasion.

Hunter donned his best black silk shirt, black breeches, and black jacket before going ashore. He wore his sword but left all but one pistol aboard the *Queen*. He also carried a hefty sack of gold coins beneath his jacket. Ostensibly he was looking for a cargo to fill his hold, but a cargo was the furthest thing from his mind as he sought directions to Water Street from a longshoreman.

Hunter located Water Street in a seedy neighborhood not far from the waterfront. Low-class brothels and saloons existed side-by-side with private dwellings and rooming houses. The buildings were mostly nondescript and rundown. Hunter inquired after the Holmes family at various businesses, and a few allowed that the name sounded familiar, though none offered an address. Hunter assumed the locals were leery of the mysterious stranger dressed in black and wearing an eyepatch.

Desperate to locate his son, Hunter decided to knock on every door until he found Enos Holmes. It was a long street, but he had no other recourse.

Just then he saw a small boy exit a saloon lugging a pail of beer. He looked pathetically thin, and Hunter felt a jolt of unaccustomed pity. He appeared to be about the same age as his own son. Something about the child was appealing, and Hunter called out to him. The boy stopped and turned around, his eyes widening when he saw the black-clad stranger hailing him. He turned to run.

"Wait! Don't run. I'm not going to hurt you. I'm looking for someone and I thought you might help me."

The lad slowed down but did not stop.

Hunter caught up with him and placed a hand on his shoulder. "I won't keep you long."

"Wha. . . . what do you want, mister?" The lad raised his head and stared at Hunter despite his fear. "If I don't get home with this beer, Enos will beat me."

Hunter barely heard the lad's words. The moment he saw the boy's vivid turquoise eyes, his heart began to pound. They were the exact color of Bliss's. He knelt on one knee before the grubby child. His hand shook as he reached out and ruffled his dark hair.

He was so choked with emotion he could scarcely speak, but somehow he managed to ask, "What is your name, son?"

"Bryan."

"Do you have a last name?"

The lad shook his head. "Enos and Meg said I was a bastard. They said no one wanted me. Meg wanted me, but then she got sick and died. There's no one but me and Enos now."

The moment Hunter had touched the lad, the sense of kinship was so pronounced, he knew the child was his son without further proof. And the boy was no bastard, no matter what he'd been told. He was legitimately born but had been deprived of both his parents by a pair of reprehensible scoundrels who justified their act with twisted logic that suited their individual purposes.

"Can I go now, mister? Enos is gonna skin me alive if I don't get back with this beer."

"Give me the pail, son, I'll carry it for you while you lead the way. I have business with Enos."

"You do? No one ever visits him." Apparently intrigued by the promise of company, Bryan skipped down the street, glancing back every so often to make sure Hunter was following. He stopped before a dilapidated two-story rooming house. "We live on the second floor. Are you sure you want to come up?"

"Positive," Hunter said. "Lead the way."

The hallway was narrow and dingy, with a strong smell of urine and rotted wood. The stairs protested Hunter's weight as he followed Bryan to the second-floor landing. At one place an entire step was missing, and part of the railing had fallen away. The thought that his son had been raised in such squalor sent rage coursing through him.

Bryan stopped before a scarred door and turned the knob. He looked back once to make sure Hunter was behind him before entering.

Harsh words greeted Bryan's entrance. "It's about time, you little bastard. You'd better not have spilled any of that beer if you know what's good for you."

The voice melded with the man as Enos Holmes appeared in the doorway. He was a tall, skinny man with thinning hair and narrow lips. He wiped the end of his reddened nose on his dirty sleeve and regarded Bryan through a blurry haze. He didn't see Hunter standing in the shadows as he grasped Bryan by the nape and gave him a vicious shake. "Where's my beer? If you lost my money, there will be hell to pay. That pinchpenny Grenville barely sends enough blunt to pay the rent and keep me in beer."

Hunter had heard enough. By now he was ready to skewer Enos Holmes. He stepped forward, placing the pail of beer on a rickety table.

Enos's eyes widened and he swallowed fearfully when he saw Hunter. "Who in the hell are you?"

"Your worst enemy," Hunter said with quiet menace.

Enos turned on Bryan, apparently blaming the boy for bringing the terrifying stranger into his home. He raised his fist as if to strike the lad. "You're gonna get it now, boy! How many times have I told you not to talk to strangers?"

Before his hand reached Bryan, Hunter grasped his wrist and shoved him away. "Lay one hand on the boy and you're a dead man."

Enos's eyes bugged out. "Who are you? What makes you think you can interfere with me and my son?"

"The boy is not yours and you know it."

Hunter wanted to beat Enos to a pulp. But not in front of the boy. "Bryan, why don't you take the beer into the kitchen and stay there while I speak with Enos."

Enos's fear was palpable. "Stay right here, kid."

"Do as I say, Bryan." Hunter's voice brooked no argument and Bryan gave none as he picked up the bucket and trudged into the kitchen.

"You're gonna pay for that," Enos called after him.

"I don't think so," Hunter said, hanging on to his temper with admirable restraint. He glanced about the sparsely furnished room, taking note of the threadbare furniture and the layer of dust covering everything, and wrinkled his nose in disgust. "I have a proposition for you, Holmes. One I guarantee you won't turn down."

"What kind of proposition?" Enos asked curiously.

"As you have probably guessed by now, Claude Grenville isn't going to send the extra money you asked for. In fact, he's stopping payments altogether."

"Did Grenville send you?"

"Not exactly."

"Then who are you and what in the hell do you want?"

"I want the boy. I'm willing to pay for your years of care, such as they were."

"You're gonna pay me for taking the kid off my hands?" Enos asked eagerly. "How much?"

"Is this enough?" Hunter asked, revolted by the man's avarice. He brought forth a sack of gold coins and spilled some into his palm.

Enos was nearly salivating as Hunter returned the coins to the sack and jangled it before his nose. "What do you want the kid for?" he asked.

"That's my business. All you need to know is that he'll have a good home and be well treated."

"Meg and I raised the lad since he was a babe. Meg would haunt me if something bad happened to him," Enos said, pretending concern.

"You have my word. The boy will be treated kindly. And you'll have enough gold to move from this hovel and make a new life for yourself. You won't have to depend upon Grenville's largess for your livelihood."

"I always wanted to go to Boston," Enos claimed. "Got a sister-in-law there. A widow woman. She always did fancy me." He rubbed his stubbly chin, apparently mulling over Hunter's offer.

"Well, now's your chance. What do you say?"

"I don't know. I'm curious, though. How do you know Claude Grenville? What do you know about Bryan?"

"I know everything there is to know. You see," he said, "Bryan is my son."

"But . . . Claude told me Bryan's father was dead and his mother didn't want him."

"Wrong on both counts. Give me your answer, Holmes."

"Take him. Without Grenville's money I ain't got no way to support the kid."

"I thought you'd agree," Hunter said grimly. "There is a condition, though."

"What condition?" Holmes asked pugnaciously. "You never said nothing about a condition."

"I want you out of this house today."

Holmes scratched the back of his neck. "Today, you say? Don't know, that's mighty quick."

"That's the way it has to be." He jingled the sack of coins in front of Holmes. "There's a king's ransom here."

Holmes licked his thin lips. "There's a ship due to sail to Boston day after tomorrow. I already checked because I'd hoped Grenville's money would arrive in time for me to book passage."

"What were you going to do with Bryan?" Hunter asked with quiet menace.

"Well, I—"

"You were going to abandon him, weren't you?"

"It ain't as if the kid's mine," Holmes whined. "Meg took care of the boy when she was alive, but the fever took her two years ago."

"I'm very close to killing you, Holmes," Hunter said, gripping the hilt of his sword. "Don't say another word. Just pack your things . . . now."

"Now?"

"Now. You can rent a room near the waterfront for a night or two, till your ship departs. I'll even accompany you down there to make sure you keep your part of the bargain."

Neither Hunter nor Holmes knew that Bryan had been listening to their conversation. He stepped forward now, his expression one of wary optimism.

"Are you taking me with you, mister?"

Another crack appeared in Hunter's tough exterior as the boy's turquoise gaze settled on him. "You heard?"

Bryan nodded jerkily. "You said you're my papa. Enos and Meg told me I didn't have a papa and that my mama didn't love me. They said my grandpa gave me away because I was a bad boy."

Hunter groaned in dismay. If Claude Grenville were here now, Hunter would have a devil of a time controlling himself. "They were all wrong, son. You do have a papa. One who wants you very much. I just didn't know about you until very recently."

Byran regarded Hunter through eyes far too solemn for one so young. "Why didn't my mama want me? Are you going to take me to her?"

"She didn't know about you, either. She was told you were dead. We'll talk about her later," he hedged. "I'm taking you aboard my ship. You'll like the *Boston Queen*."

"Should I call you Papa?" Bryan asked shyly. "I've never called anyone that before."

Hunter scooped the thin little boy into his

arms and hugged him tightly. It felt good, damn good. A tingling warmth radiated from the void where his heart had once been. He'd felt it with Bliss and now with his son. Could it be love?

"I'd like it if you called me Papa."

Chapter Nine

The *Southern Star* sailed into Mobile Bay with the tide and maneuvered into an empty slot beside one of the long piers jutting out into the water. Bliss paced the deck impatiently as she waited for the gangplank to be lowered, eager to leave the ship and begin her search for her son. Faulk joined her while the docking was in progress.

"How long before we can leave the ship?" Bliss asked anxiously.

"Not long. The gangplank will be run out in a few minutes."

"Perhaps someone on the docks can give us directions to Water Street," Bliss suggested.

"I hate for you to get your hopes up," Faulk said. "You have no idea what you'll find. The boy could be dead. Or the child's upbringing so common that you won't wish to claim him. You might decide it's better to leave him where he is if his coarse speech and crude manners prove to be an embarrassment."

Bliss rounded on him. "Not claim my own child? Are you mad? I don't care about his upbringing. He's my son and I'll want him no matter what I find. He's all I have left of Guy."

"Have it your way," Faulk said sourly. "The gangplank is in place. Shall we leave?"

The harbor master was able to provide them with directions to Water Street. Bliss had memorized the address. Number 710. The street was just a few blocks from the harbor, and Bliss decided to walk rather than wait for Faulk to hire a conveyance. As they approached Water Street, Bliss's fears for her son mounted. She thought the seedy neighborhood no proper place in which to raise a small child. Grog-shops and brothels abounded, and the houses were in desperate need of repair.

"There's the place," Faulk said, pointing to a two-story clapboard rooming house. "Shall I inquire inside for you?"

"No, I'll do it myself," Bliss said, girding herself for her first meeting with her son. She wondered what the boy had been told about his parents, and how he would react to the knowledge that she was his mother.

Heart racing, she started up the front steps. Just as she reached the landing, an elderly woman wearing a grimy white apron and carrying a broom opened the door and stepped outside.

"Are you looking for someone?" the woman asked. She looked Bliss up and down, then gave Faulk a knowing grin. "If you're wanting a love nest for you and your . . . er . . . lady, you've come to the right place. I'm not nosy like some landladies."

Bliss wanted to give the presumptuous woman the sharp edge of her tongue but decided to let the remark pass. "We're looking for one of your tenants," she explained. "Enos Holmes. Is he home?"

"The mister ain't here."

"When do you expect Mr. Holmes?" Bliss asked, cursing the bad luck that had delayed her arrival.

The landlady shrugged her plump shoulders. "He won't be coming back."

"What do you mean? I'm willing to pay for information."

"And I'd sell it if I had any. Enos paid the back rent he owed me day before yesterday and said he was going away and wouldn't be back."

"Where did he go?" Bliss asked frantically. "Did he take the boy with him?"

"Don't rightly know. I told you I'm not nosy. What my tenants do is their own business as long as they pay the rent on time. I recollect he said something about remarrying."

Bliss staggered backward as if struck. What could have happened to send Enos Holmes fleeing before their arrival? "Do you know the name of the lady he was seeing?"

"Now that you mention it, I don't recall him seeing or mentioning any lady. Oh well, tenants come, tenants go." Considering the subject closed, she began to wield the broom with more vigor than was necessary, nearly sweeping Bliss off the landing.

"There has to be something more you can tell me," Bliss pleaded. "There's a gold coin in it for you. Did you see the boy? Is he well?"

"Where's the coin?" the landlady asked slyly.

Bliss held out her palm to Faulk and he reluctantly placed a gold coin in it. She offered it to the woman. "Here it is. What else do you remember?"

The woman snatched the coin from Bliss's hand and tucked it between her ample breasts. "I didn't see the boy when Enos left, but I suppose he's well enough. He was hardly ever sick. They weren't a loving family, if you take my meaning. Meg Holmes was good to the boy while she lived, but she died and left him to Enos. Things went downhill for the boy after Meg died.

"Every year they received a sum of money," she continued. "I got the impression they were being paid to keep the boy. That's all I can tell you."

"You have no idea where Enos went?"

"No idea at all. I hope your business ain't important, because it sounded like Enos was leaving these parts for good."

"Perhaps he was taking the boy to your father in New Orleans," Faulk offered. "I suggest we leave immediately. If Enos has been raising the boy on his own, he probably wanted to get rid of him before remarrying."

Bliss's hopes soared. Gerald's words made sense. But a niggling doubt remained. "Is there an orphanage in town where Enos might have left the boy before departing?" she asked the landlady.

"None that I know of." She returned to her sweeping.

"We'll learn nothing more here," Faulk said, urging her down the steps. "I'm convinced we'll find the boy in New Orleans. Nothing else makes sense."

"Enos could have abandoned my son."

"I don't think he would. Obviously he needs money, and your father is his best chance to obtain the funds he needs. Come away. If we hurry we can sail on the evening tide."

"Not until I make a thorough search of the city," Bliss said, tilting her chin at a stubborn angle. "My son could be living on the streets and begging for his food."

Bliss could almost hear Gerald's patience snapping but she didn't care.

"Very well," he groused. "If this good woman will give me a description, I'll have my crewmen scour the city for him."

Bliss listened eagerly as the landlady gave a sketchy portrait of an active six-year-old, somewhat thin for his age but otherwise healthy.

Thick black hair and turquoise eyes were the only distinctive characteristics that might make him stand out in a crowd.

Her heart heavy, Bliss returned to the *Southern Star* with Faulk. Later that day an exhaustive search was launched. Bliss joined Faulk's crewmen as they searched the city streets for a homeless urchin with black hair and turquoise blue eyes. The hunt continued for seven frustrating days before Bliss was willing to admit defeat. Discouraged and heartbroken, she retired to her cabin as the ship slipped her moorings and charted a course for New Orleans. Though her disappointment was keen, Bliss still harbored hopes that she'd find her son in New Orleans with her father.

Suddenly she realized that she hadn't asked the boy's name, nor had it been given. Not that it mattered. He didn't need a name. The special bond between mother and son would enable her to recognize him anywhere.

Hunter learned many things about his son during the journey from Mobile to Pine Island. Through casual conversation he'd discovered what the boy's life had been like. One fact came shining through. The boy was a survivor, dauntless and courageous in the face of adversity. He possessed a strong character and an inquisitive nature. He had withstood years of neglect despite his foster mother's haphazard caring, and after Meg's death he'd suffered both physical and verbal abuse from Enos.

Food had come into the house sporadically. If there was money left after Enos spent the bulk of it in grog-shops, Meg had been allowed to stock the cupboards. When that food was gone they didn't eat. After Meg died, Bryan's life had deteriorated. He had been reduced to picking up refuse behind grog-shops.

Hunter was surprised at the tremendous amount of love he found within himself for his son. He didn't even have to search to find it. He felt revitalized, yet uncertain of the fragile emotions he'd fought long and hard to purge from his heart. He found himself dwelling on the past. Had fate not interfered seven years ago, he and Bliss would still be together, enjoying their son as a family. Perhaps there would have been other children after Bryan.

He imagined Bliss as he had left her in the bunk aboard the *Southern Star*. Lips swollen from his kisses, legs sprawled in wanton abandon, and her eyes hazy with passion. The sudden wanting the vision evoked sent heat coursing through his body. His loins hardened with painful need as he recalled the sweet scent of her skin, the taste of her mouth, the way she cried out his name at the peak of her pleasure.

God, how could he let Faulk have her? She was his wife, dammit! But the only way he could claim Bliss was to reveal his identity and risk being sent back to prison. And if the authorities learned he was a pirate, he was likely to end up swinging at the end of a rope. Piracy on the high seas was a capital offense.

Hunter's thoughts scattered when he saw Bryan climbing the ladder to the quarterdeck to join him. He grinned at the boy, noting how robust he looked after enjoying substantial meals and carefree days of playing beneath the hot sun. Sunshine and fresh sea air had given him a healthy glow he hadn't had while living in squalor in the city.

"Are we almost there, Papa?" Bryan asked, returning Hunter's grin.

"Keep watching and you'll see the outline of the island soon."

"I've never been on an island before. Will we stay there forever?"

"I don't know," Hunter hedged. He still hadn't mapped out their future. Raising his son in a pirate's world didn't appeal to him. Nor did leaving him to Bliss and Faulk to raise. Hunter had enough money to live anywhere he pleased for the rest of his life and he would still be able to leave a sizable inheritance to Bryan. He could go north to St. Louis or east to Boston. He could go to London or Paris. Places where his past wouldn't follow him.

"Do you think my mother will want me now?" the boy asked wistfully. "Will I see her someday?"

"If it's at all possible, son," Hunter promised. "There are things standing in our way. Things you're too young to understand."

Things like Bliss preferring Faulk to Hunter, Hunter thought grimly. Things like Bliss wanting Faulk to be his son's stepfather and guardian. All these obstacles and more had to be resolved before Bryan could know his mother.

And Hunter had to learn to conduct himself in society again, if and when he decided to return.

"Look, Papa, there's the island!" Bryan cried excitedly.

Hunter joined Bryan at the railing, watching his island grow larger as the ship drew closer.

"Something's amiss, Cap'n," the man in the crow's nest shouted as they negotiated the river into the lake.

The first mate, Ty Greene, handed Hunter a spyglass. Hunter scanned the approaching shoreline, his face grim. Suddenly he stiffened, cursing beneath his breath as he handed the glass back to Greene.

"Hell and damnation!" Greene swore. "We've been attacked. The village is gone . . . burnt to the ground."

"Gasparilla," Hunter said through clenched teeth. "Give me the glass."

Greene returned the spyglass to Hunter. Hunter put it to his eye and searched the beach for survivors. By now the destruction was visible to the naked eye and a great cry rose up from the crew. Some pirates had families on the island, others had women they had grown fond of.

"Do you see anyone, Cap'n?" Greene asked anxiously.

"No one. We'll put a boat ashore and search the island for the women and children. They probably took to the forest when Gasparilla fired the first shot."

Hunter asked Greene to choose a dozen crewmen to accompany him ashore and went to break out the arms. Apparently forgotten in the confusion, Bryan tagged along behind Hunter.

"Is something wrong, Papa?" he asked when he caught up with his father.

Hunter had all but forgotten the boy in the seriousness of the moment. He turned to reassure him. "Nothing to concern you, son. I have to go ashore for a while but I'll be back. You're to wait here for me."

Bryan waved from the deck as Hunter and his men climbed down the ropes to the skiff, which had already been lowered into the gently rolling surf.

The men rowed the short distance to shore in silence. The charred remains of the village were clearly visible now, and it was obvious that Gasparilla had been thorough. Not one hut or cottage remained standing. Most had been reduced to charred rubble.

The men beached the skiff and swarmed through the ruins, searching for survivors. Some of the debris was still smoldering, which led Hunter to believe that the attack had occurred quite recently.

"No bodies, Cap'n," one of the men reported when the search had been completed.

"Let's go on to my house," Hunter said. "Perhaps we'll find someone there."

Even before he reached the rubble of his own

house, the acrid stench of charred wood hit Hunter forcibly. The sight that met his eyes was nightmarish. The house was gone. All his treasures had been burned beyond recognition. Tall pine trees wearing green moss beards stood guard over the charred remains, mocking him. A lump formed in his throat, and he looked away.

"Spread out and search the mangrove thickets," Hunter ordered as the men looked to him for instructions. "It wouldn't surprise me if Gasparilla took all the inhabitants off the island and sold them into slavery," he mumbled to Greene. Apparently his men were of the same mind, for he could see despair and anger in their grim expressions.

Suddenly a man burst through the forest. Hunter gripped the hilt of his sword but released it when he recognized Caesar.

"I've been waiting for you, Cap'n," Caesar said as he stumbled up to greet Hunter. "We all prayed Gasparilla hadn't found you."

"You're safe!" Hunter cried, overcome by relief. "Where are the others?"

"At the north end of the island with the Indians. Cleo and I suspected that Gasparilla would return after his first visit and we began to prepare after you left. We warned the villagers to flee at the first sign of the *Dona Rosalia*. Then we organized the women and carried all your valuables to the Indian village. The Indians offered to help after we told them what had happened. Most of your valuables were hidden in the village long before Gasparilla came with his big guns."

Hunter was speechless. "You did that for me?"

"Aye, Cap'n, you've been more than fair to all of us."

"You say our women and families are safe?" one man asked.

"They all got away," Caesar said. "I watched as Gasparilla and his men come ashore and torched what remained of the village. Then they set fire to the cap'n's house. Gasparilla was in a rage because Hunter wasn't here. I heard him vow to hunt Hunter down and blow him from the water. Some of his men wanted to search the forest for the women, but Gasparilla forbade it. He didn't want to stir up the Calusa. He knew they were friendly to the cap'n."

Hunter was stunned. It was inconceivable that Caesar, Cleo, and the others had done this for him. He didn't deserve such loyalty. For the first time in seven years he felt gratitude toward another human being. His soul had been so empty for so long, he'd thought himself bereft of every emotion but hatred and bitterness.

"Let's get back to the ship," he said in a choked voice. "We'll sail around the island to the Indian village and pick up the survivors. Once everyone is safely aboard, we'll decide what's to be done. Gasparilla is a vindictive man; he won't rest until he's exacted his pound of flesh for my betrayal."

"We're with you all the way, Cap'n," a bearded

pirate exclaimed. This remark brought forth a bevy of cheers.

Caesar pulled Hunter aside as the others trekked back to the beach. "What about the plunder you've buried on the island?"

"I intend to take most, but not all of it, aboard my ship. Some I want to share with my crew. The rest will keep until I return for it. I've yet to decide the course of my future. I have a son to think of now. Come on, let's go back to the ship for a couple of shovels."

Three hours later, four large chests filled with treasure had been dug up from various places around the island and placed aboard the skiff. Only two remained, and Hunter decided to leave them where they were for the time being. Once the chests had been stored safely in the hold of the *Boston Queen*, Hunter took the wheel himself and set a course for the north end of the island.

Tamrah and Tomas greeted them on the beach as they stepped ashore. There was much rejoicing as the pirates and their women were reunited.

"There will be a great feast tonight in honor of your return," Tamrah said shyly.

"I thank you for all the help your people have given mine," Hunter said.

"I owe you much for giving me Tamrah," Tomas said in halting English.

"I hope I made the right decision, Tomas," Hunter said, searching Tamrah's face as he spoke to the young man.

"It was the right choice," Tamrah said. "I am happy with Tomas. I beg your forgiveness for what I did to your woman. It was wrong of me to think I could be more to you than a friend or a sister. I belong here with my people, I know that now."

"You're forgiven," Hunter said. "Your father asked me to protect you and I did my best. Now it's up to Tomas to keep you safe."

"Where is Bliss?" Tamrah asked. "Cleo said you were going to bring her back. 'Tis sad what Gasparilla did to your home."

Before Hunter could form an answer, Bryan, who had come ashore in another boat, ran up to join Hunter.

"Whose child is this?" Cleo asked curiously.

Hunter lifted Bryan into his arms so everyone could see him. "This is my son. His name is Bryan."

"Your son . . . but—" Cleo's words came to an abrupt halt as she took a good look at the boy. Serious turquoise eyes stared back at her. She gave a gasp of surprise and looked askance at Hunter.

"Aye, 'tis true what you're thinking, but I ask that you not speak her name in front of the boy."

"Have you known all along?" Cleo asked once she recovered from her surprise.

Hunter set Bryan on his feet and asked Tamrah to find him something to eat. Bryan skipped off with Tamrah, unaware of the turmoil surrounding him.

"I didn't know I had a son until the day I left in the skiff to go to Sanibel. It came as such a shock that I went off by myself to think."

"I didn't know you and Bliss were acquainted before you brought her to your island."

"I never revealed my identity to Bliss. She still doesn't know that I'm the husband she thought had died six years ago. I've changed a great deal over the years. Her child was taken from her at birth. Her father told her the babe had been stillborn, and she believed him. She just recently learned he was alive and was on her way to reclaim him when Gasparilla attacked her ship and took her to Captiva."

"Why isn't Bliss here with you and her son?"

"It's a long story, Cleo," Hunter said wearily. "One I don't wish to divulge right now. Suffice it to say Bliss still doesn't know I'm Guy DeYoung, the man she married seven years ago. She's presently with her betrothed."

"Her betrothed!" Cleo said, aghast. "How can she marry another when she already has a husband? I thought it was not allowed."

"Bliss believes her husband lies beneath a tombstone in a pauper's graveyard."

"What are you going to do? Gasparilla has vowed to kill you. If you remain a pirate, your son's life will always be in grave danger. Is that what you want for him?"

"Nay. I want a better life for him than I had. I want him to enjoy the money I've accumulated." A frown settled between his brows. "I know most of my wealth was gotten illegally but

I can't undo the past. 'Tis the future I'm most concerned about now."

The feast that night was a welcome relief from worry. The pirates had their women and children back and the rum flowed freely. Hunter put Bryan to bed in one of the grass and log huts and joined him a short while later, abandoning the celebration still in progress. Hunter had a lot of thinking to do.

Piracy was neither a practical nor a safe livelihood for him to follow. He now had a son to protect. Hunter knew how Gasparilla's devious mind worked. He was like a dog after a bone when he put his mind to something. Should Hunter remain in the Brotherhood, Gasparilla would hound him into eternity. Gasparilla was now his enemy, no matter what they had been to one another in the past.

Hunter had been aware of the dangerous consequences before he'd taken Bliss to Pine Island, but he had chosen to ignore them. At the time he couldn't think beyond the woman who had been his wife. He'd planned to seduce her, to make her love him again, then abandon her after he'd put his babe in her belly. When he revisited his motives, he wasn't too surprised to realize that he had been lying to himself about his feelings for Bliss. With painful insight he realized that he'd wanted Bliss because he had missed her, because he needed her. Because he still loved her no matter how desperately he'd tried to purge her memory from his mind and heart.

Hunter had learned a great deal about himself since Bliss had returned to his life. He'd learned that he was still vulnerable. Still able to be hurt. *That he was still married to Bliss and that they had a son*. His mind searched for answers and he found them. Sometime during the wee hours of morning Hunter mapped out his future. One that might or might not include Bliss.

The *Predator*, bearing its rightful name again and flying the black flag, raised anchor and sailed north from Pine Island. On board were the inhabitants of the pirate village and the treasures that had been rescued from Hunter's home before it was destroyed. Hunter charted a course for Barataria, Jean Lafitte's stronghold.

The *Predator* entered Charlotte Harbor, skirted Cayo Pelau, and made a wide berth around Gasparilla Island, thus avoiding a confrontation with Hunter's enemy. They anchored off Barataria on a mild fall day a week after they had set sail. Jean Lafitte himself welcomed Hunter as he walked down the gangplank onto the stone jetty.

"Welcome to Barataria," Jean said expansively. "What brings you to my home, *mon ami*? Do you have more wonderful plunder for my greedy customers? Or is the rumor true? Word has it that Gasparilla is out to destroy you."

"The rumor is true, Jean," Hunter allowed. "Gasparilla has destroyed the village and my home on Pine Island." He paused for effect. "You've helped me before, Jean, and I'm appealing to you again. But if you fear Gasparilla, I will not trouble you with my problems."

Jean tilted his handsome face upward and laughed uproariously. "Jean Lafitte fears no man. Not even Gasparilla. Come to the house, where we can speak privately."

"My son is with me. Is there someone who can look after him while we talk?"

Jean raised an elegant eyebrow. "Your son? You must tell me about him. Pierre's wife can look after him. She has several children he can play with."

Jean made his wishes known to an attractive woman standing nearby, and Bryan was taken off to join a group of children playing tag.

A short time later Hunter joined Lafitte in his elegantly appointed study, a room whose four walls were lined with bookshelves crammed with rare copies of leather-bound books. Jean poured three fingers of French brandy into two crystal snifters and handed one to Hunter.

He swirled the amber liquid in his glass and said, "Now, my friend, tell me what I can do for you."

"You can allow my men and their women to join your community. With Gasparilla on the rampage, it's not safe to rebuild the village on Pine Island."

"Do you and your son not wish to join my community also?"

"Nay. I'm taking my son to New Orleans. I don't want him exposed to the dangerous life I've led these past six years. Everything has changed since I learned about Bryan. I want to give him all that his life has been lacking. He's suffered enough for the sins of others."

"Where is the boy's mother?"

" 'Tis a long story."

"I've plenty of time."

Hunter decided to make a clean breast of it. Lafitte knew something of his story, for he'd rescued Guy DeYoung from death's door six years before. Taking a deep breath, Hunter launched into his stirring tale. When he finished, Lafitte sat back and stared at him.

"That's quite a story, *mon ami*. So now you are punishing the mother by keeping her son from her."

"His mother is marrying another man, the same man who is responsible for the loss of my eye and sending my son away to be raised by strangers," Hunter said pugnaciously.

"The mother cannot marry another when she is already wed," Lafitte reminded him.

"She is married to Guy DeYoung, and he died six years ago."

"But we both know he's very much alive," Lafitte observed. "What do you intend to do?"

"Establish myself and my son in New Orleans. My fortune and the English title I purchased years ago from a destitute viscount who bore the name of Hunter will be my entry into society. If you recall, I took the viscount captive and became intrigued when I learned we shared the same name. I bought the title on a whim, and now it will stand me in good stead. Beyond that I have no plans. My men and my ship need a home. That's why I'm appealing to you to allow them into your community. They can keep the *Predator* and choose a capable captain from among themselves.

"I would also ask for transportation for my son and myself to New Orleans," Hunter continued. "You're still wecome in the city, aren't you?"

"At the moment, but I don't know how long my welcome will last. Governor Claiborne chooses to be difficult. I hate to see you give up piracy, but that is your choice," Jean continued. "Our association has been a profitable one, *mon ami*. The day I brought you to Barataria was a fortunate one for me. I will do all that you ask. If ever you find yourself in trouble, you know where to find me. If not at Grande Terre, I can be found at 'The Temple' conducting auctions, or at the Absinthe House. I do not remain in the city long these days. Baratarians are becoming exceedingly unwelcome in New Orleans."

"I'll remember, Jean," Hunter said gratefully. "You snatched me from the jaws of death once. I hope it won't be necessary to seek your help a second time."

Hunter remained on Barataria a week, during which time he acquired a wardrobe suitable for a man of wealth and position. Unfortunately, there was little he could do to disguise his eye-patch. All he could do was devise a plausible explanation for his injury and hope no one would identify him as Hunter the pirate.

Chapter Ten

liss wanted to rush out to the plantation as
oon as she landed in New Orleans. Gerald
ired a carriage and they left together. Bliss was
n pins and needles during the short journey,
appily anticipating a reunion with her son.
he still harbored a wealth of anger at her fa-
ier and she didn't look forward to their con-
ontation.

Gerald Faulk had sulked all the way to the
lantation, obviously enraged over Bliss's re-
isal to marry him. Apparently he felt their
iarriage was to be his reward for paying her
ansom. Bliss didn't see it that way. She would
ever forgive him for joining her father in mak-
ig her life a living hell.

The plantation had just come into view when
aulk broke his brooding silence. "I've done

everything you've asked of me, Bliss," he all but shouted. "You owe me for rescuing you, whether or not you find your son with your father. Our marriage *will* take place. And soon. The bank is breathing down my neck. I'm desperately in need of money."

"I don't owe you a thing, Gerald," Bliss said evenly. "You and Father are responsible for Guy's death. We would be happily married now and raising our son together if not for your interference." Even after all these years she bled inside when she thought of Guy. "Find another heiress and leave me alone."

"Your father and I have an understanding. I allowed him to invest and share in the profits from my shipping business in return for your hand in marriage. I've waited a long time for you. There is no other woman I want. Call it an obsession, call it stubbornness, I'll have no other. I've made do with mistresses too long, but now I want a wife."

"What happened to all those profits?" Bliss asked. "Father claims you're both on the brink of ruination."

"Our profits were substantial until pirates began singling out my ships for attack." He shook his head. "I just don't understand why my ships were raided and sunk when others got through. Now our creditors are hounding us and our substantial profits have all but disappeared. Your father and I stand to lose everything. I'm a patient man. I didn't press for marriage before now because I knew you were against it."

"And you knew I couldn't collect my inheritance until I turned twenty-five," Bliss reminded him.

"I wasn't desperate for your money before now," Faulk snapped. "You're twenty-five, Bliss, I'll damn well have what I've waited all these years for."

Bliss withheld her reply as Faulk halted the carriage in front of the house and stepped down to help her alight. Rather than let him touch her, she hopped down herself and strode briskly up the steps. Mandy, the elderly slave who had been like a second mother to Bliss, opened the door, tears filling her eyes when she saw Bliss standing on the threshold.

"Oh, honey, we's all been so worried about you!" Mandy cried. She gathered Bliss to her ample breast. "Yore daddy was beside himself with worry when he got that ransom demand."

"I'm fine, Mandy," Bliss said, gently removing herself from her old nanny's arms. "Is my son here?"

Mandy gave Bliss a blank look. "Are you all right, honey? There ain't no boy here. You know yore son died six years ago."

He's not here! Bliss felt her world collapsing around her. She had so hoped . . . But now she knew her son was gone forever. She swallowed the lump in her throat and said, "No, Mandy, my son isn't dead. He's very much alive. Father gave him away after his birth and told me he'd been stillborn." Her voice rose on a note of challenge. "Were you there? Did you know what Father had done?"

"Lordy, lordy, lordy," Mandy crooned. "You know I wasn't there, honey. I was sent away to Mister Gerald's house to tend to a sick slave when you went into labor. Old Mammy Adele attended the birth. Mister Claude sold her soon afterward. He said it was her fault yore babe died."

"Lies, Mandy, all lies. Where is my father?"

"In his study."

"Let me go first," Faulk said, pushing her aside.

"No! This is something I have to do myself."

Nevertheless, Faulk followed her to Claude's study. He was right behind her when she burst into the room without knocking. Claude looked up from the papers he was perusing and leapt to his feet.

"Daughter! Thank God you're safe." He walked around his desk and tried to take her into his arms, but Bliss resisted. "Whatever made you run off like that? Where were you going? Was marriage to Gerald so repugnant that you had to go away?"

"She knows," Faulk said flatly. "She was going after *him*."

Claude blanched. "You mean—"

"Exactly, Father. I know about my son. I read the letter from Enos Holmes. All those wasted years," she lamented bitterly. "How could you let me go on thinking my son was dead when you knew he was alive?"

"I've always had your best interests at heart, Bliss," Claude cajoled. "You were too young to be tied down by a child. No one outside this plantation knew about your secret marriage to Guy DeYoung. No one ever saw you pregnant. I was careful to tell everyone who asked that you were visiting relatives in Virginia. I wanted nothing to damage your reputation. You were to become Gerald Faulk's wife. I wanted New Orleans society to welcome you. Surely you can understand a father's concern for his daughter's reputation."

"What good did it do, Father? I've been a pirate's captive. I no longer have a reputation to guard."

"No one knows about your unfortunate association with pirates. Gerald and I told all our friends that the wedding had been called off because you were ailing. Now that you're home, you're going to make a miraculous recovery. You and Gerald will attend all the social events of the season. Being seen together will squelch any gossip that might be circulating about you."

"I'm sorry to disappoint you, Father, but I don't intend to appear anywhere with Gerald. Nor do I intend to live at home. I'm no longer dependent upon you for support. I can start collecting my inheritance and live quite well on my allowance without you. You have taken something precious from me and I'll never forgive you." She spun on her heel. "I'm going upstairs to pack my things; then I'm going to visit the bank and make arrangements to collect my allowance. I'm leaving as soon as I find a place of my own."

Mouth agape, Claude stared after her as she headed for the door. Then he directed his anger at Faulk. "You've spent weeks in her company. Couldn't you change her mind? What's going to happen to us now?"

"Don't worry," Faulk said with false bravado. "Bliss is angry now but she'll come around. I have an idea that will make her see things our way."

So saying, he hurried after Bliss. He caught up with her at the top of the stairs.

"Go away, Gerald," Bliss shouted.

"Just hear me out, Bliss."

"I've heard all I care to from you."

"What do you suppose will happen when New Orleans society learns about your . . . er . . . brush with pirates?"

"I don't care what society thinks." That wasn't entirely true but Bliss wasn't going to admit it to Gerald. She wanted to live among people who respected her, but she wasn't going to marry Gerald to accomplish it. "Besides, Father said no one knows about my . . . ordeal."

"True, no one does know. But that can change." She heard a hint of menace in his voice and knew it was born of desperation.

"Are you threatening me, Gerald?"

"If that's what you want to call it. Think about it a while. Go ahead and move to town, if that's what you want. But don't expect me to accept defeat easily. If you don't come around to my way of thinking within a fortnight, I'll see that your disgrace is made public. Your name will become grist for the gossip mill."

Bliss stared at him with something akin to loathing. She knew Gerald would make good on his threat, but at this point she didn't care. If she could give Gerald and her father her money, she would. Unfortunately, she had to be married to receive more than a monthly stipend.

"Do what you must, Gerald," she said tiredly. "Just leave me alone. There are things I have to do."

"Very well. But I'll be back. You have a fortnight to decide if you want to become the subject of malicious gossip or the wife of a respected businessman."

Bliss said nothing as Faulk descended the stairs, but if looks could kill, Faulk would be a dead man.

Bliss's appointment with the banker in charge of her inheritance went smoothly. After signing several documents, she received not only her generous allowance for the current month but for the four previous months that had passed since her twenty-fifth birthday. Then she went house hunting. Though she loved the plantation dearly, she intended to move out of her father's house without delay.

Two days later Bliss signed the lease on a modest house on St. Peter Street. The neighborhood was good and the home boasted a beautiful courtyard with a spiral stairway leading up to the living quarters. A bedroom balcony surrounded by ironwork gave an unrestricted view of the gardens, and another balcony along the front of the house faced the street. She was particularly grateful for the privacy the walled courtyard afforded her.

The only bad moment came when Bliss stepped out onto the balcony facing the street and discovered that she could see the iron gates of the Calaboso, where Guy had died an ignominious death. Nevertheless, the house served her needs adequately, and she moved in the very next day. Her father offered no objection when she took Mandy with her. She placed the old woman in charge of hiring a maid and cook and was pleased when two free women of color arrived the following day to take up their duties. They were hired as day help, arriving early in the morning and returning to their families after the evening meal.

Shortly after her move, Bliss began renewing acquaintances with friends from the Academy for Young Women, which she had attended until the age of sixteen. Most were married, and though they had expressed happiness to see her fully recovered from her supposed illness, Bliss soon realized she had nothing in common with her former friends. When invitations began arriving, Bliss sent regrets to most of them, making only brief appearances at those she felt she couldn't ignore.

At one such affair, an afternoon musicale,

Bliss eavesdropped as two matrons discussed a new arrival in New Orleans.

"He's absolutely stunning, my dear," an elderly woman with two marriageable daughters confided.

"More importantly, Esmeralda, I hear he's as rich as Midas."

"Richer, Fanny," Esmeralda crowed. "He's an English viscount, by all accounts. And so eligible. Rumor has it he's a widower. Have you seen him?"

"No, but my Amanda saw him and waxed poetic about him for hours on end. Dark and mysterious, as she put it. I'll tell you, he'll be the catch of the season for some lucky woman."

"Well, my dear, I saw him and I agree wholeheartedly with Amanda. Though he appears far too dangerous for our naive daughters, that won't stop them from vying for his attention. It will be interesting to see who gets him."

Fanny lowered her voice. "He's so mysterious, so unique." She gave a delicate shudder. "I wonder whatever happened to his . . ."

No matter how hard Bliss strained her ears, she couldn't make out what made the man so mysterious or unique. Or which one of his delicious attributes caused Fanny to shudder so delightedly. Then she saw Gerald Faulk enter the room and she turned and fled. Avoiding him since she'd taken up residence in New Orleans had taken considerable skill on her part. The two weeks he had allowed her were nearly up, and she knew he was going to raise a fuss when she refused to marry him again. She wondered if he would actually spread gossip about her, and realized immediately that he was fully capable of carrying out his threat to sully her name.

Bliss left the musicale in a rush, pursued by lingering strains of a haunting, bittersweet melody that brought back wave after wave of unwanted memories . . .

Hunter.

She remembered his kisses. She touched her lips and felt them throb at the vivid memory. She recalled the hardness of his body, taut skin stretched over firm muscles. Her own skin burned to feel his hands warming her and his mouth exploring hers.

Did he miss her as much as she missed him? Did he miss her at all? During her sojourn on his island, he had consistently refused to release her. It was almost as if he were waiting for something to happen, as if he had an agenda that must be fulfilled before he would consider her release.

Bliss found her hired coach waiting at the curb and allowed the coachman to hand her up. She ignored the passing scenery as she compared Hunter to Guy, the man she'd never forget. Visibly there was little resemblance, except for their height and coloring.

But despite the glaring differences between the two men, the feeling that she'd known Hunter before persisted. The inflection of his voice. The way his head tilted to one side when he spoke. His kisses . . . Dear God! After all these years did she still long for Guy so desperately that she found similarities in two men who were as different as night and day?

Her disturbing ruminations came to an abrupt halt when the coach stopped in front of her house. She stepped out, paid the driver, and went inside. Silence greeted her. The cook and maid were gone for the day and Mandy had probably retired for the night. The stillness of the empty house made her achingly aware of the endless void within her heart.

Hunter had just arrived at the musicale when he saw Bliss fleeing the party. He thought to follow, then changed his mind. It wasn't time yet to make his presence known to her, he decided. He wanted to make a mark in New Orleans society before confronting Bliss. He was still undecided whether or not to reunite Bliss with her son. It all depended on Bliss's current relationship to Gerald Faulk. As for his immediate plans, Hunter was content to live one day at a time.

Upon his arrival in the city, Hunter had leased an elegant home on Toulouse Street, not far from the Governor's mansion. He made himself known to the citizens of New Orleans as Viscount Guy Hunter. He had returned the original Viscount Hunter to England years ago and made his purchase of the title legal through the courts. Hunter never imagined he'd have any use for the title until just recently. How ironic that he should be admired by the same people who had scorned his low standing and identity as Guy DeYoung.

Since Guy DeYoung had never traveled in society circles, Hunter knew that no one would recognize him. Besides, Guy DeYoung was legally dead and beyond anyone's reach. Viscount Guy Hunter's first act was to deposit a sizable fortune in the bank. He had just gotten settled in the elegant townhouse when invitations began arriving.

Guy had forgotten how fast news traveled in the city. He probably hadn't even left the bank before word of his arrival and gossip about the size of his fortune had spread. He'd snub his nose at the entire social scene if it weren't for his son. Guy was determined that Bryan would never be made to suffer for his father's past, or that any hint of scandal would be attached to his name.

His mind consumed with thoughts of Bliss, Guy smiled his way through boring small talk at the musicale. Every woman he met paled in comparison to Bliss. The simpering misses who sought his attention were dull and colorless, with nothing to their credit but vacuous beauty. Their inane conversation wearied him beyond bearing.

The only woman with the power to enthrall him was Bliss, the woman he had married seven years ago and had never forgotten. Originally, his seduction of Bliss had been intended as punishment, but all thought of revenge had vanished when he had found pure rapture in her arms. He'd wanted to plant his seed inside her, to humiliate her before society and her family. He'd thought it would be a fitting punishment for the agony he'd suffered. What a fool he'd been!

How was he to know he'd fall under Bliss's spell again after all he'd been through, that those powerful emotions he and Bliss had once shared had never completely died? Guy had never expected to encounter Bliss again in this life, much less experience the thrill of loving her. Encountering her on Captiva Island had been a shock. Learning that she was still married to Guy DeYoung was an even bigger one.

For many years Guy had held Bliss responsible for the suffering he'd endured, but he'd finally come to realize that Bliss had been an innocent victim of Faulk and her father. He knew now that she had suffered just as he had. She had lost a child, and he had lost his identity and his dream of the future with Bliss.

The moment Bliss lifted her head from the pillow the morning after the musicale, she knew her life was about to change. She had no solid proof, just a feeling deep inside her. She knew it the minute she opened her eyes, and the urge to spew out her guts sent her flying from bed in search of the chamber pot. She found it not a minute too soon as her stomach emptied forcefully. Weak and shaking, she rinsed out her mouth and eased back into bed until the room stopped spinning.

Pregnant!

There was no other explanation. She'd experienced morning sickness before. Counting back, she realized she had missed two monthly cycles. She must have become pregnant that last night with Hunter in Cuba. She hugged her stomach protectively and let the pure joy of her discovery overtake her. She wanted this child fiercely. But the fact that he or she would be brought into the world in disgrace and must live in shame diminished the joy and brought tears to her eyes.

She had already cut the ties with her father and expected no help there. She was fiercely determined to keep Hunter's child. This child would be hers to love and hold and keep forever. No one would ever take him away from her. But how could she manage all that on her own, without being judged and condemned by society? Was she destined to raise her child in secrecy and shame?

The solution she arrived at was simple, no matter how desperately she fought against accepting it.

She had to marry.

She had to marry quickly.

Gerald Faulk arrived on Bliss's doorstep the following day. The maid ushered him into the cozy dining room, where Bliss was enjoying a cup of strong tea and considering her future.

"Good morning," Gerald said cheerily as he seated himself without waiting for an invitation. "Your two weeks are up, Bliss. Have you set the date for our wedding? I'm tottering on the brink of ruin and will not stand for another senseless delay."

"Sit down, Gerald," Bliss invited with a hint of sarcasm.

"I'm already sitting," Gerald said, apparently oblivious to her mood as he poured himself a cup of tea. "I'm here to discuss arrangements for our wedding. It will be a large affair, of course. The event of the season."

Bliss had known this moment would arrive, had been anticipating it with dread, in fact. She'd thought of nothing else since she'd realized she was pregnant. She had examined all her choices, both rational and irrational, and had arrived at a difficult decision.

She aimed a sidelong glance at Gerald, saw that he was watching her, and decided to face her problem squarely. Despite her resolve, however, her heart and mind utterly rejected the distasteful decision she had made. But what other choice did she have? What she was about to propose was necessary to protect her child's future.

Squaring her narrow shoulders, Bliss steeled herself for Gerald's contempt and said, "I'm pregnant, Gerald."

The cup slipped from Faulk's hand, spilling hot tea into his lap. He yelped and leaped to his feet, knocking his chair over in the process.

"You're what?"

"Pregnant," Bliss said complacently.

"You can't be!"

"Well, I am."

He let loose a string of curses that fouled the air. "How dare you do this to us! What kind of woman are you? You've already given birth to one bastard."

The color drained from Bliss's face, and more than anything she wanted to slap the smirk from Gerald's face. "Guy's child is not now nor has he ever been a bastard," she enunciated slowly. She touched her stomach. "I freely admit the child I carry belongs to a pirate, but I want him as fiercely as I wanted my first child. Sit down, Gerald. I have a proposition for you, one you can't afford to refuse."

Gerald sat down stiffly. His face was red, his eyes bulging. "I always knew you were a wh—"

"Say it, Gerald, and you'll never get your hands on my fortune," Bliss warned.

"I wouldn't have you on a silver platter now," Gerald taunted. "Give me *some* credit. I refuse to acknowledge a pirate's bastard." He brushed his sleeve, as if brushing away something distasteful.

"I imagine, however, you'll accept my inheritance," Bliss retorted. "I harbor no fondness for you. What I'm proposing is a business deal. You lend me your name in return for control of my inheritance. I'm referring, of course, to a marriage in name only. I don't want my child born a bastard. You and I won't even live together. I intend to maintain separate quarters, to live a solitary existence in this house with my child.

"You may take a mistress, of course, since there will be no marital rights allowed," she continued briskly. "And I'll need adequate funds to maintain my way of life in the city. Once we settle on the amount I'll require, you'll be free to use my inheritance in any way you deem necessary."

Faulk's eyes narrowed as he considered Bliss's generous offer. "You're giving me your inheritance in exchange for my name?"

"If you agree to my terms."

He gave her a nasty smile. "So you do need me after all."

"Just your name. It's a fair trade. Your name for my inheritance."

He laughed mirthlessly. "You surprise me, my dear. I didn't know you could be such a calculating bitch."

Her chin rose aggressively. "I have a child to protect. Had I been more protective of my first child, he would be with me today. What happened to him will *never* happen again. The naive girl of my youth no longer exists. I will fight tooth and nail for myself and my child."

"Had I known it would take a pregnancy to convince you to marry me, I could have accomplished it long ago, with a great deal of pleasure. The thought of taking you now, however, sickens me. But as long as your inheritance will be made available to me, I don't see how I can refuse your *generous* offer.

"You and your child may have my name. Set the date, my dear." He stared pointedly at her stomach. "Better make it soon."

"Two weeks from Saturday," Bliss said, feeling as if her world were suddenly off balance.

For years she'd fought against marrying Gerald Faulk. Though she knew Guy would never walk this earth again, she'd never been able to accept his death. It was as if all these years she'd been waiting . . . But in two weeks she would have to lay the past to rest and make a life for herself and her child, Hunter's child. She had lost Guy's child and was determined to protect Hunter's at all cost.

Faulk prepared to take his leave. "I'll make the arrangements and alert the bank to our marriage so they can prepare the documents transferring your inheritance to me."

"While you're at it," Bliss said, "see that an agreement is drawn up addressing my demands. Leave the amount of my monthly allowance blank and I'll fill it in when I've decided how much I'll require to live comfortably."

Though his eyes were dark with suppressed anger, Bliss was relieved when he didn't argue the terms.

"To keep up appearances, 'tis best that we appear together often during the next two weeks," Bliss continued. "Parties, balls, musicales, whatever it takes to convince society that we are a couple. I don't want my child's paternity questioned."

"I suppose I can make myself available,"

Faulk allowed. "I hope you have the good sense to go into seclusion before people become aware of your condition."

"My baby will arrive two months prematurely. Not an uncommon occurrence. Fortunately, my condition can be easily hidden for several weeks yet."

"Fortunate, indeed," Faulk sneered.

"I received an invitation to this evening's ball at the Dubois mansion," Bliss said, ignoring his surliness. She hated him for what he had done to her and Guy and their child and wondered how she was going to bear his company during the next two weeks. "The ball tonight will be a perfect time to announce our wedding plans."

"I'll pick you up at precisely nine this evening," Faulk said coolly. "I've gone through hell for your money and I won't be denied now. I hope I can convince my creditors to wait two more weeks. They're threatening to take my home and business."

Bliss didn't bother seeing Faulk to the door. She wished there had been another solution to her dilemma. The thought of becoming Gerald Faulk's wife made her physically ill. So ill, in fact, that she felt bile rising in her throat. She held her hand over her mouth and rushed from the room.

Mandy found her bending over the chamber pot in her bedroom, disgorging her meager breakfast. The old woman clucked sympathetically and promptly put Bliss to bed. Then she stood back, hands on ample hips, and stared at her, her eyes dark and knowing.

"Yore increasing, ain't you, honey?"

"Oh, Mandy, I didn't want you to find out yet."

Mandy patted her hand. "It ain't yore fault, honey. You have no cause to feel guilty. That pirate, he forced you, you had no choice. I hope they find him and hang him," she said fiercely.

Bliss started to cry and couldn't stop. The thought of Hunter hanging only increased her distress. Her baby's father was too alive, too vital to die an ignominious death. Yet what other fate was there for a man who lived outside the law?

Chapter Eleven

The Dubois ball was attended by a mad crush of people that Bliss would have been quite happy to avoid. Unfortunately, being seen with Gerald was necessary if they were to present the image of a contented couple.

Gerald had arrived at her door promptly at nine, dressed in impeccable evening attire. Though he looked successful and distinguished, Bliss realized that Gerald was no longer a young man. The hair at his temples had started to silver, and his slight paunch was clearly visible beneath the close cut of his jacket.

Bliss had chosen an emerald green silk dress with a high empire waist, short puff sleeves, and a daringly low neckline that was all the rage these days. Some women went so far as to emulate Napoleon's wife by wetting their gowns before donning them, making the fabric almost transparent. It was not a fashion Bliss cared to follow.

Bliss pasted a brittle smile on her face as she strolled through the ballroom on Gerald's arm, greeting friends and acquaintances as they made their way toward the host and hostess.

"It's so good to see you two together again," Lily Dubois said enthusiastically. "We were distressed to hear about your recent illness, Bliss. You've made a remarkable recovery. Dare we hope for a wedding announcement now that you've recovered?"

"You're the first to know, Mrs. Dubois," Gerald confided, forestalling Bliss's answer. "Bliss and I have set a wedding date for two weeks from Saturday. Your invitation will be hand delivered shortly. The ceremony will take place at the Cathedral, of course. I hope you will be free to attend."

"Wouldn't miss it," George Dubois said, slapping Gerald's back exuberantly. "Would it be presumptuous of me to announce the happy occasion tonight?"

"Not at all," Gerald said. "We'd be honored to have you make the announcement." He gave Bliss a smile that didn't quite reach his eyes. "Wouldn't we, my dear?"

"That's very kind of you," Bliss murmured, swallowing the sickness rising within her. "That would be wonderful."

They moved on then, unaware that a man wearing a satin patch over one eye was intently watching them from his position behind a large pillar.

Guy had seen Bliss and Gerald enter the ballroom and he'd had to swallow the rage he felt upon seeing them together. He'd caught glimpses of Bliss alone at various functions and about town, but this was the first time he'd seen her with Faulk, and his violent reaction surprised him. Before his mind fully grasped the significance of seeing them together, he was surrounded by a group of inquisitive men and women and lost sight of Bliss.

Bliss excused herself and went to the ladies retiring room to rest her jangled nerves and repair her hair style. She was so tired of smiling and making small talk, she felt as if her face would crack. But even more unnerving had been the strange feeling of being stared at. Of course that was ridiculous, but the feeling lingered.

The retiring room was occupied. Two young women Bliss was acquainted with were discussing the mysterious stranger whom Bliss had yet to meet. They greeted her enthusiastically.

"It's good to see you out and about again after your long illness," a perky blonde said. "You look wonderful. I understand you and Mr. Faulk are still a couple. Have you set a new wedding date yet?"

"I'm fully recovered, Becky, thank you," Bliss said warmly. Becky Durbin was at least five years younger than Bliss but she had always liked the young woman. "We've set a date for two weeks from Saturday. I hope you'll attend."

"Am I invited, too?" the second woman asked.

Bliss turned her smile on the young redhead, who was even younger than Becky. "Of course, Amanda, your whole family is invited."

"Perhaps I'll be the next to marry," Becky said.

"Oh, I didn't know you had a beau," Bliss said. "Do I know him?"

A dull red crept up Becky's neck. "I have plenty of beaus, but none as attractive as Viscount Hunter." She gave a delicate shudder. "Have you seen him, Bliss? He's absolutely stunning."

Bliss went still. "Hunter?" The mysterious man's name was Hunter? No, she thought, it couldn't be! *Her* Hunter wouldn't be here. It was too dangerous. And he certainly wasn't a viscount.

"Do you know him?" Amanda asked curiously. "He looks dangerous, and *sooo* romantic. In a delicious, naughty kind of way, of course. Every unmarried girl in the city has set her cap for him."

"I've not had the pleasure of meeting the viscount," Bliss said.

"All the married women are making shameless hussies of themselves over him," Becky said huffily. "But I'm going to catch him, just you wait and see. He asked me for a dance," she said smugly.

"He did not!" Amanda contradicted. "Don't lie, Becky. He never dances with anyone. He just talks business with the men and flirts with the women."

"Well," Becky said indignantly, "I'm going to change all that. Just see if I don't."

Bliss watched Becky preen before the looking glass, curious about this Viscount Hunter. What was there about him that made all the women swoon with delight? She was still mulling over the coincidence of the viscount and Hunter sharing the same name when it suddenly occurred to her to ask, "Does Viscount Hunter wear a patch over his right eye?"

"I thought you hadn't met him," Becky said.

The blood rushed from Bliss's face and she had to cling to the back of a chair when she felt her knees begin to buckle. "You're saying I'm right? That Viscount Hunter wears a patch over one eye? Does he have black hair and gray eyes?"

Amanda snorted indignantly. "You've been putting us on, Bliss. You know darn good and well what Guy Hunter looks like. Come on, Becky, let's see if we can distract him from business."

They took their leave, unaware of the devastation they left in their wake.

Guy? Guy Hunter? Oh, God, it had to be. No, it couldn't be! Bliss could understand the Hunter part of his name, but why *Guy*? Had he used it deliberately to hurt her? Why was Hunter here, if indeed the viscount was *her* Hunter? It didn't make sense. But then nothing Hunter had ever done made sense. Realizing that all the conjecture in the world wasn't going to answer her questions, Bliss left the retiring room.

Faulk was waiting for her. "Bliss, there you are. I was beginning to worry that you'd left without telling me." He looked pointedly at her stomach. "Are you ill?"

"No, just tired. Perhaps we should make our regrets to the host and hostess and take our leave. The crush of people is appalling."

"We can't leave now. Dubois is about to make the announcement. Come along, it's what you wanted, isn't it?"

It was exactly what Bliss had wanted, but not now, not with Hunter in the ballroom to mock her. But Gerald couldn't know about Hunter. If Viscount Hunter was *her* Hunter, then no one could know his real identity. "Yes, it's what I want."

They reached the podium, where the orchestra had been playing. Dubois waited for the attention of his guests. All eyes were focused on Bliss and Faulk as Dubois announced the happy occasion of their impending nuptials. A clamor of congratulations and polite applause filled the room. Then the music began again and couples drifted away to the dance floor.

"Do you want to dance?" Faulk asked.

"I'd like to leave," Bliss replied. "I've had all of this I can take."

"We'll leave in a few minutes. There is someone I want to meet first." He tucked her arm under his. "There he is, over by that column. He's new in town; one never knows when a new acquaintance might prove beneficial. Especially a wealthy one."

Bliss looked frantically in the direction Faulk had indicated, seeing nothing but a cluster of men and women. Suddenly she knew! But it was too late to turn and run, for Faulk was pulling her through the crowd, which had parted to allow them into the inner circle.

Then she saw him. Elegantly clad in black evening wear and pristine white linen, he exuded the kind of dark mystery and energy that could only be described as dangerous. He must have spotted her at the same time she saw him, for his gaze settled disconcertingly on her.

Bliss heard Faulk say something about making his acquaintance before her vision dimmed, a buzzing began in her head, and the room started to spin around her. Then everything went black.

Guy had been talking to Banker Sanders when Dubois called the room to attention and announced Bliss's impending marriage to Gerald Faulk. He'd tried his best to contain his rage and knew he'd failed miserably when Sanders eyed him strangely.

"Are you all right, Viscount?" Sanders asked with concern. "You look like you've just eaten something distasteful."

"Sorry, Sanders, didn't think it showed. Sometimes my wound acts up and I can't control my reaction to the pain." His lie received sympathetic murmurs of distress.

"I heard you lost an eye fighting against Napoleon," Sanders said, repeating unfounded gossip.

"Something like that," Guy said, thinking it as good an explanation as any. "You were saying?"

He barely listened to what Sanders was saying. Until he'd heard the announcement, he'd been undecided about how, or even if, he should reunite Bliss with her son. The announcement had made the decision for him. There was no way in hell he was going to allow Faulk to raise his son. Guy had grown to love the boy and would never give him up to a woman married to a man like Faulk.

What was wrong with Bliss? he wondered. If she hated Faulk as much as she had claimed, why was she marrying him? There was more to this than met the eye, and he vowed to learn what it was.

From the corner of his eye he saw Faulk approaching with a somewhat reluctant Bliss in tow. Guy hadn't intended for his first meeting with Bliss to become a public spectacle, but it looked as if Faulk had taken the matter out of his hands. He broke off his conversation with the banker with an abruptness bordering on rudeness as Faulk elbowed his way through the cluster of people surrounding him.

Then she was there, standing scant inches away, as dazzling as ever. He breathed deeply;

her scent scattered his senses and dredged up memories of steamy tropical nights and heated sex. He lifted his gaze to hers, saw her eyes widen and her nostrils flare. He heard Faulk speaking to him but he didn't listen. All his senses were attuned to the woman standing before him. The woman whose lovely turquoise eyes were closing as she began a slow spiral to the floor.

Shoving Faulk aside, Guy made a mad lunge for Bliss, snatching her up before she reached the floor, long before anyone was aware of her predicament. Even Faulk appeared surprised when he saw Bliss hanging limply in Guy's arms. Fortunately, Mrs. Dubois appeared and took charge.

"Follow me," she ordered crisply as she cleared the way for Guy. They left the ballroom and entered a small sitting room. "Put her down on the sofa while I fetch smelling salts." She bustled from the room, firmly closing the door on the curious onlookers who had followed them.

"The heat and crush of people must have been too much for her," Faulk said to Hunter. "My fiancee has a delicate constitution. I'm Gerald Faulk, by the way. I've been wanting to meet you."

He stuck out his hand. Guy ignored it. "Does your fiancee usually faint in crowds?" He'd never known Bliss to be afflicted by weakness of any sort. This was all very strange. Unless . . .

Had she finally recognized him as Guy De-Young?"

"Forget Bliss," Faulk said with blatant disregard. "She'll come around. Could we speak in private some time? I'd like to acquaint you with my business ventures. Perhaps you'd consider becoming an investor."

"This isn't the time," Guy said bluntly. "I'm more concerned about your fiancee right now than I am in investing in a business of which I know nothing."

Lily Dubois returned with a vial of smelling salts. "This should bring her around," she said, uncapping the bottle and waving it beneath Bliss's nose.

Guy was gratified when Bliss gasped and turned away from the offending odor.

"What happened?" Bliss asked groggily as she pushed the smelling salts away.

"You fainted," Faulk said.

"How are you feeling, my dear?" Mrs. Dubois asked.

"Better, thank you," Bliss replied, lifting herself to a sitting position. "I don't know what got into me. I never faint."

"The heat, it happens all the time," Mrs. Dubois claimed airily. "Perhaps you haven't fully recovered from your previous illness. If you're sure you're all right, I'll go inform my guests of your recovery."

"I'm fine. By all means, return to your guests."

"Yes, well, I'm sure your fiance will take good

care of you," Mrs. Dubois said as she left the room.

"Why don't you return to the ballroom to make our excuses to the host and hostess?" Bliss told Faulk.

"Good idea. Rest here until you're fully recovered, my dear," Faulk said. "I'll make our excuses, bid farewell to a few friends, and return for you in say . . . twenty minutes. Will that be satisfactory?"

"Yes," Bliss whispered, achingly aware of Hunter's daunting presence. Why didn't he leave?

"Are you coming, Hunter?" Faulk asked when Guy gave no indication of leaving.

"Yes, of course," Guy said as he followed Faulk out the door.

Bliss gave an audible sigh as the door closed behind Hunter. She was in no condition for a confrontation. She had never fainted before and blamed it on her pregnancy and her unexpected confrontation with Hunter. Why was he here? she wondered. And posing as English nobility, no less. She was appalled at the danger in which he was placing himself and couldn't fathom his reason for doing so. Was he here because of her? Did she dare hope he truly cared about her welfare?

Oh, God, she was so confused.

Suddenly her attention was captured by a whisper of sound and she directed her gaze toward the closed door. Her breath caught in her throat when she saw Hunter standing just inside the room, leaning against the closed door. She watched in trepidation as he pushed himself away and came toward her. He reminded her of the panthers that prowled through the mangroves of Pine Island with careless arrogance and supreme confidence.

"What are you doing here?" Bliss said, finally finding her voice. "Are you mad? I'm sure you're aware that you're deliberately courting danger."

"Are you going to betray my identity?" Guy asked. She shook her head. "Then I have nothing to fear, do I?" His expression turned grim. "Why did you faint?"

She gave a careless shrug. "The shock of seeing you in New Orleans, I suppose. There's bound to be someone in a town this size who can identify you. What about the men aboard all those ships you've plundered? And how did you come by that trumped-up title?"

"The title is legally mine. So is the name I go by. I purchased both years ago. I'm pleased that you're worried about me, but I don't think you have anything to be concerned about." His glittering gray eye settled disconcertingly on her. His voice held a note of contempt. "Congratulations on your impending marriage."

"Don't mock something you don't understand, Hunter."

"Call me Guy. I'm known as Guy, Viscount Hunter now."

She dragged in a shuddering breath. "You took that name to hurt me," she charged. "You knew Guy was the name of a man I loved very much. Why? What do you want from me?"

"What I want from you is a little honesty."

"I've never lied to you."

"You told me the most important thing in your life was your long-lost son. Yet here you are, marrying one of the men responsible for taking your son away from you. Do you call that honesty?"

"Gerald took me to Mobile to find my son, but we arrived too late. He had disappeared along with Enos Holmes. I was devastated. I refused to leave Mobile until an extensive search was launched, but no trace of him was found. I had no choice but to return home without him. But that doesn't mean I've forgotten him."

Guy stared at her, as if trying to make up his mind about something. "Why are you marrying Faulk?"

"Why do you care?" she snapped with asperity. "If not for you and Gasparilla, I would have reached Mobile before my son disappeared. I'll never forgive you for making me lose the single most precious thing in my life."

"You recovered quickly enough," he shot back sarcastically. He searched her face. "You look . . . glowing," he said lamely.

She ignored the compliment. "Now it's my turn to ask questions. Why are you in New Orleans? Did you know you're the talk of the town? Your wealth is the subject of much conjecture, and women swoon at the very mention of your name."

He gave her a lopsided smile that set her heart to racing. "That's their problem. I've decided to give up pirating. An era is coming to an end, even though Gasparilla refuses to recognize it. The United States Navy is set upon ridding the Gulf of pirates. I realized that plying my trade in dangerous waters could only end tragically, and I've grown rather fond of my neck."

Bliss's spirits plummeted. She'd hoped that Guy—God, how could she call him Guy when the name brought back so many painful memories?—was here because of her. Because he missed her and wanted her.

Because he cared about her.

But that had never been the case, had it? She seriously doubted she'd ever learn the reason Hunter had held her captive on his island.

"What are your plans?" Bliss asked.

"I'm looking into purchasing a plantation. I have this unaccountable urge to become a planter." He gave her a slow smile fraught with implications she didn't want to consider. "I'm sure we'll meet again, since we seem to be invited to the same events." He gave her a hard look. "For your sake, I suggest you take care of your health. It wouldn't do to faint at every function you attend."

At a loss for words, Bliss stared mutely at Hunter's back as he took his leave. Did he suspect? she wondered. His single gray eye had stared at her so intently she had the feeling he could read her thoughts, see into her very soul. After seeing and speaking with him, she decided it would be folly to tell him about the baby. His very presence mocked her. The name he'd assumed proved his disregard for her. She would never call him Guy!

Guy left the ball soon after his confrontation with Bliss, much to the disappointment of the ladies who had sought his attention. Guy didn't give a fig about giggling young girls seeking husbands, or danger-seeking older married women searching for an affair. He was still reeling over the public announcement of Bliss's marriage to Gerald Faulk.

What was she thinking? he asked himself. How could she hold Faulk responsible for the loss of her son and then turn around and marry him? It just didn't make sense. There was much here that needed explanation. Bitterness rode him mercilessly. He thought he knew Bliss. He'd even grown to care for her again. He no longer held her responsible for the loss of his eye and his identity, or for the indignities he'd suffered in prison before his escape. But learning that Bliss was marrying his avowed enemy was too much to swallow.

Guy reached home just as the hour struck twelve and went straight to bed. He had briefly considered visiting a high-class bordello but had discarded the idea almost immediately. He hadn't had a woman since Bliss, and the thought of bedding anyone else didn't appeal to him. Finally he fell asleep, plunging headlong into an erotic dream in which he and Bliss made passionate love on a tropical sandy beach beneath a full moon.

Bliss couldn't seem to escape Hunter during the days that followed. He appeared everywhere she did; every party, each musicale, and even while strolling in the Place d'Armes on Gerald's arm. He never failed to offer a friendly greeting whenever they met, but his taunting smile completely destroyed the facade of polite interest. His mocking presence so disturbed her peace of mind that she began to dread their next meeting. Even Gerald remarked upon her edginess at the rout they attended one night.

"Ah, look, there's Viscount Hunter," Gerald said as they left the dance floor. "I don't believe I know the stunning brunette with him. Let us pay our respects."

"I'd prefer not to," Bliss said, struggling to keep the tremor from her voice. Hunter was with another woman, and it nearly killed her to think of them together . . . intimately. When would she ever get over him?

Gerald gave her a strange look. "Whenever we encounter the viscount you become green around the gills. You're not going to faint again, are you?"

"Don't be ridiculous. Why must you toady up to the man?"

"Because he is rich and it's to my advantage to cultivate wealthy friends. One day I may need to borrow again."

"When you go through my inheritance, you mean," Bliss retorted.

Gerald didn't have time to form a scathing retort, for it seemed as if Guy had found *them*.

"Good evening," Guy said. "Are you enjoying the party?"

"I've attended better," Faulk said, stifling a yawn.

"Have either of you met my companion?" Guy asked, staring intently at Bliss.

"I don't believe we've had the pleasure," Faulk said, putting on his most charming smile.

"This is Miss Carmen Delgado, a visitor from Cuba. She's staying with her aunt and uncle and was gracious enough to dance with me. Miss Delgado, may I present Miss Bliss Grenville and her fiance, Mr. Gerald Faulk?"

After a moment of polite small talk, Guy said, "Excuse us, we were on our way to the garden. Miss Delgado expressed a desire for a breath of air."

Bliss stared after them as they walked away.

"That wasn't so difficult, was it? I don't know why the man seems to upset you. He has been nothing but pleasant to you."

"I want to go home," Bliss said.

"We just got here."

"I'm not feeling well."

He grimaced, his eyes moving insultingly over her stomach. "Is that bastard you're carrying troubling you?"

Red dots of rage burst inside Bliss's head. "Don't ever call my child a bastard!" she hissed from between clenched teeth. Then she whirled and headed out the double doors into the garden, leaving Faulk standing alone to face the gossips. He didn't attempt to follow, for which she was profoundly grateful.

Cheeks burning, Bliss walked to a secluded bench in the far corner of the courtyard and sat down to cool off. If it wasn't for her impending motherhood, she'd never go through with this farce. Why, oh why, did Hunter have to come to New Orleans? Hadn't he already complicated her life enough without tormenting her with his daunting presence?

"What happened in there?"

Bliss started violently at the sound of Hunter's voice. "Nothing. Where is Miss Delgado?"

"Inside with her admirers."

"I thought you and she . . . that is, I thought she was your—"

"You were wrong. What did Faulk do to upset you?"

"Nothing, he did nothing."

"What did he say?"

He sat down beside her and tilted her face up to his, his thumbs resting upon her cheekbones. He must have felt the wetness there, for he spit out a curse and wiped away her tears.

"Why are you badgering me?" Bliss cried. "What do you want from me?"

"The truth. Why are you marrying Faulk? You can barely stand the man. Maybe it's not as obvious to others, but I know you better than anyone. You were crying."

She tried to turn her head aside, but Hunter held her fast. "Hunter, please, let me go."

"Is it so difficult to call me Guy?"

"Yes, oh God, yes."

"Do you know how devastated I was to find you gone when I returned from Sanibel?"

"I . . . you were devastated?" She could hardly credit it.

"There was much left unsaid between us."

"I asked you to take me to Mobile, and like a coward you ran off. I had no idea what you were thinking, what you intended. Then Gasparilla arrived and it was too late for us."

His eye glowed a dull silver, drawing Bliss into its heated center. She couldn't look away. His features were sharp with desire, taut with an emotion she couldn't identify. She closed her eyes, aware that he was going to kiss her even before his mouth came down hard over hers. His kiss was not gentle; it was a hard reminder of the passion they once shared, of the hunger still vibrantly alive within them. He held her so tightly and kissed her with such savagery, her whole body felt combustible.

His lips moved over hers forcefully as his hands slid down her throat to her deep neckline. He gave a tug and her breasts popped free. His mouth found a puckered nipple. He licked the aching peak with the roughness of his tongue until Bliss moaned in protest and tried to push him away.

"Don't!" she pleaded on a shaky sigh. "You

have no right. Someone could come along and see us. I'm about to be married."

"You're right, this is not the place." He rose abruptly, pulled her up with him, and straightened her clothing. She didn't resist until he began pulling her toward the courtyard gate.

"Wait! Where are you taking me?"

"Whatever happened between you and Faulk must not have upset him, for he made no effort to follow and set things right. I'm assuming you don't want to go back inside."

"No, I don't want to go inside. I'm sick and tired of smiling and pretending—"

"Pretending what?"

"Nothing. Forget I said that."

"I'll take you home in my carriage. You don't have to go back in there if you don't want to."

Bliss had little choice as her pirate dragged her through the gate to his waiting carriage. He hauled her inside and climbed in behind her.

"Where do you live?"

She gave him her address on St. Peter Street and he in turn gave it to the coachman. It wasn't far, just around the corner, actually; she could have walked the distance easily. The carriage ground to a halt. Guy jumped down and reached for her.

"No need to walk me to the door," Bliss said when he made no effort to reenter his carriage.

He appeared amused. "Are you trying to get rid of me?"

Her mouth went dry at the thought of being alone with him. "You can't come in."

"Very well."

Oh God, it wasn't like him to give in so easily. What was he planning? "Good night, Hunter."

"Guy, my name is Guy."

She couldn't bear it. Turning abruptly, she ran to the door and let herself in. Racing upstairs to the bedroom, she ran out to the balcony and looked down, breathing a sigh of relief when she saw that his carriage had departed. Seeing Hunter again, being with him, had taken a toll on her. She felt more vulnerable than she ever had in her life. She could not resist Hunter and feared for her sanity should he decide to remain in New Orleans.

Moving mechanically, she undressed without Mandy's help and donned a thin lawn nightgown. Then she let her hair down, separating the strands with her fingers as it tumbled over her shoulders and down her back. She was about to crawl into bed when a muffled sound on the balcony caught her attention. She turned toward the sound and saw the shrouded figure of a man huddled in the shadows. A shudder rippled through her when she recognized the figure that slipped through the open door.

"Hunter!"

"You didn't think I'd give up so easily, did you?"

"What do you want?"

"To make love to you. It's inevitable, you know."

Chapter Twelve

He stalked into the room, looking positively lethal. His face remained hidden in the shadows, but flickering candlelight revealed the taut set of his shoulders, his determined stance. Bliss backed away, intending to flee . . . where? She was in her nightclothes, the only other person in the house was Mandy, and it would be heartless of her to frighten the old woman.

"I'm not going to hurt you, Bliss," he said in a hushed voice. "I'd never hurt you."

"Why are you here? With all the cities in the world, why did you pick New Orleans to settle? I'm no longer your captive, Hunter. I'm trying to get on with my life. Please leave."

"I'll leave when I get some answers and not before."

Suddenly he was beside her, his hands on her shoulders, pulling her against him. Her chest constricted, making breathing difficult. She felt exposed and vulnerable, even though she knew there was no way he could possibly tell she was pregnant. There was a familiar charged tension in the room, a heat that surrounded her and made her burn with anticipation.

She blinked up at him as he caught her chin between his thumb and forefinger and raised her face for his kiss. She tried to twist away but her strength had suddenly deserted her. His mouth covered hers, hot, hard, demanding, his tongue plundering her mouth, creating a turbulence within her that left her reeling. In the moment of sanity left to her, Bliss wholeheartedly agreed with the women who thought Hunter dangerous. No one understood that better than she. A man who could render her helpless with one kiss had to be the most dangerous man alive.

He kissed her soft, trembling mouth until she was quivering all over, until she kissed him back and circled his neck with her arms. Until her pliant body melted against him in unwilling acquiescence. She sighed softly when he released the bows at the neck of her gown and pulled the garment up and away from her. She whimpered a weak protest when his arms went beneath her knees and lifted her against him. Coherent thought left her when he laid her on the bed and followed her down, pressing her into the mattress with his hard body.

His hands tangled in the silken strands of her hair as his mouth explored hers, kissing her thoroughly before slipping down to her throat to tease the erratically beating pulse at its base. His mouth moved lower, tasting and nipping her breasts with tiny love bites, laving the sweet fullness with his tongue until she was writhing and moaning and clutching him with outrageous urgency. Then his mouth slid lower, over the taut swell of her smooth belly to the burnished curls between her thighs.

He brought his hand between her legs, caressing her inner thighs, his fingers pressing inside her in arousing strokes that made her cry out and arch violently upward. She heard her own sobbing moans as he lowered his head and tasted her, his tongue parting and thrusting into her tender pink flesh as his hands lifted her up to his mouth.

Bliss couldn't breathe, couldn't think, could only feel. She was lost. Lost to feverish passion and unspeakable yearning. Rational thought fled as the hunger Hunter had summoned with his hands and mouth and body exploded into an inferno of fierce ecstasy. Bliss thought she had died and gone to heaven. Dimly she heard Hunter chuckle and glanced at him.

While she had been lost in a haze of pleasure, he had somehow managed to divest himself of his clothing. His body glowed a dull gold in the candlelight. The light shining behind him obscured his face, but instinctively she knew he was smiling, amused by her swift capitulation.

She started to rise, but he moved with pantherlike grace to cover her body.

"What's your hurry, sweetheart?" he murmured against her ear. "Dawn is hours away." He searched her face, his gaze intent, his voice harsh when he spoke again. "Have you allowed Faulk in your bed yet?"

"Bastard!" she hissed from between clenched teeth. "Why must you spoil everything?"

He snarled, a feral sound that should have frightened her, but didn't. "I don't believe he's shared your bed yet," Guy said, answering his own question. "You couldn't have responded to me as you just did if you'd been having sex regularly."

He flexed his hips; she felt the hard ridge of his sex pressing between her thighs. She knew he hadn't been satisfied yet, and the thought that he would soon be inside her made her heart begin to pound erratically. When she made an incoherent protest, he kissed her, again and yet again, shutting down her thought processes.

Then his mouth left hers and he raised himself up on his elbows, watching her face as he flexed his hips and thrust inside her. Open and unshielded, his untamed hunger reached across the charged atmosphere between them, his face revealing the fierce intensity of his need. She cried out and arched up to receive him, closing around him as she took him inside her. Her face glowed rapturously as he filled the aching emptiness with himself.

He lifted her legs around his waist and she

felt him sink even deeper into her passage. His hips moved smoothly, thrusting and withdrawing, deeper each time, increasing the rhythm of his movements and sweeping her into sweet oblivion. Then she knew no more.

Bliss opened her eyes, found Hunter staring at her, and frowned. The last thing she recalled was Hunter stiffening and shouting out her name scant seconds after she'd reached her own shattering climax.

"What happened?" she asked breathlessly.

"I think it's called *la petite morte*. The little death. Did you die a little for me, Bliss? I died for you."

Bliss looked away, too embarrassed to answer.

"Never mind," he said with a shrug. "Just answer me this. Do you think you'd have with Faulk what we just shared? I can't believe you'd marry that bastard."

"It's my life and my decision, Hunter. All you know about Gerald is what I've told you. You're acting as if you hold a personal grudge against him."

"Perhaps I do," Hunter muttered.

Bliss frowned, not understanding. "Tell me what it is."

"Perhaps one day, but not now. Do you still intend to marry Faulk?"

Bliss thought of Hunter's child growing beneath her heart and felt an aching sadness. Not once had he mentioned love or marriage to her.

If only he'd . . . But no, dreaming impossible dreams was dangerous. She waited so long for him to tell her he loved her, that he wanted to marry her himself, that the silence grew oppressive. Finally Bliss sighed and gave the only answer possible. "My plans haven't changed."

What else could she do? She'd given Hunter every opportunity to declare himself, but the words hadn't come. All he did was vent his anger at her for marrying Gerald Faulk. She wanted to blurt out that all she wanted from Faulk was his name. He could have her money, she didn't need it as long as her child was born legitimately.

Guy was too angry to say the words that would stop Bliss from marrying Faulk. He couldn't understand why she was so adamant about becoming Faulk's wife. She didn't even like the man. How could he tell her about Bryan when he knew she would want to raise the child in the same house with the man responsible for all their problems? He didn't want Faulk anywhere near his son.

Guy considered the alternative. He could reveal his identity to Bliss and tell her about their son. They were still married, after all. Would she welcome him back as her husband? Or would she expose him as a pirate and watch him hang? Bliss had been his captive, held against her will and seduced by him; how could she not want retribution?

"What are you thinking?" Bliss asked, disturbing his reverie.

He couldn't tell her. Not yet, not until he had time to think this through, to decide upon his next move. He didn't know if he was ready to trust Bliss with the two most precious things in his life; his son and his heart. Perhaps, he considered, he should just let Bliss marry Faulk and live in misery the rest of her life. Then all thought ceased as his body made him aware of other things, like Bliss lying in his arms, her nakedness pressed intimately against his.

"I'm thinking there is still enough night left to make love again," he whispered huskily. "You want to, don't you, Bliss?"

He heard her sigh, heard the tiny catch in her voice when she said, "Oh God, Hunter, yes. Yes! Don't you know by now how much I . . . Never mind, just kiss me. If we're never going to be together again, I want this night to last a lifetime."

He wanted to say the words she wanted to hear, but old doubts and fears rose up to taunt him. His voice was rough when he said, "Aye, remember this night when you're lying in Faulk's arms, knowing that he's the man responsible for giving your son away."

His words were like a dash of cold water. Bliss had been on the verge of telling him about the baby she carried when he spoiled the moment with his mockery. It was utterly heartless of him to remind her about her lost son. Not a day went by that she did not think about her child and his dead father, both lost to her forever. It would be a cold day in hell before she'd tell Hunter about the child he had put inside her.

"Damn you! Get out of here! Leave me alone. You have no right to break into my home and assault me."

"I did nothing to you that you didn't want done."

"You're wrong. Dead wrong. I thought I . . . never mind, I must have been mad to imagine I had feelings for you. Give me one good reason why I'd welcome you in my bed."

Guy opened his mouth and closed it again, shaking his head.

"Just as I thought," Bliss said. "Please leave, Hunter. I'm too tired to argue with you. Unless you can give me a reason why I shouldn't, I'm going to marry Gerald in less than a week."

Say it, Hunter, please say it, Bliss pleaded silently. How can I tell you about the baby if you don't tell me you love me? If she told him about the child now, she'd never know if he wanted her for herself or for the babe. Oh God, her life was a shambles and there was nothing she could do to make it better without Hunter's help. And he seemed disinclined to do anything but make love to her, then taunt her for her weakness.

"Very well, I'll leave," Guy said, "on one condition. I want you to call me Guy."

"You ask too much of me. That name is reserved for the man I loved with all my heart."

"Your maid is going to be mighty shocked tomorrow when she finds us in bed together," he said complacently. "Gossip travels. Think what that could do to your wedding plans."

"You wouldn't!"

"I would. I'm a pirate, remember? Say it."

Bliss bit her lip in consternation. What kind of game was he playing? she wondered. If the only way she could get rid of him was to call him Guy, then she'd just grit her teeth and do it.

"Very well . . . Guy. Would you please leave now?"

"Again. Say it again. Don't ever call me Hunter again. Unless you're referring to me by my last name."

"Guy. There, does that satisfy you? Do you enjoy tormenting me? You'll never be the man my Guy was."

He stood abruptly and stared down at her. His face was set in grim lines, his beautiful silver eye gleaming with secret knowledge. "You think not? You may be surprised."

She watched mutely as he dressed, struggling to make sense out of his puzzling words. He left the way he had entered, through the veranda doors and over the railing. Before he stepped out into the night, he paused and glanced back at her. He said nothing, not one word of farewell. He just stood there for a moment, his expression unreadable, before blending into the shadows and disappearing.

Bliss felt the terrible weight of disappointment. Her breath came in tiny pants as she gasped for air to fill her lungs. Hunter's . . . no,

Guy's last remark had sent her senses spinning out of control as she floundered for an explanation. Visions floated before her closed eyes. Images of her dead husband. Guy DeYoung had been so young when death had claimed him. Barely twenty-one. His beloved features had dimmed over the years, but not her memory of him. She tried to imagine how he would look today had he lived.

She saw Hunter's face instead.

She recalled instances when Hunter had seemed so familiar to her. The way he cocked his head, his laugh, that certain inflection in his voice. His drugging kisses . . .

Bliss dragged in a shuddering sigh, letting her imagination wander. Then she shook herself, aware that what she was thinking was preposterous. But the ludicrous thought persisted.

Oh God, she had to be mad even to consider such a thing! Her Guy wouldn't play a cruel trick like that on her. Two separate faces danced before her eyes. Moments before she fell asleep, the two images merged into one.

The following morning Bliss was lethargic and unable to focus on the wedding plans Gerald had come to discuss.

"Honestly, Bliss, this marriage is your idea," Gerald chided. "The least you could do is pay attention. Your father is anxious to talk with you. Why haven't you gone out to the plantation to visit him?"

"I have no desire to see Father," Bliss returned shortly. "You both know how I feel and why I feel that way. After you and I are married I intend to see you just enough to keep the gossip mongers satisfied."

"Claude wants to know if you're going to allow him to walk you down the aisle."

Bliss massaged her temples. She was in no condition to make decisions. Her head was pounding from lack of sleep, and her mind was awhirl with vivid memories and improbable dreams.

"I can't think now, Gerald, I have a terrible headache."

Gerald sent her a sharp look. "Don't try to back out of this now, Bliss. Your father and I are counting on your inheritance to put us back in business. I'm doing everything the way you want it, so don't even think of changing your mind. My creditors have agreed to wait until after our marriage for their money, and I will do whatever is necessary to assure your cooperation."

"Just leave me alone, Gerald. Come back tomorrow, when I'm in a better mood. Tell Father he can come here if he wants to see me."

Gerald rose huffily. "Very well, if that's what you want. I intended to spend the afternoon with you, but the time can be better spent with my new mistress. Good day, Bliss."

Bliss said nothing as he let himself out the door. It was getting so that Bliss could barely stand the sight of Gerald. Just looking at him reminded her of how he and her father had conspired together against her and Guy. How young and naive she'd been to trust their word about her baby.

The throbbing in Bliss's head increased; the walls seemed to close in on her. If she didn't get out in the air to clear her head soon, she feared she'd explode. She found Mandy in the kitchen, told her she was going out, grabbed her bonnet, and left the house in a flurry of whirling skirts.

Bliss walked aimlessly toward the Place d'Armes. Fall was in the air. The days were growing cooler, and the air entering her lungs was surprisingly refreshing. She breathed deeply, grateful when she found the pounding in her head subsiding into a dull ache. She strolled around the plaza, nodding at acquaintances she met along the way. Feeling much better now, Bliss decided to return home.

Then she saw him.

He was sitting on a bench beneath the balcony of the Cabildo. He wasn't alone. A small boy sat beside him, listening avidly to what Guy Hunter was saying. The child seemed to be about six or seven years old and resembled Guy so closely it was uncanny. She stopped to stare at them.

"They say the viscount is a widower and the boy is his son."

Startled, Bliss spun around to identify the speaker. It was Amanda. Bliss and Amanda had met often at society events, and it was no secret that both Amanda and her friend Becky had set their caps for Guy.

"Out for a stroll?" Amanda asked, her gaze intent upon Guy Hunter.

"What were you saying about the viscount?" Bliss asked. "I had no idea he had a son."

"Very few people know about the boy," Amanda confided. "Viscount Hunter asked my parents for the name of a good tutor for his son, and occasionally the viscount is seen on outings with the boy. I attempted to find out everything there is to know about Viscount Hunter, but"—she gave a harrumph of disgust—"apparently little is known about the man's past, except that he's extremely wealthy. No one seems to know where he came from or how he earned his wealth. Nor how he lost his eye."

Bliss's gaze remained riveted on the lad with Hunter. His hair was dark like his father's, but she wasn't close enough to ascertain the color of his eyes. He was a handsome boy, with a smile that reminded her of . . .

The color drained from her face and she staggered beneath the weight of her discovery.

"Bliss, are you all right?" Amanda asked, catching Bliss's arm to steady her. "You look ill. Your old sickness isn't returning, is it?"

"He's mine," Bliss gasped breathlessly.

"Who's yours?" Amanda asked curiously. "You can't be talking about the viscount, not with your wedding to Gerald Faulk just days away."

"What? No, not him. I'm sorry, Amanda, I have to go now. I'm not feeling well." She hurried off, leaving Amanda to puzzle over her strange behavior.

How dare he! How dare Hunter claim her son as his? What could the man be thinking? What was his purpose? Bliss considered confronting Hunter immediately with her knowledge, but decided against making a scene in a public place. Besides, he was already leaving the plaza and she needed time to gather her wits before facing Guy.

Why would he do such a thing to her? she fumed in silent rage. She saw everything clearly now. Hunter had reached Mobile before she and Gerald did and had taken her son, probably even paid Enos Holmes to disappear. And he'd done it out of pure malice because she'd refused to leave Cuba with him. Suddenly she recalled Hunter's last words before leaving her in Havana that night. He'd told her to make sure her husband was dead before marrying Faulk.

That memory brought her to a staggering halt. She wanted to believe, she truly did, but miracles didn't exist. No, Hunter's motive was pure spite. He'd stolen her son and was introducing him to society as his own for spiteful reasons. There could be no other answer. Unless . . . The nagging doubt still remained.

The similarities.

No, the differences were too striking.

The subtle innuendos.

No, he was but toying with her mind.

Guy DeYoung was dead, she'd be a fool to think otherwise. He'd died six years ago and was buried in a pauper's grave. If by some miracle he were still alive, he would have found a way to let her know.

Mandy met Bliss at the door. "I was getting worried, honey. You been gone a long time." Her dark eyes lingered on Bliss, as if she could see into the turbulence of Bliss's soul. "Something happened. You're pale as a ghost. Sit down, honey, and tell ole Mandy what happened."

Bliss shook her head. "I can't, Mandy, not yet. Not until I know the truth myself. I need to be alone to think this through before I can confront . . . my past."

"I'll fix you a cup of tea and something to eat. You rushed out this morning without a proper meal. You gotta think of that baby growing inside you now."

Bliss's hand flattened over her stomach. She had almost forgotten this new child after her startling discovery. But nothing had changed. This new babe was hers, just like Hunter's child was hers, and she loved both of them unconditionally. After a short rest, she decided to march straight to Viscount Hunter's house and confront the devil in his den.

Hunter's townhouse was in a much better neighborhood than hers, Bliss thought as she stood outside the imposing stone structure. Her heart was beating like a triphammer, the blood was pounding through her veins, and her mouth was dry as cotton. If she was correct, and she had good reason to believe she was, she was about to come face to face with the child she had given birth to more than six years ago, and until recently believed was dead.

Bliss had to know the truth. About Hunter and about her son. Uncertainty was eating her up inside. Slowly she mounted the front steps, her determination to confront Hunter unflagging. With shaking hands she lifted the brass knocker and brought it down hard on the wood door. Once, twice, a third time. Then she waited.

The door was opened by an elderly woman of color wearing a tignon over her graying hair. "May I help you?" she asked, peering at Bliss with bright curiosity.

"I'd like to speak to Viscount Hunter," Bliss said in a voice firm with resolve.

"He isn't in, miss. Can I take a message?"

"Are you the housekeeper?"

"I'm Lizzy, the young master's nanny. Is the viscount expecting you?"

"No." Undaunted, she stepped around Lizzy. "I'll wait."

Lizzy blinked up at Bliss, her surprise apparent; then she remembered her manners and said, "I'll show you where you can wait."

She ushered Bliss into a small parlor and left. Bliss was too excited to sit. It took all the willpower she possessed to stay in the room when what she really wanted to do was to tear the house apart until she found her son, hold him tight, and never let him go.

Long minutes passed. Minutes that seemed like hours. Bliss had no idea how long she'd been pacing the parlor when she sensed she wasn't alone. She whirled toward the doorway, and the breath caught in her throat. His eyes are turquoise, she thought, searching the newcomer's face hungrily. The same vibrant color as hers.

The lad studied Bliss with a combination of honest curiosity and caution. He must have decided she wasn't a threat, for he approached her boldly. "Are you waiting to see my papa?"

A long moment passed before Bliss could speak beyond the large lump in her throat. "Is Viscount Hunter your papa?" She wanted to take the boy in her arms so badly, she ached from it.

"Yes, do you know him?"

"I know him very well. Do you know when he'll return?"

"He said he wasn't going to be gone long." He gave her a long, thoughtful look. "You're very pretty."

Bliss couldn't help herself. She dropped to her knees before him. "And you're very handsome. What is your name?"

"My name is Bryan. Do you know my mama? Papa says she's pretty, too."

Tears blurred Bliss's vision. What in God's good name had Guy told the boy? "Where is your mama?"

Bryan looked confused. "I don't know. Papa said we were coming to New Orleans to look for her, but I guess he's having a hard time finding her."

His sad little face undid Bliss. She wanted to weep, to sing, to jump with joy, but all she could do was stare at Bryan.

Her child.

Her son.

She knew Bryan was hers with ever fiber of her being. She felt it in her soul, in her heart, in her mind. And she hated Hunter for keeping him from her. He was no better than Gerald Faulk and her father, who had taken Bryan from her at birth.

Her hand extended toward him to caress his cheek, fearing she'd frighten him if she moved too quickly. He seemed to understand her need, for he placed his small hand trustingly into hers. Then she drew him toward her, her gaze never leaving his face. She didn't know how it happened, but suddenly he was in her arms, exuberantly returning her fierce hugs. Tears streamed down her cheeks in unrestrained joy as she rose to her feet, taking Bryan up with her. She was dancing around the room with Bryan in her arms when she saw Hunter . . . no, Guy, standing in the doorway, looking positively thunderstruck. Bryan saw him too.

"Papa," Bryan squealed happily. "Look at me! I'm dancing with the pretty lady."

"Put my son down, Bliss," Guy enunciated slowly.

Unwilling to make a scene in front of her son, Bliss did as she was told.

"Go find Lizzy, Bryan. Tell her to give you some cookies and milk. I want to talk to the lady in private."

"Do I have to?" Bryan asked, clearly reluctant to leave.

"Aye, you have to."

"Can I say good-bye to the pretty lady before she leaves?"

Bliss dropped down beside the boy and gave him a parting hug. "I promise you'll see me again very soon, Bryan. You see, you're very important to me. I'm never going to lose sight of you again."

Bryan squeezed Bliss's hand and grinned up at Guy. "I like her, Papa. I hope she comes again soon." Then he skipped out of the room. Guy closed the door behind him and slowly turned to face Bliss.

Bliss didn't wait for Guy's explanation; she lit into him with all the venom she could muster. "How dare you! You're a cruel bastard, Guy Hunter. You reached Mobile first, took my son, and had the unmitigated gall to call him *your* son. How could you? Why would you want to hurt me like this?"

"I didn't deliberately set out to hurt you, Bliss," Guy said. "Why do you think I brought Bryan to New Orleans? I wanted to reunite him with his mother, that's why. While I was deciding how best to break the news, I learned about your impending marriage to Gerald Faulk.

There was no way in hell I'd allow a bastard like Faulk to raise my son."

Bliss blinked at him. "Bryan is *my* son, a fact you've conveniently forgotten," she countered. "When, if ever, were you going to tell me?"

"Sit down, Bliss, it's time you knew the truth."

"I'll stand, thank you. And when I leave here, I'm taking my son with me."

"*My* son isn't leaving this house," Guy said with deadly calm. He searched her face, aware that what he was about to tell her would shock her, but it was time. "I really am Bryan's father, Bliss. I think you've already guessed the truth, but you're afraid to acknowledge it."

Her eyes grew wide with disbelief, then narrowed in perfect understanding. Suddenly she launched herself at him, attacking him in a flurry of pounding fists and flailing feet. He allowed her to vent her rage until she was sobbing quietly against his chest.

"I know this has come as a shock," he contended. "I'm not dead, Bliss. I'm truly Guy DeYoung, and very much alive."

She backed away from him, her eyes dark with condemnation, her voice bitter with resentment. "Why didn't you tell me months ago? Your cruelty amazes me. Did you know there were times you seemed so familiar, so achingly like Guy that I hurt inside to look at you? I thought I was losing my mind. I was too old to believe in miracles."

"I tried to hate you," he explained. "I blamed you for every indignity, every beating I endured in the Calaboso. I couldn't forget the way you cried over Faulk on the dueling field, begging him not to die. I thought your father had convinced you that I wasn't good enough for you. When I was taken to the Calaboso you never once visited or inquired about my well-being. What was I to think except that you had abandoned me to a fate worse than death?

"One day I learned that an assassin was being sent to end my life. I believed you knew about it and did nothing to stop it. I believed you had already gotten an annulment and wanted me dead out of spite for wounding Faulk."

Bliss paled. "An assassin? I don't know what you're talking about. And it wasn't concern for Gerald that made me act as I did the day of the duel. I didn't want Gerald to die because I feared what would happen to you."

"I realize that now but I wasn't thinking clearly then," Guy said.

"What happened to the assassin?" she asked.

"I killed the assassin but lost an eye to his blade. He was buried in my stead. In a way, Guy DeYoung did die that day."

"So you forgot all about me and took up pirating," Bliss charged angrily. "What a fool I've been. All these years I've mourned a man who cared nothing for me, who hated me, even. Now I know why you held me captive. Revenge. You wanted your pound of flesh."

Bliss's anger sparked his own. All he could think of was that horrible year he'd spent in the Calaboso awaiting trial, barely existing between beatings, half starved and sick. "I wanted to send you back to your father and Faulk with my child growing in your belly!" he shouted. "I wanted to seduce you and make you care for Hunter the pirate. I wanted you to know how it felt to be abandoned."

He hadn't meant to be so brutally honest, but Bliss's words had riled him. Immediately he wished he could call them back. He watched in horror as Bliss turned whiter than his linen. Her eyes rolled up and her legs began to wobble dangerously. He shot forward to catch her seconds before she collapsed into his arms.

Chapter Thirteen

Cradling Bliss in his arms, Guy took the stairs two at a time, yelling at a stunned maid to summon a doctor. He carried Bliss into his bedroom and placed her gently on the bed, regarding her with concern. This was the second time she had fainted in his presence. How many other episodes had there been when he hadn't been around? he wondered. The thought was a frightening one.

It wasn't impossible for Bliss to have contracted some dread disease on his tropical island, he reflected. He'd seen brawny men felled by mysterious tropical diseases. He would never forgive himself if he had inadvertently caused her illness.

Lizzy came puffing into the room with a basin of cool water and a cloth.

"What happened to the poor chile?" she asked, clucking her tongue sympathetically.

"We'll have to wait for the doctor to tell us that," Guy said shortly. He stripped the cloth from the housekeeper's hand. "I'll do that, Lizzy. You may go and wait for the doctor."

Lizzy gave him an indignant look. "I'll stay. It ain't proper for a young lady to be alone in a bedroom with a man."

Guy gently applied the wet cloth to Bliss's forehead, paying little heed to the housekeeper, until he realized what she had said. "It's all right, Lizzy. This lady is going to be my wife."

Lizzy appeared skeptical. "If'n you say so, Mister Guy."

"Thank you. And don't forget to send the doctor up as soon as he arrives."

Guy turned back to Bliss as Lizzy quietly let herself out of the room. Bliss's color was returning and she was beginning to stir.

Her eyes blinked open. "What happened?"

"You fainted. You've been doing that a lot lately." His brow furrowed. "Is there something you're not telling me, Bliss? Are you ill?"

As if suddenly recalling why she had fainted, Bliss reared up on her elbows and gave Guy a blistering look. "There's nothing wrong with me that ridding myself of your company won't cure, Guy DeYoung! How could you keep your identity from me all this time? You must have hated me a great deal. Did it amuse you to see how much you could hurt me?" Her voice rose on a note of anger. "You even stole my son!"

"I had to," Guy said. "You were going to marry Faulk. That man is a bastard. I'd do anything to keep my son from being raised in Faulk's home."

"But why didn't you tell me months ago who you were? I loved you, Guy! I mourned your passing for six long years, living like a nun and refusing to see other men."

"I thought it best to let everyone think I had died," Guy explained. "I was consumed by bitterness. I was treated like an animal in the Calaboso and I blamed you, your father, and Faulk for my suffering. I've changed. I'm not that boy you married. Guy DeYoung was kind and considerate and caring, a decent human being. Hunter is a hardhearted, vindictive, bitter man. In the name of piracy Hunter has committed shocking acts you'd neither understand nor condone.

"I lived for revenge. Did you ever wonder why Faulk's ships were singled out for attack when other ships were left virtually unscathed? That was my doing, Bliss. I deliberately set out to ruin Faulk, and took great pleasure in my success. Then you fell into my hands and I planned a revenge far sweeter than anything I'd dreamed of."

"You willfully set out to seduce me," Bliss charged, recalling their earlier conversation. "You wanted me to conceive your child. Nothing would satisfy you but my complete humiliation. You wanted to punish me for something my father and Gerald did without my knowledge. My God! You *have* changed. You're a cruel, vindictive man, Guy DeYoung."

Before Guy could defend himself, a discreet knock interrupted the conversation.

"Dr. Lafarge is here, sir."

Guy rose instantly and opened the door to a distinguished-looking gentleman with kind eyes, and gray sideburns that matched the color of the sparse hair on his head.

"Come in, Doctor," Guy invited. "Your patient appears to have recovered but I think you should take a look at her anyway. This is the second time she's fainted in a short period of time and I'm concerned."

The doctor bustled through the door, all efficiency as he set down his bag and regarded Bliss through slightly myopic eyes. "If the young lady is ill, I'll find the cause, Viscount Hunter," he said confidently. "Kindly step out of the room so I can examine my patient."

"You called a doctor?" Bliss asked with asperity. "Why didn't you consult me first?" She started to rise. "I don't need a doctor."

"Relax, Bliss," Guy said. "Humor me. You could be seriously ill without knowing it. I'm not going to let you leave this bed until you're examined, so you may as well resign yourself to it. She's all yours, Doctor," Guy said as he let himself out of the room. "I'll be waiting out in the hallway."

Guy paced nervously, consumed with worry. He'd thought himself immune to the feelings that were eating him alive, but the possibility of

Bliss being seriously ill made him break out in a cold sweat. God, what was happening to him? He couldn't bear to lose Bliss a second time. He'd been a fool to think he could forget her, an even bigger one to believe he hated her.

He had a son to think about now. A son he'd come to love dearly. The boy needed a father and a mother, and he needed his wife. If it took the rest of his life, Guy vowed to rise above the reputation he'd so richly earned as a pirate and to lead a respectable life for the sake of his son.

A half hour later the bedroom door opened and Guy turned as the doctor stepped through the opening and closed the door behind him. He was smiling, and Guy allowed himself to breathe again.

"Is she going to be all right, Doctor?" Guy asked anxiously.

"What is that young woman to you?" Dr. Lafarge asked. "She seemed reluctant to answer my questions."

"Bliss is . . . my wife," Guy said after a slight hesitation.

The doctor visibly relaxed. "Ah, that explains things."

Panic shimmered through Guy. "Explains what? How ill is Bliss? What aren't you telling me?"

"Everything is as it should be," the doctor explained calmly. "Your wife's pregnancy is progressing splendidly. See that she takes better care of herself. She appears to be under a great deal of stress; fainting is her body's reaction to it. I'll leave some strengthening medicine for her. Try not to upset her; this is a fragile time in her pregnancy. If all goes well, you'll have a healthy child in six months."

Guy couldn't speak, could barely think as the doctor rambled on about Bliss's pregnancy. He should have known. They had made love often enough to guarantee pregnancy. In the beginning, his intention had been to impregnate Bliss and then abandon her. He'd never considered her feelings, only his need for revenge. Instead, making love to Bliss had given him unspeakable pleasure, and that soon became an obsessive need. He had realized too late that he wanted her because he cared for her, not because he wanted to punish her. It had been difficult to admit, even to himself, that he had never stopped loving her.

Years of existing for revenge had changed a carefree young man into an uncivilized pirate, but he had never forgotten the woman he had loved in his youth. And God help him, he still loved her, still wanted her. Now she was going to have his child. A brother or sister for Bryan.

"I believe I'm no longer needed here," the doctor said, sensing Guy's distraction. "I'll be most happy to deliver the child when the time comes, unless, of course, your wife prefers a midwife. You know where to reach me."

Guy acknowledged the doctor with a nod, scarcely aware of what he'd said. "Send the bill in care of my solicitor, Charles Branson, on Royale Street. I'll see you out."

"No need. Go to your wife, she needs you more than I do right now."

Guy didn't move immediately after the doctor descended the stairs. He stood a long time before the closed bedroom door, struggling to control his rising anger. How could he not be angry when Bliss had intended to marry Gerald Faulk, knowing she carried Guy's child? Was she mad? Why didn't she tell *him* she was pregnant instead of agreeing to marry a man she didn't even like? Over his dead body, Guy vowed. Faulk was never going to get his hands on Bliss or his children.

Curbing his rage, Guy opened the bedroom door and stepped inside. The bed was empty. He suffered a moment's panic until he saw her standing by the window, looking sad and forlorn.

"I suppose you know," she said, refusing to look at him.

"Why didn't you tell me? Lord knows you had sufficient opportunity."

She whirled around, her chin jutting pugnaciously. "Why didn't you tell me about my son?" she challenged.

Guy sighed. This was so damn complicated. "I was going to but . . . How in the hell could you marry Faulk? You knew you carried my child."

"You didn't want me," Bliss charged. "I had no idea you would show up in New Orleans. Or that I'd ever see you again. There's a price on your head, in case you've forgotten. I didn't know what to do. I didn't want my child to go through life labeled a bastard, so I told Gerald about the baby and struck a bargain with him. I offered him my inheritance in exchange for his name. It was to be a marriage in name only. He didn't like it, but apparently my money was too attractive to turn down. He agreed to my terms."

"I'm still your husband, Bliss," Guy said, reaching out to her.

She slapped his hands aside. "My husband died six years ago. I don't even know the man who has taken his place."

He ignored her remark. "I can't reveal my true identity for obvious reasons, but the fact remains that you're carrying my child. You're not going to marry Faulk and that's final."

"What do you propose?" Bliss asked sarcastically. "Would you prefer that I bring a bastard into the world? Or perhaps you want me to give the baby away and pretend it doesn't exist."

He spit out a string of curses that made Bliss's ears burn. "What happened to Bryan will never happen to this child. I'm going to be right here when it's born. I'm going to catch it in my hands and see it take its first breath. I would never be duped into believing the child was dead like . . ." He left the accusation hanging in the air.

Bliss rounded on him. "Go on, say it! I know you blame me for losing Bryan. Don't you think I blame myself? But you weren't there. It was a difficult birth. I was weak and ill afterward, and still mourning my dead husband."

"I'm not blaming anyone, Bliss. What's done is done. What's important now is Bryan, and the new life growing inside you. Both children are mine and I intend to claim them."

Bliss panicked. "You're not going to take my children away from me! Oh God, I can't bear it. My life has been empty so long—"Her hand flew to her stomach. "Now I have something to live for. I have Bryan, and this new babe."

"What about me, Bliss?"

"What about you?"

"Do you care for me at all?"

"Ha! That from a man who cares for nothing and no one. A pirate whose depravities are legend. I can't even bring myself to think of you as Guy, for Guy was a loving, kind, and compassionate man."

"I could tell you what changed me, but I fear the details would sicken you. Outside scars heal: it's the inner scars that change a man. I lost my soul in the Calaboso. Guy DeYoung died that day he escaped the assassin's blade. From his ashes rose Hunter the pirate. A maimed, one-eyed man, bent on revenge. Ruining Gerald Faulk and your father became my mission in life, and I succeeded beyond my wildest hopes.

"Then you came into my life again and remnants of Guy DeYoung slowly began to emerge from that place where I had buried him. I intended to use you, then discard you, but feelings I thought were banished forever seeped through the hard shell I'd built around my heart. After a while revenge no longer mattered. It was *you* I wanted. I discovered I still had a heart; it was just rusty from disuse."

Throughout Guy's startling confession, Bliss searched his face for the truth. She was startled to realize he was trying to tell her he cared for her. But caring wasn't enough. She wanted more.

"Where is all this leading, Guy?"

"You're not marrying Faulk, and you're not taking my children away from me. We'll be married tomorrow, as soon as I can make the arrangements."

"We're already married," Bliss reminded him.

"You were married to Guy DeYoung, a man who no longer exists in the eyes of the law. I have another legal name. It's Viscount Guy Hunter. The name was made legal through the courts of London. The legality of the child you carry will never be in doubt."

"What about your profession? Do you still plan to prey on unsuspecting ships?"

"I'm done with piracy for good. It's become too dangerous. 'Tis only a matter of time before the United States Navy rids the Gulf of pirates. Though Gasparilla and the Brotherhood refuse to accept it, the glory days of pirating are over. I've decided to become a planter. I've already made a bid on a plantation, and the offer has been accepted. I have only to sign the papers to make it legal. It will make a fine legacy for our children."

Despite the fact that Guy wasn't the same man she had known and loved seven years before, she offered no objection. Deep inside her was the hope that in time Hunter the pirate would become a distant memory, that one day the real Guy DeYoung would emerge and love her again.

"Do I have a choice?" Bliss asked.

"None whatsoever," Guy said tersely. "I know that might sound hard and uncompromising, but you can't expect me to change overnight. Circumstances have made me the man I am today and I can't alter what I've become. I suggest that you forget Guy DeYoung. I can never become that man again."

"I'll never forget Guy DeYoung," Bliss said thoughtfully. "I'm not sure I'd want the old Guy DeYoung back, however. You're . . . more interesting now. Seven years ago we were both children playing at being married. Today we are adults who have suffered and gained from our experience. We have one child and another on the way, and we have to go on for their sakes. I'll accept the man you are now if you allow me a glimpse of the old Guy once in a while."

"Does that mean you'll take me as I am?" Guy asked with a hint of amusement. "It's not as if we don't care for one another, because we do. Making love to you has become one of my greatest pleasures."

"I'll marry you, Guy, because I want my son. And there's our unborn child to consider. You *are* the father, which is a powerful argument for our marriage."

"Ours won't be a marriage in name only like you offered Faulk," Guy warned. "Make no mistake, ours will be a true marriage in every sense of the word. When we appear in public I want everyone to think ours was a love match, that we married quickly because we couldn't wait."

Bliss went still. "Is it, Guy? Is ours a love match?"

Guy hesitated, choosing his words carefully. "I never really stopped loving you, Bliss, not even when I hated you."

He made a tentative gesture toward her and suddenly she was in his arms. "You know I've never stopped loving Guy DeYoung," Bliss said on a sigh. "But it's going to be difficult pretending Hunter and Guy are the same man. You've changed, yet despite everything, I learned to care for Hunter. But love is a strong emotion. I loved Guy DeYoung with all my heart and I've finally accepted that he's dead to me. I'm not sure I can love the man you are now with the same intensity."

Guy gave an exasperated snort. "How can you say that when Guy DeYoung is standing in front of you? I'm not dead. I merely changed identities."

"It's difficult to accept what you've become, Guy, and I'm still angry at you for stealing Bryan. Furthermore, letting me think you were dead all these years was contemptible. It's going to take time to learn to trust you again."

His arms tightened around her. "But you do love me, don't you? Admit it, Bliss. You fell in love with me all over again as Hunter."

Bliss wanted to deny it but couldn't. "I fell in love with the part of Hunter that was good and kind and compassionate."

He gave a harsh laugh. "There was nothing about Hunter that was good and kind and compassionate."

"There was, you just refused to acknowledge those qualities in yourself. I'll always love those things in you I admire."

"Shall we seal our engagement with a kiss?" Guy whispered softly. Open desire darkened his silver gaze and flushed his skin.

He was so near, Bliss could smell the clean, musky scent of his skin and feel the moist stirring of his breath against her face. His arms were around her, holding her tightly against him, as if he feared to let her go lest she disappear. She raised her lips, offering him her mouth. She heard him groan, then closed her eyes as his mouth took hers in a searing kiss that branded her his. The kiss went on and on, his tongue exploring the moist insides of her mouth until Bliss felt almost giddy from lack of air. When he finally broke off the kiss, she had to hang onto him to keep herself upright.

"I want you, Bliss, but it isn't the right time. Bryan could come bursting in at any moment, and all the servants know we're alone up here. I told Lizzy you're my betrothed, but no one else knows. I want to tell Bryan first. Are you strong enough to face him now?"

"I'm fine," Bliss said, taking a deep, steadying breath. "More than anything in the world, I want Bryan to know I'm his mother. It pains me to think he had no one to love him until now. I want to make up for all the loneliness and hardship he's endured his first six years of life."

He took her hand. "Let's go find him."

They found Bryan in the courtyard, attempting to float a small boat in the fish pond. Bryan smiled up at them as they knelt beside him in the grass. Then his little face turned serious as his gaze settled on Bliss.

"Lizzy said you weren't feeling well. I saw the doctor leaving. I hope you're all better now."

Bliss forced herself to remain calm. She wanted desperately to take the boy in her arms and never let him go. Being with him every day, being a mother to him, was going to be pure heaven.

"I'm fine now," Bliss assured him.

"Do you have to leave?" He sounded so sad, Bliss's heart went out to him.

"We've come to tell you something, Bryan," Guy said, forestalling Bliss's answer. "Come sit on the bench where we can talk."

"Remember how we spoke about finding your mother?" Guy began once they were settled. Bryan nodded enthusiastically. "I've finally found her. I hope that makes you happy."

His face lit up. "Where is she, Papa? Please, can I see her now?"

"She's sitting beside you, son. Her name is Bliss and she's your mama."

He looked as if he didn't quite believe Guy. "She is?" When Guy nodded, Bryan sent Bliss a look that could only be described as pugnacious. "Why did you give me away? Didn't you love me?"

Bliss felt the overwhelming pain of rejection. Her son hated her. How could she bear it? She was too choked with emotion to speak. Fortunately, Guy offered an explanation.

"Your mother didn't give you away, son. She was sick after your birth and was told you had died. She had no reason to believe that you had been taken from her and given away. It wasn't until years later that she discovered you were alive."

"Why didn't *you* know about it, Papa?" Bryan asked.

"I . . . I'd been sent away," he explained. "I didn't see your mother again until just recently. She told me you were alive, and I set out to find you. Now we're together again and that's how we're going to remain."

"I've never stopped loving you, Bryan," Bliss said, smiling through a veil of tears. "Even when I thought you were dead I loved you. You're just as I always imagined you'd be. I want so much to be a mother to you. Will you allow it?"

"I've never had a real mother," Bryan said

wistfully. "I want to understand why I was taken away, but it's so hard."

"Telling you everything would only confuse you," Guy said. "But I promise to explain when you're old enough to understand."

"Do you promise to keep me with you always?"

"Oh God," Bliss moaned. She was filled with so much anguish she couldn't stop the tears from spilling down her cheeks. "No one will ever separate us again. I swear it."

"Don't cry, Mama," Bryan said, patting her arm. "I believe you. I never did believe Enos when he said my mama and papa didn't want me."

"You called me Mama," Bliss whispered, thinking it the sweetest word she'd ever heard. "You don't know how happy that makes me. May I hug you?"

She opened her arms and Bryan flew into them. They hugged one another fiercely, until Guy cleared his throat and said, "I have to leave for a while but your mama will be here with you. I'll be back in time to join you both for dinner."

"You promise?" Bryan said, obviously reluctant to let either of his parents out of his sight.

"We both promise," Guy replied. "Now give me a hug and go find Lizzy. It's about time for your tutor to show up for lessons."

"Aw, do I have to?"

"Aye, you have to. Off with you now."

Bryan gave his father a hug and scampered

off. Bliss watched him leave, her eyes bright with tears. "You're very good with him," she complimented. "You must love him a great deal."

"More than my own life," Guy said. "It enrages me when I think about the kind of life he endured with the Holmes family. If only you'd been more alert and less trusting when he was born."

"Don't you think I haven't said that to myself a hundred times since learning that Bryan was alive?" Bliss cried. "You'll always hold that against me, won't you?"

Guy sighed wearily. "Blaming you won't give me back the last seven years. Our son is with us now and our life together will begin with our remarriage. I'll put a notice in the newspapers. Tomorrow everyone will know about it. I'll return after I've made arrangements and attended to some pressing business."

Suddenly an alarming thought occurred to Bliss. "What about Gerald? He's going to be livid when he finds out."

"He won't know until it's too late."

"Mandy will worry if I don't return home. She's the closest thing to a relative I have."

"I'll take care of everything. We'll live in my house until I complete the purchase of the plantation. Your staff can join mine; this house is large enough to absorb them."

"There's just Mandy. The others are day help, but I'd like them to have a generous severance allowance if they don't choose to follow me here."

"I'll see that your wishes are followed. Mandy can begin packing. Is there anyone else you wish to notify?"

"No one. I have no close friends in New Orleans. What do you intend to do about Gerald?"

"I'll handle Faulk. The less he knows, the better."

Bliss couldn't help worrying. Gerald was desperate for money and had counted on her inheritance to pay off his creditors and revitalize his business. Depriving him of her inheritance now might send him over the edge.

"Let's go inside. You can spend time with Bryan after his lessons are finished," Guy said, taking her arm.

"This is all happening so fast," Bliss said on a sigh.

"Not nearly fast enough," Guy replied. "There's bound to be talk when our child arrives early. Don't worry," he said when Bliss sent him a worried frown. "Our child will be legitimate in the eyes of the law, and that's all that counts."

He pulled her into his arms and gave her a reassuring smile. "It's going to be all right, sweetheart. I can't promise you the same man you married seven years ago, nor the same kind of marriage you dreamed about with Guy DeYoung, but what we have now is far more exciting and a thousand times more passionate."

He brushed his lips against hers, a tender

touching of hearts and minds. "You said you loved me. Were you lying?"

She shook her head, as if to dislodge her doubts. She did love Guy. The difficulty lay in reconciling the differences between two men who were actually the same man. Whom did she love? Guy or Hunter?

The argument with herself ended abruptly. The answer was simple. She loved them both.

"I wasn't lying, Guy. I loved you as Guy DeYoung and I love you as Hunter. There are many things about Hunter I don't like. But I suppose in time I would have found a fault or two with Guy DeYoung. You're the father of my children; how can I not love you?"

"Then there is nothing to be concerned about, because I never stopped loving you. Stop trying to rationalize our situation. Didn't I say I'd take care of everything?"

Despite Guy's optimism, Bliss felt a nagging fear she couldn't shake. The possibility existed that someone would recognize Guy as Hunter the pirate and expose him for the reward. She seriously doubted that society would allow them to live in peace if his violent past was exposed.

Chapter Fourteen

The brief ceremony uniting Guy and Bliss was performed at the Cathedral by Father Pierre. Guy's solicitor acted as their only witness. Bliss felt odd standing before Father Pierre, the same priest who was to have officiated at her wedding to Gerald Faulk on Saturday. She had no idea what Guy had told Father Pierre to get him to agree to marry them and truly didn't want to know. It was bad enough having to endure the curious glances the good Father sent her from beneath his shaggy brows. Guy seemed not to notice, or if he did, he simply ignored them.

They left the church as man and wife about the same time the newspaper hit the streets announcing their marriage. Guy had just handed Bliss into his carriage and was climbing in beside her when Amanda came rushing toward them, having seen them emerge from the church as she strolled along the Place d'Armes. Her friend Becky was hard put to keep up with her.

"Is it true?" Amanda asked breathlessly. "I ran into Madame Lange a moment ago. She said she saw the announcement in the newspaper."

"If you're referring to the article announcing my marriage to Bliss Grenville, Miss Amanda, 'tis indeed true," Guy declared. He placed his hand over his heart and looked adoringly at Bliss. "What can I say? It was love at first sight."

"But . . . but," Amanda stammered, "Bliss was engaged to marry Gerald Faulk. Our invitation was delivered yesterday and our whole family planned to attend."

"We bought new dresses for the occasion," Becky said, pouting.

"As you can see, those plans will have to be changed. If you'll excuse us, ladies, my wife and I are eager to begin our honeymoon."

Bliss would have disappeared into thin air had she had the ability to do so. She could feel her cheeks burning as Guy nodded to the coachman. Almost immediately the carriage lurched forward.

"Bliss," Amanda called after them, "why couldn't you be satisfied with Mr. Faulk and leave the viscount to us?"

"Pay them no heed," Guy advised. "I wouldn't give a shilling for the lot of them."

"I'll be the talk of the town," Bliss lamented.

"Until some juicier gossip comes along. Do you care?"

She shook her head. "Not really. I haven't cared about society for a very long time. I rarely left the plantation after Guy died." As if suddenly realizing what she'd said, she quickly amended, "I mean, after . . ." Explanation defied her. "You know what I mean."

"It's all right, sweetheart. Everything is going to be fine. Just concentrate on giving me a healthy daughter or son and forget everything else. Shall we go home to Bryan now?"

"I'd like that. I can't believe he's finally mine."

The coachman left them off in front of the house, then drove the carriage down the side alley and into the carriage house. As they strode up the front steps, a man emerged from the shrubbery beside the house, blocking their path.

"Gerald!" Bliss gasped as Guy's arms came protectively around her.

"You lying little bitch!" Faulk spat. "What did you have to do to get the viscount to marry you? You begged me to marry you, to give that little bastard in your belly a name." He shot Guy a malicious glance. "Does your new husband know you're increasing? That a filthy pirate put his baby in your belly?"

Guy stepped in front of Bliss, shielding her from Faulk's fury. If he didn't have a family to protect, he would slit the bastard's throat and feel no guilt over the deed.

"You've said quite enough, Faulk. Bliss is my

wife now and I protect what is mine. If you wish to challenge me, the choice, of course, is yours. But I warn you, I'm deadly with a rapier, and despite having but one eye, I shoot straight and true."

"I wouldn't lower myself to dueling over a whore," Faulk said disdainfully. "All I ever wanted was her money. Although bedding her would have given me great pleasure," he added with sly innuendo. "I always considered Bliss mine."

It was definitely the wrong thing to say. Seconds later Faulk found himself lying on the ground, staring up at the sky and nursing a broken nose. When Faulk made no attempt to retaliate, Guy merely stepped over him as if he were a piece of offal.

"You'll pay for this! Both of you," Faulk promised, shaking his fist at them. "I hope you're happy, Bliss. You've made paupers of your father and me."

Faulk's parting shot was deadly. Bliss felt as if she'd committed a terrible crime by marrying Guy. Guy must have sensed her confusion, for he said, "You have only to remember what your father did to you to justify your actions. He and Faulk deserve everything that's coming to them."

"I—I know," Bliss said on a sob. "It's just that . . . he *is* my father."

"Men like Claude Grenville always end up on their feet," Guy said cryptically as he opened the front door and ushered her inside.

Bryan ran up to meet them, giving them such an enthusiastic greeting that Bliss quickly forgot all about Faulk and his threats. There was nothing he could do to hurt her or Guy, she told herself. Faulk had no inkling that Guy was anything other than an English viscount, exactly what he claimed to be. As long as Guy's violent past remained secret, Bliss believed he would be safe.

The cook prepared a special feast that night for the newlyweds. Guy ordered it to be served at ten o'clock in the privacy of their bedroom, after Bryan had been told about their marriage and was allowed to share in an early celebration.

Bliss went to their room shortly after nine to prepare herself for her wedding night, while Guy remained downstairs, sipping a brandy. Mandy had arrived with her clothing earlier and was waiting for her in her bedroom. Bliss hadn't had time to speak privately with Mandy and now she steeled herself for the questions she knew were sure to come.

"What have you gone and done now, honey?" Mandy demanded to know. "That viscount looks dangerous to me. Agreeing to marry Mr. Gerald was bad enough. Why did you have to go and do something foolish like marrying a man you don't even know? Land sakes, chile, you done jumped from the frying pan into the fire. What's the viscount gonna do when he learns yore with child?"

"Sit down, Mandy," Bliss said with a sigh. "You're my closest friend and I owe you an explanation. This is going to be difficult for you to understand—Lord knows I don't understand it myself—but I swear it's the truth."

Mandy lowered herself into the nearest chair. "Lordy, lordy, chile, you got me worried now. What have you gone and done?"

Bliss dropped to her knees beside the elderly woman and gripped her hands. "Have you met Bryan, Mandy?"

Mandy nodded, her eyes wary. "You mean the viscount's son? The boy said you were his mama. The pore chile must sorely miss his own mama to take to you like that. Is that why you married the viscount, because of the boy?"

"Partly. You see, Bryan truly is my son. He's the boy Papa took from me at birth and gave away."

The look on Mandy's face was one of total confusion. "I don't understand, honey. Why is the viscount passing him off as his own son if he's yores?"

"I know this is difficult, Mandy, but bear with me. Do you remember Guy DeYoung, the young man I married seven years ago against Papa's wishes?"

"Of course I do, honey. He was yore son's daddy. A pity he died so young."

"Guy DeYoung didn't die, Mandy. You can never breathe a word of this, for the knowledge will bring irreparable harm to those I love. Guy escaped from prison and another man was buried in his place. He lost an eye to an assassin's knife while he was in the Calaboso. The assassin had been hired by Gerald Faulk. I'm not certain how involved Father was in all this, but I intend to find out. Guy turned to piracy after his escape.

"We found each other when Gasparilla asked Guy to take me to Cuba after my ransom had been paid. I didn't recognize Guy as the man I had once married. He was known to members of the Brotherhood as Hunter, and that's the name I knew him by."

"It's no wonder you didn't recognize him," Mandy ventured. "Not even his own mama would know him. But I still don't understand about Bryan. How did he learn about the boy?"

Bliss then gave a sketchy explanation of the events that had taken place from the time she was captured until her release.

During the telling, Mandy's dark eyes grew as wide as saucers. "Land sakes, honey, that's some tale. Yore saying that the viscount is really Hunter the pirate, who is really Guy DeYoung. The viscount's son is yore very own chile, and yore married to the same man you married seven years ago against yore papa's wishes. That's all mighty perplexing to an old woman like me. That means—" She shook her fuzzy white head in dismay. "Oh, lordy, the chile yore carrying belongs to the viscount. I mean Hunter. No, Guy DeYoung. Which is it, honey?"

Bliss patted Mandy's hand. "I don't blame you, Mandy. I'm confused myself. All I know is that I'm carrying my husband's child, and our first son is back with us where he belongs."

"What about Mr. Gerald? He ain't gonna like this. Neither will yore papa. I been in yore papa's house long enough to know he's counting on yore inheritance to pay the back taxes and the money he borrowed from the bank. No, sir, he ain't gonna like this at all. I wouldn't want to be in yore shoes, honey. You tell Mr. Guy to watch his back."

"I'll tell him, but I doubt it's necessary. Remember, what I told you is confidential. There's a price on Guy's head. If anyone recognizes him as Hunter, there will be hell to pay."

"Yore like my own child, honey," Mandy said, clearly affronted. "I'd never do anything to hurt you." She lifted her bulk from the chair. "Turn around and let me help you outta that dress and into yore nightgown. Mister Guy don't look like a man long in patience."

"Thank you, Mandy," Bliss said, giving her a quick hug. "With you and Lizzy looking after my son and the new baby, I have nothing to worry about."

Dinner had already been set up on a table in the bedroom when Guy entered a short time later. The delicious array of food didn't tempt him in the least as his gaze found Bliss. She was wearing the lacy white nightgown he had purchased for her the day before. At first glance Guy thought she looked demure and innocent. Upon closer inspection he realized that its mod esty was deceptive. The gown was sleeveless, cut low in front, and closely hugged the elegant line of her lush figure. The modiste had told him he wouldn't be disappointed with his purchase and he wasn't.

The nightgown had been specially constructed to reveal enticing glimpses of glowing pink flesh through the sheer lacy panels. Guy groaned aloud and felt himself harden at the sight of all those luscious feminine curves. His gaze settled on the shadowy mound at the apex of her thighs.

"God, you're beautiful."

His gaze rose inch by deliberate inch over her long, shapely legs, her hips, her belly, to her ripe breasts, much larger now than he remembered. Only a very slight bulge indicated her pregnancy. A wash of heat flushed his sun-darkened skin as his erection grew and swelled beneath the tight cut of his trousers.

His breath caught in his throat as she walked slowly toward him, affording him an alluring glimpse of intimate flesh as the lace panels shifted revealingly.

"Are you hungry?" Bliss asked, indicating the food laid out on the table.

"Not for food." He stared at her. "Do you remember our first wedding night?"

She nodded jerkily. "How could I forget? We ran off at dawn and were married in a small country church in another parish. We made love in a haystack that night. We were so young," she said, sighing wistfully. "We didn't give a fig for the consequences, and learned the hard way how cruel the world can be for star-crossed lovers. We were betrayed in the worst possible way by those we trusted most."

"Forget them, Bliss. They're not worth another thought."

He reached for her and brought her into his arms, unable to keep his hands off her a moment longer. "Do you want something to eat? I'm not hungry myself, but if you—"

"No, I couldn't eat a bite."

He searched her face. "Something is wrong. What is it, love? Are you having second thoughts about marrying me?"

Bliss lowered her gaze, and Guy was astute enough to realize that she was troubled. In one graceful move he lifted her into his arms and carried her to the bed. He placed her in the center of it and followed her down.

"Tell me what's bothering you, sweetheart. I want this out of the way before I make love to you."

The tip of her small pink tongue flicked out to lick moisture onto her lips. Guy groaned, fighting hard to control the hunger gnawing at him. His need for her was like an obsession that intensified each time he was with her.

"I'm afraid I'm dreaming, or that something will happen to take all this away. I'm still in a state of shock. Finding Bryan, learning you're Guy DeYoung, getting married. I know they should be joyous occasions, and they are, but your reasons for deceiving me are difficult to understand and accept."

"I thought I explained my reasons to you."

"You did, but my mind still sees you as two different men, and sometimes I feel I don't know either of them. You're unpredictable, Guy."

"Have I ever hurt you?"

"Not physically. But keeping knowledge of Bryan from me hurt worse than physical pain. And keeping your identity a secret rates a close second."

"We've been over this before, Bliss. I thought you understood why I did those things. It's a little too late for recriminations or second thoughts. We're husband and wife, married twice to prove it. This is our wedding night, for God's sake!"

"I know. I'm sorry. I guess I'm just upset after that confrontation with Gerald. I know what he's capable of doing to us. He was counting on my inheritance, and you've deprived him of it. I know he's going to retaliate and it worries me."

"Forget Faulk. I'll handle him when the time comes, if it ever does."

She started to reply but Guy placed a finger over her lips. "Nay, don't say anything. Let me love you. It's been too long and I ache to be inside you again."

He kissed her then, trying to show her by action rather than word how desperately he needed her. He didn't blame Bliss for doubting him. Lord knows he'd given her plenty of reasons to feel apprehensive. His violent past was going to be difficult to live down.

Bliss hadn't realized how much she'd missed Guy's kisses until his mouth took hers, hot and demanding as he coaxed her lips apart with the rough tip of his tongue. She'd never been able to resist the sweet lure of seduction he wove around her, and tonight was no different. From the first time he'd seduced her as Hunter, she'd been a willing participant. Wanting him was as essential to her as eating and breathing. And at long last she knew why. Her heart must have known him even as her mind rejected the notion that Guy DeYoung lived.

She moaned against his mouth as he reached for the hem of her nightgown and slowly lifted it to her waist. She felt his hands on her bare flesh, skimming over her thighs to the moist delta between her legs. Her thighs shifted apart, allowing him deeper access.

"You're wet and hot for me, sweetheart," Guy whispered against her lips. He tugged at her nightgown. "Take this off. I want you naked in my arms."

Her gown came off easily; all she had to do was lift her shoulders and arms and let Guy strip it away. Guy's clothing took a little longer as they both struggled with buttons and ties. When they were both naked he began to kiss and explore her body with his hands and mouth as she arched up in a silent invitation to him to take her. He licked and suckled her tender nipples, creating an aching need that left her breathless and eager for a deeper union. But Guy appeared in no hurry to satisfy that need just yet.

She stifled a moan as his mouth traveled downward from her breasts to adore her stomach. But he didn't stop there. She was nearly insensate with pleasure when he took his loving to a higher level of intensity. Her body bowed sharply upward as he dragged her legs apart and placed his mouth on her.

"Guy! I can't bear this. Come inside me."

"Nay, sweetheart, not yet. Let me love you with my mouth."

The heat of his mouth found the velvety softness of her sex, sucking and licking, his tongue working maddeningly around the tiny button where ecstasy began. She screamed aloud as his mouth slid over her slick, fragrant folds, the wet roughness of his tongue teasing her, delving inside her, pushing her close to the edge but not letting her drop over. She grasped a handful of dark hair, holding him in place, fearing he'd leave her. But she needn't have worried. Guy seemed disinclined to leave her any time soon.

Then he brought his fingers into play, thrusting first one, then another inside her while he diligently plied his tongue to her sensitive nub. She burned. She tingled. Her body writhed. All her nerve endings screamed for release as time hung suspended. Her head thrashed from side to side and her body was bowed. The titillation of fingers and tongue working together produced a clamoring inside her that sent her reeling with pleasure so sharp she died a little. Then she shuddered and sobbed, her soft, guttural sounds of ecstasy filling the room.

She barely had time to catch her breath before Guy slid upward, thrusting inside her hot, wet body in a heated slide that made them both shudder. "Come with me again," he urged raggedly.

She didn't see how that was possible. She couldn't do it again. "I don't think—" Then his hips began to jerk wildly, pounding in and out of her, his breath rasping harshly in her ears, and Bliss discovered she'd been wrong. She *could* do it.

Suddenly she was there, reaching for ecstasy as her body convulsed with the sweet lassitude of pleasure. With a cry of gladness, she joined Guy in a frenzied ride to oblivion as she felt his body stiffen and his seed pump into her.

After a brief rest, they ate sparingly of the food prepared by the cook and made love again. This time Bliss became the aggressor, exploring and arousing Guy's body in the same way he had hers, kissing and nuzzling, following the path of his body hair until she reached the top of his thighs. He could feel her hands on him, her hair brushing his thighs as she bent over him. He jerked violently and nearly exploded when she took him into her mouth.

Sweat beaded his brow and his jaw clenched, making the tendons in his neck protrude. She could feel his sex grow and expand as she savored the salty taste and musky scent of him. When she increased the pressure of her lips, moving up and down the hard length of his staff, he put an abrupt halt to the erotic play.

"No more! I'm ready to—"

Lifting her up and astride him, he impaled her with the hard thrust of his shaft. She took him inside her and began to move up and down, driving him so deep she felt as if he had touched her soul.

They climaxed together and Bliss thought nothing had ever felt so right. The man making love to her might not be the man she remembered from her youth, but he still had the ability to take her to Paradise.

Resting in the sweet aftermath of completion, Bliss turned to look at Guy. His eye was closed but she could tell by his breathing that he was awake. She stared at him, wanting desperately to see his face, all of it, without the eyepatch.

"Do you never remove your eyepatch?" she asked, lightly touching the silken cloth covering his eye.

He caught her wrist, preventing her from making a more detailed investigation. "Only when I'm alone."

"I'm your wife, Guy. I want to see what you look like."

"You wouldn't like it. It's not a pretty sight. The assassin's blade did a thorough job of disfiguring me."

"One day, I vow, you'll not hide from me."

"Not in this lifetime," he said grimly.

Bliss didn't pursue the subject. Obviously it stirred up memories better left forgotten. Moments later she heard the cadence of his breathing change and knew he had fallen asleep. As she reached for that same blissful respite, she spared a brief moment to ask God to grant her and Guy happiness, and a life free from enemies and danger.

One of the enemies Bliss worried about sat with two scruffy pirates in one of the numerous grog shops lining the waterfront. They were conversing in low voices in the smoke-filled room, which reeked of cheap rum and sweat. Spittle-strewn sawdust on the floor reflected the slovenly habits of its rough-and-tumble customers. But Gerald Faulk and his coarse companions seemed oblivious to their surroundings.

"How do we know ya got the blunt to pay for our information, Faulk?" asked a squint-eyed, bearded seaman wearing a knit cap.

"Me and Squint heard that Faulk Shipping is in a heap of trouble," the second man charged. He was smaller than his companion, and uglier, with blackened teeth and sharp features. " 'Tis no secret that pirates sent most of yer ships to the bottom of the sea."

"Don't worry about the blunt," Faulk argued. "And don't call me by name. The fewer people who recognize me, the better. I'm only here because you've indicated through a messenger that you have information about a man who calls himself Viscount Guy Hunter. Over a week ago I put the word out on the streets that I would pay for information. I haven't changed my mind."

Squint scratched his chest and spat on the floor. "I don't know, mister. Our information don't come cheap. What do ya think, Monty?"

Monty rolled his eyes. "Talking could endanger our health, if ya get my meaning. If Hunter learns who told on him, we're dead meat."

Faulk's attention sharpened. "Hunter? Are you referring to Viscount Guy Hunter?" Alarm bells went off in his head. "What about him? It just occurred to me that there's a pirate named Hunter. You might as well tell me what you know. You've got me damn curious now."

"Let's see yer blunt first," Monty insisted.

Faulk was prepared. Earlier that week he had called on Claude Grenville to inform him about Bliss's marriage to a wealthy Englishman and to vent his spleen at what he perceived as Bliss's betrayal. When Faulk demanded money, Claude had reluctantly given Faulk his last valuable painting as consolation for losing Bliss. Faulk had immediately turned it into cash and spread the word that he would pay handsomely for information about a man known as Viscount Guy Hunter.

Nothing could convince Faulk that Guy Hunter was the man he claimed to be. Little was known about the stranger who had appeared out of nowhere claiming to be a titled Englishman. Had the viscount not stolen Bliss from him, he wouldn't have cared who or what the man claimed to be. But everything had changed with the viscount's marriage to Bliss, and Faulk intended to get to the bottom of it.

Faulk removed a small sack of gold coins from his vest pocket and spilled the contents into his hand. "Is this enough?"

Squint grabbed for the coins but Faulk snatched them away. "Your information first."

The pirates eyed the gold resting in Faulk's palm, communicated silently, then nodded in agreement.

"Very well, your information first," Faulk reiterated, leaning close enough to the sailors to get an unwelcome whiff of their rum-soaked breath.

"Me and Monty was down on the levee the day the viscount arrived in New Orleans on Jean Lafitte's ship," Squint confided. "We didn't know what he was calling himself then, but we recognized him right off. It were the eyepatch what gave him away."

"We got curious," Monty continued where Squint left off. "We asked around and learned he called himself Viscount Guy Hunter. We knew it weren't his real name. About a year ago we was crewmen aboard Hunter's ship. The *Predator*, it were. We only took what was owed us, but we was accused of stealing from the treasure trove aboard the ship. There are certain articles pirates abide by, and we broke the rules. Hunter set us ashore on a deserted island and left us there to die."

Faulk's eyes sparkled with excitement. "Are you saying the viscount is a pirate?"

"Aye," Squint said, "that's exactly what we're saying. Hunter, Gasparilla, and the Lafitte brothers are all members of the Brotherhood. Their ships terrorize unsuspecting merchantmen, sending them to the bottom of the sea without their cargoes. They keep their women prisoners on Captiva Island until ransom can be arranged."

"Rumor has it that Hunter betrayed Gasparilla and disappeared shortly afterward," Monty confided. "Some say Hunter is dead. Others say he's living like a king off his ill-gotten gains."

He poked Squint in the ribs. "But we know better, don't we, Squint? Hunter is right here in New Orleans, hiding behind an English title."

"Why haven't you notified the authorities?" Faulk wanted to know. "There's a price on Hunter's head."

"Hell and damnation, we can't prove he's Hunter, the infamous buccaneer," Squint contended. "It ain't like we're law-abiding citizens ourselves. We ain't exactly welcome in New Orleans. A man with a title has clout. And plenty of blunt. An upstanding citizen like yourself would stand a better chance of being believed than the likes of us."

Faulk sat back to contemplate everything he'd just learned. He'd almost made the mistake of hiring these men to kill Guy Hunter. Now he was considering ways to use this damning information to better advantage. It didn't take

Faulk long to figure out that Hunter was probably the man who had sunk his merchant ships and made a pauper of him, the man who had held Bliss captive and put his baby in her belly. Rage made him blind to everything but making Hunter pay for the huge losses he'd incurred over the years.

Killing Hunter outright was too easy a death, Faulk decided. He wanted Hunter to suffer for stealing Bliss's inheritance from under his nose. And he wanted Bliss to suffer for the mental anguish she'd caused him. But most of all he wanted money. He already had an idea about how to obtain everything he had coming to him.

"We want our blunt," Monty said, intruding upon Faulk's reverie.

Faulk tossed the bag of gold across the table. Monty snatched it up and stuffed it into the pocket of his dirty jacket. "We'll be on our way now."

"You don't plan on leaving town, do you?" Faulk asked.

Monty's beady eyes narrowed. "Why do ya ask?"

"I may have another job for you. Where can you be reached if I need you?"

"We don't come cheap," Squint asserted.

"I'm willing to pay for your services."

"Ya can find us here most nights. We rent a room above stairs when we have blunt. If we don't find a likely subject to rob, we bed down in the nearest doorway."

"I'll find you," Faulk said, rising. "Much

obliged for the information. It was most enlightening."

More than enlightening, Faulk thought as he climbed into his carriage and picked up the reins. Riveting would better describe it. He needed time now to decide how best to use the information and to explore the various ways in which he could benefit from it.

Chapter Fifteen

Two weeks after the wedding, Bliss was beginning to believe that all her fears about her future with Guy had been unfounded. Guy seemed determined to make her and Bryan happy and didn't appear to miss his old life. It helped that Gerald Faulk hadn't been back to plague them since the confrontation on her wedding day.

Their surprise marriage was still the talk of the town. They'd been invited to several social functions, however. Bliss supposed the invitations were due entirely to curiosity, and perhaps Guy's title. They had attended only two of those affairs, a musicale and a reception for the new American governor. Both affairs had proven embarrassing. Their marriage was a juicy scandal and they were often quizzed for intimate details of their courtship and hasty marriage. As a result, they accepted very few invitations.

Guy spent his days locked in meetings with prominent men who wanted him to invest in their enterprises. In addition to his business dealings, Bliss knew Guy met occasionally with his old friends Jean and Pierre Lafitte at the Absinthe House. Then there were meetings to finalize the purchase of the plantation Guy had bought. He'd told her they would be moving soon. When she'd asked which property he had purchased, he had merely smiled and said it was a surprise.

Today Guy had left early to meet the Lafitte brothers. Lizzy had taken Bryan to the park and Mandy had gone to the market. Except for the cook and two parlor maids, Bliss was alone and taking advantage of the quiet to compose a letter to her father to inform him of her marriage. Unfortunately, her mind kept drifting back to the night before, when she and Guy had made love.

Making love with Guy just got better and better. Bliss recalled how frightened she'd been the first time she'd met him as Hunter. He'd looked so fierce, so utterly ruthless. Yet she'd been attracted to him from the beginning. Even as his captive she had known there was something unique about him, despite her knowledge of his profession and the unlawful acts he'd committed. She prayed those acts wouldn't come back to haunt him now, that society would let Guy become the kind of man he was meant to be.

Bliss sighed and returned to her letter. She supposed that in time she'd make peace with her father, but it wasn't going to be easy, nor would it happen overnight. She was still agonizing over the letter when one of the maids knocked on the library door to announce a visitor. Before she could ask who it was, Gerald Faulk appeared in the doorway.

"I think you'll see me, Bliss," he said smugly as he walked into the room, shut the door behind him, and flopped into a comfortable leather chair without waiting for an invitation.

"My husband isn't home, though I expect him momentarily."

"We both know the viscount is meeting with his pirate friends, don't we? It's you with whom I wish to speak."

Taken aback, Bliss tried to pretend she didn't understand his remark about pirates. "You and I have nothing to talk about."

"I thought we might discuss money. You have it, I don't."

"There's nothing to discuss. You have no claim on my inheritance. It belongs to my husband."

Technically, that wasn't true. Guy had insisted that he didn't want her money and had placed the funds in the bank in her name. It was hers to do with as she pleased.

Faulk rose abruptly and stood over the chair

in which she was sitting. "I *know*, Bliss. I know everything."

Bliss felt her stomach lurch painfully. Faulk's cryptic words needed little explanation, but Bliss decided to brazen it out. "I have no idea what you're talking about."

His pleasant features twisted into an ugly mask. "I think you do. Nevertheless, let me enlighten you. Your husband is no more viscount than I am. Among the Brotherhood he's known as Hunter. He's one of the vicious pirates who ply their trade in the Caribbean, crippling shipping and terrorizing hapless victims. I'm well aware of his name and vile reputation. I believe he's responsible for ruining your father and me financially. There's a price on his head, you know. You, my dear, will become a widow for the second time if the authorities are made aware of the viscount's real identity."

Bliss was glad she was sitting, for she doubted her knees would have held her upright had she been standing. With as much bravado as she could muster, she retorted, "You've got the wrong man, Gerald. Guy has papers to substantiate his title."

"Titles are easily bought and sold," Faulk scoffed. "So are identities. Deny away, my dear, but I know the truth. Now I know why the viscount so readily accepted your pregnancy. He's the pirate who held you captive, isn't he? He's the man who put the brat in your belly. It all makes sense now."

Bliss felt her world crumbling around her,

but she was astute enough to refrain from verbally acknowledging Guy's guilt. "What do you want, Gerald?"

Faulk gave her a mirthless smile and returned to the chair he had occupied moments before. "Now we're getting somewhere. I'm glad you decided to cooperate. My demands are simple enough. I want your inheritance. All of it."

"And if I refuse?" Bliss asked.

"Then you can watch your husband hang. I hear it's not a pleasant sight. His face will turn purple, then black. His tongue will swell and—"

"Stop!" Bile rose up in her throat and she clapped her hands over her ears.

"Have you heard enough?"

Bliss nodded jerkily. She knew Faulk to be a vindictive and cruel man when crossed. He wouldn't hesitate to expose Guy.

"Good. Can you get to your inheritance without going through your husband?"

"I . . . yes, the money is in my name. Guy didn't want it."

Faulk gave a bitter laugh. "Of course he didn't want it. Why should he when he's grown rich on plunder and slaves he's taken off my ships and sold to the Lafitte brothers? How soon can you get the money?"

"It's going to take a few days. Guy will have to know and—"

"No! You're not to say a word to your husband. I know what he's capable of. He'd kill me in cold blood and laugh about it later. I'm not alone in this, my dear. I've instructed my two accomplices to kill Hunter should he harm me in any way. And if you fail to comply, I'll go to the authorities with what I know. Is that clear?"

"How can I keep something like this from Guy?" Bliss argued.

"I don't care how you do it as long as my instructions are followed implicitly. If I learn you've told Hunter, I'll expose him to the authorities. You have a week to get the money. I'll be waiting in a carriage in the alley behind your house a week from today. Midnight. Bring the money with you."

"I don't know if I can get out of the house without Guy knowing."

"If you fail to meet me, expect the City Guard to knock on your door and drag your husband to the Calaboso."

"I . . . I'll be there," Bliss said.

"I thought you'd say that," Faulk said with a smirk. He rose and walked to the door. "This is much better than being leg-shackled to a wife who is unwilling to share my bed. I'll see you in one week, my dear."

Suddenly the door swung inward and Bryan burst into the room. "Mama! I'm home. Lizzy let me feed the birds in the Place d'Armes."

"Well, well, well, who do we have here?" Faulk asked, his mind conjuring up all manner of possibilities involving the boy. "Those turquoise eyes look familiar. Is this your son, Bliss? How did you find him?"

"Bryan, honey, go to the kitchen and tell

Lizzy to give you some cookies and milk. Your tutor will arrive soon for lessons."

Apparently unaware of the tension between his mother and her visitor, Bryan gave Bliss a hug and skipped from the room.

"I'm beginning to understand, though I'm more than a little confused," Faulk said. "The boy *is* your son, isn't he? The reason we didn't find him in Mobile is because Hunter got to him first. Did Hunter use the boy to coerce you into marriage? I'm amazed that Hunter willingly gave up piracy to marry you, my dear." Suddenly he gave a shout of laughter. "Can it be that the bloodthirsty bastard actually loves you?"

"I don't have to explain anything to you," Bliss maintained. "Just leave Bryan out of this. You'll get your money; then I never want to see or hear from you again."

"I'm happy to know about the boy, my dear. What a stroke of luck. I can see you're a protective mama. It would be a terrible tragedy if you lost the boy after so short a reunion."

Bliss went utterly still. "You're threatening my son?"

"Take it any way you want. Just remember what I told you. Hunter isn't to know about our little arrangement. You have too much to lose by disobeying my wishes. Good day, my dear. It's been pleasant talking to you."

Swamped by panic, Bliss remained rooted to the spot long after Faulk had left. A ruthless man like Faulk wouldn't hesitate to use her son as leverage to get what he wanted. Nor would he balk at ordering Guy's death, or exposing his past.

It wasn't going to be easy taking the money out of the bank without Guy's knowledge, Bliss realized, but she hoped it could be accomplished before Guy checked on her account.

Dinner that night was a quiet affair. As the evening progressed, Guy puzzled over Bliss's uncharacteristic lack of interest in the conversation. Finally his fork hit the plate with a rattle, capturing Bliss's attention.

"What in the hell is wrong with you tonight? Did something happen today? Did someone upset you?"

Guy wasn't fooled by her wobbly smile. "Nothing is wrong," she said brightly.

"You've hardly touched your food, or heard a word I've said."

"I'm not very hungry. Pregnant women are often moody. You weren't around when Bryan was born and weren't subjected to my bad humor."

He stared at her. This was the first sign of "bad humor" he'd noticed, and he thought her pregnancy a lame excuse for her preoccupation. Nevertheless he decided to give her the benefit of the doubt, since he knew damn little about pregnant women.

"Why don't you go on up to bed, sweetheart, you look tired. I'll join you later. There are some papers I need to look through first."

Bliss didn't need a second invitation. Looking

somewhat rattled and distracted, she excused herself and hurried off.

Guy stared thoughtfully after her. Something was definitely wrong, but he didn't know what. No one had reported anything unusual or out of the ordinary happening at the house today to explain Bliss's odd behavior.

Suddenly a dreadful thought occurred to him. Could Bliss be having second thoughts about marrying him? He knew he'd acted like a tyrant by insisting that they wed, but he had been determined not to let her walk out of his life.

He wandered into the library and spread out the contract for the plantation he was buying. After poring over the papers for several minutes, he signed both the contract naming the sum that was to be paid to the owner and an agreement to pay off the existing mortgage. Guy knew he could buy a plantation for far less money, but he wanted this one because it was a place where he knew Bliss would be happy.

Setting the papers aside, Guy rose, stretched, and thought of Bliss waiting in bed for him. In his mind's eye he pictured her as she had been last night, her lips swollen from his kisses, her lithe body writhing beneath him, the room filled with her soft moans of pleasure. A shaft of heat speared through his body, gathering below the belt and causing a painful tightening in his groin.

He started toward the stairs, as eager as a green lad about to make love to his first woman.

He wanted to feel her soft lips opening for his kisses. Wanted to set her lush body afire with his hands and mouth, until her hunger was as great as his. Wanted to watch her face as she shattered for him.

He took the stairs two at a time, literally shaking with need, his erection swollen and painful. Despite his eagerness, he forced himself to make a dignified entrance instead of bursting into the room as he wanted to do, leaping into bed and thrusting into her hot, welcoming center.

She appeared to be sleeping, and disappointment speared through him. He approached the bed, making as much noise as he dared without rousing the entire household. She didn't stir. Guy frowned. He hadn't realized she was so tired. Then he saw her eyelids flutter and wondered if she was only pretending. He watched the rise and fall of her chest and realized it was too erratic, not at all what one would expect from someone in a deep state of sleep. Why did Bliss need to pretend with him? he wondered. He didn't like the answer.

"I know you're awake, Bliss," he said as he sat on the edge of the bed to remove his shoes and stockings. "Are you going to tell me what's bothering you? Pretense isn't necessary with me. If you didn't feel like making love, all you had to do was tell me. I'm not the ogre you seem to think. I'd do nothing to hurt you or our child."

Bliss's eyes fluttered open. The last thing she wanted was to hurt Guy. She was so confused.

Making love with Guy while she harbored a secret would be dishonest, as dishonest as not telling him about her conversation with Faulk. She had always given unstintingly of herself and she knew Guy would know she was holding back and demand to know the reason. Faulk's instructions had been specific. If Guy was told about their deal, Faulk would seek immediate retribution. Either Guy or Bryan would suffer for her lack of discretion and she couldn't allow that to happen. She knew what Faulk was capable of.

"I'm sorry. I didn't mean . . . that is . . . I'm not in the mood tonight. Do you mind?"

"Are you ill? Because something sure as hell is wrong with you. You just aren't yourself. Perhaps I should send for the doctor."

"No! I'm fine. Just tired. I'm sure I'll feel better tomorrow."

He stepped out of his trousers and climbed into bed beside her. She didn't resist when he took her into his arms. She could feel his erection throbbing against her thigh and felt like a traitor, but she just couldn't pretend that everything was fine when it wasn't. She could lose her son, her husband, everything she loved in the world if Guy had the slightest inkling she was dealing with a man like Faulk. The Guy she knew would immediately retaliate, and that could set off events that would result in disastrous consequences. Too much was at risk.

"Go to sleep, Bliss," Guy said. "Perhaps you'll tell me tomorrow what's bothering you." He was silent a long time, then he asked, "Are you sorry you married me? I'm not exactly the kind of man you deserve."

"You're everything I want, Guy, never forget that."

It was the way she said it that worried Guy.

Bliss managed to sneak away from the house twice during the following week without anyone asking questions about her destination. The visits to the bank were necessary since there were all kinds of difficulties involved in removing so large a sum of money from her account. There were papers to sign and accounts to close. Fortunately, no one had to approve the withdrawal, for the money had been under her control since her marriage. She brought a carpetbag along the day she picked up the money and hid it beneath the bed when she returned home.

This entire week has been a living hell, Bliss thought as she checked beneath the bed to make sure the carpetbag was still there. Deceiving Guy hadn't been easy, but telling him was not an option. She could tell he was puzzled and resentful of her odd behavior; she would be relieved when this was all over and she could get on with her life. She prayed the money would satisfy Faulk, that he would keep his word not to expose Guy to the authorities. She didn't trust him. Not at all.

That night, the night she was to deliver the money to Faulk, Guy didn't attempt to make love to her. Bliss was more distraught than usual and she appreciated his sensitivity to her mood, even though she knew he sensed her distress and had countless unspoken questions about the cause. She lay beside him, stiff and unyielding, as he pulled her into the curve of his body.

"How long is this coldness between us going to last?" he asked as he pushed himself away from her. "Is there something you wish to tell me?"

He sounded annoyed, as if he expected an answer from her. Bliss wanted desperately to tell him what was troubling her, but the consequences frightened her. "There's no coldness, Guy. It's just . . . I'm pregnant."

"I'm the one who made you that way. Is that the problem? I'm at my wit's end, Bliss. Do you resent me for getting you pregnant?"

"No! God, no! I want this child. I've always wanted it."

"Then it's me you don't want."

"I love you, Guy. You're just going to have to trust me."

"Will you ever tell me what's bothering you?"

He sounded offended, and with good reason. "I don't know. Soon. When I can."

He gave a ragged sigh. "I don't like this, Bliss, but I suppose I'll just have to be patient until you're ready. Don't wait too long," he warned, "I'm not a patient man. I want my wife back. I want her soft and yielding beneath me. I want to hear her sweet moans, watch her face when I bring her to pleasure. I miss that, sweetheart."

"I miss it, too," Bliss said on a sigh. "We'll be close again, I promise. Just give me time."

"Let me fix what's bothering you."

Oh God, did she dare? Faulk's threat came back to haunt her. If she valued Guy's life, she had to hold her tongue. "There's nothing for you to fix," she said brightly. "Go to sleep, Guy. I'm sure things will look better tomorrow."

Tomorrow Faulk would have his money, and she wouldn't have to explain until Guy found out about her depleted bank account. She hoped that by then Faulk's greed would be satisfied and he'd forget all about revealing Guy's past.

Bliss lay awake, waiting for the clock to strike twelve. She could tell by Guy's deep, even breathing and relaxed body that he was sleeping soundly, and her relief was immense. If all went well, she'd be able to meet Faulk and return to bed before Guy realized she'd been gone. Moments later the clock struck twelve and she eased out of bed.

Guy felt the mattress shift and awoke instantly. Long years of living with danger had conditioned him to remain alert even in sleep. Then he felt Bliss leave the bed and he opened his eyes. Moonlight streamed through the window, providing sufficient light for him to see Bliss moving noiselessly about the room.

He watched with growing alarm as she pulled

a dress over her nightgown, threw a shawl over her shoulders, and stepped into her shoes. He thought she might be ill and was about to ask if he could help when he saw her pull a small carpetbag from beneath the bed.

Alert now, Guy could think of no use Bliss would have for a carpetbag in the middle of the night unless . . . Nay, the answer didn't bear consideration. Bliss would never leave him and Bryan. Then a horrible thought occurred to him. What if Bliss left him and took Bryan with her? She had her own money and could do just about anything she wanted. Anger churned through him.

Guy wanted to leap out of bed, to stop her from doing something she'd regret, but he bided his time, waiting, wondering. Struggling to control his rage, Guy imagined the worst when he saw Bliss hug the carpetbag to her chest and let herself out of the room. Seconds later he was out of bed and pulling on his pants and boots. Then he left the bedroom as quietly as she had.

Guy's first surprise was Bliss's destination. It wasn't Bryan's room. He couldn't conceive of Bliss leaving without Bryan after she'd gone through hell to find him. He hugged the walls as he trailed her downstairs and through the kitchen to the back door. He clung to the shadows and watched as she cast a furtive glance behind her and opened the door. She stepped outside. He waited a moment, then quickly followed. She seemed to know exactly where she was going as she hurried down the path to the gate that opened into the alley.

Guy slipped out the gate behind her and darted behind a clump of shrubbery when he saw a carriage waiting in the alley. Shock and disbelief warred within him when he saw Bliss walk straight for the carriage.

It was true! he told himself. Bliss was leaving him. But for whom? Suddenly a man stepped out of the carriage and motioned to Bliss. Guy's hands clenched into fists when he recognized Gerald Faulk. How could Bliss do this to him? Had she deceived him from the very beginning? What kind of sick relationship did she have with Faulk? He sidled closer, hoping to hear their conversation, but they spoke too quietly to be heard. When he saw Bliss hand the carpetbag to Faulk, everything became very clear to Guy. The bag held Bliss's clothing and she was indeed leaving him.

Black, gut-wrenching fury raged through him. Never had he felt so betrayed. Not even when he'd held Bliss responsible for his misfortune years ago. He didn't want to believe it of her, but the proof was there before him. Faulk took the carpetbag from her hands and turned to place it in the carriage.

Now Guy knew the reason why Bliss had been so distraught lately. Obviously she'd been conniving behind his back with Faulk ever since Guy had forced her into an unwanted marriage. It hurt to know that she couldn't bear the thought of making love with him anymore. God! How could he have been so stupid?

After the initial shock passed, Guy felt a violent urge to kill Faulk. Hunter the pirate would have snuffed out the repulsive bastard's life without a second thought, but Viscount Hunter had too much at stake to kill indiscriminately. He had an innocent child to protect. No, he would not kill Faulk, but he could still confront his enemy.

He stepped out of the shadows, quickly closing the distance between himself and Faulk. Faulk saw him approaching and tried to enter the carriage, but Guy was too fast for him. Grasping Faulk's arm, he pulled him out and away, at the same time stripping the carpetbag from Faulk's hands and throwing it into the bushes behind him. From the corner of his eye he saw Bliss gasp and step away, and with good reason, he thought dimly. She had never seen him in a rage before.

Grasping Faulk by the lapels, he dragged him forward roughly until they stood nose to nose. "Did you think I wouldn't find out?" he said in a voice that would have done the Devil justice.

"Bliss swore she wouldn't tell you," Faulk gasped through chattering teeth.

"I'm not stupid, Faulk. I knew Bliss was up to something. I just never imagined you were involved."

He shoved Faulk backward, pressing him against the carriage. He wanted to knock Faulk senseless but settled for a hard punch to the gut, satisfied when Faulk grunted and doubled over.

"I'm probably making a mistake by not killing you, but I don't want my son to suffer for my sins. Get out of here, Faulk. If you ever sniff around my wife again, I won't be so lenient the next time."

"Your threats don't frighten me, Hunter," Faulk gasped, obviously still in pain. "I'll get even. You're going to be sorry you interfered."

"Go ahead and do your worst, Faulk," Guy challenged. "Your threats don't scare me."

"You're a fool," Faulk sneered. Before Guy had a chance to react, he leaped into the carriage, slapped the reins against the horse's rump and raced off. Guy watched him disappear down the alley, fearing he'd made a terrible mistake by letting the bastard live.

"Why did you do that?" Bliss cried on a note of panic. "You don't know what Gerald is capable of." Her voice became shriller and shriller. "You've ruined everything!"

Guy rounded on her. "You're my wife, Bliss. Did you think I'd just stand by and watch you leave with the bastard? Do you care nothing for our son?"

Bliss stared at him as if he'd just lost his mind. "Did you think I was going to leave you?"

"Drop the pretense, Bliss," he sneered. "I saw you myself. I watched you leave our bed with a carpetbag you'd apparently packed earlier in anticipation of your rendezvous with your lover."

"Lover! Oh, God. Please listen to me, Guy. You don't understand."

"I don't want to hear it, Bliss. I'm tired of your lies."

"You *have* to listen."

Her voice had become so loud Guy knew he had to get her back to the house before she became hysterical and awakened the neighbors. Sweeping her up into his arms, he carried her into the house, stopping briefly to retrieve the carpetbag from the bushes. He negotiated the stairs and entered their bedroom, refusing to listen to her pleas. Then he set her on her feet, struck a light to the branch of candles, and shoved the carpetbag into her arms.

"Here. Unpack your clothing. You're not going anywhere. At least not until our child is born. Then you can go wherever you please, without the baby, of course. Your inheritance will provide you and Faulk with a nice living."

Dumbfounded, she stared at the bag. "Clothing? Are you mad? I don't want Gerald Faulk. I'd never leave my baby."

"You could have fooled me," he sneered. "I just don't understand how you can want Faulk after what he did to you, to our son, to us. He's a sickness inside you, one that has no cure."

"Let me explain," Bliss pleaded. "It's not what you think."

"Nay. Don't say anything. I can't bear it."

He removed a clean shirt from the drawer and began to dress.

"Where are you going? It's the middle of the night."

"I have to get out of here. I won't be responsible for my actions if I remain. You don't want to see me when my temper explodes, and I'm so damn close right now I'm afraid I'll hurt you."

His face took on a hard-edged remoteness. He felt as if nothing she could say would ever make it right between them again. The ache inside him grew into a churning, grinding pain that he would carry with him the rest of his life. He couldn't look at Bliss, couldn't speak for fear of exploding into violence. He started to walk away, knowing that no matter the contempt in which he held Bliss, he would never hurt her or risk harming his babe.

"Where are you going?" Bliss repeated shrilly.

"I don't know. I can't stay here tonight. Do I need to hire a guard to make sure you don't trot off with Faulk the moment I'm gone?"

Bliss reeled beneath his harsh words. "I told you, it's not what you think. Don't go. Let me explain. Then you'll understand why—"

"Answer my question, Bliss. Do I need to hire a guard?"

"No! I'm not going anywhere. I never intended to leave."

He nodded curtly. "Very well. I'll leave you to your cold bed."

"Wait! When will you return?"

"When you see me."

Without a backward glance, he strode from the room.

Chapter Sixteen

Facing the stern visage of the captain of the City Guards, Gerald Faulk pounded his fist on the desk, trying to make his point and apparently not succeeding.

" 'Tis the truth, I tell you!" he sputtered. "Viscount Guy Hunter is the buccaneer known as Hunter. He's hand in glove with Jean Lafitte and the Brotherhood."

"That's a rather inflammatory remark, Mr. Faulk," the captain replied. "What proof do you have to substantiate your claim?"

"He was recognized by two sailors and identified as the infamous pirate. The buccaneer is alleged to have sent countless ships to the bottom of the sea. Believe me, Captain Fargo, Viscount Hunter and the pirate are the same man."

"Where are your two witnesses?" Fargo asked with obvious skepticism.

"They . . . er . . . that is, they declined to appear in person. But many of Hunter's victims have reported that he wears an eyepatch over his right eye. So does the viscount. What more proof do you need?"

" 'Tis a war injury, I hear," Fargo maintained. "See here, Mr. Faulk, I can't arrest a man for piracy without solid proof. Many men wear an eyepatch. The man is a viscount and I have no reason to doubt him. He has made some powerful friends since his arrival and is involved in business dealings with many of them. I could get into a lot of trouble for accusing an innocent man unjustly. Bring me proof and I'll be more than happy to arrest him."

"You're making a big mistake," Faulk blasted, furious. "Have you checked his credentials to see if he's who he claims to be?"

"There was no reason to doubt him. I repeat, unless you bring me positive proof, my hands are tied. If you'll excuse me, I have work to do."

Faulk fumed in silent indignation. There had to be some way to prove his claim. "One more thing," he said, earning a frown from the captain. "What kind of proof would you require?"

"A signed confession," Fargo suggested facetiously.

"Very well," Faulk said, "you'll have it."

His face set in determined lines, Faulk stomped away, leaving an amused Captain Fargo in his wake.

* * *

Bliss hadn't seen Guy since he'd left in a rage two days before. She was worried sick and was running out of excuses to tell Bryan when he asked about his missing papa. She hadn't expected Guy to be gone so long. She didn't think he'd be able to stay away from his son. When he returned, she vowed to make him sit down and listen to her, even if it meant she had to sit on him to hold him still.

It hurt to think that Guy trusted her so little. Hotheaded to a fault, Guy had jumped to conclusions and refused to hear her explanation. She couldn't imagine where he had slept the past two nights and didn't want to think about the places a man could spend a pleasant night. The city was filled with high-class brothels. For all she knew, Guy was keeping a beautiful quadroon mistress on Rampart Street.

Gerald Faulk hadn't returned after Guy had threatened him, but Bliss's greatest fear was that he had carried out his threat to expose Guy. She knew Faulk must be furious and that he probably hadn't wasted any time spilling his guts to the authorities. Her nerves were frazzled; every time she heard a noise on the street, she was sure it was the City Guard coming to arrest Guy.

It wasn't long before Mandy grew suspicious and confronted Bliss about Guy's continued absence. "What have you gone and done now, honey?" the old woman asked. "Look at you, yore a sight. I ain't never seen you so upset.

Where is that man of yores? He's been gone a mighty long time."

"I don't know where Guy is, Mandy. We had a terrible misunderstanding. Guy never gave me a chance to explain. I don't think I've ever seen him so angry."

Mandy took Bliss's hand and led her to a chair. "Sit down, honey. I'll fetch you a nice cup of tea and you can tell ole Mandy all about it."

Bliss composed her thoughts while Mandy went to fetch the tea. When she returned, she poured two cups of tea, sat down across from Bliss, and placed her feet on the footstool. "Now talk, Bliss."

Bliss related everything between sips of tea, until the whole mess was placed before Mandy. When she finished, Mandy shook her head and clucked sympathetically. "You done wrong not telling yore husband. That man looks like he can take care of himself. You gotta explain the minute he steps foot in the house. Don't let him go on thinking you betrayed him a minute longer than necessary. If he loves you like I think he does, he'll listen. Then everything will be fine again."

"That's good advice, Mandy, but Guy has to return before I can explain. And I have no idea where he is."

"He'll return, honey, trust me. That man loves you."

At the end of three hellish days, Guy's temper had cooled enough to allow him to face Bliss without blowing up. He had spent the first night following his abrupt departure in the carriage house. The next day he'd gone to visit the Lafitte brothers, hoping to find a place to stay with them. His search proved futile. The Lafittes were not at the Absinthe House, nor at their blacksmith shop, nor at Pierre's house. He learned from Pierre's mistress that the brothers had returned to Barataria to make ready for their weekly illegal auction held deep in the swamps at a place called "The Temple."

Since the Lafittes weren't available, Guy had rented a room at the Pontalba Arms and spent the following two nights trying to make sense out of Bliss's behavior. After a time, he'd begun to regret leaving without listening to Bliss's explanation. Nothing about the strange affair made sense.

Once his initial anger gave way to clearer thinking, Guy begun to suspect there was more to the midnight tryst between Faulk and Bliss than he'd supposed. He'd been a pirate too long to change overnight, and had reacted violently. At one time he would have heedlessly hacked down a man he considered his enemy. He'd been adversely affected by years of sinful living and had spilled a sea of blood, but he saw his willingness to let Faulk live as a positive step toward giving up his old way of life and embracing the new one.

Then he'd jumped to conclusions, judging Bliss without giving her a chance to explain. She'd begged him to hear her out, but his foul temper and distrustful nature had sent him into a rage. It was time now to return home and do what he should have done in the beginning. Listen and pass final judgment after he'd heard all the facts.

Grappling with his thoughts, particularly about the irreparable damage he might have done to his relationship with Bliss, Guy failed to notice the two seedy-looking men trailing him on the opposite side of the street. Nor did he see them cross the street and duck into an alley when he stopped to admire an attractive carving of a wooden horse in the mercantile window and ducked inside to buy it for Bryan.

Guy was smiling a few minutes later when he left the shop with the horse safely tucked under his arm. The last thing he expected was to be pulled into the alley and struck over the head with a stout cudgel. The package fell to the ground, he dropped to his knees, then fell flat on his face.

Bliss paced the drawing room like a nervous tigress. Mandy had been wrong, she silently lamented. Three days had passed without a word from Guy. She didn't know where to look or what to do. Her one consuming fear was that Guy had made his way to Barataria and returned to piracy, even though he'd vowed never to return to his former profession.

Bliss knew Guy loved Bryan; she couldn't conceive of him leaving the boy behind. Or abandoning the new babe she carried inside her. In fact, Guy was so possessive of his family, she couldn't imagine him giving up anything he considered his property. The only conclusion she could reach was that his misconception about her meeting with Gerald had sent him fleeing back to his former life.

Guy had been hurt so badly, she imagined it was difficult for him to trust again, but she hoped that once his temper cooled he would realize she wasn't capable of betrayal. The idea that she would take up with Gerald Faulk, a man she despised, was ludicrous.

God, where was he? Bliss wondered despairingly. Bryan had asked for his father so often she was running out of excuses. At first she'd been resentful of Guy's abandonment, but when she'd calmed down and considered his violent past, she blamed his behavior on those undisciplined years he'd spent engaged in piracy and seeking revenge for the injustices done him. She sighed wearily. She'd wait forever if that was how long it took for Guy to come to his senses and realize she loved him and no one else.

Guy regained consciousness slowly, painfully aware of his aching head and uncomfortable position. His back was to the wall and his wrists were bound, stretched above his head and attached to a hook. His feet barely touched the floor. Dim images began to form before his good eye, and what he saw did little to cheer him.

"Where am I?" he asked hoarsely.

"In my warehouse," Gerald Faulk said, stepping into Guy's line of vision.

Still groggy, Guy shook his head and was immediately sorry as pain pierced him from temple to temple. "What happened?"

"You're my guest for the time being."

Guy yanked on the ropes binding him. "Why am I fettered? What's going on, Faulk?"

"You don't know, do you? Did Bliss tell you nothing?"

"Dammit, Faulk, I've had enough of this foolishness. Tell me what's going on. But first, cut me down. This is damn uncomfortable."

Guy heard someone snicker and glanced in the direction of the sound. He immediately recognized two former crewmen.

"Are those two cutthroats your hirelings, Faulk?" Guy asked disparagingly. "I take it they did your dirty work for you. I suppose they told you who I was. I wouldn't trust them if I were you."

"See here, Hunter, we ain't no cutthroats," Monty claimed. "You had no right to punish us. All we wanted was our fair share of the plunder."

"I can see you're wondering how my association with these two came about," Faulk said. "I had a strong suspicion you weren't who you pretended but couldn't prove it. I put word out on the streets that I was paying for information about a man calling himself Viscount Guy Hunter. These two came forward."

"Why didn't you go to the authorities?" Guy spat.

Faulk shifted uncomfortably, and Guy could tell he was annoyed about something. "I did, but they wanted more proof than I could give them," Faulk groused. "Your title fooled them, but I'm not so gullible. If you hadn't interfered the other night, this wouldn't be necessary."

"I have no idea what you're talking about," Guy said as he tested the ropes binding his wrists to the hook. Whoever had tied him had done a good job.

"I visited Bliss the other day and told her I knew who you were. I threatened to expose you if she didn't turn over her inheritance to me."

"Bastard!" Guy snarled, pulling futilely on the ropes. "How dare you frighten my pregnant wife?"

Faulk laughed. "It worked. She got the money from the bank and would have delivered it to me if you hadn't come charging after her like a jealous husband. You shouldn't have interfered, Hunter. You forced me into this, you know."

Guy absorbed everything Faulk had just told him and came to a horrifying discovery. He'd wrongly accused Bliss of betraying him with Faulk. He'd been too hotheaded to listen to her explanation and had left in a fit of anger. Oh, God, he'd never forgive himself for hurting her. He prayed she would forgive him for acting the jealous fool and accusing her unjustly.

"So your little ploy was foiled and the authorities wanted solid proof of my identity,"

Guy taunted. "What now? How do you propose to obtain the proof you need?"

"You're going to sign a full confession," Faulk said smugly. "You've taken everything from me and I demand retribution. You're not leaving this room until I have what I want. You will acknowledge your identity and confess to the crime of piracy on the high seas. You will also acknowledge guilt for the plunder you've stolen and the lives you've taken. When I take you before the City Guards, I'll have all the proof I need to establish your identity. I'll be a hero."

Guy laughed, which seemed to enrage Faulk. "Don't hold your breath. I'm not going to sign a damn thing."

"Laugh all you want, Hunter. After my boys finish with you, you'll beg to sign, won't he, mates?"

"Aye," Monty and Squint said in unison. "Hunter left us to die on that island. And we nearly did before we were picked up by another ship."

"It's going to take more than a couple of scurvy water rats to make me do something I don't want to do," Guy said stubbornly.

"We'll see about that," Faulk sneered. "Squint, you first. See what you can do to make our guest tractable. I want that confession signed."

Squint's ugly features contorted into a grotesque smile. "Sure thing, Mr. Faulk. Leave Hunter to me. I'll have him willing to sign in no time."

He swaggered forward, taking a position before Guy. Faulk retreated out of harm's way, licking his lips in avid anticipation as Squint hauled his arm back and punched Guy in the gut. Guy barely had time to recover before Squint landed a fist in his face. After that it was all a blur as Squint aimed blow after blow to various parts of Guy's anatomy. Time hung suspended as the abuse continued, until Guy finally lost consciousness.

"Enough," Faulk said, stepping forward with a bucket of water. "Move away so I can douse him with water. Maybe he'll be ready to sign when he comes to."

Guy struggled upward though an ocean of water, unable to breathe, unable to move his arms so he could swim to the surface. He was drowning; his life was racing before him. Then he felt stinging blows to his face and realized he could breathe again. He opened his eyes and knew he was in hell. There wasn't a place on his body that didn't hurt.

"Ah, you're awake, good," Faulk said, gloating. "Have you had enough? Are you ready to sign now?"

"Got to hell!" Guy spat.

Faulk's eyes darkened with fury. "Very well, perhaps Monty can persuade you." He motioned the second pirate forward. "He's all yours, Monty. I hope you're better at persuasion than your friend."

Monty gave Guy a truly evil grin. "I got something here that's guaranteed to make Hunter agreeable," he said, slapping a riding crop against his palm. "Turn him around, Squint."

Faulk moved to help Squint. They loosened the rope just enough to enable them to turn Guy around to face the wall. Though Guy struggled valiantly, he was too weak from the previous beating he'd received to prevent the ropes from being tightened and reattached to the hook. He stiffened when he felt someone cut through his coat and rip apart his shirt.

"Should I begin?" Monty asked with an eagerness that made Guy begin to sweat.

"Wait!" Faulk said, stepping closer to peer at Guy's back. "This isn't the first time the bastard's been whipped. Look here. See those white lines crisscrossing his back? Want to tell us how that happened, Hunter?"

"Use your imagination," Guy said through clenched teeth.

"Go ahead, Monty, use the crop. It doesn't look like Hunter wants to cooperate."

Guy steeled himself for the first blow. It came swift and hard, followed closely by another, then another, until they were coming so fast he lost count.

"Are you ready to sign?" Faulk asked, apparently underestimating Guy's stubbornness.

"Go to hell," Guy grunted, nearly insensate with pain but determined to sign nothing.

The beating continued several minutes more, until Guy slumped against the ropes, oblivious to the brutal punishment he'd endured.

"Cease," Faulk ordered. "No sense continuing when he can't feel pain."

"You want me to douse him with water, Mr. Faulk?" Squint asked, reaching for the bucket.

"Nay, he's immune to beatings. There's got to be some other way to get what I want." Suddenly his expression brightened. "I know! Hunter is inordinately fond of his wife and her brat. If I can get them here, it would be just the kind of leverage I need to persuade Hunter to sign the confession."

"You want us to get them for ya, Mr. Faulk?" Squint asked. "That will cost ya more, but me and Monty are willing."

"I need some time to think this through," Faulk mused. "I'll be in my office if you need me. Stay here and watch Hunter. Don't do anything further until I tell you."

Faulk sat in his office at the front of the warehouse, pondering his problem. Hunter was proving to be uncooperative and obstinate, more so than he had anticipated. The pirate seemed inured to pain. Faulk wasn't thrilled with the prospect of killing Hunter, for that would prove nothing and could even land him in the Calaboso, a daunting prospect. Nay, his intent was to prove that Viscount Guy Hunter was an impostor, that he was Hunter the pirate, a man with a price on his head. The reward for Hunter's capture was bound to be a substantial one.

But Hunter's stubbornness and threshold of

pain were proving more troublesome than he'd anticipated. There had to be a solution to his dilemma, and Faulk suspected the answer lay with Bliss and her son. If he was correct in his thinking, Hunter would be willing to do anything to keep them safe.

Then it came to him. There was but one person who could bring Bliss and the boy here. Taking paper and ink from the drawer, he scribbled a note, then returned to the warehouse and gave it to Monty to deliver.

It was almost dark when Monty returned with Claude Grenville.

"Claude, I'm glad you came so quickly," Faulk said affably. "We need to talk."

Grenville appeared haggard, as if he had aged ten years in the past few weeks. "What's this all about, Faulk? Your note said it concerned Bliss. Have you seen her recently? She claims she doesn't want to see me again."

"As a matter of fact, I have," Faulk said.

"How is she?" Claude asked. "What do you know about this Viscount Hunter? Does Bliss love him?"

Faulk chose his words carefully, aware that Claude was too soft when it came to his daughter. If it wasn't for his urging, Claude would have let Bliss keep that brat she'd had with Guy DeYoung. His thoughts skidded to a halt, thinking it odd that Hunter and DeYoung shared the same name. Then he shrugged and turned his attention to the problem at hand.

"Listen carefully, Claude, I asked you to come

here because I need your help. The man who calls himself Viscount Hunter isn't who he pretends to be. He's the pirate known as Hunter. The same pirate who singled out our ships for attack and caused our financial ruin. He's the same man who held Bliss captive and is most probably the father of the child she's carrying."

Claude's expression was one of shock. "Bliss is pregnant? You knew that and were still willing to marry her?"

"Let me explain, Claude," Faulk said, sitting back in his chair with his fingers steepled before him. Then he proceeded to explain about the deal he had struck with Bliss and how Hunter had ruined his plans.

"My daughter must love this pirate," Claude mused thoughtfully.

"To her misfortune," Faulk said with derision. "Hunter is a wanted man. He wouldn't have come to New Orleans if not for Bliss. He even went to Mobile and got her son from Enos Holmes. The boy is with Bliss now."

Claude appeared stunned. "Bliss mentioned the boy in her letter, but I assumed he was the Viscount's son."

"No one but Hunter, Bliss, and myself know the child is actually Bliss's son by that fellow who died in the Calaboso six years ago."

"The fellow you had killed, you mean," Claude contended. "That wasn't my idea."

"Don't go soft on me now, Claude," Faulk said. "We're still going to come out of this with sufficient funds to reestablish our business."

"How do you propose to do that? I refuse to hurt Bliss again. I lost a daughter when I gave away my own flesh and blood. I committed a grave error in judgment; my daughter will never forgive me. If I had it to do over, I wouldn't have listened to you."

"It's too late for regrets now. I need your help. I've already gone to the authorities and exposed Hunter, but the fools require solid proof of his identity. The word of my two witnesses won't hold up against that of a viscount, so I'm determined to get a confession from Hunter. Unfortunately, the bastard is being obstinate."

Claude's eyes widened. "You can't mean . . . You haven't . . ."

"But I have," Faulk said, laughing at Claude's apparent shock. "Hunter is in my warehouse right now, tied up like a Christmas goose. In fact, he's in no condition to go anyplace anytime soon."

"You mean . . . torture?"

Faulk shrugged. "He has but to sign the confession and my men will stop. As I said before, he's being obstinate and no amount of . . . er . . . persuasion has changed his mind."

"What do you expect me to do?"

"Hunter needs a subtle nudge to make him amenable. If he thought harm might come to Bliss or the boy, I'm sure he'd see things my way. You are the only one who can bring Bliss to me without using force."

Claude leaped to his feet. "See here, Faulk, I refuse to place my daughter and her son in danger. I may not be the best of fathers but I love my daughter. I refuse to let you use her to get to Hunter."

"Sit down, Claude," Faulk cajoled. "I don't intend to hurt Bliss. Bringing her and the boy here is merely a ploy to show Hunter I mean business. Once he signs the confession, all we have to do is take him to the authorities and collect the reward. Afterward, you can press to have the marriage annulled and I can marry Bliss and claim her inheritance. It's the only way to save both of us from total ruination."

Claude appeared to be mulling over Faulk's proposition. "I want to see my daughter's husband before I make up my mind."

"Why?" Faulk asked suspiciously.

"I want to be able to tell Bliss her husband is alive and well. If she loves this pirate, she'll want to know he's alive, else you can kiss her fortune good-bye."

Faulk shrugged and stood up. "I don't suppose it will hurt. Follow me."

Claude was close on Faulk's heels as they left the front office and entered the yawning darkness of the empty warehouse. Faulk led him directly to a place sheltered by crates. Claude stopped abruptly when he saw two seedy characters beside a man hanging limply from a hook.

"Is he dead?" Claude asked in a hushed voice. "What in God's name have you done to him?"

"Naw, he ain't dead," Monty grunted. "He's

got a thick hide and the stubbornness of a mule."

"He's a close-mouthed bastard, all right," Squint agreed.

Claude approached Guy cautiously, his eyes drawn to the bloody stripes marring his back. "You had him whipped."

"He's a bloodthirsty pirate," Faulk said. "He's ruined us, Claude. You can't pity a man like that."

"He's my daughter's husband."

"So was that DeYoung fellow we got rid of."

"I didn't order his assassination," Claude argued. "That was your doing."

"That's water under the bridge," Faulk said, growing tired of Claude's whining. Guy chose that moment to groan and move his head. "As you can see, Hunter is still alive and breathing. I'm convinced that further punishment isn't going to loosen his tongue. We need Bliss and the boy, Claude. You're in too deep to pull out now. I suggest you cooperate."

"Are you sure you won't hurt them?"

"You have my word."

"I'll bring them on one condition. Don't inflict any more torture on Hunter."

"It wouldn't do any good if I did," Faulk said disgustedly. "The man is immune to pain. How soon can you have them here?"

"I don't know. It's too late to see her tonight. It's not going to be easy to convince her to come with me and bring the boy. Give me a couple of days."

"That's preposterous!" Faulk sputtered.

"You want Bliss, don't you?" Claude contended. "I'll need time to convince her to trust me. She doesn't think much of me now. And it will give Hunter time to heal somewhat, so she won't be shocked when she sees him. My daughter is no fool."

"Very well," Faulk grumbled sourly. "Don't let me down."

"I won't. Meanwhile, cut him down and give him food and water."

"I'll take it into consideration. You'd better go now. Bring Bliss and the boy here as soon as you can manage it."

Claude hurried off. There was much to be accomplished in the little time Faulk had allowed him.

Bliss felt the crushing weight of disappointment when Guy failed to return. She didn't even have friends or family to turn to for help. Earlier today she and Mandy had gone to the office Guy had rented on Royale Street, but he wasn't there. Furthermore, his secretary told her Guy hadn't been to his office in two days. He'd even missed an important meeting that morning.

Bliss began to suspect that something other than anger was detaining him. She imagined all kinds of dire circumstances that could have kept him away. She feared that Faulk had gone to the authorities, and that Guy had been taken to the Calaboso, but since she'd heard nothing about his arrest, she decided that wasn't the case. Nevertheless, Bliss had a frightening premonition that Faulk was behind Guy's prolonged absence.

"Yore gonna make yoreself sick, honey," Mandy said when she found Bliss pacing the drawing room. "Why don't you get some sleep? You gotta think about the babe."

"I couldn't sleep, Mandy. I know something terrible has happened to Guy. After his temper cooled he would have seen reason and come home to listen to my explanation. I don't know what to do or who to turn to for help."

"I wish there was something—" Her sentence was abruptly cut short by the sound of someone rapping furiously on the door. "Who would be calling at this time of night?"

"Guy!" Bliss cried, flying across the room. She reached the door, flung it open, and nearly collapsed in disappointment when she saw her father standing on the doorstep.

"Father, what are you doing here at this time of night? I thought it was—"

"You thought I was your husband," Claude said, pushing past her into the house. "We need to talk . . . in private."

Mandy bristled indignantly. "I ain't gonna leave her alone, Mr. Claude."

"It's all right, Mandy," Bliss sighed wearily. "I'll speak with Father in the library. See that we're not disturbed."

"I ain't going far," Mandy said tartly. "I'll be just outside the door."

"I don't blame you for not trusting me,

Mandy, but I'm here to help Bliss, not harm her."

Mandy gave a loud harrumph, apparently unimpressed.

"What is it you wish to say to me, Father?" Bliss asked once they had gained the privacy of the library. "I've got a lot on my mind right now."

"I know," Claude said, "and I'm sorry. I've not been a very good father to you. But I'm here to help now."

"Help?" Bliss asked cautiously. "What makes you think I need help?"

"I've just seen Gerald Faulk. He sent for me, insisting that I come to the city immediately. He wants me to bring you and the boy to his warehouse."

"Whatever for?" Bliss asked, thoroughly confused.

"Sit down, Bliss."

"I'll stand." Bliss knew she wasn't going to like what her father had to say. "Does this concern my husband?"

"Faulk is holding a man he insists is Hunter the pirate in his warehouse."

Bliss paled and staggered backward. Claude supported her weight as he guided her to a chair.

"What does he hope to gain by holding Guy prisoner?" Bliss asked shakily. "Faulk threatened to expose Guy to the City Guard. Why didn't he?"

"I understand Faulk *did* go to the City Guard,

but the authorities wanted proof before arresting a member of English nobility. Since he had no proof, Faulk had Hunter kidnapped, hoping to force him to sign a confession."

"Force him?" Bliss whispered, grimly aware of what her father implied. "Is Guy . . . ? Is he—"

"He's alive, Bliss, but we have to work fast if he's to remain that way. I've come to help you."

"Help me? Why would you do that?"

After a long pause, Claude said, "Whether you believe it or not, I love you."

Chapter Seventeen

"You love me?" Bliss repeated. Her voice was thick with scorn. "You have a funny way of showing it, Father."

"I don't blame you for hating me, daughter. I've done nothing to earn your forgiveness or your trust. I conspired to separate you and the man you loved, and then I took your child from you. You were so young. I wanted the best for you and thought Gerald Faulk would be the proper choice."

"You've never listened to me, Father. You've always thought of your own greedy needs. You took my husband and then my son from me. You and Gerald paid an assassin to kill Guy DeYoung."

Claude started violently. "Who told you that? Nay, Bliss, that was none of my doing. All I did was use my influence to keep DeYoung from being brought to trial. Faulk was the one who had DeYoung killed. He knew you'd never marry him while DeYoung lived. But I won't absolve myself of guilt, for I realize what I did was reprehensible."

"And yet you say you love me," Bliss scoffed.

"It's because I love you that I only pretended to agree to Faulk's plan to bring you and the boy to the warehouse. He intends to use you to coerce Hunter into signing the confession. I don't trust Faulk. He's become obsessed with money and blames your husband for bankrupting Faulk Shipping. I refuse to hurt you again, Bliss; that's why I'm here."

Bliss wanted to believe her father, but it was so difficult after the pain he'd caused her. "How do you propose to help? Have you seen Guy? Is he well?"

"There's no easy way to tell you, and I won't lie to you. Your husband has been severely beaten. But the beatings have stopped because Faulk thinks more desperate measures are necessary to get him to sign."

A choking sob rose up from Bliss's throat. "Oh, God, he's been hurt enough. How can I stop it?"

"I've bought you some time, daughter. Perhaps together we can find a way to free your husband. Do you love him so much?"

"Oh, yes, with all my heart."

Claude smiled. "I'm glad. 'Tis time you stopped mourning the young man you wed against my wishes. I'm happy you've found your son. I understand Hunter helped. I—" He hesitated. "Do you suppose I might meet him?"

Bliss stiffened, recalling all those empty years she'd thought both Guy and Bryan lost to her. Her father was to blame for all her anguish. Her father and Gerald Faulk. But he was still her father, so she searched her heart for a tiny spark of forgiveness . . . and found it. Faulk was not so lucky. She found nothing inside herself but contempt and hatred for Gerald Faulk.

"Do you really expect me to believe you wish to help me and Guy?" Bliss asked skeptically.

"I hoped you would. Does Hunter have friends in town who would be willing to help him? If not, we could appeal to the City Guard for help."

"Enlisting help from the City Guard is too risky. There is still a bounty on Guy's head. I'd hate for them to launch an investigation into his background."

"Guy," Claude mused thoughtfully. "That was DeYoung's given name."

Bliss's chin lifted defiantly. "Yes, it was." She said nothing more and Claude didn't ask. "To answer your first question, Guy has no close friends in New Orleans. He has business acquaintances, but no friends who would be willing to risk their lives for him. Unless . . . Of course," she cried, her eyes sparkling. "The Lafitte brothers! They would help if they were made aware of Guy's predicament."

"Aye, I'm sure of it," Claude concurred. "I've

heard the Brotherhood takes care of its own. Do you know where to find the Lafittes?"

"Handbills have been posted all over town advertising an auction to be held at 'The Temple' tomorrow. It was signed by both the Lafittes. Many people will be flocking to the site. Merchants, slave traders, all those interested in obtaining a bargain. I'll go to them and ask for their help. I only pray it won't be too late."

"I'll come with you."

"Very well, but I won't leave Bryan behind. Gerald might grow impatient and send his henchmen for him in my absence. I don't want Bryan to become their pawn."

"We'll leave first thing tomorrow," Claude said. "Shall we go by pirogue or carriage? Pirogue will be faster."

"Bryan will be with us; carriage is safer. Pray God the Lafittes will be there."

After Claude ate a late meal, they sought their separate beds. Bliss had no idea what had brought about her father's change of heart, but with Guy's life at stake, she had no other choice but to trust him.

The narrow, rutted road took them through marshland and ancient cypress trees whose gnarled roots protruded from the murky brown water like knobby knees. Theirs wasn't the only carriage on the narrow road, but one of a long line of many. Eerie fingers of mist lifted upward from the swamp, swirling through the trees and gilding the silvery Spanish moss hanging from their branches. Shadows and sunlight flirted with the mist, dancing from tree to tree in a breathtaking display of mystical beauty.

The road ended abruptly at a path composed of white shells. Carriages were parked haphazardly on whatever dry piece of land their drivers could find here at the edge of the marsh. Those who came on horseback had tethered their horses to tree limbs; already the path was crowded with people who had arrived early for the sale.

Bryan regarded the outing as a great adventure and danced excitedly around Bliss and Claude as they left the carriage and started down the path. Bryan had met his grandfather just this morning and apparently still hadn't reached a decision concerning his feelings for the older man, for he'd spoken hardly at all to Claude.

"Stay close to your grandfather and me," Bliss warned as Bryan skipped ahead of them.

Bryan gave Claude a considering look as he waited for them to catch up. "Is he really my grandfather, Mama?"

"He is indeed, Bryan."

"Why haven't I met him before? Didn't he want to see me?"

Bliss sighed. "It's a long story, son. I'll tell you when you're old enough to understand."

Bryan stared up at Claude, his expression mutinous. "Papa said Grandfather gave me away when I was a baby. I don't think I like him very much."

Claude winced as if in pain.

"I deserve your scorn, Bryan," Claude conceded. "What I did was wrong, and I'll understand if you never forgive me. But I want you to know I regret what I did. I want to make amends, even if it takes the rest of my life."

"It's going to take time, Father," Bliss said, speaking for both herself and Bryan. She couldn't speak for Guy. Guy had suffered intense physical pain and mental anguish because of her father.

The shell path led them deeper into the swamp, to an ancient Indian mound composed of white shells surrounded by live oak trees. The site was believed to have been the scene of human sacrifice when Indians gathered there in bygone years for ceremonies.

Now it was used by the Lafitte brothers as a storehouse and auction place for their illicit goods. A wide platform that extended over the shallow waters of the marshland had been built; and here the privateers unloaded their boats and spread out the contraband merchandise taken from prize ships and brought to Grande Terre for disposal. Standing to one side of the platform, a large group of male and female slaves waited for the auction to begin.

"Do you see Jean Lafitte?" Claude asked.

"No, not yet. He may still be on one of the boats," Bliss guessed.

"I've never been to one of these auctions before," Claude said, eyeing the large array of valuable merchandise on display. "I had no idea they were so well attended."

"Piracy pays very well," Bliss said grimly, recalling the chests of plate and specie Guy had shown her. At first she'd been disconcerted to realize they would be living off his ill-gotten gains, but when she recalled how Guy had been treated by Gerald and her father and more or less forced to join the Brotherhood, it no longer mattered.

"There's Lafitte now!" Claude said, pointing to a satin-and-brocade-clad man swaggering through the throng of people gathered for the auction.

Bliss had never seen Jean Lafitte up close and thought him handsome in a dandified sort of way. But she knew better than to judge him by his appearance. Guy had told her Lafitte could be vindictive and cruel toward those he considered enemies. Beneath Jean's handsome face and peacock-bright attire lay a dangerous, ruthless man. She hoped he considered Guy a friend.

"Stay here with Bryan while I go speak with Mr. Lafitte," Bliss said, steeling herself for the meeting.

Lafitte was speaking with a portly gentleman and his elegantly clad wife when Bliss approached. Lafitte must have seen her from the corner of his eye, for he excused himself and turned toward her.

"Mr. Lafitte," Bliss said hesitantly, "may I speak with you?"

Lafitte swept off his hat and executed a courtly bow. "Most certainly, mademoiselle. I never turn away a beautiful lady. What can Jean Lafitte do for you? Is there some item you covet and can't afford? Or a slave you fancy? Perhaps we can strike a bargain, eh?"

Despite Lafitte's unspectacular height, he was imposing. His elegant attire wasn't the only thing about him that was impressive. Sparkling dark eyes, shoulder-length black hair, and neatly trimmed mustache combined to make his darkly handsome features memorable. The cruelty just below the surface was clearly discernible, however, in the sardonic curl of his full upper lip.

"I'm not here for the auction, Mr. Lafitte," Bliss began nervously. "You don't know me, but you do know my husband. Guy speaks of you often."

Lafitte's dark brows drew together. "Your husband? I do not believe I know anyone named Guy. Please elaborate, madame."

Bliss cast a furtive glance at the people milling around them, and Lafitte correctly interpreted her need for privacy. "Walk with me toward the boats, madame, where we can speak without interruption."

Bliss gave him a grateful smile. "Thank you. I'd prefer to keep our conversation private."

"And so it shall be." He led her off to the boats, away from the crowd inspecting the merchandise. "Now, what can I do for you and your husband? You said I know him."

Bliss nodded eagerly. "You know him as Hunter."

Lafitte's expressive face registered surprise. "Indeed I do know Hunter." He looked past Bliss to where Bryan and her father stood waiting. "Ah, you've brought Bryan with you, I see. I carried both Bryan and his father to New Orleans aboard my ship. And you must be the woman he told me about. What kind of trouble has Hunter gotten himself into now?"

A delicate pink stained Bliss's cheeks. She wondered what Guy had told Lafitte about her. But she couldn't worry about that now; she had more important matters to deal with.

"I understand Guy has confided in you about his past." Lafitte nodded. "Do you recall his mentioning a man named Gerald Faulk?"

"*Oui*, I remember. Faulk hired an assassin to kill Hunter. If I didn't have a skilled surgeon on Grande Terre, Hunter would have died. Unfortunately the doctor wasn't able to save Hunter's eye. What has Faulk done now?"

"He has abducted Guy and is holding him prisoner in his warehouse."

"For what purpose?"

"He wants Guy to confess to being a pirate and has used torture to make him comply. Not only does he want to collect the bounty on Guy's head, but he intends to marry me after Guy is hanged for his crimes. He will use my inheritance to rebuild his business. I dare not appeal to the City Guard. Someone might get suspicious and investigate Guy's past."

"So you came to me for help," Lafitte said, stroking his mustache.

"There was no one else," Bliss choked out. "I can't lose Guy again. He's been severely beaten; God knows what condition he's in. He's a stubborn man, he'll never sign a confession."

"How do you know all this?" Lafitte asked, apparently unwilling to commit himself until he knew all the facts.

"Faulk sent for my father. Father was supposed to bring Bryan and me to the warehouse. Faulk intended to use us to make Guy sign the confession. Lord knows what Faulk would have done to us if Father hadn't had a change of heart and told me what Faulk intended."

"Hmmm, sounds suspicious to me," Lafitte mused. "Hunter told me your father was against your marriage, that both Grenville and Faulk planned his demise. Are you sure you can trust your father?"

"It was difficult at first, but I . . . I believe him," Bliss said, hoping she hadn't misplaced her trust. "He says he's sorry for hurting me and wants to make amends."

"What is it you wish of me?" Lafitte asked.

"I need your help to rescue Guy. Without a confession, Faulk can do nothing to hurt Guy, and Guy will never sign such a damning document. He'd die before bringing shame upon his family. The torture will continue and Guy could die. Will you help us?"

"Your Guy still belongs to the Brotherhood, despite the fact that he no longer plies his trade.

I will endeavor to rescue him because I hold a special fondness for your husband and son, madame. Do you have a plan?"

Bliss was so grateful, she wanted to fall on her knees and thank him but knew it would embarrass both of them. "I haven't planned beyond the fact that I want Guy rescued before it's too late," Bliss said.

"Let me find Pierre and explain things to him," Lafitte said. "He can handle things here while I return to Grande Terre for my ship. You will accompany me, of course. We can discuss plans as we travel down the canal to Barataria."

"What about Father and Bryan?"

"Bring Bryan. 'Tis best he's not left in the city where Faulk can find him. We don't know to what lengths Faulk is willing to go to make Hunter sign the confession."

"And my father?" Bliss asked.

"Does Faulk still believe your father is doing his bidding?"

"Father thinks so. There is something else that might be helpful. Faulk thinks Guy and I had a . . . misunderstanding shortly before Guy was abducted."

Lafitte thought a moment, then said, "Send your father back to the warehouse. Tell him to say that you refused to accompany him to the warehouse because you're angry and don't care what happens to your husband. That ploy might confuse Faulk, or send him searching for another way to force Guy to sign."

"Faulk will resort to more torture," Bliss

whispered shakily. "I don't want Guy to suffer any more than he already has."

"It's a chance we'll have to take."

"Very well," Bliss agreed worriedly. "I'll speak to Father."

"Meet me back here with Bryan. We'll take one of the pirogues back to Grande Terre for my ship. By tomorrow night you'll have your husband back or my name isn't Jean Lafitte. I assume you know where Faulk's warehouse is located."

"Yes, but I'll ask Father for directions just to make sure."

"Ah, there's Pierre," Lafitte said, raising his hand to hail his brother. "Go and speak to your father, madame."

Bliss allowed Bryan to inspect a table laden with merchandise while she pulled her father aside to speak with him in private.

"Mr. Lafitte is going to help us, Father," Bliss said in a hushed voice. "Bryan and I will accompany him to Grande Terre and sail aboard his ship to New Orleans. I don't know how he intends to rescue Guy, but he seems confident."

"He can do it if anyone can," Claude said sagely. "What am I to do in the meantime? Shall I accompany you to Grande Terre?"

"No, Mr. Lafitte wants you to return to the warehouse and tell Faulk you couldn't persuade me to accompany you. He knows Guy and I had a misunderstanding a few days ago. Try to convince Faulk that I don't care what happens to Guy. Lafitte thinks that ploy will throw Faulk's plans into disarray. But I'm afraid, Father. What if he resumes his torture of Guy?"

"Your husband is a strong man. He'll survive. Meanwhile, I'll attempt to alert him to the rescue attempt."

"That's what Mr. Lafitte had in mind. Oh, Father, don't let them kill Guy. I love him so much."

"More than Guy DeYoung?"

"Yes, more than Guy DeYoung."

It was true, she realized. She'd loved the youthful Guy DeYoung with the budding love of an immature girl. What she had with Guy Hunter was a deep, enduring love, a love with none of the giddiness or uncertainty of youth.

"I'll do what I can, Bliss," Claude promised. "Trust me."

Bliss kissed him on the cheek. "Thank you, Father. Tell me exactly where to find Guy before I collect Bryan and join Mr. Lafitte."

Claude gave Bliss specific directions and watched as she and Bryan climbed aboard the pirogue. Then he returned to the carriage for his trip back to the city.

Guy felt as if his back were on fire. His gut ached and he knew his face must look a bloody, swollen mess. His eyepatch had become dislodged and with his hands tied behind him, he hadn't been able to push it back into place.

Guy remembered little of what had happened after he'd passed out, except that he could have sworn he'd heard Claude Grenville's voice. Just what I need, he thought as he shifted uncomfortably on the cold damp floor, another of my enemies joining the game.

Guy shifted again, groaning when his raw back scraped against the wall upon which he was leaning. He saw Squint and Monty watching him as they ate the food Faulk had brought them. His mouth watered hungrily but he wouldn't give them the satisfaction of asking for something to eat.

Faulk had been in earlier, demanding that he sign the confession, and had left in a rage when Guy once again refused to sign. But Guy expected him back, for he never stayed away long. As if that thought had conjured up his image, Faulk stalked into the warehouse from his office. He wasn't alone. Claude Grenville was with him, and they appeared to be arguing about something.

Guy listened intently to the angry words flying back and forth between his captors. His attention sharpened when he heard Bliss's name mentioned.

"Damn you, Claude! I can't trust you to do anything. What in the hell am I going to do now? Without Bliss and the boy, Hunter will never agree to sign the confession. We're paupers, Claude! I hope you like the feeling."

"You may be a pauper, Gerald, but I'm not," Claude asserted. "I've found a buyer for my plantation. I sold it lock, stock, and barrel. The new owner wanted it so badly that he paid off the note at the bank and gave me enough money to buy a small place in town."

"Bastard," Faulk hissed. "There is no hope of finding a buyer for my home, it was repossessed by the bank yesterday. I was allowed to take nothing but my clothing and a few personal items. I've been reduced to living in a single room at the Pontalba Arms."

"I'm sorry, Gerald," Claude said.

"Not sorry enough, apparently. I'm without funds, ruined, and it's all that bastard's fault," he raged, stabbing a finger at Guy. "I asked one little thing of you, Claude, and you failed me. Didn't you impress upon Bliss the importance of accompanying you here? Did you tell her that her husband's life depended upon her cooperation?"

"Apparently they had a falling out. Bliss doesn't seem to care what happens to him," Claude claimed.

"Am I going to have to storm Bliss's house and take her and that brat by force?" Faulk threatened.

Guy came to life when he heard the threat. "Touch one hair on their heads and you're a dead man, Faulk!"

Faulk aimed a vicious kick at Guy's ribs, laughing when Guy grunted in pain and doubled over. "You're in no position to make threats, Hunter. I'm desperate. The bounty I collect for you will enable me to reclaim my plantation from the bank. I'm going to enjoy seeing you hang for your crimes. Bliss will be a widow, and I'll claim both Bliss and her inheritance after you're dead."

Guy gave a wobbly smile. "You have to have proof first, and I'm not in the mood to sign a confession."

"You will be when I return with Bliss and her son. I think you'd do anything to protect them," he said slyly. "I'd hate to have to hurt them, but you're giving me no choice."

Guy tried to surge to his feet, but Faulk pushed him back down. "Damn you! How dare you threaten my family?" He directed a malevolent glare at Claude. "What kind of father are you?"

"Claude will do as I say, Hunter," Faulk claimed. "Don't expect help from him."

Claude flushed but said nothing.

"Monty and I should encounter no trouble gaining entrance to the house. You can be damn sure I'll have Bliss and her son with me when I return. You wouldn't like to see them hurt, would you? I predict you'll be eager to sign that confession."

"What do you want me to do?" Claude asked.

"Stay here and keep Squint company. You can help him guard Hunter. If I'm not back tonight, you and Squint can bed down on the pallets I've provided."

"I'm sick of this warehouse," Squint grumbled after Faulk departed. "I ain't had a drink in three days, or a woman in longer than that. And I ain't seen any of that blunt Faulk promised."

Suddenly Claude saw a chance to redeem himself in his daughter's eyes. "Why don't you go out and have a little fun, Squint? I'll take care of things here while you're gone."

Claude allowed himself to hope as Squint considered his suggestion. But Squint must have thought better of it, for he shook his head, shattering Claude's hopes.

"Naw, Faulk wouldn't like it. When the woman and kid gets here, Hunter will sign quickly enough, and I'll have money in my pocket again."

Claude's mind worked furiously. There had to be some way to let Guy know help was on the way.

Guy listened to the conversation in grim silence. He'd been jubilant when Claude had returned without Bliss and Bryan and was proud of her gumption. Refusing to accompany her father to the warehouse had been a gutsy move on her part. He didn't even care that Bliss hadn't come to his aide because she was angry with him. He applauded her stubbornness even though it meant she hadn't forgiven him.

Guy saw Claude rise and approach him, bracing himself for further abuse. Since his capture he'd been kicked, punched, and whipped. He suspected Claude wanted his turn.

"What are ya gonna do?" Squint asked when he saw Claude crouch down before Guy.

"Spit in his face," Claude said, pretending anger.

"Be my guest," Squint guffawed as he turned back to the meal.

Claude hawked up a wad of spittle and made a noise with his mouth, pretending to let it fly into Guy's face. Guy flinched, but his eye narrowed in surprise when his face remained undefiled.

Then he saw Claude stiffen and stare at his face as if he'd just seen a ghost. What Claude did next utterly baffled Guy. He bent low and whispered, "Be prepared. Help is on the way."

"What?"

"Bliss and Bryan are safe. Jean Lafitte is—"

His sentence ended abruptly as Squint lurched to his feet and stalked over to them. "What are you two jabbering about? Get away from him, Grenville."

"I was cursing him," Claude improvised.

"Didn't sound like no cursing to me," Squint muttered.

Claude rose reluctantly, trying to convey a silent message to Guy with his eyes.

The look Guy returned gave no indication that he had understood Claude's communication. Actually, Guy had heard every word.

Guy had distinctly heard Claude mention Lafitte before his words had been abruptly cut off by Squint. Where did Lafitte fit into the scheme of things? Nothing made sense.

"Grenville," Guy called out to the older man. "What did Bliss say when you told her my life was in danger?"

"She said she didn't care what happened to

you," Claude replied. "What did you do to my daughter to make her so angry?"

"It was a small misunderstanding," Guy explained.

Guy found it impossible to believe Bliss cared so little for him. Nay, that didn't make sense at all. Bliss loved him, he had to believe that. He had hurt her, he knew, but he prayed that Bliss realized he'd been speaking from anger and jealousy the night they had argued.

That thought gave him small comfort as he fretted over the possibility that Faulk might actually hurt Bliss and Bryan should he refuse to sign the confession. He felt so damn helpless.

Without Bliss and his son, life wouldn't be worth living.

Chapter Eighteen

Faulk burst into the warehouse the following day in a rage. Monty followed close on his heels, looking as disgruntled as Faulk. Faulk marched directly to Guy and gave him a vicious kick in the ribs.

Guy groaned as he heard a loud crack, and pain exploded through him. He knew that at least one and maybe two ribs had fractured beneath Faulk's booted foot. But the pain wasn't nearly as great as his relief. He'd fretted most of the night, fearing that Faulk's plan to abduct Bliss and Bryan would succeed. Seeing Faulk arrive without either of them made him jubilant, despite the punishment he knew he'd have to endure because of it.

"She's gone!" Faulk ranted. "We broke into the house after all the lights went out and found the family bedrooms empty. We waited outside the house for Bliss to return, but she never showed up. We remained until it became obvious that she wasn't coming back."

"I'm glad," Claude contended, thankful that Bliss and Bryan were with Lafitte. "I can't bear the thought of having my daughter hurt again."

Faulk turned on Claude, his face ugly in his rage. "This is your fault, Claude! You should have forced Bliss and the boy to accompany you here. Instead, you let her slip out of our hands. How in the hell am I supposed to convince Hunter to sign the confession without proper inducement? He would have agreed to anything to keep Bliss and the boy safe. You're just a maudlin old man who can't control his own daughter."

"Perhaps you should let Hunter go," Claude suggested.

"Let him go! Are you crazy? He'd kill me without the slightest hesitation." A nerve twitched in Faulk's jaw and his eyes burned with rage. "Either Hunter signs the confession and dances at the end of a rope or he dies right here in my warehouse."

He glowered at Guy. "What's it to be, Hunter?" he asked, his voice raising shrilly. "Are you going to sign or shall we commence with the flogging?"

"Go to hell!" Guy gasped. "I'll never sign that damning piece of paper."

"String him up, boys," Faulk ordered.

"Now yer talking, Mr. Faulk," Monty said as

both he and Squint hastened to obey. They hefted Guy to his feet and attached his bound wrists to the hook, turning him to face the wall. Then Monty smiled and reached for the riding crop, slapping it against his palm with resounding menace.

Claude stepped forward in a last-ditch effort to stop them. "The man has suffered enough. You've already proved that torture isn't going to change his mind."

"He hasn't suffered nearly enough," Faulk snarled. "He's sunk my ships, stolen my cargoes, and put me out of business. I still don't know why he singled my ships out for attack when ships from other lines got through unscathed."

"Don't you?" Claude asked cryptically.

Guy listened to all this through a haze of pain. His arms were leaden, his back was on fire, and his ribs were a constant ache within his chest. But he was lucid enough to hear and wonder about Grenville's statement. It sounded as if Grenville was actually arguing for his life; strange behavior for someone who had once wanted nothing more than to be rid of him.

"We're ready, Mr. Faulk," Monty said, swishing the riding crop back and forth through the stagnant air.

Faulk sent a threatening glance at Claude. "I'll take care of you later. Proceed, Monty," he ordered, turning back to Guy with a malevolent smile.

Guy sucked in his breath, waiting, wondering

how long he could endure another flogging without passing out. His teeth and fists were clenched, his eyes tightly closed when the first stroke whistled through the air and landed on his back. He bit his bottom lip nearly through to keep from crying out. The next stroke dragged a groan from him, and after that he lost count.

The pain . . .

His body was a throbbing pillar of agony, no longer human, not yet dead. Then the beating stopped and he was swallowed by blessed darkness.

Night had fallen when the *Carolina* slipped into a berth beside the quay. Jean Lafitte was at the helm, maneuvering the ship into place. Bliss stood on the prow with Bryan, watching anxiously as the ship completed the docking process. She had argued that she should accompany Lafitte to Faulk's warehouse, but Lafitte had flatly refused, insisting that she remain safely aboard his ship with Bryan. Bliss didn't know how she would bear the waiting, but for Bryan's sake she knew she must.

When the docking was complete, Lafitte materialized at her side. He no longer appeared the dandy. He looked deadly and dangerous; armed to the teeth with sword and pistols.

"I'm taking two men," Lafitte said. "More than that will bring the City Guard out. The governor has banned Baratarians from the city. Unfortunate deaths have occurred during free-for-all fights with Mississippi flatboatmen and Kaintucks. Robberies and fires have been blamed on my men whether or not they are responsible, and the citizens of New Orleans have asked the governor to bar Baratarians from entering the city."

He gave a snort of disgust. "The citizens buy our goods, yet clamor to have us declared outlaws. Pierre and I are still welcome in some of the best homes, but we cannot enter the city without an outcry being raised. 'Tis best to keep my nocturnal visit as quiet as possible."

"I wish I were going with you," Bliss sighed. "I'm so worried about Guy. Father said he's been severely beaten by Faulk's henchmen."

"Fear not, madame, your husband will be with you soon. If he is not in good health, I will personally see to Gerald Faulk's punishment."

Bliss watched in hopeful anticipation as two stalwart pirates joined Lafitte and descended the gangplank. Moments later they reached the levee and blended into the shadows. Faulk's warehouse was built opposite the levee, and Bliss knew it wouldn't take long for Lafitte to locate it. And even less time for the pirate to rescue Guy from the three men holding him prisoner.

"Do you think Mr. Lafitte can find Papa?" Bryan asked after the men had melted into the night.

"I'm sure of it," Bliss said, trying to remain cheerful for Bryan's sake.

"I hope Papa is all right."

"I'm sure he is, love."

"Why would anyone want to hurt Papa?" Bryan wondered.

"There are bad men all over the world," Bliss said for lack of a better explanation. "Think good thoughts. Papa will be back with us soon."

Bliss wanted to protect her son from any ugliness that might occur and thought it best to send him below to the cabin until everything was resolved and Guy was back safely. She spotted Dobbs, Lafitte's young cabin boy, and called to him.

Dobbs hastened forward. "What can I do for you, ma'am?"

"Please take Bryan below, Dobbs. There must be something down there to keep him occupied."

"Aye, ma'am," Dobbs said, taking Bryan's hand and leading him off despite the boy's protests.

Once Bryan was gone, Bliss turned her gaze toward the shore, worry etching her smooth brow. By now Lafitte and his men would be at the warehouse, and she uttered a prayer for their success.

Guy had regained consciousness but remained still. He'd been released from the hook and was now lying on the floor. He opened his good eye. It was night. He knew it because of the blackness reflected against the high windows and the circle of candlelight spilling over the men seated on the floor with their backs resting against a stack of crates.

He saw Monty and Squint and Claude, but not Faulk. He turned his head slightly, felt the abused muscles of his neck and shoulders protest, and stifled a groan as pain exploded through him. His hands felt like chunks of raw meat attached to his arms. He lay motionless, resting and regaining his strength, painfully aware that the beatings would begin again when Faulk returned.

Time passed slowly. His eye half closed, Guy watched the three men, waiting for someone to make a move. He was surprised when he saw Claude rise cautiously and move toward him. Guy waited with bated breath, expecting Monty or Squint to interfere, and was grateful when they didn't.

"They're sleeping," Claude whispered, squatting down beside Guy. When he brandished a blade before Guy's face, Guy feared his days on earth were about to end. He released a long-drawn-out sigh when Claude merely slit the ropes binding his wrists together.

Blood rushed to his arms and hands. The pain was excruciating, but Guy gritted his teeth and flexed his fingers until the pain subsided somewhat.

"Why are you doing this?" Guy asked hoarsely.

"For my daughter. To atone for all the pain and heartache I've caused. 'Tis only right that you and Bliss should be allowed to raise your son together."

The breath slammed from Guy's lungs. "You know?"

"Apparently Faulk didn't recognize Guy DeYoung, but I did," Claude confided. "Oh, not immediately. It wasn't until your eyepatch slipped that I recognized you."

Guy was stunned; then he became angry. "Am I to believe that you suddenly regret what you did seven years ago?" he asked sardonically. "I find that hard to credit. You wanted me dead badly enough to hire an assassin to kill me. Why the sudden change of heart?"

"I had nothing to do with the assassin," Claude claimed. "Left to me, I would have had the marriage annulled right after the child was born and forgotten about you. But Faulk wasn't satisfied with that. He wanted you permanently done away with so Bliss would be free to turn her affection elsewhere."

"You gave our son away," Guy hissed.

"Aye, I'm guilty of that and deeply regret hurting both Bliss and the boy. I've met Bryan. He's a fine lad despite the difficulties he's encountered during his young life. Bryan knows what I've done to him, and I hope one day he'll find it in his heart to forgive me."

Guy sat up gingerly, flexing his hands, heartened when he felt mobility returning.

"You're free. Can you walk?"

"I think so. Do you have a weapon?"

"Nay, just the blade I used to free you."

"Give it to me. I might need it."

"You're in no condition to make it out of here on your own. Listen," Claude said, leaning close, "there's a plan afoot. Help is on its way."

Guy gave him a puzzled look. "Help? What are you talking about? Who would risk his life in my behalf? Help me up; Faulk might return at any time."

"Please, Guy, listen to me for once."

"There's no time. Just promise me you'll keep Bliss and Bryan safe from Faulk if I don't make it."

"You have my promise," Claude said, "but there's no need—"

The sound of approaching footsteps brought Claude's words to an abrupt halt. Both men turned in the direction of Faulk's office.

"Damnation!" Guy hissed as he returned to his position on the floor and thrust his arms behind his back as if they were still bound. "It's Faulk. Quick. Get back to your place."

"What are you doing there, Claude?" Faulk roared as he stormed into view.

"Just wanted to see if he was still alive," Claude said, scuttling away.

"Wha . . . What's the matter?" Monty asked, blinking awake.

"I thought I told you to stay awake," Faulk groused. "I'm not paying you to sleep."

"We gotta sleep sometime, Mr. Faulk," Squint muttered, rubbing sleep from his eyes.

Faulk's attention turned to Guy. "Any trouble from Hunter?"

"Naw, he ain't moved a muscle. We ain't been sleeping long, I swear it. Ya want us to flog him again?"

Faulk didn't answer. Instead, he walked over to Guy and poked him with his foot. "Wake up, Hunter. Shall Squint begin the flogging again? Or are you finally ready to cooperate?"

Hunter pushed himself up, resting his back against the wall as he glared up at Faulk. "Do your worst, Faulk, I'm not signing a damn thing."

Guy grew apprehensive when Faulk leaned closer to stare at his face. He knew his eyepatch was no longer in place. Faulk said nothing for a very long time. Then Guy saw Faulk's eyes narrow in sudden comprehension, and he realized that Faulk had finally guessed his secret. Faulk's hand streaked aggressively forward and Guy flinched, assuming that Faulk meant to strike him. But Faulk had other intentions. With a flick of his wrist, Faulk ripped off Guy's eyepatch and flung it away.

"Good God! I know who you are!" Faulk shouted. "You should be dead. How in hell did you escape the assassin? Who is buried in your grave?"

"The assassin you sent to kill me," Guy said, smiling despite the twinge of pain it caused. "A fitting end for him, wouldn't you say?"

"It will give me great pleasure to finally put you in that grave where you belong," Faulk said, drawing a pistol from his pocket and aiming it at Guy's heart. "Say your prayers, Guy DeYoung. You're a hard man to kill."

Two things happened at the same time. The gun discharged into the air as Guy kicked it from Faulk's hand, and three armed men burst into the warehouse.

"Where are you, *mon ami*?" called a voice that Guy recognized instantly.

"Lafitte!" Guy called out. So that was what Claude had been trying to tell him.

Faulk, stunned by Lafitte's unexpected visit and determined to end Guy's life, grasped the hilt of his sword and pulled it free from the scabbard strapped to his waist. Guy barely had time to fend off Faulk's initial attack as he rolled sideways, causing Faulk's blade to thud into the floor scant inches from his head. Then he brought his arms from behind his back, wielding the short blade Claude had given him. It was woefully inadequate compared to Faulk's more substantial sword, but it was all Guy had.

Faulk raised the sword and launched another attack. Guy dodged and slashed forward with his own blade, groaning when his cracked ribs protested the sudden movement.

"How in the hell did you get loose?" Faulk hissed. "Nay, don't tell me. 'Twas Claude, wasn't it? As soon as I'm finished with you, I'll take care of him."

Guy was far too occupied to answer. But he wasn't the only one fighting for his life. From the corner of his eye he saw Squint and Monty leap to their feet to defend themselves against

Lafitte and his men. They fought a losing battle. Within minutes the two had been cut down and lay on the floor in a widening circle of blood.

"I'm coming, *mon ami*, hang on," Lafitte cried as he rushed to Guy's defense.

"Nay, stand back!" Guy warned as he leaped aside to parry Faulk's next blow. "I've waited too long for this moment. Faulk is mine."

"Be careful, *mon ami*," Lafitte cautioned. "You look as if you've gone through hell. Here," he said, tossing Guy his own trusty blade, "use this."

Guy caught the sword handily, then spun around to deflect Faulk's upward thrust. The sudden pain caused by the sharp movement brought a grimace to his face, but he gritted his teeth and concentrated on Faulk's next move. Guy knew he was courting death by taking on Faulk in the condition he was in, but the thought of someone other than himself killing Faulk was objectionable.

Guy could tell that Faulk was growing desperate. His movements were jerky, his expression one of unrestrained hatred. And he looked frightened.

Guy felt himself tiring, but he refused to give up. He was weak and hurting and hungry enough to eat sawdust, but he knew that somewhere inside himself he'd find the strength to defeat his avowed enemy. He'd waited seven long years for this day, and now revenge was his. That thought empowered him as nothing else could.

Guy's good eye followed the erratic path of Faulk's blade, waiting for the moment Faulk lowered his guard so he could deliver the lethal blow. The opportunity came abruptly when Faulk crouched and feinted, preparing to sink a killing thrust into Guy's gut.

"Die, you one-eyed bastard!" Faulk screamed as he lunged forward for the kill.

Guy saw it coming, prepared for it, and retaliated with deadly accuracy. He danced sideways and sucked in his gut as Faulk's blade missed him by scant inches. While Faulk was still in a forward lunge, Guy brought his sword around and upward, sinking it into Faulk's left shoulder, just above his heart. He'd aimed for Faulk's heart, but Faulk's momentum had carried his body lower than Guy had anticipated and he'd missed his mark. Faulk's blade clattered to the floor as he clutched his shoulder and staggered backward.

"Will you finish him off, *mon ami*," Lafitte asked in a bored voice, "or shall I?"

Guy stared down at Faulk. He had fallen to his knees, head bowed, blood running through his fingers onto the floor, and suddenly Faulk's death no longer seemed important. All Guy wanted was to find Bliss and Bryan, take them home and spend the rest of his life with his family. Since giving up piracy he'd not taken a life, nor done anything else that would shame his children. And now, after years of patience, of playing cat and mouse with Faulk's ships, he couldn't kill the man in cold blood and still expect Bliss and Bryan to respect him.

"I'm finished with killing, Jean," Guy said wearily. "Faulk's death will bring me no honor. I'm free now. Look at him. He's a defeated man. He may even die of his wounds."

"Are you sure?" Lafitte asked. "It would take little effort to end his miserable life."

"I'm sure. Thank you for coming to my rescue. Even if I had slain Faulk, Monty and Squint wouldn't have allowed me to live. You arrived in the nick of time. How did you know where to find me?"

Suddenly Claude stepped out from behind a crate, where he had watched the one-sided battle from a safe distance. "Bliss and I traveled to 'The Temple' to find Lafitte," he explained. "We had no one else to turn to."

"This was Bliss's doing?" Guy said, stunned. "After the way I treated her, I didn't think she'd ever want to see me again."

"Bliss never stopped loving you, Guy DeYoung," Claude said. "I'm glad you found one another again. I want my daughter to be happy, and if you're the man she wants, I'll not interfere this time. There have been too many lies, too much sadness in her short life."

"Let's get out of here," Lafitte said. "Your wife is waiting for you aboard my ship. She has probably chewed her fingernails to the quick by now." He placed an arm around Guy's shoulder.

"Let me help you, *mon ami*. You don't look too well."

"Truth to tell, Jean, I feel like hell." The swordplay with Faulk had exhausted him. His entire body was a mass of pain, and he didn't even remember having lost his eyepatch when Faulk had ripped it away.

"Let's go," Lafitte said, supporting a staggering Guy as they left the carnage behind.

Still very much alive, Faulk lifted his head, his eyes glittering with rage as he watched the men walk away, leaving him to die. But he wasn't going to die, he vowed. His wound was serious, not fatal. He rose, swayed unsteadily, then seemed to rally. All his woes had begun and ended with Guy DeYoung, and this time he intended to put Guy DeYoung back in the grave where he belonged.

Faulk had more on his mind than Bliss or money. Nothing less than DeYoung's death would satisfy him now. This time he'd make damn certain the man met his maker. But first he needed to tend to his wound before he bled to death. He removed his coat and shirt with difficulty, made a pad of his shirt, and pressed it against the wound above his heart. Then he pulled on his jacket and buttoned it. The tight garment held the compress firmly in place, effectively stanching the bleeding. Satisfied with his handiwork, Faulk found his sword on the floor and staggered out of the warehouse.

* * *

Bliss paced the deck, peering into the misty darkness for a glimpse of Lafitte and Guy, praying unceasingly for Guy's well-being. Anxiety gnawed at her as long, fretful minutes passed, turning into a half hour, then an hour. Suddenly the watch gave a shout and Bliss's heart nearly thudded to a stop when she saw five dark figures emerge from the dark shadows and approach the ship.

She recognized Guy immediately. He was leaning heavily upon Lafitte, their steps slow and deliberate. She watched with trepidation as Lafitte gently lowered Guy to a crate while the others, save for her father who remained behind, continued on to the ship. Bliss ran to the gangplank to await the arrivals, blood roaring in her ears, her heart beating a wild tattoo.

The two pirates who had accompanied Lafitte ashore hit the deck first. Lafitte followed close behind. Bliss would have flown down the gangplank to Guy if Lafitte hadn't grasped her arm to stop her.

"A word first, madame," Lafitte said. "Your father is with Hunter, or Guy, if you will. He's in no danger of dying but he's in need of a doctor's care. Perhaps you should consider returning to Barataria with me and letting my surgeon see to him. The choice is yours. I didn't want to bring him aboard until I knew your preference."

Bliss swallowed past the lump growing in her throat. "How badly is he hurt?"

Lafitte shrugged. "His back will need attention. Faulk became overzealous with the whip."

"There's more," Bliss guessed, reading between the lines.

"He may have a cracked rib or two. And don't be shocked by the swelling around his eyes and cheekbones. There's nothing that won't heal with time."

"I don't know how to thank you," Bliss said tearfully. "What about Gerald Faulk? Is he . . . ?"

"He was still alive when we left the warehouse. I would have run him through, but your husband wouldn't let me. When we left, he was bleeding rather profusely from a wound delivered by your husband. I don't know where Hunter found the strength, but he performed magnificently."

"I should like to return home, Mr. Lafitte," Bliss decided. "Mandy has considerable knowledge of healing, and since Guy has no serious wounds, we will trouble you no further."

"As you wish. Do you need help?"

"I'll send Father for a hackney. Our home isn't far from here; we can even walk if need be. I'm going down to Guy now. Would you send Bryan to us? We'll wait for him on the levee."

"I'll send him down with Dobbs," Lafitte said. "Adieu, madame. Should we meet again, I hope it will be under happier circumstances."

He kissed her hand and went below for Bryan. Bliss paused at the top of the gangplank and gazed down at Guy. He saw her and rose slowly, as if movement pained him. Then he started forward to meet her. Claude made as if to follow, but Guy said something to him, and he turned and walked down Market Street. To hail a hackney, Bliss supposed.

Bliss's heart sang with joy as each step carried her closer to Guy. Guy appeared to gain strength and his steps seemed to drag less as he walked up the gangplank to meet her. They met in the center, and suddenly she was in Guy's arms, crying and laughing at the same time.

"Are you all right?" Bliss asked, tears streaming down her cheeks.

"I am now," Guy said on a ragged breath. "I'm sorry, Bliss. Can you ever forgive me? I was a jealous fool for not trusting you. I would have returned and told you sooner, but I became careless and let myself be taken by Faulk's men."

"Don't explain, Guy, it's not necessary. I know you love me as much as I love you."

"You're a wise woman, Bliss DeYoung. Shall we get our son and go home?"

He hugged her again, as if loath to let her go. Bliss hugged him back, too choked for coherent speech. Through a veil of tears, she happened to glance over Guy's shoulder and saw a figure detach itself from the shadows and walk toward them. At first she thought her father had found transportation and was coming to tell them. She looked away a moment as she disengaged herself from Guy's arms.

"I think Father has returned," she said, glancing back at the approaching figure.

"Good, and I see Bryan at the top of the gangplank with Dobbs."

Lafitte's cry came without warning. He had been standing on the quarterdeck, watching the touching reunion.

"*Mon ami*, look out!"

Glancing once again over Guy's shoulder, Bliss saw Gerald Faulk pounding up the gangplank, wielding a sword. Rational thought fled, and Bliss reacted spontaneously.

Scant seconds before Faulk's blade would have embedded itself in Guy's vulnerable back, Bliss gave her husband a hard shove. Guy dropped heavily, grunted in pain, and rolled down the gangplank, tripping Faulk on his way to the bottom. Momentum carried Faulk forward, toward Bliss, his blade thrust out in front of him. It all happened so fast Bliss had nowhere to go. Faulk's sword pierced her thigh cleanly. She screamed and staggered backward, right into the arms of Jean Lafitte, who had left the quarterdeck at a run when he realized the danger.

Bliss didn't remain long in Lafitte's arms. Lafitte handed her to one of his crewmen, who had followed him down the gangplank, and turned his attention on Faulk, who had regained his feet and was starting down the gangplank to finish Guy off.

His lips curling into a snarl, Lafitte shouted a challenge to Faulk. "You'll not find me as lenient as my good friend. En garde!"

Bliss watched the unfolding drama in a haze of pain and disbelief as the crewman placed her on her feet. Her thigh throbbed. She could feel wet, sticky blood dripping down her leg and her head spun dizzily, but she wouldn't allow herself to pass out until she knew Guy was safe. She wasn't worried about Lafitte; he could take care of himself. All her fears were for Guy, who lay still as death at the foot of the gangplank. All her enmity was for Faulk, the man who had put her through seven years of hell. She hoped God would forgive her, but she wanted Faulk dead.

Her sight was dimming now, but she clung to the sailor like a lifeline, absorbing his strength, refusing to faint. Her stubbornness was rewarded when she saw Lafitte feint to the right and bury his blade in Faulk's heart. Faulk stumbled sideways, then tumbled over the edge of the gangplank into the roiling river.

That was the last thing Bliss remembered.

Chapter Nineteen

A persistent ray of sunlight stabbed at Bliss's closed eyelids. In an effort to escape the annoying disturbance, she turned her body away from the light and groaned when she felt a sharp jab of pain.

"Lie still, sweetheart."

Bliss recognized Guy's voice and forced her eyes open. It took several minutes for her vision to clear before she saw his beloved face. His brow was creased into a worried frown, and she noted with surprise that his eyepatch was missing. She raised her hand and gingerly touched a fingertip to the puckered scar that ran diagonally from above his brow to just below his empty eye socket.

Guy gently grasped her wrist and pulled her hand away. Bliss sensed his embarrassment and didn't persist. "How do you feel?" Guy asked.

"I hurt. What happened?" Her gaze left his swollen face and traveled down his body. "I remember now. Gerald tried to kill you again. I saw you lying at the foot of the gangplank and thought you were dead." Her brow furrowed in concentration. "How was I hurt? Is Bryan all right?"

She tried to sit up, felt a stabbing pain in her upper right leg, and touched the thick bandage swathing her thigh.

"Bryan is fine," Guy assured her. "He's playing on the beach with the other children."

"Playing on the beach? Children?" She sounded confused.

"We're on Grande Terre, in Lafitte's house. Lafitte took us aboard the *Carolina* and brought us here to recuperate. His doctor is skilled in treating wounds."

"How was I wounded? I don't remember much about it."

"I didn't see it myself, but Jean told me it happened very fast. You saved my life when you pushed me out of the way of Faulk's sword. Unfortunately, you took the wound Faulk intended for me. His blade pierced the fleshy part of your thigh."

Bliss's hands flew to her stomach, expelling a ragged sigh when she felt the small bulge beneath her shift.

"The babe is fine," Guy assured her. "The doctor said he was never in any danger."

"Thank God. Is Father here?"

"Nay, he returned to our townhouse to reassure the servants and inform our friends and my business acquaintances that we're on an extended honeymoon."

"Father truly is sorry for all the heartache he caused us," Bliss confided. "He told me that you were Gerald's prisoner and advised me to flee with Bryan. If not for Father, Gerald's plan to bring me and Bryan to the warehouse would have succeeded. You would have signed the confession to save our lives, but that wouldn't have saved your life. You would have been hanged."

"Now we truly have a second chance to find happiness together. It's not going to be easy to turn my life around, but I'm willing to try for the sake of you and our children. I love you, Bliss. The moment you walked into my life again, I knew my love for you had never died, despite seven years of denying my feelings. I convinced myself that making you my captive was a fitting retribution. I intended to put my babe in your belly and send you back home in disgrace."

"You must have hated me a great deal," Bliss said. She could readily imagine the pain he'd suffered over the years to make him the hard, vindictive person he'd become. "I've seen the scars on your back. I know how badly you were hurt."

"I suppose I did hate you, until I saw you again. Then it was inevitable that I would fall in love with you all over again. It was as certain as the sun rising and setting, and I was swept up by the forces of destiny."

He took in a fortifying breath and continued. "I should have told you who I was in the beginning. I've hurt you in countless ways. I hope you can find it in your heart to forgive me."

"How can I not? Even when I knew you as Hunter, I loved you. There were so many similarities between you and the man I thought I'd lost forever that I began to question my own sanity. Your laugh, the way your eye turned from gray to pure silver when you made love to me, the way you tilted your head when you smiled, the deep resonance of your voice. My heart recognized you long before my mind dared to hope."

"I have much to make up to you and our son," Guy said. "Bryan is an exceptional child. He turned out remarkably well for a child whose formative years were controlled by Enos Holmes. I swear to you that from now on Bryan and our future children will have a home and stability and all the love they need."

"What about me?" Bliss asked teasingly.

"That goes without saying. You're my love, my life, my future. There isn't a man alive who loves a woman more than I love you. I've done something I hope will make you happy."

"What have you done?" Bliss asked curiously.

"How would you like to live in the place where you grew up?"

Bliss's heart constricted. "What are you talking about?"

"I discovered that your father had placed his plantation on the market. When his business dealings with Faulk failed, he obtained a second mortgage on his land. It was in danger of being repossessed if he couldn't sell it. I instructed my agent to offer your father a deal he couldn't refuse. It was a fair offer, love."

Bliss was stunned. "I don't know what to say. I love the plantation and all its people, and I know Bryan will too. Does Father know you're the buyer?"

"He does now. I told him before we left the city, and he's accepted that it's no longer his. He's staying at our townhouse during our absence."

"That was very generous of you," Bliss said, blinking back tears. "I've never loved you more than I do right now."

Bliss's gaze returned to Guy's sightless eye, her expression grave as she studied the damage done by the assassin's blade. Guy turned his face, apparently unable to bear what he must have considered Bliss's pity.

"No, don't turn away from me, love," Bliss pleaded as she turned his face toward her.

"It's hideous," Guy responded. "I'm sorry you have to see me like this. One of Lafitte's women is making another patch to replace the one Faulk tore away in the warehouse. I shouldn't have let you see me like this, but I wanted to be here when you awakened."

"It's not hideous," Bliss huffed indignantly. She raised herself up slightly and kissed his closed lid. "It's part of you and I love everything about you."

"Dr. Rochet removed the damaged eye and sewed the lids together when Lafitte brought me to Barataria. I was severely injured and barely alive. Someone fashioned a patch for me and I've worn it ever since. It's a part of me now, I'll never appear in public without it."

"Then wear it if you must, but know that it isn't for my sake. With or without the patch, you're still the man I love." She searched his swollen face, concern mirrored in the depths of her turquoise eyes. "How badly did Gerald hurt you?"

Guy shrugged her concern away. "A couple of cracked ribs, a lacerated back, a few bruises. Nothing that won't heal. You didn't ask me about Faulk. Would you like to know what happened to him?"

Bliss sighed. "I was saving that for last. Just thinking about him makes me ill. I know he's dead. I saw Lafitte skewer him and watched him fall in the river."

"Lafitte killed him. His body never rose to the surface. Good riddance, I say."

"It's sad in a way," Bliss said. "None of this would have happened if Gerald and Father hadn't objected to our marriage. You wouldn't have turned to piracy, Gerald would still have a prosperous business, and Bryan would have been raised by parents who loved him."

"We can't change the past, sweetheart," Guy

contended. "But we can control our future. No one will ever hurt you again, I swear it."

"When can we go home?" Bliss wondered.

"I thought we might go on a short cruise before returning home. Lafitte has generously offered to loan us one of the prize ships he keeps hidden in the back bay. We both need time to heal, and I want to return to Pine Island for the chests I left behind when I departed."

"I'd love to return to Pine Island," Bliss said dreamily. "Are you certain it's safe? Gasparilla is still out there."

"By all accounts, Gasparilla is playing hide and seek with the American Navy," Guy said. "Piracy no longer exists as we once knew it. I saw the end coming and was smart enough to get out with my skin intact. Gasparilla won't give up without a fight. He'll continue to terrorize the Gulf and die a violent death for his obstinacy. It might not be this month or this year, but it's coming."

"Thank God you're no longer involved," Bliss breathed gratefully. "How soon can we leave?"

"A few days. As soon as the doctor says you can travel. That will give me time to get a crew together. We'll sail under the American flag; that should gain us a measure of safety."

"Bryan will love the island."

"I want to make love to you on the beach, beneath the full moon, with the stars reflected in your eyes and the sun-warmed sand heating your skin. It's been a long time, sweetheart, and I need you desperately."

Her eyes sparkled with happiness. "Lie down beside me."

He shook his head. "I don't dare. You're still too sore and I'm too weak to do either of us justice. But soon, love, very soon."

He bent his head and brushed her lips with his. Though the touch was feather-light, Bliss felt her lips tingle and burn, and wanted more. She grasped his head between her palms and drew it back down toward her lips. Guy chuckled and gladly obliged, deepening the kiss as he half reclined on the bed and drew her into his arms.

She felt a shudder go through him as he disengaged her arms from around his neck. "This is exactly what I was trying to avoid," he said in a voice raw with need. "When you're fully recuperated, I promise you'll have no complaints concerning my ardor. I intend to keep you in my bed and in my arms until you beg me to leave you alone."

"Is that a promise?" Bliss asked archly.

"I give you my word on it."

Pine Island

Bliss sat on a tuft of grass with her bare feet buried in the warm, sugar-white sand, watching the sun set over Pine Sound. She watched, enthralled, as the huge red ball dipped below the horizon, scattering diamonds over the sparkling water.

Since the ship had arrived at Pine Island

seven days ago, Bliss's recovery had been nothing short of miraculous. Guy's swollen face had returned to its normal contours and he sported a new eyepatch. His ribs weren't completely healed yet, but he experienced only minor twinges of discomfort from time to time. As for Bryan, he was deliriously happy exploring the island.

Bliss sighed contentedly as she watched the sun all but disappear, creating a breathtaking canvas of blood-red splashes on a purple background. She felt as if she were sitting on the edge of the world as a shimmering moon replaced the sun. The sound of footsteps crunching in the sand disturbed her introspection, and she smiled as Guy dropped down beside her.

"I thought I'd find you here," Guy said.

"But for the trill of night birds, the buzz of insects, and the sound of the sea, it's so quiet I can actually hear myself think," Bliss said. "You and I could be the only people in the world right now."

"Tamrah was here," Guy said conversationally.

Bliss nodded. When they'd arrived, she'd been surprised to see Tamrah waiting on the deserted stretch of beach that had once held a bustling village.

"Was she alone?"

"Nay, Tomas was with her."

"They've really taken a shine to Bryan," Bliss said. "By the way, where is the little scamp? I thought he was on the ship with you."

"Tamrah wanted to take him home with her to meet her people, and I consented. She'll bring him back tomorrow." His arms went around her, pulling her against him.

"Remember what I said about making love beneath the moon and the stars?"

Bliss's breath lodged in her throat. They hadn't made love for weeks. She was all healed now, and so was Guy. She couldn't imagine why he was holding back. She'd thought it was because of her expanding girth and hoped he wasn't the kind of man who didn't enjoy making love to a pregnant woman. She didn't want to believe it of him but could think of no other reason why he hadn't touched her, though they'd slept in the same bed every night.

"I remember. I was wondering if you did."

"I've forgotten nothing I've ever said to you. I've been waiting a long time for this moment. I'm going to make love to you now. Here. In our own private paradise."

He undressed her slowly, then laid her down on the warm sand. Moonlight reflected against her skin, making it as luminescent as a Florida pearl. Her vibrant hair rivaled the sunset. Her stomach was gently rounded with her pregnancy, and her slender legs were long and shapely. Her breasts were ripe and full and tipped with large, dark nipples. Everything about her excited him, and he throbbed with anticipation as his gaze flowed over her like warm honey.

Fierce, hot desire pounded through him as he

made love to her with his eyes. His mouth literally watered for a taste of her as he leaned forward and trailed tiny nipping kisses down her throat and across her breasts. He inhaled her sweet aroma as his tongue lingered lovingly on her nipples, tracing wet circles over the protruding buds, savoring her taste, her scent, finding her delicious.

He felt her shudder, heard her make unintelligible noises deep in her throat as he took a full, ripe nipple into his mouth and suckled. She arched her back, as if offering herself upon the altar of his adoration as his hands played upon her heated flesh.

Her muted cries and churning hips created a fever inside Guy as he slid his hand over her stomach to the apex of her legs, coming to rest on the moist lips of her sex. She called out his name when he slid one finger along the outer seam, opening her to his intimate caress. Then he thrust a thick finger inside her, setting off vibrations within her that nearly brought him to culmination.

Desire hot and desperate burst through Bliss. She was wet with it, nearly mad with the need to feel him embedded deep inside her.

"Guy, please!" The hunger, the urgency, was almost more than she could bear. She clawed at his clothing, wanting to feel him against her, hot flesh to hot flesh.

"Aye, sweetheart, 'tis time," he grated, sounding nearly as desperate as she.

Together they tore off his clothing until he

was gloriously nude, his hard, wildly aroused erection prodding against her thigh. She was quivering uncontrollably as he lay full length upon her, her breasts against his chest, her legs against his. She opened her thighs to him and raised her hips, inviting him without words to enter her heated center.

"Nay, not this way," he panted hoarsely as he got to his knees and eased her onto her stomach.

Confused, Bliss squirmed and murmured a protest when he lifted her bottom in the air, folded her legs beneath her and positioned himself behind her.

"Don't be afraid, love," he whispered raggedly. "There are many positions in which to find pleasure. Nothing is wrong between husband and wife."

When he did nothing but stare at the dewy petals of her sex, she wiggled impatiently and pushed herself backward against him. She heard him groan, then felt his shaft opening her feminine passage. She cried out, pleasure pounding through her as he thrust his erection deep inside her velvet softness, sheathing himself completely. Then he grasped her hips and rocked her gently back and forth on her knees, each thrust bringing him deeper, tighter, until ravaging pleasure filled her every pore, consumed her every thought.

He began slowly, then quickly gained speed, plumbing her deeply, his tempo becoming hard and fast and frenzied. Bliss felt a tumultuous thrumming begin inside her, expanding to a wild crescendo as her cries rose to a high, sweet wail. The tightness inside her grew, becoming so intense Bliss could no longer contain it within her body. A wild, keening cry exploded from her lungs as she shattered and soared to sweet oblivion.

Moments later she heard Guy's hoarse cry, felt his fingers digging into the soft flesh of her buttocks, rocking her against his groin. His shaft throbbed deep within her, and then she felt the hot spurt of his seed filling her.

Neither of them moved for several long minutes as the sound of heavy breathing stirred the air around them and pleasure undulated through them, drenching them in the heat of their love. She was still dazed when Guy withdrew from her, gently turned her, and laid her upon the warm sand. Then he stretched out beside her and took her into his arms, holding her close as she floated back to reality. She opened her eyes and smiled at him.

"I love you, Bliss," he whispered against her lips. "I'm going to devote the rest of my life to proving I'm worthy of you and our children. I know you don't approve of my ill-gotten gains, but it wouldn't be practical to leave my remaining wealth buried on this island. I've made a decision I hope will please you. What do you think about giving a portion of the money I've accumulated to the Little Sisters Of Charity to start an orphanage? I don't ever want our children to feel shame for what I've done in the past."

"I won't tell them if you won't," Bliss murmured contentedly as she snuggled deeper into the curve of his body. "I think an orphanage is a wonderful idea."

"Consider it done. Now, my sweet bride, shall we go back to the ship and make love again in our bed?"

"The night is warm, the moon is bright, and I don't want to wait that long. Love me now, my bold pirate. But first, remove your eyepatch. There is no need to hide yourself from me. Everything about you is perfect."

He slipped his eyepatch over his head and tossed it onto the sand. Bliss stared at him and blinked, convinced that the moonlight was playing tricks on her. She no longer saw Guy's terrible scars. They had disappeared as if by magic, and both of his beautiful silver eyes were open and regarding her with heartrending tenderness.

She smiled dreamily. In the eyes of love, anything was possible.

Epilogue

Guy pushed the doctor aside at the last moment and caught his child as it slid from Bliss's body. He knew such behavior was frowned upon but he didn't care. He'd missed Bryan's birth and much of his childhood and was determined to be on hand every blessed moment of this new child's life. He hugged the squirming babe to his chest, so filled with raw emotion, he felt tears rolling down his cheeks.

Aye, tears from a reformed pirate who had once been so feared that people shuddered in terror at the very mention of his name.

"Put the child down, Viscount," the doctor ordered curtly. " 'Tis time to tie off the cord and deliver the afterbirth. This is highly irregular. Most men are content to remain well away from the birthing room until it's all over."

"I'm not most men," Guy said as he knelt at Bliss's side and reluctantly placed the babe on her stomach.

"Do I have a son or daughter?" Bliss asked groggily.

"A son, love. A beautiful boy with hair the color of burnished gold." Just then the babe let out a loud wail, his little fists flailing and his legs churning. Guy gave a laugh of pure joy. "It looks as if he's going to be as feisty as his mother."

"Is he healthy? Did you count his fingers and toes?"

"He's beautiful. All his fingers and toes are intact, and judging by the noise he's making, his lungs are strong and healthy. What shall we name him?"

"Hmmmm?" Her eyes were closing as sleep threatened to claim her.

"A name, love, what shall we call our son?"

Her lids fluttered open and she gave him a drowsy smile. "Anything but Hunter. One pirate in the family is enough."

Connie Mason

Highland Warrior

She is far too shapely to be a seasoned warrior, but she is just as deadly. As she engages him on the battlefield, Ross knows her for a MacKay, longtime enemies of his clan. Soon this flame-haired virago will be his wife, given to him by her father in a desperate effort to end generations of feuding. Of all her family, Gillian MacKay is the least willing to make peace. Her fiery temper challenges Ross's mastery while her lush body taunts his masculinity. Both politics and pride demand that he tame her, but he will do it his way—with a scorching seduction that will sweep away her defenses and win her heart.